Christie Barlow is the number one international bestselling author of seventeen romantic comedies including the iconic Love Heart Lane Series, *A Home at Honeysuckle Farm* and *Kitty's Countryside Dream*. She lives in a ramshackle cottage in a quaint village in the heart of Staffordshire with her four children and two dogs.

Her writing career came as a lovely surprise when Christie decided to write a book to teach her children a valuable life lesson and show them that they are capable of achieving their dreams.

Christie writes about love, life, friendships and the importance of community spirit. She loves to hear from her readers and you can get in touch via Twitter, Facebook and Instagram.

facebook.com/ChristieJBarlow
x.com/ChristieJBarlow
bookbub.com/authors/christie-barlow
instagram.com/christie_barlow

Also by Christie Barlow

Puffin Island Series

A Postcard from Puffin Island

The Love Heart Lane Series

Love Heart Lane

Foxglove Farm

Clover Cottage

Starcross Manor

The Lake House

Primrose Park

Heartcross Castle

The New Doctor at Peony Practice

New Beginnings at the Old Bakehouse

The Hidden Secrets of Bumblebee Cottage

A Summer Surprise at the Little Blue Boathouse

A Winter Wedding at Starcross Manor

The Library on Love Heart Lane

Standalones

Kitty's Countryside Dream

The Cosy Canal Boat Dream

A Home at Honeysuckle Farm

A WINTER WEDDING AT STARCROSS MANOR

CHRISTIE BARLOW

One More Chapter
a division of HarperCollins*Publishers* Ltd
1 London Bridge Street
London SE1 9GF
www.harpercollins.co.uk
HarperCollins*Publishers*
Macken House, 39/40 Mayor Street Upper,
Dublin 1, D01 C9W8, Ireland

This paperback edition 2024

3

First published in Great Britain in ebook format
by HarperCollins*Publishers* 2023
Copyright © Christie Barlow 2023
Christie Barlow asserts the moral right to
be identified as the author of this work
A catalogue record of this book is available from the British Library

ISBN: 978-0-00-841321-7

Printed and bound in the UK using 100% Renewable Electricity
by CPI Group (UK) Ltd

For Estelle Maher
A truly inspirational woman.

Loveheart La...

Primrose Park

The Lake House

CLOVER COTTAGE ESTATE

The Old Bakehouse

The Boat

Bumblebee Cottage

Starcross Manor

Scott's Veterinary Practice

THE GREEN

HIGH STREET

Primary School

Post Office

Ham... Vill... Sh...

Peony Practice

Callie's apartment

Solicitors Office

Dolores' apartment

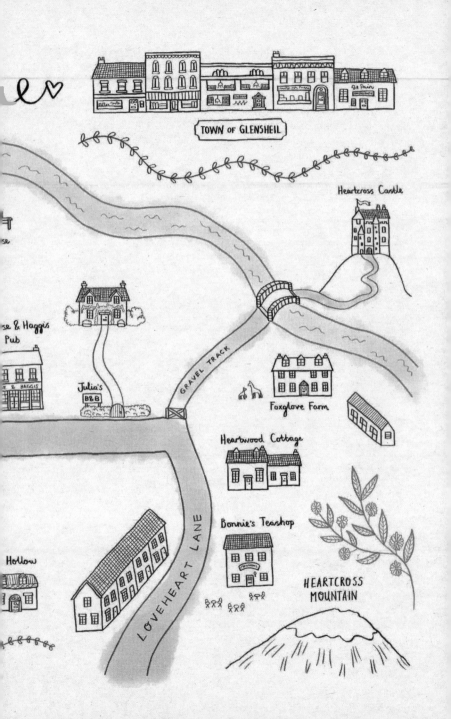

Prologue

Flynn Carter was sitting at his office desk, perplexed. As Monday mornings went, this one was full of the unexpected.

Staring out through the window over the grounds of Starcross Manor he took in the wintry scene typical of a November day in the Scottish Highlands. He watched the hypnotic flurry of snowflakes falling to the ground, which was already covered with a light dusting, before staring back at the letter in his hand. It just didn't make sense to him. He placed it back on the desk and checked his watch, willing Julia to hurry. He needed to talk to her.

Finally Julia opened the door and breezed into his office. 'It's beginning to look a lot like Christmas!' she trilled.

'It's November,' replied Flynn, smiling indulgently. He knew how much his fiancée loved Christmas.

'Which means it's nearly Christmas! It's a beautiful winter wonderland out there. I just love this time of year. Have you heard the news this morning? Trains are delayed and the gritters are out. You'd think we'd be used to this kind of weather by now; it's so predictable.'

The weather in the past week had been on the chilly side and looking at the grey sky through the window Flynn knew the snow was only going to get heavier. Julia unravelled her scarf as she walked over to him and playfully touched his cheek with her cold hand.

'Get off me,' he said, good-humouredly. 'You're freezing.'

'You love it. Now, what's up with you? You've picked the worst time to have a crisis – right in the middle of breakfast.' Julia owned the local B&B and had received the distress call from Flynn just after she'd finished cooking forty full Scottish breakfasts for her guests. 'I've left Eleni in charge but I can't stay away long as it's a big changeover day and the bedrooms need cleaning. Coffee?' she asked, pointing at the coffee machine in the far corner of the office.

Flynn nodded. 'A strong one.'

'You have me intrigued,' she replied, glancing back over her shoulder.

'We need to talk weddings. One wedding in particular.'

Julia paused, clearly noticing the grave look on Flynn's face.

'Okay,' she replied, sitting down on the chair opposite him and sliding a mug of coffee towards him. 'I know you've been under a lot of strain lately, but this wasn't quite the romantic conversation I've been anticipating.'

Even though the two of them had been engaged for the last twelve months they'd still been unable to pin down a date for their wedding. With all their business commitments, and the fact they wanted to go on honeymoon straight after, not to

2

mention Heartcross becoming ever more popular with tourists year-round, it was proving increasingly difficult.

Flynn's face softened. 'I'm not talking about us. I'd like nothing more than to marry you right now but with business being so busy—'

Julia opened her arms wide and interrupted. 'My dream is a whimsical winter wedding.' She laid her hands on her heart. 'I can perfectly picture my outfit, which obviously I can't tell you about except to say that it will be complemented by a faux-fur jacket and bold berry lipstick, all festive glam.' She glanced towards the window as she continued. 'There will be a sprinkling of snow on the ground, snowflakes in our hair, and we'd be surrounded by the silvery mountainous landscape, the icy waters of the lake, a magnificent manor house…'

'You sound like you're writing a feature for a wedding magazine! It all seems wonderful to me and I can't wait to make you my wife. There's nothing I want more.'

'I know, I know, but finding a time in the schedule to organise it all, and then to take time off work to go on honeymoon… Thank goodness you have your wedding planner now. That must make things a little easier? Surely we can take the pressure off us and hand everything over to her? It's not as though we don't have a lovely venue to get married in and the best chefs to cater for us—and our friends can walk here.'

'Correction: I *had* a wedding planner. That's part of the reason I called you.' Flynn pushed the letter he'd been re-reading over the desk towards Julia.

'What's this?' she asked, picking it up and glancing over it.

'Jenny has resigned, leaving the competition winners without a wedding planner.'

Starcross Manor had just launched a national competition, the winners receiving the wedding of their dreams this coming Christmas Eve with no expense spared.

'It's an absolute disaster.' Flynn exhaled. 'The competition winners have just been announced and are due in at the end of the week to meet the now non-existent wedding planner. What am I going to do now?'

'Let's not panic; it's going to be okay,' Julia reassured him soothingly. 'Jenny's resignation letter doesn't give much away, does it? But I do know her mother was poorly. Maybe she's taking time to care for her.'

'Maybe,' replied Flynn. 'But why wouldn't she just come and talk to me and ask for compassionate leave? I have tried to telephone her but it just goes straight to answerphone, and now I'm stuck with a real dilemma. I don't suppose—'

'Absolutely not,' cut in Julia, knowing exactly what Flynn was about to suggest. 'As much as I love you and would love to help you out on this occasion, my B&B is going to be just as busy as Starcross Manor in the run-up to Christmas. I have no time to be organising weddings.'

'You can't blame a man for trying.' With a look of despair on his face, Flynn raked his hand through his hair and leaned back in his chair.

'Is there a possibility you could explain to the winning couple that there's been a change in staffing and unfortunately the wedding needs to be postponed?' enquired Julia.

Sitting up, Flynn turned the computer screen towards her and tapped on an email. It was from the winning bride and it oozed excitement. She couldn't thank Flynn enough for making their dreams come true. 'Would you like to have that conversation?'

'After reading that email, probably not. I can understand her excitement. Christmas Eve, Starcross Manor … it's a fairytale come true for any couple and for it to be all expenses paid? A dream!'

'The competition was meant to put Starcross Manor on the map. A one-stop shop, with the best wedding planner in the business. All the publicity would be a huge boost for the business and every step of their journey was meant to be filmed for our promotional video showcasing the outstanding service we provide to make all your wedding dreams come true. I was hoping this would lead to Starcross Manor becoming the top wedding venue in Scotland. I managed to persuade one of the best independent film-makers in the country to help me out on this project, even though he's normally filming wildlife, not weddings.'

'Guy's work is exceptional, but I've seen comments on social media that he didn't attend the film awards and Isla was saying last time he was in the village he seemed preoccupied and a little unsociable.'

'He's not here to make friends; he's here to put Starcross Manor on the map.'

'What about starting the recruitment process again?' suggested Julia, trying to prevent Flynn from wallowing.

'I don't think we have enough time to readvertise, sort through the applications, arrange interviews… The wedding is in five weeks' time, so it will be here before we've selected someone.'

'There's got to be another solution, someone else who can step in. What about another member of the staff you already have?'

'I've thought of that, but the staff that I'd trust with this project are already flat out with their own jobs during the run-up to Christmas. The hotel is fully booked and we have all the normal festivities that need to be catered for. Can you imagine how many guests we have to look after on Christmas Day?'

For a moment they sat in silence, both of them thinking.

Flynn's phone pinged. 'It's Libby,' he said, glancing towards the screen.

'And how is that gorgeous sister of yours?'

'Christmas crazy as usual. She's got a few weeks off work before she starts her new job with Frazier. I still can't believe she was headhunted by them and that they want to incorporate her fashion business into their brand.'

'What? How have I missed this bit of news? That's so exciting! They're one of the biggest fashion houses in New York and it's such a great opportunity. Hang on a minute, is she moving?'

'It's all happened within the last forty-eight hours and yes, I believe they've allocated her an apartment. It will be a fantastic opportunity for her. I think she said her new title is "chief fashion designer" and she'll be leaving for New York just after New Year's. I'm very proud of her after everything she's been through.'

'She's a superstar and deserves the world. But New York... I'm going to miss her. We *must* celebrate Christmas together and I'm going to call her and arrange a catch-up soon so she can tell me all about the new job. I want to hear all the details —' Julia stopped mid-sentence and held Flynn's gaze. 'Oh my...' Julia began flapping her hand in excitement. 'Did you just say that Libby has a few weeks off work before she starts her new job? That might be a solution to your problem: wedding-loving Libby! She designs dresses—including wedding dresses—she's organised, has a great eye for detail, and if she's not leaving for New York until January, she could be your temporary wedding planner! Give her a ring! You have nothing to lose by asking.'

For a moment, Flynn was quiet as he mulled over the suggestion. Then a smile began to spread across his face. 'You may be right. This might be the ideal solution and I know I can trust her to do a good job but…' He exhaled. 'Remember the last time I offered her a job?'

'I do, but that was in completely different circumstances. Libby needed to stand on her own two feet and bounce back on her own terms. I know all you were doing was looking out for her, but at the time she viewed it as you taking pity on her. It's different now. She's a strong, independent woman who doesn't settle for anything or anyone less than she deserves. She believes in her own ability and has created a successful fashion business that has put her on the map. And now she's been headhunted by one of the top fashion houses in America! Plus, this would be just a temporary situation to help you out.'

'I'm suddenly feeling guilty that I haven't spent more time with her. I know we've both been busy, but Edinburgh is only twenty-five minutes away by helicopter, whereas New York is a long-haul flight away.'

'I hear you. We just need to make sure we spend as much time as possible with her over Christmas, and if she agrees to the idea of planning this wedding for you, we'll see her a lot more over the next few weeks. I'm telling you, this is the perfect solution. Libby would be a brilliant wedding planner.'

Before Julia could finish her sentence, Flynn was shutting down his computer and pulling on his jacket. He swigged back his coffee and grabbed his wallet from the drawer before slipping his phone into his inside pocket.

'Where are you going?'

'I'm going to Edinburgh.'

'What, now?'

'Yes, now. I think I've got more chance of persuading Libby face-to-face rather than by a telephone call, because you're right, she would be perfect for the job. We could put her up in one of the lodges in the grounds and we'd get to spend more time with her before she leaves. I'm praying she agrees.' Fastening his coat and pulling on his gloves, he grabbed his hat and pressed a swift kiss to Julia's lips. 'Did I tell you that you're simply the best?'

The door swung closed behind him, leaving Julia smiling. 'Fly carefully,' she bellowed after him. 'The snow is coming down.'

'I love you,' he shouted back.

Walking to the window, Julia drank her coffee and looked over towards the helipad. Flynn was already striding across the white ground towards the navy-coloured helicopter, which displayed his initials in bold gold lettering on the side. It didn't take long before the blades spun round and the machine lifted effortlessly off the ground. Julia hoped the snow would stay light until Flynn was safely back at Starcross Manor.

Within minutes Flynn was out of sight. After pulling on her coat and wrapping her scarf around her neck, Julia picked up from his desk the framed photograph of him, Libby and their dad, Wilbur. Thinking about everything that Libby had gone through in the last ten years brought tears to Julia's eyes. Despite being put through hell she'd picked herself up and was now heading to New York. Julia was proud of her and she knew Flynn was too.

Noticing a stack of wedding magazines on the shelf behind the desk, Julia glanced at the top one. The model looked stunning wearing ice blue. The long-sleeved tulle gown featured floral sequin artwork that allowed the dress to sparkle from top to toe. To complement the dress, the model had a fake fur jacket over her shoulders. At that moment a thought crossed Julia's mind: if Libby accepted Flynn's offer, maybe while she was here Julia could ask her to make her future wedding outfit.

Julia laid one of the magazines in the middle of Flynn's desk and stuck a Post-it note on top. She wrote:

Life's too short. Let's get that date fixed. Marry me! X

Chapter One

Five weeks to Christmas

Libby stepped over the cardboard boxes that were dotted about the living room and made her way towards the kitchen. She hadn't even managed to have a cup of tea yet so she switched on the kettle. She asked Alexa to play *Heart Christmas* and immediately Christmas songs began to filter through the living room, adding to the festive feel.

For the last few days she'd been slowly packing her possessions. She was looking forward to her move to New York in the new year.

'I declare it's officially Christmas,' she sang to herself as her favourite Christmas song, 'Fairytale of New York', began. Jigging over to the fridge, she grabbed the milk.

Once upon a time Christmas had brought her painful memories, because it reminded her of the time when her life had changed for ever. But time was a great healer and she'd come to terms with the past. She was now at a very good place in her life, with a successful career, and about to embark on a whole new adventure. With a cup of tea in her hand, she looked around at the boxes that held her life. She couldn't possibly take all this stuff with her to New York, could she?

This rented house had served her well in the last ten years. Between these four walls she'd laughed – though no doubt cried more – and it had been her safe haven, allowing her to rebuild her life in the wake of everything she'd gone through. Feeling suddenly proud of how far she'd come, she picked up the letter that had changed her life and re-read the job offer from Frazier. She'd applied for the job on a whim and never in her wildest dreams had thought she would be offered the position. But here she was holding the confirmation letter to her brand-new life.

Her obsession with clothes had started when she was just a little girl. Her father was a man of outlandish suits and hats, which fascinated her, and most weekends – much to her brother's discomfort – she would make Flynn stand still for hours while she dressed him in outfits that she'd concocted from local jumble sales.

Finishing her drink, she looked towards the bay window. Even though it was still November, the next job on her list was putting up the Christmas tree. Libby was hoping Flynn and Julia would invite her to spend Christmas with them, but in the meantime, she still wanted to be surrounded by twinkly fairy lights and decorations in the run-up. Climbing the stairs, Libby pulled down the loft ladder and clambered into the attic. The artificial tree and a box of favourite decorations were just in front of her but as she was about to grab them, she stopped in her tracks. Above her there was a deafening drone and a whirl of rotors – a noise Libby recognised instantly. There was a helicopter above her house.

After lowering the tree and decorations onto the landing, Libby shut the loft and dragged them down the stairs. Moving towards the bay window she could immediately see a sea of bobble hats on the edge of the green, their owners pointing up at the sky. The crowd was both amazed and amused.

'I can always rely on you to make an entrance, can't I?' she murmured to herself. She watched the helicopter with her brother's initials descend onto the blanket of snow that covered the green and then went to open the front door. Smiling in the face of the cold blast of air that greeted her, Libby leaned against the door frame and folded her arms. She was always happy to see her brother.

Within seconds, Flynn had shut the door of the helicopter and hurried over the fresh, undisturbed snow. As soon as he noticed Libby waiting for him in her doorway, he grinned and bent down, scooping snow up in his hands.

'Don't you dare!' she shouted.

'I dare!' He laughed, playfully throwing a snowball in her direction, making her shriek.

'Hey!' She laughed, stepping back as the snowball hit the step in front of her.

'Hi, sis! Surprise!' He kissed her on both cheeks before stamping the snow off his boots.

'A surprise indeed!' She pointed towards the helicopter. 'You do know you're testing your luck with the local constabulary, don't you? That is not legal.'

'They all love me, and anyway it's worth the risk if it means I get to come and see my sister.'

Libby opened the door wide and Flynn stepped inside.

'And what are you doing here in this weather? I texted you only this morning and you never mentioned you were coming.'

'A brother can come and see his sister just because, can't he?' His tone was jovial as he took off his coat and hung it in the hallway.

'He can, but in this weather? I reckon it means you need a favour and it's such a big favour that you can't ask by text. Don't forget, I've known you all my life.'

'Funny that,' he replied, following Libby into the living room and walking straight into a cardboard box. 'You've been busy.'

'I'm just trying to sort out everything before I go to New York. You really don't realise the volume of crap you acquire until you have to pack it all up.'

'Where are you going to store all this? Surely you're not taking everything with you?'

Libby screwed up her face then gave Flynn a cheeky smile. 'I was actually going to ask if my favourite brother could help in any way.'

'I'm your only brother,' he pointed out. 'And of course I can! I could even go one better than that.'

Libby narrowed her eyes.

'I can get someone over to pack up all the rest of your stuff for you.'

'And why would you do that? Call me suspicious but you've flown here, in this worsening weather, without prior warning, and now you're offering to do me a good deed? I'm not complaining, mind you. Packing up a house is possibly one of the worst jobs in the world. But it is definitely suspicious.'

'Can a brother not help out his sister without there being an ulterior motive?' he replied, knowing full well he was telling a little white lie and about to ask Libby for an enormous favour. 'And can I just add how proud I am of you? You've come so far.' He placed a supportive hand on her elbow. 'This job sounds amazing and you deserve it.'

'Mmm, showering me with compliments now too? Don't be too nice, you'll have me getting all emotional. Now, let's make you a drink and you can tell me the *real* reason why you're here.' Libby lightly nudged his shoulder. 'You can also help me decorate the tree.'

A few minutes later, Libby handed Flynn a mug of tea. While she boiled the kettle he'd slotted the artificial Christmas tree together, and it now had pride of place in the bay window. Its twisted, threadbare branches had seen better days.

'This tree has certainly had its day,' Flynn said wryly.

'It's well loved,' Libby argued. It was like an old family friend. Its lights had twinkled in this living room for the past ten years. 'I still remember trundling off to the garden centre to buy it. My first Christmas on my own in this place. At first, I struggled to fit it in the car.'

'No shit, Sherlock, you drive a Mini!'

'A convertible Mini, which was a lifesaver. I put the roof down and got the tree home. I'm surprised I didn't catch pneumonia though, as it was minus two outside and a fifteen-minute drive.'

Flynn laughed. 'Only you. Where's the box of decorations?' he asked, placing his drink on the table.

'Right there.' Libby pointed to a cardboard box.

Delving into the box she pulled out anything that sparkled. 'Wait, we need to put the lights on first. Here they are,' she said, dragging out a reel of fairy lights. 'Every year I tell myself off for not putting them away properly,' she said as she yanked them apart. She noticed Flynn smiling and paused, her eyebrows raised in question.

'They won't have a cat in hell's chance of working if you pull them like that. Give them here.'

Libby watched Flynn untangle the lights, weaving them in and out of tangled loops of wire with ease.

'Right, there you go. All you need is a little patience. Plug them in.'

'Here goes,' she said, bending down and pushing the plug into the socket. They both stood and waited. Absolutely nothing. Not a flash of light or a glimmer of hope.

'I think you might have to try and switch the plug socket on,' shared Flynn, cocking an eyebrow.

'Oh, yeah!' She giggled, flicking the switch. Instantly, the lights began to twinkle. 'Look at those. Isn't Christmas just a magical time of the year?'

'It is.'

'Now that's sorted, you best tell me why you're actually here.' She gave him a sideward glance as they began to wrap the lights around the tree.

'Okay,' he said, taking a breath. 'I'm here to talk weddings.'

Flynn had Libby's full attention now and she stopped in her tracks. Her mouth fell open then she grinned. 'Oh my God, you and Julia have set a date? Finally!' She gave a little shriek, threw her arms open wide and hugged Flynn tightly. 'This is brilliant—and about time. When? Where? I'm assuming Starcross Manor? Winter or summer? Look at me, I'll already be asking for time off from my new job the second I arrive.'

'And breathe.' Flynn laughed. 'It's not Julia.'

Immediately the smile slipped from Libby's face and her

mouth fell open for a second time, though this time for different reasons. 'Please tell me you haven't been—'

'Of course I haven't been cheating on Julia!' Flynn was quick to interrupt, looking aghast that she would even suggest such a thing. 'I can't wait to marry her.'

Libby held her hands against her fast-beating heart. 'Thank God for that.'

'But I *am* in a bit of a dilemma. Jenny, my wedding planner, has quit with no explanation and left me in a predicament. I launched a competition to give one lucky couple the wedding of their dreams—all expenses paid—on Christmas Eve. The couple are being filmed through the whole process and I was going to use the video for promotional marketing, maybe TV ads or possibly a one-off TV programme highlighting Starcross Manor as *the* elite wedding venue in Scotland. My hope was that the footage would help to attract celebrity and high-net-worth clients, putting us on the map, but now I have no wedding coordinator to plan the whole thing. Jenny picked the winner out of the hundreds of entries, announced their names, then resigned...'

'Blimey! That's not good timing. If she'd have hung fire, you would have had time to rearrange the wedding date and employ someone else.'

'Exactly, and now I have a couple that are overjoyed and excited ... but no means of giving them the wedding they've been promised.'

'You're in a mess. But what are you doing here? You should be recruiting a brand-new wedding planner instead of hanging baubles on my tree. And why are you looking at me in that way...'

Flynn gave her a hopeful smile. 'I thought wedding-loving

Libby, who is obsessed with Christmas, could possibly come to my rescue.'

The penny had well and truly dropped. 'Me? You want me to be your wedding planner? But I've got a job, not to mention I have to pack this house up and tie up all of my loose ends here before I fly to the Big Apple.'

Flynn perched on the arm of the sofa. 'Just hear me out. I only need five weeks—max—of your time and I don't trust anyone else to do it. I know you won't let me down and if you take on the job you can come and live at Starcross Manor and spend the whole holiday season with us. Dad will be over the moon to see you.'

'Except Dad won't be there. His feet haven't touched the ground since his retirement and he's touring Spain, Portugal and the Canary Islands on a winter cruise for the next month or so.'

'He arrives back on Christmas Eve, just in time to devour the best Christmas feast he's ever laid eyes on, and we could all be waiting for him. Like I said, I can arrange for your belongings to be boxed and stored, taking the pressure off you here. For the wedding, we can source the cake from Rona at Bonnie's Teashop, the flowers from Buttercup Barn, and, to top it all off, we have Andrew Glossop on board for the catering... You're brilliant at interior design, coordinating colours and you love Christmas! I honestly can't think of anyone better to step in. Please at least think about it?'

Libby was completely taken by surprise at the request but she could see the predicament that Flynn was in. 'I wasn't expecting this. It's a lot to take in.'

'I know, but as well as your accommodation, I can pay you and offer you all your meals for free at Starcross Manor. I'm ready to offer anything you want to get you to help me pull this off. Christmas at Starcross Manor will be fabulous and Julia would love to hang out with you before you go to New York. We both would.'

'But coordinate a wedding? This is someone's big day. The day they've dreamed about all of their life. And I'm meant to be taking a few weeks off, not making myself busier than ever. I've been working flat out and I was looking forward to some down time before I started my new job.'

'Just think of it as co-ordinating a large fashion show. You dress the room and flowers according to your collection. It wouldn't be that much different, surely?'

'But what about dress materials, sewing machines, portfolios of ideas for the bride and groom to look through?'

'Anything you need, you will have. There's a studio in the grounds of Starcross Manor where everything can be planned from, and a workshop for yourself.' Flynn put his hands together in a prayer-like pose and the hopeful smile made another appearance.

'And how long have I got to think about this?' asked Libby.

Flynn looked at his watch, then out of the window. The snow was still falling. 'About thirty minutes while we finish decorating the tree.'

Libby laughed. 'Oh, the pressure. You'd best get decorating!' she ordered, throwing bright red tinsel at him. 'In the meantime, I'll have a think.'

Twenty minutes later, Libby stood on tiptoe and placed the fairy on top of the tree. The fairy, too, was ancient, bought the same time as the tree. 'We've been through hell and back, this fairy and me.'

Standing side by side, Flynn and Libby admired their work. The tree had been transformed and it sparkled before their eyes, magnificent with its glittery baubles and multi-coloured tinsel. Libby smiled at the twinkly lights. She felt the same as she did every year: a little emotional by the time she had finished decorating the tree. It was always a welcome reminder of her strength and determination … and how far she'd come.

'It looks beautiful – and what a perfect backdrop.' Libby looked out of the bay window over the green. The snow was still falling and she watched as smoke spiralled out of a neighbour's chimney and disappeared into the grey sky in the peaceful silence. She turned back towards Flynn.

'And I get all my meals for free, you say?'

Flynn's eyes widened. 'Yes! Does this mean…?'

'As if I'm going to leave my brother in the lurch. I mean, it's a win-win. I get to help you out, design and make a wedding dress, co-ordinate someone's special day, and after we've watched them get married on Christmas Eve, I get to spend Christmas with my family. I can't wait to see Dad.'

Flynn picked Libby up and hugged her. 'I blooming love you! Thank you!'

She patted his shoulder. 'Put me down. To be honest I can't wait. It's going to be so much fun, and as I love weddings and Christmas, it's the perfect combination.'

'I can't wait to tell Julia. She'll be over the moon to see you.' Flynn's smile couldn't be wider.

'And me her, but you best give me some details. When do you want me to arrive?'

They both sat down on the settee. 'I've not even looked at

the file of the competition winners. All I know is they are called David and Miranda and they are looking forward to their once in a lifetime wedding. They are coming in next week to meet the wedding planner and Guy is arriving some time Wednesday, I believe.'

'Who's Guy?

'The film-maker. He's going to be following and filming your every move along with the happy couple. As I mentioned, some of the footage will hopefully be used to promote and market Starcross Manor as the go-to wedding destination, while the rest will be for the bride and groom, a reminder of their special day. So … anytime late this week, does that work for you?'

'I'll pack my suitcase and be with you by Wednesday.'

'I promise I'll take care of everything here. I'll even get the Christmas tree transported if you wish.'

Libby laughed. 'The extremes you'll go to so I won't change my mind.'

'I can send the helicopter back for you?'

'I'm okay travelling by train,' replied Libby, who was not keen on any mode of flying. Already the thought of the long flight to New York was filling her with dread.

'You're a lifesaver.'

'I know!'

Flynn hugged Libby again. 'I don't mean to disappear on you so soon, but the weather isn't great and Julia will be worrying until I'm back.'

'It's okay. You just get yourself back safe.'

Flynn grabbed his coat from the hallway and kissed Libby on the cheek. 'I'll get the winners' file ready for you and sort the essentials—sewing machine, et cetera—and I'll leave the rest in your capable hands.'

'See you Wednesday!'

Libby stood and watched Flynn stride across the snowy green. Within a couple of minutes, the helicopter had lifted off the ground. Libby waved and closed the front door. Wandering back into the living room, she smiled at the cardboard boxes and switched on the TV. If Flynn was going to arrange for her house to be packed up, she might as well make the most of her free afternoon. With a box of chocolates perched on the arm of her chair, she got comfy on the settee and snuggled under the heated throw. There was only one thing on her agenda: to find a romantic comedy to watch, one that combined Christmas and weddings. She considered it crucial research as her aim was to organise the winter wedding of the century.

Chapter Two

At the train station, the buildings were already shrouded with Christmas decorations, and a gigantic tree led the way to the platforms. As Libby weaved her way through the festive travellers, pulling her suitcase behind her, she noticed all the loved-up couples, hand in hand, and felt a pang in her heart. She wondered if she could ever let herself be loved by anyone again. This was her tenth Christmas being single and she was more than okay with that … most of the time. Her work was her lifeline and the only constant in her life, outside her family.

In the last couple of days, there had been numerous travel disruptions on the railways and buses, the continuous fall of snow making it difficult to travel anywhere. But thankfully Libby's train was still running and on time. She made her way to the ticket machine and after purchasing her ticket she sought the shelter of the waiting room and texted Flynn.

Your Knightess in shining armour is on her way!

His reply pinged back almost immediately.

I can't wait to see you but the snow has taken over Heartcross. There are no buses or taxis running at Glensheil Station but don't worry, I'll send transportation.

Flynn followed up his text with a winky face.

Libby smiled; she wouldn't put it past Flynn to send reindeer pulling a sleigh. Just at that moment there was an announcement over the tannoy that her train was arriving. Libby stepped onto the platform and saw the train rumbling towards her, followed by a sound of the brakes squealing as it slowed to a stop. Slipping her phone into her bag she held tightly onto her suitcase as her fellow passengers began to flood the platform.

Making her way to the first-class carriage, she located her seat and pushed her luggage into the hold before settling in. The journey by train was just over four hours but with a good book and a stack of wedding magazines in her bag Libby was looking forward to relaxing, reading and taking in the spectacular views of the Scottish Highlands. Libby loved Heartcross and catching up with all the gang in the village. She loved everything about the olde worlde feel of the place, from the River Heart to the impressive castle standing tall in front of the magnificent mountains, to the delicious cakes from Bonnie's Teashop and the roast dinners at The Grouse and Haggis. Flynn had tried many times to entice her to join his team and even though his offers had always been tempting, she knew her passion was for fashion and designing dresses.

Taking a wedding magazine out of her bag, Libby began to flick through the pages. The only thing she knew about the competition winners was their names—Miranda and David—and she was eagerly anticipating their first meeting. Libby couldn't wait to share her ideas. She was going to embrace this winter's plush colours, glittery décor, roaring fires and a frosty sprinkling of snow. It was going to be so romantic. Regardless of the theme of the wedding, Libby knew it was essential to design the dress first, knowing its colour and design would guide the bride and groom to choosing all the other wonderful wintry details. Libby had pinged an email to Flynn late on Tuesday afternoon, listing everything she needed including contacts that would showcase all things festive. 'Be glitzy, go quirky' was always Libby's motto at the beginning of any dress design. In the fashion world glittering gold was really hot right now, and luxe precious metal tones would make the bride and the wedding decor look radiant.

Flicking through the magazine she stopped at a feature on bridal jewels. Libby already had pearls in mind. Freshwater pearls were unique, and paired with gold they would give a luxurious modern nod to the festive season.

Libby was going to do everything she could to ensure this couple got to live their fairytale by creating the perfect winter wonderland wedding. She envisaged a secret winter garden, an ideal place for the guests to toast marshmallows and grab a hot chocolate. They could possibly even have a churros station. Warm blankets could be on hand, with a sign next to them saying: *to have and to hold in case you get cold.* For the reception, Libby was already imagining the juxtaposition of rustic oak beams and delicate fairy lighting. She knew she was going to have so much fun during the coming weeks and she couldn't wait to watch the lucky winners walk down the aisle.

The woman sitting opposite Libby on the train ordered a

cup of coffee then pointed to the magazine. 'Whoever he is, he's a lucky man.'

Libby shook her head. 'It's not me getting married but I do have the job of organising a Christmas Eve wedding.'

'How romantic,' replied the woman. 'I'm sure it will be very magical.'

Libby smiled, but inside she felt that old familiar pang. There was a time when she thought she would get married, but things didn't work out that way for her and for many years she'd blamed herself. Pushing the past out of her mind, she determined to focus on the present. 'I see you're married, how many years?' she asked the woman.

'Would you believe fifty years next year?' The woman gave a warm smile.

'That is true love right there.'

'Believe me, there's been many a time I've wanted to commit murder,' the woman said with a laugh. 'But I have to say, I think it's a lottery and a happy marriage is based on luck. As much as I joke, I've had a very happy life and wouldn't change a thing.'

'You're indeed lucky,' replied Libby.

As the train pulled into the next station, the woman said goodbye to Libby and made her way to the platform. A ticket inspector with a rosy-cheeked smile appeared in the aisle and checked Libby's ticket.

'Glensheil, right by Heartcross. Such a beautiful part of the world.'

'It is,' agreed Libby.

'The snow has fallen quite heavily in those parts and the buses and taxis aren't running from the station. Do you have transportation arranged?'

'I do, thanks.' Libby smiled. 'My brother is sending someone for me.'

The inspector nodded and continued down the carriage. Numerous doors slammed a few moments later and then the whistle blew followed by a shout. As the train set off again, Libby watched the snow-covered trees and houses whizz past the window. Feeling tired she rested her head against her scarf on the window pane and closed her eyes.

The next thing she knew the ticket inspector was lightly shaking her.

'Excuse me, ma'am, we are in Glensheil. You've nearly missed your stop.'

Startled, Libby looked out of the window and immediately recognised the station. She couldn't believe she'd been asleep all this time. 'Oh my, thank you so much for waking me,' she said, jumping up, collecting her suitcase and making sure she had all her belongings. As she made her way to the door, she saw the carriage was nearly empty and she was the only one to disembark from the train at Glensheil. She stepped on to the platform. There wasn't a soul in sight.

Knowing she was lucky to have arrived as planned despite the worsening weather, Libby pulled her suitcase across the gritted platform and headed towards the exit, hoping someone was waiting for her. The view, as ever, was stunning, with Heartcross Mountain in the distance, the peak covered in snow. It was breathtakingly picture-perfect, looking like a painting she'd once seen in an art gallery.

Reaching the station exit she saw that the snow was untouched and there wasn't a vehicle anywhere. Libby knew it was going to be impossible for a car to travel in these conditions and she reached into her bag to ring Flynn, but she had no mobile signal.

Debating whether to abandon her case and start walking, Libby heard the drone of an engine and the beep of a horn. She looked up to find Drew was waving madly at her through the window of his tractor. He pulled up just in front of her and left the engine running.

'Lib! It's great to see you,' he said, jumping down from the cab. 'I see you've brought the good weather with you.'

Libby smiled. 'Look at this place. I'm surprised *you* got here, never mind me.'

Drew opened the passenger door. 'I know. There are transport cancellations everywhere today. Flynn sent me as there's no other vehicle getting through here at the minute. The snow ploughs are out in force so hopefully things will be better within the next few hours.' Drew was his normal happy self, his tight blond corkscrew curls springing from underneath his woolly hat. As usual he was wearing his khaki farm overalls. 'You climb in, I'll get your suitcase.' The snow crunched under Drew's boots as he quickly retrieved the case and threw it into the back of the tractor before jumping back behind the wheel. 'It may be a little bumpy when we reach the track.'

'Don't worry about that, I'm just glad I'm not stranded at the station.'

The tractor began to move through the snow with ease and Libby held on to her seat as they bounced along.

'So you're here for Christmas?'

'Yes, and I can't wait to spend some time with the family.'

'And I believe after Christmas you're off to the Big Apple?'

'I am.'

'Flynn has been telling us all about it and that you're now

dressing and designing clothes for celebrities. I know Isla can't wait to catch up with you and hear your news.'

'I can't wait to catch up with everyone.' Since her brother opened up Starcross Manor, Libby had spent lots of time in the village of Heartcross. She'd attended the annual boat race and summer fair alongside Flynn and Julia, and established good friends during her visits, in particular Isla, with whom she'd become close friends. They often chatted on Facetime and interacted with each other's social media.

Isla's best friends were Felicity, who part-owned Bonnie's Teashop, and Allie, whose parents owned The Grouse and Haggis. They were a close-knit group but had always welcomed her every time she returned.

'I'm looking forward to the new job. It's an amazing opportunity, but I have my work cut out for the next month.'

'I believe so. You've recued Flynn from staff shortages, I hear. A wedding on Christmas Eve, though … you have the perfect backdrop for it.'

'I know, this is an amazing part of the world.'

'I know Flynn would love to have you on the team full-time. Every opportunity, he's singing your praises.'

'Mmm, that might change in the next few weeks as the only thing I've ever organised is a fashion show. I'm hoping the bride and groom are very easy-going. I get to meet them at the end of the week. Let's hope I can pull off the wedding of the century.'

The track leading to Love Heart Lane was covered in a thick blanket of snow that was already inches deep.

Thankfully, Heartcross was used to this kind of weather, though it did mean that the route into the village would be restricted and depending on the amount of snowfall some vehicles would find it difficult to climb the half-mile track between the town of Glensheil and Heartcross. Libby looked out of the window, there wasn't another vehicle in sight.

The tractor travelled along the High Street before following the winding lane through the woodlands, manoeuvring past the gatehouse and approaching the tree-lined driveway—the trees dressed with twinkly fairy lights—leading to the impressive, elegant Starcross Manor.

'This place takes my breath away every time.'

Libby gave a tiny gasp, pointed, then put her hands on her heart. The lake was frozen over and the secluded snowy wood was the perfect sanctuary for the herd of red deer that had suddenly appeared and lolloped across the snow-covered ground before just as swiftly disappearing amongst the trees.

The Georgian manor house standing in front of the tractor was magnificent, set in a hundred acres of lush green grass that included formal gardens, a deer park, woodlands and a wildflower meadow. The driveway leading to the entrance was grand, sweeping into a wide circle with an ornate fountain in the centre that wouldn't look out of place in the grounds of a royal palace. Huge stone steps led to the large double oak doors and a broad porch of stone pillars that housed the most beautiful Christmas trees Libby had ever seen.

'This place is just magical and those Christmas trees put mine to shame,' Libby confided.

'In the next couple of weeks, I'll take Isla and the boys to choose ours from the forest. We go through the same rigmarole every year. Isla always chooses a tree way too big and I have to saw most of it off to fit it in the living room. Isla will be ordering me about throughout the whole ordeal and then we'll bicker ... but I wouldn't have it any other way.'

Libby laughed.

'Here we are. Safe and sound.' Drew parked the tractor at the bottom of the stone steps. After helping down Libby, he grabbed her case.

'Thank you for collecting me. I'm not sure how I'd have got here in this weather.'

'It's my pleasure. You get yourself in the warmth and I'll bring your case up.'

'Thank you, and please tell Isla I'll be in touch as soon as I've settled in.'

The stone steps had been gritted but all around her the landscape glistened with snow. Already imagining the bride walking up the steps towards the entrance on Christmas Eve, Libby began to feel even more excited about the upcoming wedding.

Admiring the Christmas trees, she approached the entrance and a doorman dressed in a smartly cut black suit, top hat and gloves opened the door and officially welcomed her to Starcross Manor. Libby stepped onto the red carpet inside and did everything in her power not to gasp out loud. It was decorated to perfection with such class. The foyer was grand and to the side of the reception a beautiful winter wonderland scene had been created, the floor laden with fake snow and another enormous Christmas tree towering and sparkling over the scene. The grand staircase was wrapped in holly and crimson garlands with fairy lights tumbling all around them.

She was just about to make her way to the reception desk when she heard her name being called from the top of the grand staircase. Glancing upwards, she saw Flynn was racing down the stairs towards her with a huge grin on his face.

'You're here!'

'I am,' she said, hugging him tight when he reached the bottom.

Drew appeared with the suitcase just then and Flynn immediately shook his hand. 'Thanks for collecting Lib.'

'Not a problem. It was either me or a sledge and alpacas. I'll catch you later and good luck for the coming weeks,' Drew said, looking towards Libby.

'Thanks.'

As soon as Drew disappeared, Flynn picked up Libby's suitcase. 'You must be hungry and in need of a drink. Do you want to eat first or…'

'Can I settle into my room first and freshen up, and then we can grab something to eat and drink?'

'No problem,' Flynn said as he walked towards the reception desk.

The receptionist hung up her call and smiled at them both. 'Welcome back to Starcross Manor, Miss Carter.'

'Please, call me Libby.'

The receptionist smiled and opened the desk drawer, handing a bunch of keys to Libby. 'Anything you need, just ask.'

'Thanks so much.' Libby turned towards Flynn. 'I could get used to this.'

'I'm just grateful you're here. Let's get you settled in, fed and watered, then I can show you the studio you will be working from.'

'Sounds like a great plan.' Libby held up the bunch of keys. 'Why have I got keys and not one of those fiddly card things that I can never open the door with?'

'Because you're not staying in the main hotel.'

Libby looked at him quizzically. 'Where am I staying then?'

Flynn grinned and turned back towards the receptionist. 'Will you send Libby's suitcase over, please?' he said before turning back to Libby. 'Follow me.'

Libby had no idea where they were going but she followed Flynn through a maze of grand corridors with artwork on the walls. On her other visits to Starcross Manor, Libby had never ventured into this part of the hotel, so she did her best to take it all in. Finally, they reached a set of double doors and stepped outside. She was pleased to see that the snowflakes were still falling.

'Please tell me you're not putting me up in a garden shed.' She narrowed her eyes at Flynn.

'As if I'd dare.'

Flynn led the way through the illuminated gardens then took a gravel path that led to a woodland and then a clearing.

Stepping out from the darkness of the woods, Libby couldn't believe her eyes. 'Oh my... Look at this!' She stared at the circle of log cabins, all swathed in fairy lights hanging from their crooked roofs. Outside each log cabin was a small real Christmas tree waiting to be decorated. It was picture-perfect.

'I thought you might like to stay in one of the log cabins instead of a hotel room. There's more space and more character. You can obviously use the hotel facilities and eat in the restaurants—use the spa and gym—but I thought you could make this into a proper home for the next few weeks.'

Libby was overjoyed. 'This is just amazing. I actually feel like I'm in the middle of the Swiss Alps. It's like something out of a romantic novel. It's utterly gorgeous. I didn't even know these log cabins existed. How did I not know?'

'They're a relatively new addition. I wanted to make sure they were perfect before showing you. Now, as I know you love this time of year even though it's still November, I've organised a tree,' he said, pointing to it. 'There's another one inside and a box of decorations and believe me, if you like the outside, you haven't seen anything yet.' He took the bunch of keys from Libby and held up the silver one. 'This is for the front door.' Flynn put the key in the lock, opened the door and stepped to the side, sweeping his arm towards the inside of the lodge. 'After you.'

Libby stepped inside and gave an incredulous stare. 'Christmas has arrived!' Everywhere was dressed in crimson and gold, from the soft furnishings to an enormous bouquet of red roses and berries dressed in a huge ribbon on the table in the middle of the room.

'Just a small token of my appreciation. I can't thank you enough for helping me out with this wedding.'

'Flynn, this is all too much.'

'Don't be daft! You're doing me a huge favour and it also means that Julia and I are going to get to see lots of you during the festive period. That's priceless to me.'

Libby couldn't take the smile off her face. 'It's me who feels like I've won a competition. I can't believe you've done all this for me.' She was still looking around the room, completely taken with the cosy interior. There was a wood-burning stove in the living room, which was already lit and giving out a welcoming warmth to the room, a huge window at the far end that beautifully displayed the snowy mountainous terrain in the far distance, a flat-screen TV and a top-of-the-range kitchen with a wine rack full of bottles.

'The fridge is stocked with essentials and there's also tea and coffee just here,' he said, opening a cupboard.

'You really have thought of everything. I'm certainly going to be living my best life in the next few weeks! Thank you.'

Flynn smiled. 'I just want you be comfortable.'

The bellman appeared in the doorway, dropping off Libby's suitcase before tipping his cap at Flynn and disappearing again.

'Take a look outside,' urged Flynn.

Libby walked towards the back window and took a closer look at the outdoor space. The wooden terrace was festooned with hanging coloured bulbs and just to the right was a hot tub with a hedge either side, giving extra privacy but not blocking the view of the spectacular scenery. Libby could already picture spending her evenings sitting in the hot tub, sipping a glass of fizz with the snow falling lightly around her.

'I think this is going to be the best job in the world.'

'Through there are a couple of bedrooms, a bathroom and a small study where I've set you up with a sewing machine just in case you needed one here as well as the studio … which I can show you after lunch.'

Libby wandered through to the bedrooms and couldn't quite believe the study, which was bigger than her bedroom at home. Flynn had thought of everything; along with the sewing machine were a mannequin, scissors, pins, tape measures and an ironing board. Attached to the wall was a large whiteboard planner, outlining the weeks and jobs that would need to be co-ordinated to ensure smooth planning of the upcoming wedding.

'There's similar in the studio. I also took the liberty of arranging numerous materials and rails of wedding dress samples to give the bride ideas and choice. We have connections with a local tailor that has an outstanding reputation. There are also lots of brochures in the studio for places like Buttercup Barn, the florist based at the Heart of the Village at Foxglove Farm. The owner is going to pop in with some winter flower bouquets that could help with the colour scheme of the wedding.'

'Perfect.'

'Keeping all the business local will help to cement the business relationship we have here at Heartcross, and of course there's nobody better to bake the cake than Rona.'

Libby agreed. Rona, owner of Bonnie's Teashop, baked cakes to die for.

'She's already agreed to make the cake, so we don't have to worry about timing, but as soon as the colour scheme is confirmed, and the bride and groom have agreed on the type of cake and number of tiers, do let Rona know. Between you and me, she's a gem and is only charging me for the ingredients. In return she has free use of the spa through the festive season.'

This was exactly what Libby loved about Heartcross: everyone looked after each other.

'Shall we grab you some food and then I can show you the studio you'll be working from?'

'Sounds like a plan.'

After eating lunch in the restaurant, Libby was excited to see the studio. It was another separate building that was a short walk through the walled garden. The studio was at the end of the snowy path with yet more Christmas trees either side of the door, both dressed with twinkly lights.

'You have seriously created the best place to plan weddings. This is so romantic.'

'That's the plan. This studio is going to be the main hub for future weddings. It's going to be a one-stop shop. Dresses can be designed here, suits, flowers, cakes and transportation options provided, even including hot-air balloons or brides arriving by helicopter.'

'It sounds like you've got it all worked out.'

Flynn put the key in the lock but hesitated. 'I've been told off.'

'What do you mean?' asked Libby.

'Julia made a good point and I should have thought about it, but my only excuse is I'm a man.' He gave Libby a warm smile. 'Are you okay organising this after … everything?'

Libby touched his arm. 'I'm ten years on and life goes on. Don't worry, I love weddings and I'm happy to be here helping you.'

As soon as the words left her mouth she felt that tiny pang in the pit of her stomach that only crept up on her every so often. She quickly dismissed it and focused on her brother.

'Anyway, you haven't got another sister to help you out of this hole and I do design dresses for a living.'

'You're the best,' said Flynn enthusiastically. 'Come inside and let me know what you think.'

A wall of floor-to-ceiling mirrors reflected a long line of wedding dresses and tuxedos, all with different coloured accessories, hanging from a rail to one side. A stock of wedding shoes were displayed on the wall opposite the mirrors along with a bookcase and a table bearing a number of coloured files. Comfy plush chairs and settees were ready to welcome future brides and grooms, along with a display unit full of champagne. At the far end of the room was the essential bit of kit that Libby needed: a sewing machine and work table. The huge displays of the most beautiful blooms in each corner of the studio were just as stunning as the view through the large window overlooking the grounds of Starcross Manor and the mountains in the distance. Everything about this place oozed romance.

Libby sank into a plush sofa and stared around the room. 'I get to work in here up until Christmas? I've had worse jobs,' she joked, then stood up again and walked over to inspect the large books on the table. The first was navy blue with gold lettering, the title reading *Weddings at Starcross Manor*. Libby opened the book. There was every type of wedding cake possible. Square, round, sheet, rectangular, hexagon, single, mini, one-tier, two-tier... Libby turned the pages. 'These are amazing.'

'Aren't they just? All those have been baked by Rona.'

'She is a marvel.'

'We also have images of flower options if you look at the book just to your left. The florist at Buttercup Barn has photographed flowers for all seasons and colour co-ordinated the bouquets.'

Libby opened the second book on the table. 'These are stunning,' she said as she turned the pages slowly. 'This is fabulous and really is going to make my job a lot easier.'

'In that one,' Flynn said, pointing at a third book, 'there are table decorations and wedding invites—again, all colour co-ordinated—plus little extras including candles, different ideas for welcome drinks, seasonal cocktails and mulled wine. And as we are in Scotland, most grooms want to get married in a kilt...' Flynn pointed to the last book. 'We have a great working relationship with the tailor in Glensheil. I've tried to make it as easy as possible for you.

'The wedding is going to take place in The Grand Hall. It's an awe-inspiring room with gigantic floor-to-ceiling windows overlooking the snowy grounds. I can picture the publicity brochure and footage we can share on social media: huge open fires, a rustic feel, holly garlands, mulberry colours, the bride in white and—'

Libby laughed. 'It sounds to me like you've got it all planned out.'

'I know it's a cost but if we get this right, it will bring in a hell of a lot of business. I want all the brides and grooms in the world to be getting married here. I want the venue to be at the top of everyone's list. I want an A-list feel, bigger than Kew Gardens or Blenheim Palace.'

'That's what I love about you. You get an idea and boom! You make it happen. I'm in no doubt that within twelve months this will be the number one wedding venue in the world.'

'Now you're just making fun of me.'

'I'm not! Maybe after here, I can take a look at The Grand Hall. Do we know how many guests the couple will have?'

'There is a budget for that as I didn't want to end up bankrupt. The total number is one hundred and twenty.'

'That's the perfect size. I was also thinking about a secret garden, with mulled wine, cranberry winter cocktails, blankets and fairy lights.'

'Would you believe I have one of those, just off The Grand Hall? In fact, let me show it to you because it's something we've been working on recently and I'm really proud of how it's come together.'

A moment later, they sailed into The Grand Hall. The open fire was roaring away and there was an exquisite dining area laid before them. Libby looked up to the ceiling where oak beams arched regally. Starcross Manor was indeed a year-round showstopper.

'Stars will twinkle through the section of glass roof at that end,' said Flynn, pointing. 'Chairs will be laid out in rows, here, here and here.' He reminded Libby of a flight attendant, the way he manoeuvred his hands. 'They will be married overlooking the grounds and the mountains.'

The elegance, panache and charm of the room had made an instant hit with Libby. She knew the competition winners were going to be blown away by it.

'And this door leads through to the secret garden where winter cocktails can be served beneath the swaying lanterns.' Flynn swung the door open to reveal the most beautiful hideaway. The grey slate floor led to a number of rustic pews and chairs scattered around, dressed with damson plush velvet cushions that complemented the mulberry harlequin Shetland throws, the palette of colours exquisite in the wintry space. A huge fire pit was positioned in the middle of the garden and a path of round flagstones led through a wooden archway to a stunning glasshouse, which would provide warmth along with a whimsical ambiance. There also a small bar at the far end.

'WOW! What an amazing place and space.' Libby spun around, taking in the whole scene before her. 'They are very lucky people,' she said, walking up to the fire pit. 'I can picture it now. Logs burning, drinking hot chocolate while roasting marshmallows. I think I need to get myself an invite to this wedding.'

'As the wedding planner I think you'd be top of the list,' replied Flynn with a warm smile. He pointed to something behind Libby and she turned around.

'There she is!' Julia was hurrying towards Libby and enveloped her in the biggest of hugs. 'I can't believe you're here and we get to keep you for Christmas too!'

'I know! Christmas with my favourite people.'

'Eek!' Julia gave a little squeal as she hugged Libby again. 'And we must make sure we spend quality time together before you head off to New York. Huge congratulations on the new job, by the way. I can't believe you're leaving us … and selfishly I don't want you to.'

'Thank you and I know. It's a little surreal that I was chosen from all the applicants. I honestly didn't think I'd have a cat in hell's chance.'

'Of course you did. Your designs are amazing, your business is booming and everywhere I look on social media someone is wearing something of yours. I bet that that's exactly what our competition winners think too, that they didn't have a cat in hell's chance. What do you think of this place?' Julia swung her arms open. 'It's breathtaking, isn't it.'

'I think it's utterly gorgeous and decorated to perfection. This is the place dream weddings are made of,' Libby said, attempting to dismiss memories of the past from her mind. The last and only wedding she'd ever organised was her own. She had thought Daniel was her life, her soulmate. They'd spent many hours discussing their future, the type of house they were going to live in and how many children they wanted. They even imagined what their children would look like. Would they have curly hair and blue eyes like Libby or fair hair and brown eyes like Daniel? But during that time, Libby had begun to feel poorly. She was exhausted, often irritable and very emotional, and after several tests the consultant shared news she was not expecting. She was going through premature menopause. It wasn't something that happened to everyone; in fact, it only happened to 0.01 per cent of the population. And unfortunately Libby was one of those people. Overcome with grief at the realisation she would not be able to have children, Libby had broken down. All she'd ever wanted was her own family. She had thought Daniel would stand by her but instead he'd ended things, abandoning her at the time she needed him most. He said he had no choice, that he wanted children of his own and that was something Libby could never give him.

Facing double heartache, Libby had turned to her family for support. Thankfully, they were there to catch her as she fell. It took her a long time to process the fact that she would never be able to carry her own child, while also dealing with Daniel's abrupt disappearance from her life. Without Flynn and her dad it would have been near impossible to survive, let alone come out the other side stronger. They were by her side every step of the way, providing the love and support she so desperately needed. They held her while she sobbed, supported her while she raged at the injustice of it all, and—most importantly— they made her understand that it wasn't the end for her. She had options for the future, including adoption, fostering or falling in love with someone who already had children. Libby knew she had so much love to give but what she feared most was meeting the man of her dreams and being rejected again simply because she couldn't have children.

The date for Libby and Daniel's wedding had been set for over a year and though he didn't call it off on the wedding day itself – he had done it six months before – it still didn't make it any easier when the day finally arrived. The weather had been perfect, the temperature a whopping twenty-five degrees. The dress had been hanging in Libby's spare room as she didn't know what to do with it, and she'd wandered in and stared at it for some time. It was quite simply a gown fit for a princess, with layers of ruffles that floated to the ground, a bateau neckline and a floral beaded bodice. At the time it had been Libby's ideal dress.

Ironically, it was the same dress that had landed her her dream job in New York. She'd stored it in a suit carrier in the wardrobe in the spare bedroom for ten years and when she applied for the position, and the brief was 'a modern-day take on Cinderella', Libby had taken great pleasure in hacking the dress to pieces and redesigning the whole thing.

Julia must have noticed Libby's smile had slipped and touched her arm. 'We do appreciate you helping us out. We know—'

Libby interrupted. 'Honestly, all that is a distant memory. It seems like it never really happened, and could you imagine if I had actually married Daniel?' She rolled her eyes and laughed. 'I, for one, am glad I didn't. And believe me, I'm going to have fun organising this wedding.'

After giving Libby another quick hug, Julia smiled beatifically. 'This secret garden was my idea and all the interior design was left to me. Probably because I always wanted a secret garden at my wedding and I want to be married on a winter's day with the snowy mountains towering in the distance. I've had my wedding mapped out since I was a little girl—I even have a scrapbook with my own plans and designs. There are magazine cut-outs and everything.' Julia laughed.

'Really? That's amazing! I'd love to take a look at that,' enthused Libby.

'I'll dig it out. With this winter over soon, there's no excuse for next year. I'm taking charge of your diary,' Julia teased Flynn. 'We *will* be married next winter.'

'And that's you told.' Libby jokingly pointed at Flynn before turning back to Julia. 'If you're free tonight, maybe you could bring your scrapbook over to the lodge and we can have a proper catch-up over a glass of wine.'

'Lovely! Sounds like a plan,' replied Julia.

'You're obviously invited too,' added Libby, glancing at Flynn.

'Girly chat and scrapbooks? I think I'll leave the pair of you to it.'

'What he means is that Drew and Fergus have organised a game of cards at the pub and given the choice—'

Flynn held his hands up. 'I can neither confirm nor deny.'

Leaning towards Flynn, Julia kissed him on his cheek. 'I need to get back to work but, just so you know, I saw Guy in the foyer when I arrived.' Looking in Libby's direction, she added, 'He's the film-maker you'll be working with. He's very easy on the eye, but can be a little aloof,' she said mysteriously, giving Libby a look.

'He's not aloof,' chipped in Flynn. 'He's just dedicated and wants to do a good job. It's called being professional.'

'Believe me, us women have a sixth sense about these things.' She looked towards Libby for support. 'There's more going on in his life than meets the eye. In every interview I've seen him do recently there's been a certain sadness behind the eyes.'

'Don't be ridiculous, it's probably the lighting,' retorted Flynn.

'I should be in for an interesting month,' Libby said. 'What's his surname?'

'Hart,' replied Flynn.

'A very apt name for a guy filming a wedding,' replied Libby.

'He's well known in his field,' insisted Flynn. 'Look him up.'

Libby had every intention of doing so.

'I really have to get back to work,' Julia said as she edged towards the door. 'I'll see you tonight around seven thirty. Does that suit you?'

'Perfect,' replied Libby, watching Julia disappear through the door.

'And I've got a meeting in thirty minutes. Are you okay to amuse yourself?' asked Flynn.

'Absolutely.' Libby already had plans to relax with a book and maybe venture into the hot tub after unpacking her clothes. 'I'll catch up with you later.'

Watching Flynn leave, Libby took another look around the secret garden. She walked over towards the private bar and poured herself a gin and tonic then sat in one of the comfy-looking chairs, pulling a throw around her shoulders. After taking a sip of her drink, she googled Guy Hart on her phone and was amazed to see that not only was he a film-maker, he was an *award-winning* film-maker for wildlife programmes he'd filmed in Africa. His career was impressive: he'd also been to the Antarctic and made films about the ocean and mountainous terrains. Libby couldn't fathom why he would be filming a wedding video, given that it seemed a step back in his career, but scrolling through his images, she saw that Julia was right: he was very easy on the eye and it wouldn't be any hardship working alongside him for the next few weeks even if he was, in Julia's words, 'a little aloof'.

Looking at his social media she saw that his Instagram followers were off the scale. Each image was expertly photographed but there was one thing that Libby noticed immediately: there were no photos showing anything to do with his personal life.

After finishing her drink, Libby headed back towards the lodge. It wasn't long before she'd unpacked her suitcase and made a plan for the rest of the afternoon, which included taking a dip in the hot tub and curling up on the sofa to read a book before Julia arrived later tonight.

Feeling like she was on a winter holiday, Libby poured herself another drink and slipped into her bikini. Shivering, she grabbed her robe and pulled a red bobble hat over her curls, her breath misting the air as she stepped outside.

'This is the life,' she murmured, lifting the lid on the hot tub and flicking the switch to turn it on. There was a loud gurgling sound and bubbles began to rise to the surface. Taking off her robe, she slipped into the water, letting its warmth soothe her body. Being surrounded by the rural beauty and the tranquillity of the place, Libby felt relaxed and happy. She was going to make the most of her time here, as she knew that when she arrived in New York, the city that never sleeps, her life would take on a hectic pace.

After balancing her drink on the side, she lowered her shoulders under the water and tilted her head upwards, attempting to blow away the light snowflakes that were fluttering all around. Her ears pricked up as she heard a door slam and she sat up straight, looking towards the lodges. She quickly realised that the noise hadn't come from her own lodge but from next door, where her neighbour had evidently stepped outside to take a call.

'Yes, I've arrived. Do we really need to talk about this now? Do you not think it's bad enough I have to film a wedding and spend every waking hour watching it being planned? And here you are again, ramming it down my throat. I need a stiff drink.'

Libby gave a tiny gasp. From the conversation she knew this must be Guy, which meant he would be staying in the lodge right next door to hers. His accent was posh. She couldn't quite place it but it reminded her of an elite public schoolboy or even royalty. Out of curiosity – and not wanting to draw attention to herself – Libby lay perfectly still, listening to whatever she could hear over the noise of the hot-tub jets.

'We all know why I don't want to be here,' continued Guy.

Libby didn't. She was intrigued; why he didn't want to be here? Surely it wasn't that bad a prospect, spending the next few weeks in a luxury lodge in a beautiful part of the world? The scenery was stunning and if his lodge was like hers, it was cosy and radiated winter and Christmas perfectly.

Knowing she shouldn't be listening to someone else's conversation she felt a twinge of guilt. Guy's voice began to peter out as he wandered back towards his lodge and Libby took her chance to escape. The last thing she wanted was for him to notice her through the hedge. It would be embarrassing to introduce herself wearing just a bikini and a red bobble hat. Stepping out of the hot tub she switched off the bubbles and was just about to grab her robe when…

SPLASH!

Libby nearly jumped out of her skin and immediately spun round, letting out a scream and wrapping her arms round her chest, her heart racing. There was a large furry thing splashing around in the hot tub.

'Oh my God!' she squealed then froze.

Narrowing her eyes, she took a closer look then let out a hearty laugh. Her beating heart began to calm. In the water, looking like it was having the time of its life, was a dappled Dachshund paddling and diving under the water. It gave an excited bark while swimming around in circles.

'Aren't you the cutest thing! Where have you come from?' Libby looked all around but couldn't see anyone. She was just about to climb back into the water to rescue the puppy when she heard Guy's voice shouting from his lodge.

'Where the hell are you?' he bellowed, his voice getting louder. 'You'll be the death of me.'

The posh accent and angry tone made Libby smile. Hearing Guy's voice the dog barked and immediately she heard footsteps.

Guy appeared on the other side of the picket fence and Libby met the eyes of the handsome stranger. She swallowed, then her mouth fell open. She knew she was catching flies but she couldn't help it. She was too busy getting lost inside the dark hazel eyes that were staring back at her. The photos on

Google Images didn't do him justice. He was the first man in a very long time that had stopped her dead in her tracks.

'Breathe,' she murmured to herself, thankfully quietly enough that he didn't appear to hear.

He walked through the gate. 'I'm so sorry, I didn't know anyone was here,' he said apologetically, averting his eyes as he hurried forward and passed Libby her robe. 'I can't have anyone dying of hypothermia on my watch.'

Suitably embarrassed by standing there wearing only a bikini and a bobble hat, Libby thanked him and quickly pulled the robe around her body.

'Nice hat,' he said, looking back in her direction. 'You need that in this weather to keep you warm.' There was a spark of humour and a glint in his eye. He grinned at her and instantly Libby felt herself blush. She hoped he would attribute it to the cold.

'My thoughts exactly,' she replied, giving back a little banter.

'I was looking for...' Guy glanced towards the hot tub. 'I was looking for my dog, who seems to be swimming in your hot tub.'

'Aww, it belongs to you.'

'She does. Every time I look at her, I wonder how I got so lucky.' Guy rolled his eyes in jest. 'I'm Guy.'

'Libby. And this is...'

'Branston.'

Libby raised an eyebrow. 'Branston. That's an unusual name for a dog.'

'Named after Branston Pickle. For two reasons: the first reason being that the day I brought her home I was eating cheese and crackers for lunch with Branston Pickle and after I left the room for two seconds, she managed to knock the jar off the coffee table and lick out most of the contents. The second reason speaks for itself.' Guy nodded towards the hot tub. 'She's always getting herself into a pickle. I tend to call her Pickle.'

Libby laughed.

'I suppose I better get her out of there, before she overcooks. But she doesn't seem to mind the hot water.'

'Are you going in?' asked Libby, clutching the neck of her robe tighter. She had no intention of slipping it off and climbing back into the hot tub in front of Guy.

He looked down at his outfit, a classy mixture of designer brands.

Libby continued with a straight face. 'I think it's a bit soon in the relationship if I'm in a state of near undress for the second time in five minutes,' she joked before her face broke into a warm smile.

'Oh, I don't know, I'm up for that,' he teased, giving her a wolfish grin that revealed a perfect set of white teeth. They stared at each other for a moment, and Libby's stomach gave another little flip.

She watched as he turned, walked to the rear of the lodge and unhooked a large blue net that was attached to the wall. Pickle was still ducking and diving but not for much longer as Guy extended the net and scooped her straight out of the water. Libby was on hand with a towel, which she passed to Guy, who wrapped Pickle up tightly then balanced the net against the wall. After a quick towel dry, Guy placed Pickle on the ground. She woofed playfully and tried to grab the towel but with no luck. Pickle then turned her attentions to Libby and the energetic whirlwind began to tug at the bottom of her robe with surprising force, her bum waggling as she growled softly then rolled over on her back, waving her paws in the air.

'She has no shame,' announced Guy, tickling Pickle's damp stomach.

Pickle was the cutest ball of dappled brown that Libby had ever seen. 'Oh my life, just look at those eyes.' Libby scooped up the potbellied puppy in her hands and took the towel from Guy, wrapping Pickle tightly once more. 'She's absolutely gorgeous.'

'Don't let her good looks fool you. She leaves a trail of destruction everywhere she goes. She's chewed several pairs of shoes, armchairs, rugs, a laptop charger ... the list is endless. Get a dog, they said, it will enhance your life. It's costing me a fortune. Do you have any pets?'

Libby had always wanted a dog and on many occasions had come close to getting one, but with the change in her lifestyle next month, she was glad she hadn't.

'Me? No. I have trouble keeping the three potted plants on my kitchen window alive. They're constantly fighting for survival.'

Guy laughed. Taking Pickle from Libby's arms, he said, 'Sorry again for the intrusion.'

'I don't mind. This one is cuteness overload,' she said, giving Pickle one last pat.

'No doubt we'll see you around.' He raised his eyebrow hopefully.

'I'm here until after Christmas,' she replied.

'Late Christmas Eve for us, as soon as my work commitment is completed. And if I'm truly honest, that can't come soon enough.'

'Surely it can't be that bad?'

'Believe me, it is. I've been roped into a job that isn't going to be... Oh it doesn't matter, you need to get inside before you catch your death.'

Libby *was* beginning to feel chilly. She had every intention of grabbing a shower and sitting in front of the log fire as soon as possible, but something made her pause. Why wasn't Guy looking forward to the next few weeks? All he had to do was trail around after the happy couple catching their magic moments on film. This was her opportunity to drop into the conversation that actually the next few weeks might not be as bad as they seemed, since they were going to be working together, but she decided to keep that snippet of information to herself for now, wanting to find out a little more about Guy first.

'Life is what you make it. You might not be looking forward to it but who knows, you might just have the best time. And even if you have a bad day at the office, you can always look forward to enjoying the scenery in the evening.'

'That I can,' he agreed, holding eye contact, his eyes sparkling and his stubble glistening from the spotlights shining up from the decking.

They exchanged smiles and stared at each other for a moment in a contemplative silence. When he finally turned and walked away, he looked back over his shoulder and Libby grinned. She watched him until he disappeared, then with a spring in her step hurried back into the warmth of the lodge. There was something mesmerising about Guy Hart, but Libby gave herself a little shake. The last time she'd found anyone intriguing, he'd upped and left when she needed him most. And she certainly wasn't here to find a man.

Standing in front of the log fire, which emitted a welcoming warmth, she thought about the conversation she'd overheard and how Guy had openly admitted he wasn't looking forward to the next few weeks. Libby was always up for a challenge, and now that she was fully aware of this fact, she was going to make sure that this was the best job he'd ever worked on. Whatever it took, she *would* put a smile on Guy Hart's face.

Chapter Three

Libby was wrapped up in her favourite cosy sweatshirt and thermal fleece leggings with her feet snug inside her fluffy slippers. After all the travelling she'd felt tired and had fallen in and out of sleep on the settee for a number of hours. Now it wouldn't be long before Julia arrived, and Libby decided to prepare some nibbles and chill a bottle of wine. Flynn knew her well and she was pleased to see that the fridge was full of all her favourites—a selection of cheeses, pickles and cold meats with fresh salad—and in the bread bin was a fresh crusty bloomer. This was just the kind of picnic tea she loved.

With everything laid out and ready for Julia, Libby glanced out of the front window of the lodge to see if she was coming. Thankfully, for the time being, the snow had stopped falling. The snow in front of the lodge was untouched except for one set of footprints and two long lines imprinted in the fresh dusting. Just a little further up the path she spotted Guy, shuffling along in the snow pulling a bright red sledge with Pickle sitting proudly on top of it. The sight of Pickle lording it up on the sledge made Libby laugh out loud. Guy stopped a little further on and lifted Pickle onto the ground. The snow was nearly touching her belly. Libby realised that Pickle must have needed the toilet but was refusing to walk in the cold snow.

'The things you have to do,' she murmured, still watching.

Guy turned around and began walking back to the lodge, and Libby quickly moved away from the window, not wanting him to catch her watching. Her thoughts turned to his personal life. Guy Hart was established and famous in his field yet the Internet provided information only about his career—nothing personal.

As she poured herself a glass of wine there was a knock on the door. Her heart began to beat faster as the first thing that popped into her head was that it might be Guy. She quickly checked her appearance, dabbed on a tiny amount of lip gloss and puffed up her curls before hurrying to the door.

Opening it, she came face to face with Julia.

'Come on, it's freezing out here!' Julia's hat was pulled way down low on her head and her scarf was wrapped tightly around her face with only her eyes peeping out.

'Oh, it's only you!' exclaimed Libby, having forgotten their plans for a brief moment. Libby looked over Julia's shoulder to see if Guy was anywhere to be seen.

Julia followed her gaze. 'What do you mean, it's only me? Who were you expecting? You look a little disappointed to see me.'

'Don't be ridiculous,' replied Libby opening the door wide.

'Come on in. I've prepared us a few nibbles and the wine is chilling.'

'Mmm.' Julia waggled her finger round in a circle in front of Libby. 'I know you, there's something you aren't telling me.'

'I'm just excited at the thought of spending the evening with my favourite sister-in-law-to-be and of course catching up with all your gossip.'

'And I need to catch up with yours.' Julia handed Libby a bottle of wine, then held up the book she was carrying. 'Here's my wedding scrapbook,' she said.

Libby took it from her as Julia took off her boots and slid her feet into a pair of slippers she'd brought with her. 'Always have to be comfy.'

'You sound like an old married woman already,' joked Libby, taking Julia's coat and hanging it on the hook.

'Chance would be a fine thing. I just need to pin your brother down to set the date.'

'With all this talk of weddings, let's hope it's sooner rather than later.' Libby gestured towards a chair before poking the embers and throwing a couple more logs on the fire. 'Take a seat. I'll pour the wine and grab the food.'

With the wine poured and food laid out on the coffee table, Libby sat cross-legged on the rug in front of the fire. 'This is blooming good wine,' she said.

'That's the joy of having a fiancé who owns a hotel with the biggest wine cellar I've ever seen in my life.'

Libby laughed, then picked up the scrapbook and placed it on the rug in front of her. 'I can't wait to look through this.'

'It's been a work in progress for many years. I've never shown this to anyone before.'

'I'm privileged. I can't wait to see what you have in here.

Before we start though, I know Flynn probably wants you to ask me if there's anyone special in my life … because he's always asking! Please let him know my strongest connection is with the Wi-Fi.'

Julia laughed. 'You have so much to give and share with someone special.'

'I do and I will when the time is right. For now, I've a job waiting for me in New York and that's my main priority, along with spending Christmas here in Heartcross with my family.'

'I have to say, you're the only person I know who has escaped the Heartcross curse.'

'"Once you arrive in Heartcross you never want to leave,"' chanted Libby with a smile. 'I do love it here; I always have. It's a beautiful part of the country with the most spectacular views and just the best people. And of course, there's the bonus of you, Flynn and my dad being here.'

'Wilbur has kept himself busy since he retired from the Little Blue Boat House. Bea, who now manages it, has raised hundreds of thousands for the new lifeboats and the Heartcross Rescue Station. Hopefully, everything will be up and running in six months or so. She's worked so hard and Wilbur wants to come out of retirement and help man the switchboards. Your dad has more energy than all of us put together!'

'He just doesn't know when to stop, does he? But it's a very good cause and I think the busier he is, the younger he seems.'

'Libby, I've got something to ask you. I know it's not happening anytime soon but I was thinking, as my father has passed away and I don't have another father figure in my life, when the time comes, and Flynn and I finally get a date in the diary … do you think Wilbur would give me away? I didn't want to ask him before I ran it by you first.'

'Why would you need to run it by me first?'

'Because he's your father and I don't want to step on your toes. Surely the first person he should walk down the aisle should be you.'

'Aww, that's such a lovely thought. Thank you for asking me first but I think if it's left to me, he might never get the chance to walk anyone down the aisle!' replied Libby. Julia looked relieved. 'You really aren't treading on my toes. But I'll tell you now, with my father's eccentric dress sense, we need to make sure he doesn't outshine the bride.'

'Thank you.' Julia looked genuinely touched that Libby was more than okay about it.

'Before I leave for New York we will be pinning that brother of mine down for a date.'

'We will but as I want a winter wedding'—Julia pushed the scrapbook forward towards Libby—'it will have to be next Christmas. That gives me plenty of time to organise it though.'

'Let's have a look at your scrapbook.'

Side by side, they sat and turned the pages.

'Flynn's attire will be easy: kilt, dirk and sporran, three-button waistcoat, white shirt and bow tie. He's going to look so handsome. I can picture it now. I arrive by a wooden sleigh pulled by reindeer across the grounds of Starcross Manor…'

Libby raised an eyebrow. 'I'm hoping the competition winners don't request reindeer. Where am I going to magic those up from?' She was beginning to feel worried as it suddenly dawned on her that the winning couple could request absolutely anything and she was going to have to make their dreams come true.

'You'd have a number of options. The first is obvious.'

'Go on.'

'Duh! Ask Santa,' joked Julia, bumping her shoulder against Libby's. 'But failing that, you could catch the wild deer from the grounds at Starcross Manor or dress up Isla and Drew's alpacas from Foxglove Farm. You never know, you might not even be able to tell the difference if you put faux antlers on them. The third option is to speak to Grace and Andrew. They look after a herd of reindeer every year up at Heartcross Castle. It's open to the public and children can go and feed them.'

'The third option it is. Absolutely perfect!'

'Everyone knows someone who knows someone. Believe me, within the network of the Heartcross community, there is nothing that can't be sorted.'

'I think I believe you.' Libby tapped a cut-out from a magazine that was glued to the next page.

'Pipers! I've always wanted bagpipes. I can picture it now. I arrive at the steps of Starcross Manor in the sleigh pulled by reindeer and step out onto the red carpet that travels up the stone steps between the most beautiful decorated Christmas trees. The pipers are standing at the top of the steps and will play as I walk towards them.'

'Very Scottish. It sounds to me as if you have it all worked out!'

'The colour scheme is classic white. The Grand Hall will be filled with white blossom trees, fairy lights, candles and white chairs. The food is all about comfort. Dainty canapés are lovely but on days like today when it's chilly outside, guests want comfort food. A cheese fondue or mini beef Yorkshire puddings would be perfect, and for the main meal it has to be a roast dinner with a joint carved at each table. And for the dessert, sticky toffee pudding is always a winner.'

'You're making me so hungry!' admitted Libby, thinking it all sounded so utterly perfect.

'And before the guests head off home into the cold night, they will be served something warm and hearty. Maybe a hog roast, bacon rolls, sausage rolls or even cheese toasties,' enthused Julia. 'And now on to my outfit.'

Libby couldn't wait to see what Julia had in mind.

'I want to push boundaries and be a little different. You know I'm not a girly girl. I prefer jeans and trousers, and trainers on my feet. I've never been one for a pair of heels.'

'Go on, I'm encouraged.' Libby wondered what Julia was going to say next.

'My dream is a two-piece bridal suit that's seriously bold and contemporary. There's no photograph or cut-out as such, but I've tried to draw what was in my head.' Julia bit her lip and turned over the page, waiting for Libby's reaction.

Libby stared at the drawings, silent for a moment, taking in every detail. She was blown away.

'You aren't saying anything. You hate the idea, don't you? Do you think it's too out of the ordinary and I should stick to a traditional dress?' Julia asked, concern evident in her tone.

Libby looked up and met Julia's gaze. 'Hate it? Far from it. Julia, this is what you call fashion forward, on trend and truly a vision. I absolutely love it! Have you ever thought of becoming a fashion designer?'

'They're just scribbles,' Julia replied humbly, but from her expression Libby could tell she was secretly chuffed at the validation.

'In that case, these scribbles will turn heads. This outfit is striking.'

'That's the plan!' Julia wore a huge smile. 'For a second I honestly thought you didn't like it. My heart was beating so fast.'

'A champagne bodice and ivory trousers—the perfect combination.' The drawings showed the bodice with long lace bubble sleeves and a high boat neckline. 'These details bring it all to life.' With dozens of 3D florals covering the top and all the way down the arms and back, it was truly breathtaking. It was finished perfectly with pearl clasps down the back. The wide plain trousers were a contrast in their elegance and minimalist style.

'And to wear on top for any outdoor photos, I was thinking something like this.' Julia turned over to the next page.

'I'm glad my new boss hasn't seen this because I think I'd be out of a job,' teased Libby. She was looking at a stunning jacket in silver feather plumes with a three-quarter sleeve. It was the ultimate lightweight cropped jacket that complemented the trouser suit perfectly without compromising on shape and detail. 'I absolutely love the colour!'

'I thought with a soft satin lining and covered in delicate faux feathers,' added Julia, looking at Libby for her approval.

'I think you've nailed it. It will hang softly against the body but will also give you that extra warmth. We can attach the front of the jacket with a discreet hook-and-eye fastener so it can be worn open for maximum exposure of that fabulous suit. You've made my job so easy,' admitted Libby, taking a sip of wine.

'Your job?'

'Yes, my job. You have to let me make this design for you.'

Julia gave a tiny gasp. 'Are you sure?'

'Of course I'm sure. I'd be offended if you didn't let me.'

'Eek!' Julia gave a squeal and hugged Libby tightly. 'Thank you, thank you, thank you.'

'You don't have to thank me. It's what sisters-in-law are for.'

Julia held up her glass and chinked it against Libby's. 'You have really made my night.'

'These 3D flowers on the bodice will all be hand sewn and I have just the perfect material in mind.'

'But that will take for ever.'

'I best get started then!'

Libby could see the happiness written all over Julia's face. 'You're going to knock the socks off Flynn when you walk down the aisle.'

'*When* is the very question, but that is the plan!'

'And this wedding cake looks scrumptious,' exclaimed Libby. 'Those frosted fruits look incredible on that white cake and those sugar crusted cranberries are striking. You have made the wedding planner's job very easy.'

'And because it's a winter wedding I was thinking it would be fun to place a sprig of mistletoe in the men's buttonholes so anyone could sneak a quick kiss if they dare.'

'Brilliant! I love that idea and all of these. You have such a clear vision. It makes me wonder what the competition winners are like and what type of wedding they want. I need to read up on them before I meet them.'

'I don't know anything about them. But it must have been a hard job and a tough decision to wade through all the entries and pick a winner.' Julia placed the scrapbook back on the table and began tucking into the food. 'I have to say though, I find it so strange that Jenny resigned so abruptly. She loved her job. I was talking to her only forty-eight hours before and she never said a word. Let's just hope you and Guy don't follow suit.'

'I'm not going anywhere. Free accommodation, food and a wedding … what's not to like?'

'You're smiling,' Julia noticed. 'I mentioned his name and now you're smiling.'

'I'm not,' protested Libby, but she was finding it hard to tame the smile on her face.

'Have you met him yet or just stalked him on social media?' Julia tilted her head to one side waiting for an answer.

'Both,' admitted Libby. 'And his pickle!'

'I beg your pardon?' Julia looked amused.

'His dappled Dachshund—who is called Pickle—decided to go for a swim in my hot tub, which was completely embarrassing as I was standing there in my bikini and red bobble hat when his dog came from nowhere and launched herself straight into the water.'

Julia let out a hearty laugh. 'No way! I bet that was quite an introduction.'

'It was downright embarrassing, but he did comment that I had a nice hat.'

'Oh, I bet he did.'

Libby pointed to the wall and mouthed, 'He's staying right next door.'

'He can't hear you,' Julia said. 'Why are we whispering?'

'I don't know,' replied Libby. 'But I have to say I didn't find him aloof. In fact, he was friendly and funny. What gave you the impression he was aloof?'

'Maybe it was the wrong choice of word,' Julia admitted. 'But the boys were saying that the last time he was in town, he just seemed very preoccupied and not his usual cheery self. But then, I suppose we can't be cheery all of the time.'

'You're right, we all have bad days and we never really know what's going on in other people's lives. Well, aloof or not, it'll be good for me to have company on a daily basis. My job can be quite lonely and there are days when I don't even speak to another human, except when I shout answers at Bradley Walsh when *The Chase* is on in the background.'

Julia laughed. 'But all that is about to change.'

For the past ten years, Libby had kept costs down and worked on her designs out of the spare room of her home. Most days, she threw her hair up in a messy bun and stayed in her PJs unless she had to venture out for a meeting. She absolutely loved her job, but the one downside was that she missed the day-to-day conversations and interactions you had when working with other people. But Julia was right, all that was all going to change now. The fashion house in New York City was spread over six floors with hundreds of employees.

Libby smiled to herself, remembering how when she was growing up she'd thought a 'fashion house' was a giant house that everyone lived in, not that it housed many famous designers under one brand.

Libby had always been into textiles and started making her own clothes as a teenager, becoming the envy of her friends, who loved her designs. As soon as she left school, she went to college and studied fashion design. She started out doing clothing alterations at home after work while also working full-time in a department store as a personal shopper, advising customers about what looked good on them. After a while she began to get more creative and fashioned her own line of clothes, which she promoted on social media. Once she had built her reputation online, the demand for her designs was huge and before she knew it her business was growing rapidly. Within a year, she was making good money and had booked her first fashion show. Soon the press couldn't get enough of her and she started spotting people from reality TV shows wearing her outfits to media events. Before she knew it, Libby had received a DM and had signed up to create an exclusive outfit for her first celebrity client.

Her dream had always been to showcase her designs at New York fashion week and with this new job she was one step closer to achieving it.

'It is. It'll be very strange working in a busy, noisy environment, but I'm looking forward to it too.'

'Let's hope you aren't too busy for me in the coming month. I want to see you at every opportunity before you fly off to New York.'

'I'll be making all the time in the world for you and Flynn in between working my socks off.'

'I do hope we're going to get lots of enquiries when all the promotion stuff goes out. This is going to be a truly amazing wedding on Christmas Eve with you at the helm.'

Libby smiled at the compliment. She knew if she could pull this off for Flynn it would be such a win for Starcross Manor.

'It's a good job I love weddings and putting a smile on people's faces.'

'Libby Carter, your infectious personality and work ethic should be bottled. Talking of bottles, this one is empty!' Julia waved it in the air.

'There's plenty more where that came from.' Libby got up

and fetched another bottle from the fridge. 'So how did Guy end up with the gig? What's his connection to Flynn?' she asked, intrigued. She didn't mention that she'd overheard Guy's telephone conversation and that he wasn't looking forward to the next few weeks.

'Flynn has met Guy several times through Rory. Rory knows how much Flynn needs this to be a success and as Guy owed Rory a couple of favours, Flynn became one of them.'

'That's decent of him. I've checked out his profile and trailing a bride and groom for a few weeks seems a little mundane compared to his usual line of work.'

'"His usual type of work" … someone *has* been doing their research.'

'I only wanted to know more about who I'd be working with … and, in my defence, I looked him up before I actually met him.'

'And what was Guy's reaction when you shared that you would be working together over the next month?'

'I've not actually got that into the conversation yet. Hopefully, it'll be a nice surprise.'

'I'm sure it will be more than a nice surprise.'

For the next couple of hours they gossiped, and Julia's hilarious stories about the villagers' latest antics had Libby laughing non-stop.

'This is what I love about this place: it's a real community. You all work hard, laugh together, cry together and are always there for each other. I've lived where I've lived for the past ten years and I barely know my neighbours. In fact I can count on the fingers of one hand the number of times I've had a conversation with any of them, and that's usually only when I've taken a parcel in for them.'

'We're lucky in Heartcross. I think we all realised just how special this community was when the bridge collapsed. That winter was the worst ever.'

The village of Heartcross had become famous when the worst weather in Scottish Highlands history had caused the bridge to collapse. It linked the village to the next town, and the stranded residents of Heartcross were catapulted into the national news.

'And wait until you catch up with Isla. Foxglove Farm has expanded! The old barns have been converted and rented out to local businesses. It's like a small countryside shopping emporium nestled in the heart of Heartcross and is called exactly that: The Heart of The Village. You're going to love it. Buttercup Barn, the florist's, is right in the centre. It's beautiful. Fresh flowers every day, and Florrie, the owner, is just a gorgeous individual. You'll love her. Flynn has given the contract to Florrie for all the wedding flowers that are organised through Starcross Manor.'

'I can go and explore it tomorrow.'

'Then there's a couple of small boutiques including countryside clothing, a gift shop, the farm shop – which Drew has expanded to include a small butchers – and there's a pet store, a baked potato van and a crêpe shop.'

'Sounds heavenly.'

'And not forgetting there's the fairy wood for the children and if you feel like walking an alpaca there's always that option too!'

Libby laughed. 'I'll put that on my list of things to do

before I go to New York. I can't see much chance of that happening down Fifth Avenue. Oh, it's such a treat to catch up with you, Julia. I've had a lovely evening.'

'Is that because I'm here or because you've met the boy next door?'

Libby rolled her eyes playfully. 'Because I've spent the evening with you.' But she had to admit that Guy had been in the back of her mind for most of the evening.

After they'd washed up the glasses and plates, Julia put on her coat and pulled on her boots. 'There's going to be plenty of opportunity to catch up. I can organise a Christmas girls' night too.' This is what Libby had missed, proper girlfriends whom she could spend quality time with, exchanging gossip and having a great laugh. It wasn't as though she didn't have friends, but her college friends had settled all over the country and many were now married and busy with their own families, and although Libby always sent birthday and Christmas cards, over time their invitations to meet up had dwindled and they'd drifted apart.

'You can count me in, it'll be great to catch up with everyone.' Libby opened the door.

'Keep the warmth in,' said Julia, pressing a swift kiss to each cheek. 'Oh, I've forgotten the scrapbook.'

'Would it be possible to leave that with me for a while? I want to take a closer look at your designs.'

'Of course you can.'

Libby watched Julia walk down the path, the fairy lights twinkling and leading the way back towards Starcross Manor. She stood for a moment enjoying the silence and took in the view. There was something very magical about this place; she felt it every time she visited her family. It was so peaceful. She hadn't felt this relaxed in a long time. After closing the door, she switched on the TV and curled up with the throw draped over her on the settee. With the scrapbook resting on her knees, Libby began to turn the pages again, looking over Julia's designs. Along with the wedding that she had to organise for the competition winners, she wanted to surprise Julia and turn her sketch into the wedding suit of her dreams before she left for New York. Even though Flynn had already sourced and provided a large number of amazing fabrics in the studio she knew the precise fabric she was looking for—and if she remembered rightly there was a fabric shop on the other side of the town, approximately a twenty-minute walk away. Her plan was to head there first thing. The delicate 3D flowers on Julia's design would be time-consuming and she wanted to start on them right away. On the way back from the fabric shop, she planned to visit The Heart of The Village and call in to Buttercup Barn and introduce herself to Florrie.

The weather report followed the news and she was unsurprised to see more snow being forecast. Even though the weather was absolutely perfect for a winter wedding, providing a stunning backdrop, Libby knew that once the snow began to arrive in the Scottish Highlands it was here to stay, and one problem that she could envisage for the upcoming wedding was the travel arrangements for the wedding guests. There were bound to be disruptions and cancellations to public transport and she needed to get contingency plans in place.

Placing the scrapbook on the table, Libby reached for the remote and switched off the TV. It had been a full-on day and sleep was calling.

It wasn't long before she found herself sinking into a

comfortable bed. Exhausted after a long day she reached across and switched off the lamp then jumped as she heard a bark outside followed by a muffled voice.

Libby got up and dared to peep through the gap in the curtain. Outside in the freezing cold was Guy standing in nothing but a pair of lounging pants and boots.

'Will you hurry up and go to the toilet? This is not a game. It's freezing out here.'

Libby didn't want Pickle to hurry up—she was too busy staring at Guy's toned torso as he wrapped his arms around his body to keep warm!

Pickle was now crouched down and was excitedly trying to catch the fluttering flakes in her mouth.

'This is not playtime! Now do your business so we can go inside.'

But Pickle had other ideas and was busy running around in circles, still trying to catch the snowflakes. 'Right, I've had enough. I'm not playing this game.'

Libby smiled watching the calamity outside.

'Pickle! If you carry on like this, I'll be sending you next door to live with Libby.' Guy's voice was firm.

Pickle barked one last time and Guy leaned forward, scooped her up under his arm and headed back inside his lodge.

Hearing Guy speak her name made Libby smile, and knowing she was on his mind caused a tiny flip in her stomach. Climbing back into bed she pulled the duvet up to her chest and closed her eyes. The moment she met Guy she was intrigued by who he was, and wanted to know more about him and his personal life. The next month was going to be a lot more interesting with him around. A fleeting thought took her by surprise: what would it be like to be on the arm of Guy Hart? She instantly gave herself a little shake. That could *not* happen. Her path had been chosen for her ten years ago and after all the heartache she'd suffered, she'd vowed never to put herself in that position again.

And she wouldn't.

But there was no doubt that Guy was the last thing on her mind before she fell asleep...

Chapter Four

B ashing the top of her boiled egg with a spoon, Libby was feeling refreshed after a good night's sleep. It didn't take long to finish her breakfast and after washing up her dirty plate and mug, she brushed her teeth and sprayed herself with perfume. Glancing out of the window, she noticed it had finally stopped snowing. It was bright outside and according to her weather app the temperature was minus four outside.

Slipping on her coat, and slinging her bag across her body, she placed her hat on her head and wrapped a scarf around her neck. Feeling ready to face the icy outdoors she stepped outside and shook the snow from the branches of the Christmas tree standing tall by the front door. When she returned later, she had every intention of throwing some decorations on it.

Burying her chin in her scarf she walked across the grounds of Starcross Manor towards the main entrance. For the past few years, Heartcross Castle had set up an ice rink in the castle grounds for the tourists and villagers to use during the festive season but this year it had moved to Starcross Manor. As she contemplated the backdrop of Heartcross Mountain and the Manor House, Libby wondered if the bride and groom could ice skate. It would be a magical moment to include them skating in their wedding video.

Now heading towards the high street, she reflected that this village really was perfect in every season. In the distance smoke was spiralling out of the chimney pots of the whitewashed houses on Love Heart Lane, and all the fields of Foxglove Farm were veiled in a layer of white candy-floss snow. The frost had polished the trees and the bushes with its glittering silver sheen. It was pure winter magic. A sign erected at the foot of Love Heart Lane listed the new businesses that occupied the barns at The Heart of the Village, which had opened since the last time she'd visited. There was definitely going to be a crêpe with her name on it after she'd introduced herself to Florrie.

With her hands buried deep inside her pockets Libby headed across the bridge that linked the village of Heartcross to the town of Glensheil and noticed a familiar figure walking towards her. The sight of Guy pulling Pickle on the sledge was just as hilarious the second time, the dog sitting upright with the wind tossing her ears, her nose in the air. She sported a red fleece coat to match the sledge, and Libby couldn't help but smile. Guy was focused on the road in front of him, and on avoiding the mounds of snow piled along the edge, so didn't see her coming.

'Good morning,' trilled Libby as she approached him.

He lifted his gaze. As soon as he saw her, his eyes sparkled and his smile grew.

She pointed and gave a little chuckle. 'Is this the latest fashion accessory for dogs?'

Guy rolled his eyes. 'I must have the only dog in the world who doesn't like going for a walk. People keep pointing at us and taking photos. Pickle is about to become the latest TikTok sensation.'

'A very well deserved honour.' She laughed. 'You can't really blame them. It's a very comical sight.'

The second Pickle heard Libby's voice she was up dancing on her hind legs, bum waggling, tail wagging. Libby bent down and scooped her up in her arms. 'I think you've got the right idea. I mean, when you can have your own chariot and be pulled along, who would want to get their feet wet in the snow?' Libby gave her a quick hug before placing her back on the sledge.

'Don't go encouraging her, she's a diva at the best of the times. Also, why is it that when humans talk to puppies, their voice rises an octave and they sound all babyish?'

'It's one of the mysteries of life.'

'Where are you heading? Despite the weather, it's quite busy in town.'

'I'm just off to the fabric shop then I'm going to have a look around The Heart of the Village. I believe there's a pet shop there; you might be able to get Pickle some Wellington boots.'

'You really aren't that funny.'

Libby pinched her thumb and forefinger together. 'Just a little.'

'The jury is still out,' he said. 'I best get this one back.' He hesitated. 'I don't suppose you have plans this afternoon?'

The only things that Libby had planned this afternoon were chasing Flynn for the file on the competition winners so she could familiarise herself with their background, and decorating the Christmas tree outside the front door of her lodge.

'Nothing, absolutely nothing.'

'If you're free I'm walking over to the deer park. I'm hoping to shoot some fantastic footage before the snow begins to fall again.' He glanced up at the sky, which was still looking heavy with snow. 'But it might not be your thing,' he quickly added, giving her the option to decline.

The invitation had left a warm flush running through Libby's body and she paused for a moment, trying to calm her racing pulse.

'I mean, if you're here with someone else, they are more than welcome to come too,' he said, interpreting her silence for hesitation.

'No, I'm on my own, it's just me.' Libby noticed the corners of his mouth immediately lift, and turn into a full-on smile that had such intensity it made her heart beat faster. He was a vision of total gorgeousness and Libby had to remind herself to breathe. How did he do that?

'And you?' she asked in anticipation.

'It's not just me... I come with a Dachshund and that, unfortunately, is non-negotiable.'

'Absolutely. Pickle is non-negotiable. What time?' she asked.

'Would 2pm suit you?'

'It would,' she replied, patting Pickle on her head before walking away. A little further on, she dared to glance back over her shoulder. Guy looked back too, with a lopsided grin. Libby gave a tiny wave and immediately felt embarrassed. 'What are you doing? Stay cool,' she admonished herself, but there was no budging the huge smile on her face.

With a new spring in her step, and Guy still very much on her mind, she crunched snow under her boots as she made her way through the town towards the fabric shop.

Guy was right. Despite the weather, Glensheil was already busy. Libby navigated her way through the pedestrians on the slushy pavements past all the fancy boutiques. She took in the aroma of the coffeehouse and admired the freshly baked pastries in the window of the bakery. Following the tree-lined pavement that looked all wintry with the frost shimmering on the branches, she saw the fabric shop just up ahead. It was small and was called The Fabric Vault. As she stepped inside, the old-fashioned bell above the door alerted the sales assistant to her arrival.

'Good morning,' she chirped. 'Come on in out of the cold.'

'Good morning and thank you,' replied Libby, taking off her gloves and scarf. 'It's a bit chilly out there, isn't it?'

'It certainly is. Is there anything in particular I can help you with today?'

Libby explained the type of fabric she was looking for and exactly what it was for. The sales assistant pointed her through an archway that led to a room housing some of the most exquisite fabric Libby had seen. She began to browse through rolls and rolls of material, knowing exactly what she was looking for: a crisp, smooth, sheer ivory cloth.

Within seconds, she stumbled across two perfect textiles, one for the main bodice of the jumpsuit and the second for the 3D flowers. 'Perfect,' she said out loud, running the fabrics through her fingers. The second she set eyes on the ivory material Libby felt a tad emotional. This was exactly what she was looking for and she knew that Julia would look breathtaking wearing the finished wedding suit.

Happy with her finds she quickly worked out how many metres she would need of each and within five minutes she was walking back down the high street swinging a carrier bag full of fabric. Libby couldn't wait to surprise Julia with the finished garment. After working with hundreds of models over the last few years Libby had the ability to estimate measurements extremely well, and while Julia was with her last night, she'd looked over her body shape and made notes on her phone after she'd left.

Heading back over the bridge she heard a horn beep and a car slowed down as it approached her, Isla waving madly from the driver's seat. Pulling into a lay-by, Isla wound down the window. 'There she is! Drew said he'd picked you up from the train station. Where are you heading?'

Libby had liked Isla from the second they'd met. She was always full of fun and someone you just instantly warmed to. 'Actually, I'm heading your way. I'm off to check out The Heart of the Village and introduce myself to Florrie at Buttercup Barn.'

'Jump in! I'm heading home.'

Libby didn't need telling twice and was thankful for the heated passenger seat as they set off towards Foxglove Farm.

'How are you? You're back for Christmas and then off to New York, I hear. How exciting is that?'

'I have to keep pinching myself,' admitted Libby. 'It's so surreal. A little scary but exciting too.'

'I bet and, in the meantime, you're here organising the wedding of the competition winners after Jenny resigned, I believe?'

'Yes, Flynn said it was a little out of the blue and took him by surprise but he's hoping the publicity from this wedding will secure future bookings, possibly even celebrity weddings.'

'That would be good business! Starcross Manor will host the weddings and you will design the dresses for the stars…'

'Except I'll be in New York.'

'But wouldn't that be the perfect partnership?' Isla suggested, driving through the gate of Foxglove Farm.

Libby cast her mind back to this time of year a decade ago, when things were difficult and she had been going through the biggest change in her life. Even though her family had held her together through such a painful period, she had still been fiercely independent and so when Flynn had offered her a job at one of his other hotels, she'd refused. She knew it wasn't a pity offer, that he genuinely thought she would be perfect for the role, but Libby wanted to succeed in her career by standing on her own two feet.

'It would be the perfect partnership. Never say never,' she said with a shrug. Who knew what the future held? There was always a possibility that if she had continued success as a fashion designer she would get the chance to help Flynn out if he had a celebrity client who needed a wedding dress designed.

'And can you keep a secret?' she added.

Isla glanced in her direction. 'Of course I can.'

Libby crumpled the carrier bag on her knee. 'I'm making Julia's future wedding outfit as a surprise and this is the material.'

'Oh my gosh, have Flynn and Julia set a date?'

'No, not yet, but I'm hoping they do before I go to New York. Julia had sketched out her own creation for her big day and I'm going to make that dream come true. It'll all be ready and waiting for her when the time comes.'

'How romantic! And she doesn't have a clue?'

'No, and I can't wait to see her face when she sees it.'

'It's so exciting! I love a good wedding!'

'Let's just hope I can pull off this wedding at Starcross Manor on Christmas Eve first.'

'You will. I believe you have gorgeous Guy working with you? I've met him a couple of times.' Isla pointed beyond Heartwood Cottage, which was next to Bonnie's Teashop, and following the direction of her finger Libby saw another cottage in the distance. 'Rumours have it that Guy is interested in Weathervane Cottage. It's only just come on the market.'

Libby looked towards the cottage in the distance. It was standing alone just off the mountain pass. 'What a stunning location. Could you imagine waking up to those views every morning?'

'I'm surprised you didn't end up in Heartcross.'

'I do love it here. It always feels like I'm coming home when I arrive.'

The car travelled slowly up the drive and headed down a track at the side of the farmhouse. It turned the corner into the most beautiful courtyard that Libby had ever seen.

'Gosh, you have been busy. Look at this place!' she enthused.

The refurbished barns were in a horseshoe shape, all draped with twinkly lights and with Christmas trees scattered around, giving a festive feel. There was even a group of reindeer feeding on bales of hay in a nearby paddock.

'This place is amazing!'

'We're very happy with it. Drew and Fergus worked hard

to get this place up and running, with help from Jack, who owns the local building company. With the tourist traffic in the area increasing tenfold over the past few years, this is perfect for business. It took nearly the best part of a year to convert the barns and sort out all the legal stuff, but each business is doing so well. Buttercup Barn is in the corner.' Isla pointed. 'And over there we have The Village Closet, a ladies' boutique, and The Quirky Emporium, which sells vintage collectables. We also have Heartcross Pets and Grooming, the crêpe place and Ivy House, home to gifts, candles and unique cards for all occasions. That one there is the new library, and then we have the hot potato van and the farm shop, which stocks a wide variety of meat and cheeses. There's something for everyone,' Isla said proudly as she finished giving Libby the verbal tour.

'And already it's so busy.' The doors to each business were open and a queue was forming outside the farm shop.

'It's all been like this since we've opened, and long may it continue. I've got to go and do a few hours in the farm shop but we must catch up properly. I'll text you with some dates.'

'That would be lovely, and thanks for the lift.'

Libby climbed out of the car eager to explore The Heart of the Village but looking at the time she realised she couldn't stay long, as she wanted to cut out the flowers that needed hand-stitching for Julia's wedding suit before this afternoon so she could make a start on sewing them later tonight.

Delicious scents wafted past her from the crêpe barn, making her stomach rumble, and she realised how hungry she was, but her first visit needed to be to the florist. Crossing over to the path towards Buttercup Barn, Libby was taken by surprise when she heard raised voices behind her. Glancing back over her shoulder she saw a man and woman arguing in the car park. The face of the man was hidden as he was sitting behind the wheel of a car and the woman was standing on the pavement peering through the driver's side window. At a guess, she was in her mid-twenties, with distinctive flame-red hair. As Libby watched on, the woman turned and walked away. It was an unusual scene for first thing in the morning— or at any time in peaceful Heartcross, really—and Libby tried to shake off the unsettled feeling it had prompted as she made her way across the courtyard towards Buttercup Barn, which looked delightful with its olde worlde charm. The beautiful shop front was full of colour and happiness, with artificial flowers tumbling around the oak beam porch. The display highlighted the natural beauty of the season with two wooden cartwheels adorning each side of the duck-egg-blue door, and a wooden heart hanging in the centre, entwined with holly and berries. Just outside the shop on the flagstones was a wheelbarrow laden with hessian-wrapped floral arrangements.

Libby pushed open the door and was pleased to find that the inside was as beautiful as the outside. It reminded her of a quaint little florist's hidden away in Covent Garden that she'd stumbled across when working on a fashion project in London.

Inside were wooden crates, ivy plants and plaques with homely sayings on them. There was a staging area for creating arrangements with spools of ribbon, wire, green florist tape, flower wrap and rolls of tissue paper all carefully arranged for easy access.

Florrie was standing behind the wooden counter wrestling with a hand-tied bouquet of berries, red roses and rustic manzanitas, giving the arrangement a Christmas vibe. 'That is stunning,' Libby said admiringly as she walked towards the counter.

'Isn't it just?' replied Florrie with a warm smile.

Florrie had a style that was entirely her own. Her mousy hair was tied up in a messy bun with fresh snowdrops giving it an extra touch of charm. Her jeans were baggy and rolled up at the ankles, with coloured flowers embroidered down the side of each leg. Her layered tops in crimson and orange were striking, and she wore red woollen fingerless gloves with a matching scarf to keep her warm.

'And I'm about to pair them with these white roses and pale green foliage. Are you looking for anything in particular?'

'You must be Florrie. I'm Flynn's sister, Libby.'

'Hello! I've heard so much about you from Flynn and Isla. The famous fashion designer about to take New York by storm. It's lovely to finally meet you.'

'You too, and in the meantime, I'm turning my hand to wedding planning. That's why I'm here to introduce myself.'

'Of course! Jenny was telling me there were thousands of entries for the competition that she'd had to sift through and the choice was a difficult one.'

'Apparently so. I've not met the winning couple yet so I've no clue about the theme or colour scheme of their dream wedding. I have the first meeting with the bride and groom next week so as soon as I know I'll pop back in and maybe we can get some samples made up?'

'Of course. I've told Flynn that this wedding will be my priority. I'm looking forward to working together and adding the perfect flowers to the perfect day, along with any other requirements.' Florrie handed over her business card. 'My phone number is on there. I'm here to help you in any way I can.'

Libby had instantly warmed towards Florrie and was glad

they'd have a chance to get to know one another better as they worked together. Her manner was friendly and professional. 'That is so kind and makes my job a lot easier. Thank you.'

'Hopefully all the publicity Starcross Manor gets will be good for Buttercup Barn too. I don't know if he's mentioned it, but I've agreed with Flynn to supply all future flowers for the weddings that are planned up at the manor.'

'He did, and with his plans to make Starcross Manor the go-to wedding venue for as many happy couples as possible, I think you're both going to be run off your feet.'

Florrie laughed. 'I hope so. Owning my own shop has been my dream for years and working with Flynn will hopefully keep this little business afloat.'

'It's a beautiful name for a florist's shop. How did you decide on it?'

'When they were converting these barns into our units I came to view them and this one had clumps of buttercups growing through the ground. I thought it looked so pretty and instantly asked for this one to be mine. Buttercup Barn seemed the perfect choice after that.'

'It was meant to be.'

'It was and I'm so happy here. I mean, what's not to like, being surrounded by fresh colourful blooms all day every day?'

'You're living the dream,' Libby agreed.

'Are you heading back towards Starcross Manor?' Florrie asked as she wandered around picking different flowers from the numerous buckets that were standing in the shop window. Libby watched as Florrie put together a handful of rich red roses with delicate waxflowers and dainty hypericums along with fronds of rhododendron and hemlock with harmonious foliage, the fragrant eucalyptus and festive pine cones giving it extra structure.

'Yes, I'm staying in one of the lodges and am just on my way back now … after I've grabbed a crêpe, of course.'

'Savoury or sweet?' Florrie quizzed.

'Definitely sweet this morning,' Libby replied, watching Florrie secure the flowers with a ribbon before wrapping them up in the seasonal paper on the counter.

'Good choice. They have the best hazelnut spread with strawberries. Now, here you go … these are for you.'

Libby took in the aroma of the bouquet as Florrie handed it over. 'They're beautiful … and the smell is divine. Are you sure?'

'Of course I'm sure. Just my way of saying welcome and good luck. I'm looking forward to working with you on the wedding.'

'Thank you.' Libby was genuinely taken back by such kindness.

'Before you go, can I give you these to give to the accounts departments at the manor? Jenny was meant to collect these invoices at the end of last week but she didn't appear.'

'That would have been after she resigned.'

'Which came as a total surprise to me. In fact'—Florrie looked out of the window—'she seemed a little preoccupied this morning. She usually pops her head around the door but even though I gave her a wave she carried on without stopping.'

A thought struck Libby. 'Is Jenny the girl with long red hair I saw in the car park?'

'Yes, that was probably her. She used to pop next door for a crêpe before she started work.'

'Does she live around here?' Libby asked, still thinking about the argument in the car park.

'I believe she lives on the other side of Glensheil, but I'm not sure where. I have to say, the last couple of times she popped in she wasn't her usual self. In fact, she seemed a little harassed, subdued, maybe. I remember thinking at the time that something wasn't quite right.'

'And she didn't say anything to you about her plan to resign?'

Florrie shook her head. 'Nothing at all.'

'I suppose circumstances can change overnight.'

'Maybe, but when she got the job she was ecstatic. It was her dream job and told me she couldn't ever imagine working anywhere else. Starcross Manor was her life and she only had good things to say about the management team there.'

'How odd. And now she's gone and the wedding of the year has been left in my hands. Hopefully I'm up to the task. Let me grab those invoices.'

With the bouquet of flowers and a Nutella crêpe in her hands, Libby headed back towards the lodge. She was thinking about Jenny and wondered what had changed for her in such a short time to cause her to resign. According to Flynn and Florrie she loved her job there and had worked hard for her promotion. Libby knew it must have been a hell of a task wading through all the wedding competition applications. If she was struggling why hadn't she approached Flynn? Libby didn't know much about Jenny's background but she couldn't wait to meet her choice of bride and groom and see what had made them stand out from the rest of the applicants. Eating the crêpe as she walked back along the high street towards Starcross Manor, she suspected that her waistline was likely going to expand in the coming weeks as she worked her way through every crêpe concoction possible.

It wasn't long before she arrived back at Starcross Manor and she was heading up the path towards the lodge when she noticed Guy. He had his back to her as he talked on his phone and his voice was raised, a heated exchange evidently in progress.

'I'm not going. Please listen to me. I've been through enough humiliation as it is.' Guy's voice cracked with emotion as he hung up without saying goodbye to whoever was on the other end. Hearing the crunch of Libby's boots behind him, he spun round. Immediately, Libby noticed he looked drained and visibly upset but as soon as he saw her, his face softened.

'You okay?' she asked, watching him slide his phone into his back pocket.

'Flowers and chocolate. Someone has had a good morning,' he replied, deflecting the conversation from her question.

'Chocolate?' she queried, looking down at the bunch of flowers and the carrier bag of fabric she was holding.

Guy began to grin and tapped his lips then pointed towards hers. Straightaway, she wiped her mouth with the back of her hand. 'Busted! Nutella crêpe,' she said, smiling. 'And it was blooming delicious. You should check out The Heart of the Village. There's a great flower shop too.' She held up the bunch of the flowers.

'Noted for future reference.'

Libby was flattered by his flirtatious smile. He had a

wonderful air of confidence about him and a twinkle in his eye.

'I'll see you this afternoon,' he said. 'Wrap up warm.'

'You will and I will,' she replied, juggling the items she held while she rummaged in her bag for the key.

'Here, let me help.' He reached out, his hand brushing against hers as he held the flowers, causing tiny shock waves to course through her body. He hadn't taken his eyes off her and she coyly lowered hers. Surely he must have felt that too? Her heart began to beat a little faster as she opened the front door then took the flowers back from him. 'Thank you,' she said.

'You're welcome,' he replied, walking towards his door. They each hesitated on their doorstep and Libby felt herself mirror his contagious smile. She slowly shut the door, kicked off her boots and hung up her coat. Guy was still very much on her mind.

For the next few hours Libby kept busy. The fire was roaring, the TV was on in the background and she had set up camp in the living room. Julia's scrapbook was open on the table and dressmaking tools were scattered all over the floor. Libby had calculated how many hand-sewn flowers were needed for the bodice of Julia's design and had begun to trace them on the paper before sewing the very first flower and sitting back to admire her work. It was perfect—possibly the most delicate work she'd attempted by hand.

At 2pm, Libby wrapped herself up warmly and pulled on her boots. Stepping outside the lodge with a flutter of nervousness in her stomach, she realised how much she was looking forward to the afternoon ahead. She was just about to knock on Guy's door when it opened to reveal him standing there with a wide smile and a couple of camera bags thrown over his shoulder.

'Let's hope we get some good footage.'

'No Pickle?' asked Libby, looking past him.

'She's asleep in her crate, exhausted after her morning sledging,' he joked, placing his hand in the small of Libby's back to guide her towards the path. They took the route that led them to the front of Starcross Manor and then past the frozen lake towards the edge of the field. There wasn't another soul in sight.

'We're heading just up there.' Guy pointed.

The snowy woodlands were up ahead, the whole place silent and idyllic. The air was crisp and fresh and Libby was thankful for her warm cable-knit jumper and thermal socks as they trekked across the untouched field of snow.

Guy nodded to the left of them. 'I'm sure I saw a deer, just over there.'

Libby turned in that direction but saw nothing. From the corner of her eye she spotted Guy bending down and she turned around quickly as he cupped snow in his hands and playfully threw it in her direction. She raised her arms to shield herself, and let out a peal of laughter.

'Stop!' she cried, pretending to object even though she was secretly enjoying herself. She began to run across the field and Guy hot-footed it after her, both ducking and diving as they continued to launch snowballs at each other. By the time they reached the edge of the field Libby was desperately trying to catch her breath. 'No more! I have nowhere to run to.'

Guy laughed and held up his hands. 'Okay! Me neither! You got me good and proper.'

Both were still laughing as they approached the stile. To her surprise, Libby felt comfortable in his company, like she'd known him for years. Guy climbed over and extended his hand towards her. She wobbled as she climbed over too, and he immediately put both hands on her waist and lifted her safely to the ground. For a moment, she was conscious their faces were close and their eye contact was strong.

'It's just up there, through those trees,' Guy said, breaking the contact between them. 'And can you smell that?'

There was a hint of woodsmoke in the air, which instantly took Libby back to her grandparents' house. They had lived in the mountains with their faithful Labrador and always had a log fire burning. Her grandfather had loved nature and wildlife and Libby thought that if he were alive today, he would really like Guy; they would have had so much in common.

'What got you into filming?' she asked, still thinking about her grandfather.

'My father. There was always a camera lying around when I was a kid. It was a hobby for him but I think he would have liked to make a career out of it.'

'Aww I suspect you were a cute kid … and how things change,' she joked. 'And I bet he's proudly followed every step of your career.'

Guy suddenly went quiet and Libby got a tiny glimpse into his personal life. 'Things are actually a little difficult between us,' he said abruptly. 'Be careful on this stretch, it's very icy.'

Just at that second, Libby wobbled and Guy slipped his hand firmly into hers. He didn't say any more about his father, leaving her wondering what was so difficult between them. They walked over the icy stretch then Guy let go of her hand. 'Here we are. Flynn told me about this place.'

In front of them stood a one-storey observatory nestled into the branches of a giant tree. It was surrounded by other tall trees, their branches bowing under the weight of the snow. Libby was glad to see a purpose-built staircase instead of a rope ladder and carefully followed Guy up the steps. He brushed the settled snow off the railing as he went, ensuring she had a firm handhold, a gesture that warmed her further.

'Are you sure this is safe?' she asked, holding on to the rail, her boots feeling unsteady on the ice.

'Of course, it's purpose-built so if the trees sway, this place sways too.' Guy must have noticed the look of horror on Libby's face. 'Don't worry, you're in safe hands.'

'And there are no spiders up there?' The only fear Libby had in life was spiders and this place looked like it could house hundreds of them.

'If there are, I don't mind being chief spider catcher for the afternoon. I'm not very fond of them myself but I've seen some pretty damn big ones in some of the countries I've visited and the UK ones don't tend to scare me anymore.'

Libby shuddered at the very thought.

When they reached the top of the steps Guy unlocked the padlock with a combination code that Flynn had supplied. Libby stepped inside and looked all around. 'It's like a proper den.' It was simple yet cosy. Positioned in front of a huge window were a couple of red tartan chairs, separated by a small table, with blankets resting on their arms, and a telescope and a pair of binoculars nearby. On the floor were a number of large fake fur rugs.

Libby stood at the window and gasped. The last time she'd seen anything as magnificent as this view was after her recent interview in New York. She'd ridden to the 102nd floor of the One World Observatory, a three-storey destination on top of the western hemisphere's tallest building, and enjoyed the sweeping views across the city. Even though the two places were worlds apart this view was equally breathtaking. 'We live in an amazing country. What a view.'

'It's gorgeous, isn't it?' Guy looked at her as he draped a blanket around her shoulders.

The view was indeed spectacular. The mountainous terrain had been showered with snow, and on the hill in the distance Heartcross Castle towered above trees and fields that went on for what seemed like miles. Guy opened one of his bags and took out an old fashioned camera. Libby was surprised to see it was old-school. She was expecting top-of-the-range equipment.

'You use old-fashioned film,' she observed, watching him flick open the back of the camera.

'I do, and I also have the latest technology.' He waggled his phone. 'But sometimes it's the more primitive technology that captures the best footage in its entirety. Simple yet breathtaking.' Once again, he was looking at Libby in an intense way that created a flutter of giddiness in the pit of her stomach.

'I have the equipment to transfer the stills to my phone and laptop and create a slideshow. That camera I've had since I was a teenager.'

'I'm impressed. You've been into photography and film-making for a long time then?'

'I've always been obsessed,' he replied. 'I wasn't your

typical teenager. I spent my weekends walking hills and mountains, watching and waiting for a perfect shot of wildlife. I loved the branches of the trees, the flow of the streams tumbling over the rocks—all of nature. There is nothing more rewarding than developing the film and discovering that you've captured the perfect photo. I never dreamed it would turn into a proper job. I've been so lucky. Some of the places I've travelled to have been out of this world.'

'Is Heartcross on that list?' she asked.

'Without a doubt.' He gave a wolfish grin, pointed the camera at her and clicked. 'You have a perfect smile.'

'Why, thank you.'

'Here, let me show you how to use it.'

Guy stood behind her at the window, his arms resting on her shoulders as he held the camera out in front of her. She breathed in, savouring his delicious aroma, and noticed her heart had begun pounding a little faster.

'First thing is to take the cap off, otherwise there will be no photos.'

Libby stayed focused on what was in front of her; she didn't dare look behind her, knowing that Guy's face was centimetres from hers.

'Here, like this. Focus through this window, then pull this lever back.'

Click.

'Now you have a go.'

With his hands hovering over hers for a brief moment Libby took the camera from him. Feeling an instant pull towards him, she summoned up enough courage to meet his gaze. He stared at her for a moment and then his eyes dropped towards her lips for a split second before he looked away. Her heartbeat quickened, her mouth dry. There it was again, that electrical feeling fizzing away in her body. Focusing forward, she smiled, knowing the attraction between them was mutual, but then frowned. These feelings were unexpected and ones that she hadn't experienced for a very long time, and the last thing she needed right now was any complications before leaving for New York. She would need to keep her emotions in check.

Slowly, Guy moved from behind her and extracted a tripod from the second bag. 'If your hand begins to shake, put the camera on the tripod.' He slid a chair across the wooden floor nearer to the window and Libby did the same.

'I'm hoping to catch the herd of deer that live in this area. I think it will add some nice texture to the wedding film I'm here to create.'

Libby couldn't help but notice the lack of enthusiasm in his voice at the mention of the wedding and decided to probe a little. 'I'm sensing you aren't a fan of weddings.'

He looked towards her. 'It's not my favourite topic of conversation at the minute so let's not spoil the afternoon.'

Libby knew there was more to his story but didn't want to press him further. She dared a sideward glance towards him and recognised that haunted look on his face. It was one she'd seen many times in her own reflection—one of hurt and pain.

However, Libby had a piece of news that she hoped would put the smile right back on his face.

'What if this job turned out to be more enjoyable than you thought?' She bit her lip to suppress her smile.

'How could that possibly happen?'

Libby held his gaze, wanting to observe the exact second he processed the next bit of information, and held out her hand.

Guy looked at her in amusement.

'Let me introduce myself properly. Libby Carter, pleased to meet you.'

Guy narrowed his eyes as he reached out to grasp her proffered hand. 'Carter? Are you related to Flynn Carter?'

'Yep, I'm his sister and temporary wedding planner,' she confided, shaking his hand.

Guy's eyes widened, a look of amazement on his face as his smile broadened. 'You're joking.'

'Absolutely no joke.'

Guy exhaled then raked his hand through his hair. 'You mean we're going to spend the next five weeks together?'

'We are.'

Guy was still smiling but also shaking his head in disbelief. 'You may be right. It may just be a little more enjoyable than I thought.'

'Only a little?' she teased, pleased by his reaction.

'Maybe a lot,' he replied, his eyes glowing with an inner light that instantly made Libby sure that the next few weeks were going to be a whole load of fun.

'That's good to hear. Now, it's a little on the chilly side in here, isn't it?' Libby shivered.

'Warm drink?' asked Guy.

Libby looked around and couldn't see any electrical outlets or kitchenette. 'How are you going to magic up a warm drink?'

From the side pocket of his bag he pulled a flask with two plastic cups. 'And I've got two slices of chocolate flapjack from Bonnie's Teashop.'

'Now you're talking!' Libby was impressed. 'Nutella crêpes and now chocolate flapjacks—I'll need to watch my waistline.'

'I don't think you have anything to worry about,' he

replied, causing Libby to blush a little as she remembered the bikini and bobble hat.

After Guy poured two cups of tea and handed Libby a slice of flapjack they stared out of the window, just taking in the view. A robin redbreast jumped onto a branch right in front of them and Guy videoed it from his phone as it hopped up and down before taking flight.

'So, tell me about Libby,' said Guy, taking a sip of his drink. 'You said you're the "temporary" wedding planner?'

'Flynn's wedding planner resigned at short notice and I couldn't leave him in the lurch. My usual job—when I'm not rescuing my family from staff shortages—is fashion designer.'

'That sounds very impressive.'

'I set up my own fashion label about ten years ago and it's gone from strength to strength.' Not wanting to seem like she was boasting, Libby kept the news to herself that she'd just landed a job with one of the biggest fashion houses in New York.

'Even more impressive.'

'It sounds grander than it is. I've worked out of the back bedroom of my own home for most of the time but it's saved on costs and I've managed to create a recognisable brand with a pretty good following. I'm doing all right.'

'Sounds like you're doing more than all right. A ten-year successful business sounds good to me.'

Libby knew she was doing more than all right. She hadn't been an overnight success; she'd worked hard to create her brand, and with her new life waiting for her in New York it was something to be incredibly proud of.

She took a bite of flapjack. 'It is and I'm happy.'

'What makes your life a happy one?'

Now there was a question that Libby hadn't anticipated being asked when she woke up that morning. 'I'm happy because I like myself. I spend a lot of time with me and I think I'm actually okay.' She smiled. 'I also have a job I enjoy and a great family. Flynn, Julia and my dad mean the world to me. My mum passed away when I was a young girl and I don't have many memories of her, just photographs from my dad, but my dad did everything he could to fill the gap. He's just an amazing man—selfless and full of love for his children—and having a brother who looks out for me the way Flynn does...' Libby thought for a second. 'It makes me feel safe and loved.' As the words left her mouth, two things happened. First, she realised she'd meant every word, acknowledging also for the first time that she felt a little scared about moving thousands of miles away from the people who were always there for her. Secondly, the smile slipped from Guy's face.

'And how's being single for you? Isn't romance meant to be the key to happiness?' he asked.

'That's a deep question,' she replied, thinking about it. 'Maybe one day there will be a person who complements my life, not complicates it, and wants me just for me, but in the meantime I'm more than content being on my own.'

Libby had once thought she was indeed with the man she'd just described, thought they had each other's backs and would stick by each other no matter what. But she'd been wrong. He hadn't loved her just for being her, and it had broken her heart to discover that. Everyone told her there would be someone else out there who would love her unconditionally and would understand her situation, but even now there was tiny part of her that didn't know if she could ever let herself be vulnerable like that again.

'And, for the record, I think you hold the key to your own happiness. Being in a relationship shouldn't be society's default expectation of us. Being happy and secure within ourselves is what we should all aspire to.'

'And if someone special comes along?'

'Then I'd reconsider. But they would have to be damn special.' Libby gave him a warm smile.

Guy looked deep in thought and Libby wondered what his story was. He was handsome, easy to talk to, funny, and very successful. She knew she hadn't shared with him her full story but they had only just met. Apart from her immediate family, Libby had found it difficult to open up about her situation to anyone. Feeling a lump in her throat, she swallowed and stared fixedly at the window, not daring to look in Guy's direction in case he noticed the tears in her eyes.

'Look!' He pointed towards the clearing through the trees.

Libby couldn't see anything but had the camera poised and ready just in case.

'I can't see anything,' she whispered. 'And why am I whispering?'

Guy gave her a sideward glance and smiled. 'Just behind the trees on the far left.'

All of a sudden, a herd of wondrous dappled deer with impressive antlers that looked like the bare branches of trees bounded across the snowy ground. They moved with such grace, it was the most beautiful sight Libby had ever seen.

'They're all legs! Oh my, look at that one.' Libby quickly brought the camera up to her eye to capture the moment and began to click. The baby of the pack followed at the tail end of the herd. 'It looks like it's dancing,' observed Libby, watching as it skipped and jumped across the ground. 'It looks like Bambi.'

'My guess is that the fawn is around six months old.'

'This place feels like a million miles from real life,' Libby murmured.

'This is my real life. The wildlife programmes are the best to make. Animals are majestic and simple.'

'You have a wonderful job,' she said, her eyes still firmly fixed on the field as the herd disappeared into the woods.

'I do. Do you think you got some good photos?'

'I hope so, but how do I look back at them?' she asked, looking down at the camera in her hand.

Guy grinned. 'It's not like your phone. You can't swipe back through the digital photos. And that's what I love about this type of photography. You don't know what magic you've captured until you develop the film. Hopefully, I've captured some magical moments on my phone and after a little bit of editing the slideshow could be a breathtaking introduction to Starcross Manor and what it can offer, if Flynn decides to use it for promotional purposes. I still can't quite believe you're his sister.'

Libby smiled and placed the camera on the table. 'I think the next few weeks are going to fly by.' She couldn't wait to spend the days with Guy, but she also didn't want them to go too quickly. Finishing off her drink, she pointed to the camera. 'I'd like to see how you put it all together,' she said.

'Of course you can. I'd like that,' he said, smiling at her and reaching for his phone, which had begun to ring. He looked pensive as he stared at the screen before declining the call. The phone pinged again a moment later with a text message.

'Everything okay?' Libby asked.

Guy stood up and walked to the door. 'I'm sorry, I'm going to have to make a call.'

He left the observatory and she watched him walk down the steps. With his leg bent and his foot resting on the trunk of a tree he made a call. The conversation didn't last long and Libby could tell by the look on his face that something had rattled him.

She was right.

The second he appeared back in the doorway, he announced, 'I'm sorry, something's come up and I'm going to have to cut our afternoon short.' He didn't offer any further explanation, simply began to pack up the equipment.

Libby felt her own mood slump a little. She was disappointed their afternoon was coming to an end earlier than they'd planned. She wanted to spend more time getting to know Guy. Standing up, she folded the throw and placed it on the back of the chair. 'That's okay, these things happen. Some sort of emergency?' she queried.

'You could say that,' he replied, but didn't elaborate or look in her direction. He clearly had something on his mind.

'I hope everything's okay,' she added. 'Maybe another time?'

'I'd like that,' he replied, giving her a genuinely warm smile. 'Are you ready?'

Libby nodded and followed Guy down the steps of the observation tower. She shivered. The air now seemed chillier, matching the atmosphere. She wished he'd never received that phone call but there was nothing she could do about it now.

They walked back in silence, the mood sombre, and the first thing that Libby noticed when they approached the lodges was that the lights were on in Guy's, which she thought was strange as they hadn't been when they'd left.

He stared towards the lodge before he turned towards her.

'Thanks for this afternoon. I'm sorry to have cut it short. I'll catch you later,' he said, putting the key in the lock of his front door. Before Libby could reply he'd stepped inside and closed the door behind him.

Even though they'd had a good time, it wasn't entirely the afternoon that Libby had hoped for. Putting the key in her door she heard Pickle's bark and looked over towards Guy's front window. She was surprised to see Guy facing a woman. Wondering who she was, Libby stepped into the warmth of her own lodge.

Chapter Five

'Daddy!'

Holly ran towards Guy and clung to his legs. His smile was wide the second he laid eyes on her, the feeling of love towards her overwhelming as he lifted her up and hugged her tightly. After kissing both his six-year-old daughter's cheeks he blew a long raspberry against her skin, making her giggle uncontrollably.

'Eww, get off!' Holly placed her hands on Guy's chest and attempted to push away from him before wiping her cheek with the back of her hand. 'Put me down!' she playfully squealed as Guy swung her to her feet. 'Mum has had to go away so me and Granny are staying with you.'

'I know,' he replied, thinking back to the heated conversation with his mother only moments before. 'And how lucky am I to have you for extra time?'

'Very lucky,' replied Holly with her lovable, cheeky grin.

For Guy, what Holly's arrival meant was that, once again,

his daughter was not her mother's first priority. His ex-partner, Sophie, didn't understand what co-parenting was all about. In his eyes, she was selfish, booking time off when it suited her and not bothering to check with him. Guy spent a good portion of his time rearranging his schedule to accommodate Sophie's whims. Sophie had never come to terms with the typical schedule of a school day, claiming it left her with no time to broaden Holly's learning, so she'd decreed that their daughter would be homeschooled, and Sophie would make time for play, projects and experiments. Real-life skill-building was big on her agenda and she'd said that Holly would learn in different places like museums, parks and science centres. Guy hadn't agreed; he felt that Holly should have friends her own age, not just adult company. He'd also pointed out that their daughter needed the routine and stability of school life. Sophie had triumphed in the end, however, and Holly had never started school, but now his ex was beginning to lose interest in homeschooling and more often than not would take off at a moment's notice, leaving Guy in the situation that he was in now.

With her feet firmly back on the ground, Holly picked up a toy that Pickle had dropped and they had a game of tug of war, which Pickle won easily.

'Why don't you watch TV for a moment while I talk with Grandma?'

Holly jumped on to the settee, her little legs—wrapped in multi-coloured tights—dangling over the edge. Pickle jumped up next to her and rested her head on Holly's knee.

Guy knew he hadn't made eye contact with his mother, Cynthia, since he'd returned. After the argument on the phone, he had nothing different to say. They had had their own feud going on for the last four years and he was exhausted by the situation. There were no more words he needed to say to either her or his father. They had both made their choices and Guy had to live with that, the pain still twisting in his gut at the very thought of the last few years.

After switching the TV on, he walked over to the kitchen area and noticed his mother's small suitcase. Could this situation get any worse? Leaning against the sink and folding his arms, he finally looked over in his mother's direction. Guy had spent his whole life avoiding confrontation. He was the one always keeping the peace and putting others first … and look where that had got him. Good guys always came last.

His mother broke the silence. 'That sort of behaviour is unbecoming. Shouting at me on the phone like that … I can hardly believe it.'

He looked at her, speechless. What had he done wrong except be a loyal, honest individual who worked hard to provide the best for his family? But his efforts had never been good enough. He glanced over to Holly. She was the only good thing to have come out of the last six years.

He was trying his best not to react to his mother's outburst but that was proving difficult as immediately he felt his hackles rise. Already she'd managed to push his buttons. 'It's lovely to see you too,' he replied with a hint of sarcasm and was immediately annoyed with himself for reacting.

The annoying thing was that he *knew* he was behaving like an idiot. But who could blame him? He'd been through hell and back and was still trying to come to terms with all the deceit and the lies of the past. It was bad enough that he'd discovered his wife-to-be had cheated on him but what had happened next … he still found it difficult to comprehend, and didn't think he would ever accept the situation.

Growing up, Guy had been close to his family—or so he thought. His mother's words still rang in his ears from when he was a little boy: 'Family is for life. You can always rely on us no matter what.' That couldn't be any further from the truth.

'There's something you should know.'

Guy braced himself for whatever his mother was going to say next.

'Sophie has no other family and she's asked your father to walk her down the aisle. I know you're going to say, "How could he?" after…'

Guy was speechless, shaking his head in disbelief. He exhaled. Just when he thought that nothing else could shock him, his own father was about to walk his ex down the aisle.

'We are her only family and for Holly's sake…'

Guy held up his hand; he couldn't cope with any more of this conversation. He could still feel the tightness in his chest, his blurred vision from fighting off the tears, the pain in his throat the night he'd discovered Sophie's infidelity. His family unit had been destroyed in a matter of seconds.

'I just thought you should know and … Sophie asked me to give you this.' She reached into her handbag and handed Guy a cream, embossed envelope. 'A save-the-date notification. They've booked the wedding.'

He turned it over in his hands and put it down on the worktop. 'I will not be going to the wedding.' Guy shook his head in disbelief. 'Why do you all want to keep inflicting pain on me?'

They stared at each for a second, neither of them saying a word until Cynthia broke the silence. 'Look, I'm here to look after Holly while Sophie is away, and with your father being poorly at the moment he needs his rest. It's only for a short while and if we don't talk about the situation, I'm sure we can rub along nicely, for Holly's sake.'

It was bad enough that he was here to film a wedding, which was a constant reminder of what he had going on in his personal life, but now this? He was still hoping to wake up and discover it was all a bad dream, but even though this wasn't what Guy needed right now, he knew there was no other choice.

Cynthia looked around the lodge. 'Can you show me where to put my things, please?

'The bedrooms are through there. Yours is the first on the left.'

After watching his mother disappear towards her room, Guy glanced across the living room to find that Pickle and Holly had fallen fast asleep, their bodies cuddled up together. Holly was unaware of the situation around her, and despite the challenging circumstances and the way he was feeling, he had tried his best to keep everything as normal as possible for her.

Four years ago, Guy's life had descended into complete darkness. He'd always been a self-assured person, comfortable in his own skin, but the infidelity had broken him to his core, and anxiety and trust issues were now affecting his mental and emotional state. It had destroyed him, and the only thing he could do was throw himself into work. He hadn't spoken about the way he was feeling or what he was going through, and the worst part about it all was that he felt as though he'd lost his family. People say that time is a great healer but Guy couldn't see a way out of this situation any time soon.

With her favourite red bobble hat firmly pulled down around her ears and her coat zipped up to her chin Libby juggled the box of decorations and a mug of mulled wine. Getting into the Christmas spirit, she was on a mission to decorate the little tree outside her front door.

She was also hoping for a glimpse of Guy.

After sorting through the different coloured baubles, she switched on the battery-operated fairy lights and began to weave them around the tree. As soon as the lights were symmetrical Libby began to hang the baubles, transforming the tree in seconds until it glittered before her very eyes. With only the star left to fix to the top she stood back to admire her work and took a sip of her drink.

Hearing a tiny gasp behind her, Libby spun round. Standing behind her was a small human with a multi-coloured scarf wound round her neck, that matched her multi-coloured tights. Her hair was in pigtails and a string of russet freckles dotted the bridge of her nose. She was adorable.

Wide-eyed, she looked at the tree. 'Wow!' she exclaimed.

'That's Christmas right there,' replied Libby, looking all around for the girl's family, but there was no one else in sight. 'Where have you come from?'

Holly pointed to the lodge next door. The door was slightly ajar and Libby suddenly recognised Guy's boots on the girl's feet.

'I'm Libby,' she said, wondering who the little girl was.

'I'm Holly.'

'That is a very Christmassy name.'

'I saw you through the window.' The little girl peered inside the cardboard box and looked a little disappointed.

'I've got one last thing to hang: the star. Would you like to put it on top of the tree?' asked Libby, reaching inside the box and holding it up.

'Yes please!'

Libby passed the star to Holly, who took a step forward in the oversized boots and carefully balanced the star on top of the small tree.

'Now make a wish,' whispered Libby.

With a huge smile on her face, Holly squeezed her eyes shut and made a wish, her fingers crossed.

As soon as she opened her eyes Libby asked, 'And what did you wish for?'

'I can't tell anyone, because if I do it won't come true.'

'How about a little clue?' probed Libby with a smile.

The little girl shook her head and waggled her finger. 'Nope.'

'Holly! Where are you?' Guy shouted and soon appeared at the door, spotting Holly standing next to Libby. 'There you are. You shouldn't go outside without telling me,' he said as he tugged at her scarf to wrap it more warmly around her. 'Get yourself into the warmth.'

Holly turned back towards Libby. 'Thank you for letting me make a wish,' she said, leaving Guy looking puzzled.

'You're very welcome, and whatever you wished for, I hope it comes true,' Libby said, watching Holly attempt to stomp back indoors. The boots were way too big for her and she stumbled but Guy caught her. As he lifted her up, her feet waggled in the air, the boots stuck in the snow.

'Daddy! I've lost the boots! Don't put me down,' she squealed.

'Then stop wriggling!' He laughed, swinging her round and lowering her slowly onto the mat inside the front door.

'Daddy, can we put up a tree?' Holly said hopefully, tilting her head to one side.

'Don't look at me like that, you know it's too early. We can put the tree up a couple of weeks before Santa arrives.'

'But Daddy, Libby has her tree up.'

'Into the lodge!' He pointed, leaving Holly screwing up her face before she ran back inside. Turning back towards Libby, he said, 'She's got character, that one.'

Libby met Guy's gaze. 'Daddy?' she said, surprised.

'Yes, Holly's my daughter.'

'And adorable.'

'She is, but I'm biased.'

'Daddy! Pickle has pickled the carpet.'

Guy rolled his eyes. 'Never a dull moment. That's my cue to leave.' He pointed towards the door and began to walk backwards. 'I'll catch…'

'You later,' Libby finished his sentence as the door shut behind him.

She stood there for a second with her arms wrapped around her body, staring at the Christmas tree. Once upon a time she'd made a wish on a star just like Holly, but her wish hadn't come true. She blinked back a tear as there it was again, that very familiar tug at her heart. The word 'mum' pulsated inside Libby's mind. She responded to the empty, sad feeling that had suddenly crept back in by immediately turning it into a positive, remembering all the love, support and advice that Flynn and her father had given her. It had been difficult acknowledging that she would never have a biological child of her own, but she'd allowed herself to cry and be angry, and sharing her fears with her family had helped her understand that the future might hold other possibilities. She was looking forward to exploring them when the time was right, because in her heart she knew she would make a pretty awesome mother.

Chapter Six

Four weeks to Christmas

I t was Libby's first day on the job. Holding a mug of coffee, she stared at the mountain of clothes piled on her bed. This was a disaster; what the hell did a wedding planner wear? She held up some sort of baggy green tweed dress against her body and looked in the mirror. How did she ever think this was a good idea? She wasn't used to dressing for work. Her usual attire was comfy lounge wear or her pyjamas, as often there were days when she didn't bother to get changed after waking. Having changed outfits what seemed a million times she texted Isla, feeling exasperated.

What does a wedding planner look like?

Almost immediately her phone beeped and Libby glanced at the screen to see a line of laughing emojis.

You don't struggle with style! You're a fashion designer!

This was very true. Libby knew how to make clothes look good on others, but wearing her comfies wasn't going to appeal to the competition winners. She needed them to have faith in her ability. So, knowing she needed to dress the part, she was after a look that was professional yet not stuffy. She texted back.

You're no help!

Black oversized jacket, white top, skinny jeans, nice belt, always does the trick

came the instant reply.

Five minutes later, Libby had settled on that very outfit and checked her reflection in the mirror one last time before heading into the hallway. With her curls bouncing above her shoulders, she grabbed her bag, slipped her feet into her heeled boots and declared herself ready. With a racing heartbeat and a look of excitement on her face, she tried to imagine the day ahead. She pressed her lips tightly together to suppress a smile as Guy's front door opened at the same time as hers and he emerged with his duffle coat on and his camera equipment slung over his shoulder. He smiled at Libby.

'Look at us, work buddies. Are you ready?' she asked, locking the door behind her.

'I am,' he replied.

'Can I borrow your arm?' she asked, linking hers through his. 'I'm not trusting these boots on this ice. The last thing I need is to be slipping over.'

'Very true, we can't have you falling at my feet just yet.' His eyes sparkled, leaving Libby wondering what he meant by 'just yet'.

They began to walk side by side down the path and through a stone archway, which led to a tiny courtyard at the rear of the hotel. Above their heads was a purpose-built lattice with twisted vines of holly and berries, the whole thing laced with snow.

'How beautiful does that look?' said Libby admiringly, looking upwards. Just then she stumbled on the edge of the stone step and Guy clutched her arm tightly to steady her.

'Nearly,' he said teasingly, and caught her eye, causing her stomach to give a little flip. 'I bet this place is equally beautiful in the summer,' he said when she was steady on her feet once more.

'It is. I fell in love with it the first time I visited Starcross Manor. The history and the grounds are intriguing. It must have taken many years to nurture and cultivate it into such a gorgeous place of beauty.'

'It is indeed a gorgeous place of beauty,' he said, still looking at her. 'It's just something else, isn't it?'

Libby realised he was flirting with her a little. They carried on walking, still arm in arm. 'The studio is just up here.'

'And there's another step just ahead,' joked Guy.

'And you're telling me that because you don't want me falling at your feet?'

'That's your assumption,' he replied playfully.

Libby bit her lip to hide a smile and took the opportunity to steal a sideward glance at him. He was looking at her with a twinkle in his eye that made her heart race faster ... if that was even possible.

'We're here now.' Libby pointed to the studio at the end of the snowy path. 'Just look at those Christmas trees. Don't you just love all the twinkly lights?'

Guy pulled away slowly from her linked arm. 'It seems I have no choice but to love twinkly lights, considering they're everywhere.'

'That's because it's that time of year.'

'It's November.'

'And only four weeks until Christmas!'

Libby unlocked the door and they stepped inside, where they were welcomed by the warmth of the heating.

'What do you think of this place?' she asked, shutting the door behind them and taking off her coat.

Guy looked around the room. 'Very wedding-y! If that's even a word.' He put down the camera bags and hung up his coat.

'That's good then because that's what I'm here to do: organise a wedding! I'm not sure what it is you don't like about weddings, but by the time I've organised the most perfect wedding and we watch the happy couple walk down the aisle, I hope to have changed your mind.'

'Mmm, I'm not sure that will ever happen,' he murmured. 'But let's see if lovely Libby can work her magic,' he added, looking up from under his floppy fringe.

'Lovely Libby?' she questioned, feeling a tingling pulse that she couldn't control race through her body. She was fully aware of how captivating Guy was and that the smile on her face was widening.

'Lovely Libby,' he repeated.

'If nothing else, the next few weeks should be entertaining. Let's hope I can pull off all the wedding planning.'

'I think you're going to do a pretty amazing job.'

'You can keep the compliments coming,' she replied. 'Now, where do you think the best place is to set up the recording equipment? Every moment of the happy couple's journey needs to be captured.'

Guy looked around the room then pointed. 'That raised area will be perfect. The camera will capture it all and I can sit there, out of the way.'

'Tea and coffee are over there, toilets that way and—'

'Never mind tea and coffee, look at all that fizz! I've seen some wine racks in my life but nothing as full as that one.'

'No drinking on the job, but maybe after we've got through the first day we should sample a small one.'

'Sounds like a plan.'

'And where is adorable Holly today?' asked Libby.

'Still asleep and being looked after by my mother,' he replied, but then he steered the conversation in a totally different direction. 'Flynn said something about a schedule he'd put together and that I was to ask you for a copy. Have you seen it?'

'Yes, he's left it by the computer. It's just here.'

The schedule had made Libby's life easier. Certain tasks needed to be done by certain dates—the dress, the groom's attire, bridesmaids, flowers, cake, menu, room décor et cetera —and it was all outlined and ready to be accomplished.

'That all seems simple,' Guy said once he'd finished reading. Cocking his head as if hearing something, he pointed towards the door. 'I can hear voices. Here we go.' He pressed a button on the video recorder and gave Libby an encouraging smile. 'Break a leg!' he mouthed.

Libby suddenly felt nervous as the door opened and in walked Lisa the receptionist, holding the file with all the information on the winning couple.

'Libby! Lovely to see you! Let me introduce you to our competition winners.'

Lisa's eyebrows rose and her eyes widened as she stared at Libby in a way that was clearly meant to signal something, but Libby wasn't sure what Lisa was trying to tell her. Libby narrowed her eyes but couldn't grasp what she was missing until the winning couple walked through the door.

'Here comes the bride!' sang Lisa, gesturing towards the door. 'And of course, the groom. Let me introduce you to Miranda and David.'

Libby painted on her biggest welcoming smile, her eyes firmly fixed on the couple in front of her. She extended her hand to the tallest woman she'd ever seen—and she'd worked with a lot of models in her time. At a guess, Miranda was over six feet tall, her heels adding even more inches, and she was entirely in black—from her heels to her clothes to her make-up and her jet-black hair, which fell to the bottom of her spine. Libby looked up—and up—to meet the bride's gaze and shook her hand. 'I'm Libby, pleased to meet you.'

'Me as well. And this is my gorgeous husband-to-be, David.'

Even with Cuban heels David was five foot three at best and he was dressed in jeans with a black shirt and neon green tie. It crossed Libby's mind that they looked as though they had just rolled in from a fancy dress party from the night before. Their attire reminded her of a pair of villains in a cartoon. She gathered herself quickly and hoped the look of surprise wasn't written all over her face. Daring to look over in Guy's direction she saw he was filming every second as planned.

'Hello, David, lovely to meet you. Are you good?' she asked.

'I am,' he replied, his deep voice taking Libby by surprise, again.

Miranda had a huge smile on her face as she clasped David's hands in hers. 'We can't quite believe that we've won the competition.'

Libby knew she shouldn't judge a book by its cover and that the couple standing in front of her might be very much in love, but were they really right for the publicity that Flynn had hoped to create for Starcross Manor? She was sure he had been hoping for a model-like couple who wouldn't look out of place on the front of a bridal magazine.

'And you're the woman who is going to make all our wedding plans come true,' added Miranda.

'I'll do my very best,' replied Libby, still smiling. 'Let me introduce you to Guy. Guy will be recording every step of your journey for your very own wedding keepsake video.'

Guy stood up from behind the camera and shook both of their hands. 'Congratulations!' he said. 'It must be a dream come true for you both.'

'Oh it is,' enthused Miranda. 'I told David I was going to enter us in the competition and he said we didn't have a cat in hell's chance, didn't you, David?'

'I did.'

'But I told him you had to be in it to win it and that's what we did!' Miranda clapped her hands together like a performing seal, and Guy beat a hasty retreat behind the camera.

'I need to be getting back to reception. But here's the file. Apologies for not getting it to you sooner,' Lisa said as she made to leave.

'That's okay,' replied Libby. She'd chased up the winners' file at the end of last week but had been told it had been mislaid. At least they'd found it now.

'Good luck with everything,' added Lisa.

Libby took the file, thanked Lisa and watched the door shut behind her.

'Tea or coffee?' she asked, turning towards Miranda and David. 'Let me get you both a drink and then we can talk weddings! It's so exciting!'

Miranda had unbuttoned her coat and already hung it on the coat stand, and was now running an approving eye over the collection of fizz. 'Why settle for tea or coffee when you have such an extensive fizz collection? It's never too early for a glass, is it, David? After all, we *are* celebrating.'

'Never too early,' he replied, joining her and pointing to certain bottles in the wine cooler.

'You choose, David,' suggested Libby, wanting to accommodate them in every way possible.

After selecting a bottle, Miranda and David sank down on to the plush sofa while Libby took crystal glasses from the cabinet next to the wine cooler then popped the cork, which immediately flew up in the air and landed at David's feet.

'We need to keep this to remind us of the first day planning our wedding,' he suggested, slipping it into his trouser pocket.

After handing Miranda and David a glass each, Libby

poured herself a drink and, looking towards Guy, held up a glass. He shook his head.

'Let's make a toast. Firstly, congratulations! Here's to the happy couple! And secondly, I promise I will do everything I can to make this a wedding to remember.' She clinked her glass against theirs.

Libby took a sip, trying her best to push her first impressions of the couple out of her mind. After all, even though they might not be the conventional couple she was expecting, they did look very much in love and deserved the same chance as anyone else to have the wedding of their dreams. There was still a slight niggle in the back of her mind, however, and she was eager to read the file to discover what had set them apart from all the other entries.

She opened the file that was lying on her lap and was amazed to find it nearly empty. Quickly flicking through the sparse pages she couldn't find their initial application form or any background information. 'You must be thrilled to have won the competition,' she murmured, stalling for time.

'Absolutely thrilled! I mean, we get the wedding of our dreams and all expenses paid. Christmas Eve can't come quick enough, can it, David?'

'It certainly can't! I'm marrying my dream girl. I'm a very lucky man.'

'Starcross Manor is the perfect venue too. We have such stunning views of the mountains and it's particularly breathtaking at this time of year. I'm looking forward to working with you both. Now, tell me all about you,' Libby enthused. 'How long have you been engaged? And are you from around these parts?' she asked.

At the question, Miranda placed both hands on her heart

and gave a tiny sigh. 'David and I fell in love at first sight seven years ago and we've been inseparable ever since. You know when you just click with someone in an instant? I knew I was going to spend the rest of my life with him.'

Libby smiled at them both and took a sip of champagne. Despite what she'd been through in her personal life she still warmed to a good love story.

'We met at the races, the Scottish Grand National. We just knew the second that we laid eyes on each other in the hospitality box. He looked hot to trot, dressed up to the nines, and afterwards he asked me to spend some time with him. He whisked me off to Cameron House, one of the most luxurious hotels in Scotland—you should give it a visit—it's on the banks of—'

'Loch Lomond,' Libby finished her sentence. She knew exactly where the hotel was, with its stunning views and world-class cuisine.

'You know it?' Miranda seemed surprised.

Libby knew it well. It was the same hotel her ex, Daniel, had booked when they went away for their first night together.

Libby also knew how special a day at the races could be, as that was where she'd met Daniel. Her girlfriends at the time had organised a day out and though they could only afford the cheap seats they had had every intention of having the best day. With hip flasks tucked away inside their bras and wearing outfits that Libby had made for the occasion, they felt on top of the world as they cheered for their favourite horse. Libby won her bet on the very first race and as she went to cash in her winnings, she met the eye of a guy who was looking down on her from the VIP box. He smiled. She smiled. He gestured for her to come up and pointed to a set of stairs. Libby had looked over her shoulder at her friends, who'd just hooked up with a group of men on a stag do. Without giving it a second thought, she slipped away to meet the stranger. After the last race he whisked her away to Cameron House and the rest was history … until he broke her heart and called off their wedding.

'I haven't been to the races for a very long time,' replied Libby, having no intention of watching a horse race again as long as she lived.

'After the races, we spent three exhilarating days together at the hotel. I'll spare you all the details but it was a match made in heaven and here we are now. Together for ever. We go back often, don't we, David?'

'We do,' replied David.

Libby was a little perplexed. She knew for a fact that that hotel was one of the best luxury hotels in Scotland and if anyone was staying there for several days at a time, they weren't strapped for cash, which left her wondering what had motivated them to enter a competition to win a free wedding. But of course everyone loves a freebie, and more often than not, the rich were rich because they knew how to avoid spending money.

'We've both been unlucky in love but not anymore. We were destined to be together and since we've found one another we aren't letting each other go. How about you? Is there someone special in your life?' Miranda was twirling the large diamond engagement ring around on her finger while looking at Libby. 'A beautiful girl like yourself must have them falling at your feet.'

'Not at the moment,' replied Libby, who automatically thought of Guy. Taking a quick glance towards him, she saw he was looking at her through the lens of the camera.

'And it's our dream to start a family as soon as we get back from honeymoon,' gushed Miranda. 'I entered the competition on a whim and who'd have thought we would actually win? We thought our wedding planner was called Jenny though. Will there be two of you?' Miranda swung a glance around the studio as though expecting Jenny to appear at any moment.

Thinking quickly on her feet, Libby said, 'Jenny has moved to another position but I'm so excited to work with you to make your wedding dreams a reality.'

'That's such a shame. We got on like a house on fire when she called to tell us we had won and even had a little chat about our plans for the wedding.'

'I'd love to talk through your ideas for the wedding and work together to make this a very special day for you both,' Libby said encouragingly, reaching across to the table to grab a notebook and balancing it on top of the file on her knee. After spending time with Julia and her scrapbook, Libby was thinking cosy winter elegance with a red ruby bouquet boasting a mix of King Protea, roses, gerbera daisies, fritillaria, waxflower, silver brunia, tulips and gorgeous greenery, or an exquisite frosty blue theme, again featuring roses, anemones, berries, dusty miller and silver brunia.

'Black,' replied Miranda.

'Black?' queried Libby, not quite understanding and taking a quick sideward glance towards Guy.

'Black,' Miranda repeated. 'Everything has to be black. Ever since I was a little girl, I've always wanted a black wedding; it just seems like it would be so elegant and elevated. I've never conformed to the status quo or social expectations. I've always enjoyed being bold, being different and trendsetting, and I can't believe you're actually going to make this happen. I can't thank you enough, Libby.'

Libby looked between Miranda and David, waiting for their faces to break into a smile and tell her that they were joking, but after a few seconds had passed, Libby realised they were deadly serious. She was hoping that she didn't look as shocked as she felt. Trying not to get flustered, she wrote BLACK in capital letters on the top line of the notebook, remembering Flynn's words: *Whatever the client wants, the client gets.*

Libby couldn't understand why they'd been selected if they'd stated this on their application form. Surely Flynn and Jenny would have had a meeting about the image that Flynn was looking for? She knew he wanted a wedding that would appeal to the masses, with winter berry blooms and burgundy bridesmaids' dresses. Or black-tie elegance with a beautiful, classy interior, twinkly lights, winter warmers and possibly a horse-drawn carriage that would deliver the bride to the entrance of the countryside manor house.

'Black,' repeated Libby again. Just in case she hadn't heard right the first few times.

'Black,' echoed Miranda. 'Black dress, black cake, black flowers. No colour at all.'

'But with lots of sparkles and all things shimmery,' added Libby. Despite the challenge ahead, Libby was not going to be beaten. With sparkles at least she might have something to work with.

'No sparkles, no shimmer. Just black. Plain black.'

Libby looked sideward at the rails of gorgeous wedding dresses on the far side of the room. Not one of them was black.

Miranda gave David a loving smile and placed a hand on

his knee. 'It's not all about the bride though, is it? There's two of us getting married here. David has had his own wedding dreams too and it's only fair we should both be able to have what we want on our special day.'

Libby had no idea what was coming next, but she had a feeling that whatever it was, it was going to throw another huge spanner in the works. She turned her attention to David. 'Absolutely! Tell me all, David.'

'Neon green,' he replied with a huge smile, putting his hand under his tie and flicking it upwards.

'Neon green,' repeated Libby, turning the words over in her mind. Her mind flicked back to a few years ago when actress Blake Lively had stepped out in a neon green Versace suit, which she wore with a chic pair of multi-coloured pumps to promote her latest film. Unafraid of taking risks when it came to fashion, she'd looked self-assured, and the look became even more vibrant as the night went on, with the bright lights accentuating the outfit's unusual colour. But David wasn't Blake Lively ... or even Harry Styles, another global superstar who could pull off any outfit.

Miranda began to laugh. 'We had you there for a moment, didn't we?'

Libby exhaled then threw back her head and laughed. Relieved. 'You did! I mean, a black and neon green wedding!' She placed her hand on her heart.

'Even though it's David's favourite colour we do appreciate that it may be a little out there, so we have decided to stick with just all things black.'

Libby could feel the smile sliding from her face again. For a moment she'd thought they'd been joking about the whole colour scheme. She didn't know whether to laugh or cry.

Hearing a stifled cough from the corner of the room, she knew that Guy was finding this all very amusing.

'If it's black you want, then it's black you shall have,' declared Libby, trying to stay upbeat about the whole situation but wondering how Flynn was going to take the news.

'Just to clarify, the whole theme is black, even down to the baubles on the Christmas tree,' added Miranda with a smile.

'I'm sure we can do whatever you want,' replied Libby, silently processing it all. 'This is one of the most special times in a couple's life, planning a celebration of your love and sharing it with your nearest and dearest. I'll work with you as best I can, bringing everything together for your special day. Now, do you have your diaries with you? We need to pencil in a few dates where we can chat about your flowers, cake, guest list and invitations…'

Miranda reached down to her bag. 'I'm one step ahead of you there.' She pulled out a ream of paper and handed it Libby. 'Our guest list, along with their addresses.'

Libby was surprised and impressed at how organised Miranda was. With the wedding being on Christmas Eve the invites would need to go out as soon as possible, so it was fantastic to already have all the addresses to hand.

'Everyone invited to the day is invited to the reception and here are some extras for the evening.'

'Thank you,' replied Libby.

'And as I'm sure you've already guessed, the invites are to be black with white writing to maintain the theme. Oh, and before I forget…' She delved into her bag once again and pulled out a folded piece of paper. 'Here's the contract. Signed, sealed and delivered.'

'Contract?'

'Yes, it was sent out to us after Jenny rang us to say we were the lucky winners.'

Libby took the contract from Miranda and scanned it. It outlined the day and the date of marriage, the venue, how many guests were included and all the things that Flynn was willing to organise and pay for.

'Excellent,' she said, slipping it into the empty file. 'Now let's get our diaries co-ordinated.'

Once they'd got everything scheduled Libby handed over a note card with all her contact details. 'If there is anything else you think of before our next meeting, here's my card. My number is on there and please don't hesitate to ask any questions. Is there anything you'd like to add?' she asked as she turned towards Guy.

'I think you've covered everything but it would be great if I could film you shaking hands with Libby. And then if you could walk down the path hand in hand as you leave that would be perfect.'

Everyone was all smiles as Libby shook their hands and after Miranda put on her coat, she and David headed down the path. As soon as Guy stopped filming, he walked back into the studio to find Libby pouring the rest of the fizz into two large glasses. She handed one to him and they stared at each other for a moment before they both burst out laughing.

'I'm not sure why I'm laughing,' Libby admitted, gulping down a huge mouthful of fizz. 'Because when I tell Flynn all about this, I can already see his face. He's not going to be happy. He wants the classic romantic fairytale winter wedding.'

'It honestly sounded more like a funeral than a wedding.' Guy shook his head in disbelief. 'Black and colourless. It's not often I am lost for words but I don't know what to say except it's a good job you're creative. Let me show you your face when Miranda declared the wedding was going to be all black. Hold this.' Guy passed his drink to Libby. After he pressed a few buttons on the camera he turned it towards her so she could see the screen.

She watched the video play out. As soon as Miranda said the word 'black', the smile slid from Libby's face. She looked horrified. 'I didn't hide what I was thinking very well, did I?'

Guy was still grinning.

'Who in their right mind wants a black wedding? With a black cake and flowers too.

You're right, it sounds more like a funeral.'

'Maybe she's going to walk down the aisle to the song "Another One Bites the Dust",' added Guy, laughing.

'Don't! It's not funny! What am I going to do? I'm not sure Flynn will be happy with this.'

'You're going to have to give them what they want. After all, they won the competition.'

'But *how* did they win the competition? I don't even have the application form. How is a wedding in black and a couple of such height difference—'

'You can't be heightist, if they love each other…'

'I know and I don't mean to be, but I know what my brother was thinking when he launched this competition. Black with no shimmers… It's going to be a wedding to remember, but not in the way Flynn was likely hoping.'

'And here was me thinking this was going to be the worst job that I've had this year. Now I can't wait to see how this one is going to pan out.'

Libby rolled her eyes and took another sip of her drink. 'We need to go and tell Flynn.'

'We?' queried Guy.

'Yes, *we*! Remember, we're in this together. We made a deal. Don't let me down now.'

Guy grinned.

'Please,' Libby quickly added. 'I need back-up.'

He clinked his glass against hers. 'Even though I think you're more than capable of going by yourself, I wouldn't miss Flynn's reaction for the world. There's no time like the present.'

Chapter Seven

Libby knocked on Flynn's office door and waited.

'Come in,' he shouted.

Guy did the gentlemanly thing and held the door open. 'After you,' he said, giving Libby a look of reassurance, knowing what she was about to reveal.

Flynn was sitting behind his desk, papers spread out in front of him, while Julia was leaning against the window sill, her hands wrapped around a steaming mug of tea. 'Here they are! We were just talking about you. How did the first meeting go? Was it all hearts and flowers, romance and twinkly fairy lights?' Julia asked.

'Not quite,' admitted Libby, screwing up her face before sitting down on the chair opposite Flynn. Guy grabbed another from the far side of the room and parked it next to her.

Julia's eyes flicked between the two of them. 'They did turn up, didn't they?'

'Yes,' Libby said, hesitantly.

'I can feel a "but" coming on,' Flynn said, folding his arms and leaning on the desk.

'I'm not sure it's going to pan out exactly how you're imagining it.'

'How can a beautiful romantic winter wedding in the most stunning of settings with everything Christmas and all things festive not be quite how I imagine it?' he asked, looking puzzled.

'Because that's your ideal wedding, and Julia's too, but unfortunately the winning happy couple don't quite share your vision.'

'What do you mean? How can anyone not share that vision? I gave a specific brief to Jenny.'

'Possibly one that may have got lost in communication. The bottom line is your bride is over six foot tall – I'd say around six-foot-four without heels – and your groom is pushing five-foot-four *with* heels. Not only that, but they also want a colourless wedding.'

Flynn looked confused. 'What do you mean? What's a colourless wedding?'

'Exactly what it says on the tin. No colour. Everything at the wedding is black. Black dress, black cake, black flowers, even black invitations.'

Flynn looked horrified. 'Black? It wasn't Halloween or April Fool's Day last time I looked. You're winding me up, right?'

'Of course they're joking!' Julia chipped in, looking between Libby and Guy before realising that both of their expressions were serious.

'Not joking,' confirmed Libby. 'I wish I were.'

'I've captured it all on film, if you want to take a look?' added Guy, holding up his camera.

'I think I best had,' replied Flynn.

Julia went and stood behind Flynn's chair as Guy turned the viewfinder towards them both and the footage began to play.

Libby watched a slow crimson blush crept up Flynn's cheeks, a look she knew only too well. He wasn't happy. As soon as the short clip was over, Guy switched off the camera. A look of disbelief was written all over Flynn's face.

'What are you thinking?' Julia asked him.

'I'm thinking this is a complete disaster. I understand that we all have different ideas about our wedding day and we can't all be the same, but ... black? We can't use this wedding to promote Starcross Manor and that was the whole point of the competition. This wedding was meant to be the most romantic winter wedding in the world, not a version of the *Rocky Horror Show*. We'll have to cancel and then take a second look through the applications and see who came a close second.'

Libby opened the file and slid the contract across the table. 'No can do. You've already signed the contract and unless there's a clause in there that says you can get out of it, you have to honour the promise that clearly states what the bride and groom want, the bride and groom get.' Libby tapped the form.

'Damn. Pass me their application form. I need to see what they put on there for Jenny to have chosen them.'

'I'm afraid there is no application form in the file. It's missing. I have no information about the winning couple whatsoever except what they've told us today. All that was in this file was details of the competition and the closing date for entries.'

'How is there no information about the winning couple? I need to check with Lisa where she found the file. Their application form has to be somewhere. There was a section where they had to describe their dream wedding and if they described this all-black nightmare there's no way they should have been chosen. You don't think...' he began, suddenly looking panicked. 'Surely Jenny actually *read* all the application forms before choosing the winner, right?'

Libby felt bad for her brother. It was clear that Flynn was in disbelief and trying to reason his way out of this disaster.

'Maybe there's a way to disqualify them,' he said, sounding hopeful.

'You can't disqualify them,' Julia replied. 'I know it's disappointing that you probably can't use the footage to promote future weddings but if they have been chosen to win—'

'By someone who no longer works here,' interrupted Flynn.

'Disqualifying them for any reason would create a whole lot of negative publicity that you and Starcross Manor don't need. There will be uproar. Just think about what that could do to your reputation and the reputation of this place. I hate to say it, but these people won and are entitled to the wedding they want.'

Flynn briefly closed his eyes. 'I can't believe this is happening ... and different heights, did you say?'

'Miranda towers over David. This may be a little disappointing but we are going to have to work with it the best we can.' Libby looked hopefully towards Guy. 'With Guy's skills, maybe we can film something a bit more abstract that gives them the promised video of their day but could also be repurposed as promotional material. What do you think?'

'We could make it more of a professional video showing what Starcross Manor has to offer with its unique wedding planning services. Put a different spin on it,' Guy chipped in, building on Libby's idea.

'But ... this competition has been advertised across all our social media channels, and people will be waiting to see the wedding of the century. I can't post a colourless Christmas Eve wedding with no festive touches whatsoever. This was meant to entice future brides and grooms, not scare them away.'

'I know the main point of the competition was to publicise this wedding and use it for marketing purposes but there are other options,' said Julia.

'Such as?' enquired Flynn, winding his hand around in a circle to hurry Julia in sharing her thoughts.

'Stage a pretend wedding for the promotional stuff. It doesn't have to be a real wedding. Just enough for Guy to put a video together while we have him at Starcross Manor.'

'But where I am going to get a pretend bride and groom from, and what chance is there that they'll be available for filming as and when we need them just before Christmas? There also needs to be chemistry between them and they have to look good together. That's a big ask on short notice.'

'You could hire a couple of models or actors from an agency and tell them exactly the look you want,' Libby chipped in. 'That might work.'

For a moment, Flynn was quiet, mulling over the suggestion. Before he could say anything, Julia put down her mug and began flapping her hands in his direction. There was a huge smile painted across her face. 'When I suggested Libby would be the perfect planner for this job...'

'So it was *your* suggestion,' said Libby.

'You don't think Flynn comes up with all the good ideas himself, do you?' she teased.

'Oi, I am here, you know!' remarked Flynn, pretending to look hurt.

But Julia was no longer looking at Flynn; she was staring at Libby and Guy. 'Stand up, the pair of you,' she said, gesturing towards them both.

Perplexed, Libby and Guy looked at each other before standing up.

'Your perfect couple is right here! Libby is gorgeous and Guy extremely handsome. The height difference is perfect and just look at them together. Why hire models when you have these two? Libby can pick any dress from the studio and, with Guy kitted out in a kilt, you have your textbook couple. We can dress The Grand Hall, even ask the villagers to come up for a glass of wine and mingle as pretend guests. We would get some wonderful footage, I'm sure of it. The community of Heartcross will probably be eager to get on board and help us out. I bet Florrie would be happy to do the flowers and Rona the cake. Surely it's a no-brainer?' The enthusiasm in Julia's voice was evident to everyone.

Flynn's beam widened but Libby noticed the smile had slipped from Guy's face.

Standing up, Flynn planted a kiss on Julia's lips. 'You're a genius. This is a brilliant suggestion.' He turned to face Libby and Guy. 'Julia's right, you would be perfect for the promotion video. You pair look like you're made for each other! This would really help us out. What do you think?'

Flynn was unaware of the slight tension that was radiating from Guy but it hadn't escaped Libby. Flynn looked at them earnestly, waiting for an answer. 'Libby?'

Hesitantly, she suggested, 'It might be fun to dress up and drink champagne and be on the arm of a handsome man.' She smiled towards Guy but he'd already picked up his camera and was walking towards the door.

'Sorry, I can't' was all he uttered before the door shut behind him.

'What's just happened here?' Flynn asked, looking at Libby.

'I'm not quite sure,' she replied, but she knew something had triggered Guy.

'I thought it was an excellent idea. You pair just look so natural together and the photos would have been perfect for our promotion. But it was only a suggestion. I'll go after him. Something has clearly upset him,' Flynn said, getting up to follow Guy.

'No, I'll go. Leave it with me,' Libby replied, speedily leaving the office to chase down Guy.

Driven by frustration, Guy strode across the grounds of Starcross Manor, the snow muffling his frustrated strides. He felt angry and betrayed by the recent events in his life and it hurt. In fact, at times it hurt so much it would take his breath away. At the moment, everywhere he turned, it was all about weddings. It was hard enough filming a wedding, with what was going on in his personal life, and now they wanted him to play the pretend groom? Absolutely not!

He knew his behaviour must have looked a little erratic but

he couldn't help the way he was feeling. It was as if he had been stabbed in the heart. He needed to keep his emotional walls high and strong, because he could never face going through anything like this again. The easiest thing would be to cut himself off from everyone in his past, but he knew that wasn't possible because of Holly. They were still her family too.

As he opened the front door of the lodge, Holly ran into his arms. She squealed in delight as he hoisted her onto his back, and wrapped her arms around his neck. 'I do love you,' he murmured, knowing he would never let his little girl down as his own family had let him down.

'I love you too, Daddy.'

Feeling Holly hugging him tightly and hearing those words was comforting. With his thoughts still very much on the past, he was overcome by a deep sadness, but looking over his shoulder at a smiling, happy-go-lucky Holly helped him thrust those feelings towards the back of his mind.

'Lunch is ready. Granny was hoping you'd be back in time. She's made your favourite sandwiches and we've taken Pickle on the sledge to The Old Bakehouse for cake.'

'This is what I love about you, you always make me smile when—'

'There's Libby!' Holly started waving madly and Guy looked over his shoulder, knowing she must have come to talk to him. He lowered Holly to the ground as Libby walked towards them.

'Hi, Holly, how was your morning?'

Holly leaned in towards Libby as though she was going to tell her a huge secret. 'We've been to The Old Bakehouse for cake and Granny has been trying to make me a dress...' Holly looked over her shoulder then back towards Libby. She leaned forward again and this time whispered, 'But it's not going well.'

'Oh no, why's that then?' asked Libby, just as quietly.

'Because her glasses don't work anymore, and Granny has trouble threading the needle. Then there's Pickle who keeps getting up to mischief. It's stop, start, stop, start, but she tries her best.'

Libby laughed. 'As long as we try our best, that's all that matters.' Her glance turned to Guy. 'Is it possible to have a quick word?' she asked.

'We're just about to have lunch.'

Right on cue, Cynthia called, 'Lunch is ready' from inside the lodge and Pickle escaped through the door, her tail wagging and her bum waggling as she weaved frantically in and out of Libby's legs. 'I believe you've been up to mischief?' said Libby, scooping up the pup. Pickle immediately licked Libby's face, making Holly laugh.

'Libby can come for lunch; there's loads. Granny always makes too many sandwiches.' Holly tugged on Guy's hand before he took Pickle from Libby's arms.

'I'm sure Libby has her own plans.'

'Have you?' asked Holly. 'Because we have cake too.'

'Cake, you say? What type of cake?' Libby looking inquisitively towards Holly.

'Cream and jam cake.'

'That happens to be my favourite. Is it a Victoria Sponge?'

Holly nodded. 'Yes.'

'Well, I haven't made any plans for lunch…'

Guy glanced down at Holly, with her adorable eyes and her hands in a prayer-like stance. 'Please, Daddy.'

'How can anyone resist that face?' He opened the door wide. 'You best come in then. Holly, please go tell Granny we have one more for lunch.' He lowered Pickle to the ground and she immediately chased Holly as she ran into the lodge shouting, 'Granny!' leaving Guy and Libby standing outside alone.

Libby was just about to ask if everything was okay, but Guy beat her to it.

'I don't want to talk about it and the answer is still no.' His tone was firm.

Libby held her hands up. 'Talk about what? I'm just here for the cake. What girl doesn't love free cake?'

Guy's face softened. He looked relieved and gave a smile. 'Noted,' he said.

'That's more like it. You do look lovely when you smile. You get a tiny dimple, just here.' Libby waved her finger just near his cheek. 'Looks kind of cute.'

Guy rolled his eyes and gently pushed her inside. Libby looked back over her shoulder. 'I'm excited I get to meet my future mother-in-law already,' she teased, watching with delight as a horrified look crossed Guy's face. 'Was that too soon? Sorry, I was only joking!'

'Yes, definitely too soon. The subject of weddings is off the menu.'

'Sorry! Noted,' she said, mirroring his choice of words.

Guy shut the door behind them and followed Libby into the living room.

Holly slipped her hand inside Libby's. 'Come and sit next to me.'

'Of course I will,' replied Libby.

Guy introduced his mother to Libby before Holly and

Libby sat down next to each other at the table. 'Dad, you sit next to Libby,' Holly ordered, pointing to the chair on the other side of her.

'I will, but I'll just get the drinks first.'

While doing so, Guy watched Holly and Libby laughing and joking. Taken by surprise, he suddenly felt emotional and swallowed a lump in his throat. Six years ago, this was how he'd imagined his family life: all of them sitting around the table, enjoying each other's company. How things had changed in such a short time. Placing a jug of water on the table, he slipped into the chair next to Libby and watched the conversation flowing between her and Holly. They began clapping their hands with each other while singing a rhyme they both knew.

Out of the corner of her eye Libby caught sight of Guy watching and she gave him a warm smile. He smiled back.

'Do you want to have a go?' asked Holly, looking at her dad.

Holly was beautiful, Libby thought, the image of Guy with the same nose and lips.

'It's okay; I'll leave you girls to it but thank you.'

'Have you got any children, Libby?' asked Cynthia. 'You're such a natural.'

Libby shook her head. 'It's just me.'

'You're still young, there's plenty of time yet,' Cynthia said.

Libby just smiled. Over time she'd learned to cope with conversations like this.

'And while I'm here, you can have me and Pickle to keep you company,' offered Holly.

'Thank you, that would be lovely, but I think I'll borrow Pickle only when she's asleep.'

'Good plan,' replied Holly, holding her hands up for another clapping game.

As they ate, Cynthia asked questions about Heartcross. Libby couldn't sing its praises enough, nor those of the community that lived here. During the conversation she glanced in Guy's direction a couple of times and caught him watching her. Then Cynthia's phone began ringing in the living room and, apologising for the disruption, she took herself off to answer the call.

'I like Libby. Daddy, can she come for lunch more often?' Holly looked between the pair of them. 'It's nice to have new friends.'

'That's okay by me, if it's okay by Libby.' Guy smiled at them both but held Libby's gaze longer, making her heart beat a little faster. He'd stretched out his legs under the table and one brushed against hers as they looked at each other.

'It is,' replied Libby. 'And what are your plans for this afternoon?'

'Granny is going to attempt to sew my dress again.'

'And where is your dress?'

Holly ran off in the direction of the bedroom and returned with a pile of material and a half-sewn sleeve.

'And what occasion is this dress for?' asked Libby, turning the material over in her hand.

'Mummy's wedding,' replied Holly.

'How lovely,' Libby said. Was this the reason Guy wasn't very keen on weddings? Was it possible that Guy still had feelings for his ex, and that's what was causing the tension? 'I bet you're excited. I could get this dress finished for you this afternoon. I have a sewing machine in the studio and all the equipment I need.' She looked over towards Guy. 'If you have no plans, Holly could join me for the afternoon and watch her dress being made.'

Before Guy could answer, Holly was jumping up and down with excitement at the prospect. 'Please, Daddy?'

'I don't want to tread on anyone's toes, of course,' Libby added. 'I just thought it might take some pressure off your mum?'

'Between you and me, I think my mum would be secretly chuffed to have this task taken off her hands. But are you sure? Haven't you got other wedding things to coordinate? We don't want to put you out.'

'All I was planning on doing this afternoon was making a secret outfit,' Libby replied.

'What's a secret outfit?' asked Holly.

'It's a secret,' said Libby with a wink. 'But I can sew your dress first.'

'Then my dress will be finished!'

Guy looked from Libby to Holly. Holly had her eyes squeezed shut and her fingers crossed on both hands.

'Are you sure it's okay with you?'

'I'd love to spend my afternoon with Holly, but first I'd just like to remind you I am actually only here for one reason.'

'Which is?' Guy narrowed his eyes.

'Cake! I was promised cake!'

Guy laughed and began to clear away the plates before cutting enormous slices of cake. Cynthia was still on the phone and had moved into the bedroom to continue her call.

'Thank you, it's very kind of you to help out with the dress.'

'It's my pleasure, and it's what I do best.' Libby checked

her watch. 'Do you want to come and pick Holly up from the studio in a couple of hours?'

'Perfect. That'll give me time to go for a wander and snap some photos.'

After they'd devoured their cake, Guy helped Holly put on her boots and fasten up her coat. Libby was holding a carrier bag with the dress inside.

'Will you thank Cynthia for lunch?' said Libby, looking in the direction of the bedrooms.

'I will, and you girls have a good time this afternoon.'

'We will!' Libby and Holly chorused.

Guy stood in the doorway and watched them walk down the path side by side. Holly looked up at Libby as she chattered away, and slipped her hand inside hers. Libby was stooping over listening to every word. She was an absolute natural with children. There was a kind of generosity and warmth to her and Holly had taken to her instantly. As they were about to disappear around the corner, Libby glanced back over her shoulder and flashed Guy a tender smile. He waved before shutting the door. After his break-up, he'd removed himself from the dating scene, putting Holly first, and hadn't even considered the prospect of another woman in his life after all the pain he'd suffered. But Libby made him feel strangely at ease, She was intriguing, markedly intelligent and alarmingly attractive. He'd been thinking about her more and more ever since they met.

With Libby very much on his mind, he headed into the kitchen and began to load the dishwasher. Cynthia had finished her call and when she joined him, Guy could feel a slight tension in the air. He turned around. Cynthia's face was grave.

'Libby has taken Holly to finish her dress. I hope you don't mind but she'll get it done in a couple of hours and it would take—'

'Yes, of course,' interrupted Cynthia, her voice shaky.

'Is everything okay?' Guy asked, sensing that his mother needed to say something.

'That phone call, it was your sister. Her health is—'

Guy put up his hand in an attempt to stop his mum talking about this but it didn't deter her.

'This feud with her—'

Guy sighed. 'Mum, I can't do this. It's all too much.'

'Something has to give. It's not just you it's having an effect on.'

Guy raked his hand through his hair and briefly closed his eyes. 'When I said I can't cope with this any longer, I meant it. I came here for a break from the whole situation.' Feeling defensive, his heart begin to beat faster, the irate and anxious feelings rising inside him once again. He didn't want to think about his sister. Grabbing his coat and his camera, he said, 'I need some air, I'm going out.' As he left, he avoided eye contact with his mother but he knew she had that familiar look of disdain on her face. But she couldn't make him talk about Lydia. Guy stepped outside, closed the door behind him and took a deep breath.

Chapter Eight

'Look at all these dresses! It's a princess shop.' Holly pointed towards the beautiful wedding dresses hanging on the rail.

'They are gorgeous, aren't they?' replied Libby, taking the material for Holly's dress out of the bag and grabbing the child size dressmaker's dummy.

'That's weird, it has no head.' Holly walked inquisitively around the mannequin. 'What does it do?'

Libby smiled. 'Most weddings have beautiful flower girls like yourself and I'm going to use the dummy to make your dress. I'm going to measure you then check over the fabric and cut out what pieces we need. Then I'll pin the fabric around the dummy so we can see what your dress is going to look like. When it's pinned in place, we will carefully try it on you and make sure it's the right size and fit before I sew it all together. Oh dear, I forgot to ask your daddy or granny what the design of the dress is like.'

'It's whatever I want,' stated Holly. 'I'm the only flower girl.'

'Do you want to have a look through a couple of magazines to see what you might like?' Libby asked. Then she noticed that Holly had spotted the glass cabinet of tiaras at the far end of the room. 'Go and have a look,' she said, and watched Holly joyfully skip over to the cabinet.

'Look at these, they are so pretty.' Holly was standing on tiptoe with her face pressed against the glass.

Libby brought over a chair and helped Holly to step onto it. She stared into the cabinet. 'Which one is your favourite?' she asked.

'That one right in the middle. It sparkles.'

Holly was pointing to a glamorous tiara. The comfortable headband was accented by elaborate floral elements and the floral segments were set with iridescent freshwater pearls and small, glistening, round cubic zirconia.

'It does indeed sparkle. When we finish your dress you can try it on.'

'Can I?'

'Of course you can,' said Libby, lifting an excitable Holly down from the chair. 'But first let's choose the design of your dress.'

Libby gathered a number of magazines from the shelf and spread them out on the white fur rug in the middle of the studio. Holly lay on her stomach, her legs in the air, her face in her hands. Libby sat cross-legged next to her. 'Have a look and see what design you like best.'

'And I can have any design?'

'You can have whatever dress you wish.'

'You're very clever,' Holly replied, as she began turning the pages. Every dress that Holly saw was her new favourite. 'They all look so pretty.' Holly turned over another page. 'This one is the same colour as mine.'

'And the same material. Do you like that one?'

Holly nodded.

The fluttery crimson crinkle chiffon material was ideal for the dress featured in the magazine. With its A-line silhouette, scooped neckline, cap sleeves and the bowknot embellishment, Libby knew it would be perfect for the little girl. 'That's the one, you're going to look utterly beautiful. Holly Hart will go to the ball,' announced Libby, standing up and switching on the radio. She took hold of Holly's hands and gently pulled her to her feet. As the next song came on Libby twirled Holly around and they jigged along until the song finished.

'I'm out of breath,' Libby admitted. After taking in some deep breaths, she walked over to the water dispenser, poured two cups of water and handed one to Holly before taking a sip from her own. 'Right, let's get this show on the road.'

'What show?' asked Holly, puzzled as she looked all around.

Libby laughed. 'It's just a figure of speech.'

'What's a figure of speech?'

'It just means: let's begin making your dress!'

Holly helped Libby to lay the material out on the table then once again stood on the chair for a better view. Libby could see that Cynthia had tried her hardest to follow some sort of pattern and had attempted to sew the back of the dress to the front. It wouldn't take Libby long to unpick the stitching and start again.

'I'm going to be a dressmaker when I grow up,' Holly announced. 'I can make all my own clothes.'

'It's a brilliant job to have. I was about your age when I decided what I wanted to be when I grew up and that's exactly what I do.' There was a small part of Holly that reminded Libby of herself. Holly was concentrating closely, watching everything that Libby did. 'Go over to the top drawer of that table and you'll find a measuring tape.'

Immediately Holly fetched the tape and handed it to Libby.

'Thank you. And now I need to take some measurements. This might tickle. I need you to stand like this.'

Holly mirrored Libby's stance, her arms open wide and feet apart. Libby began to take the measurements and scrawled them on a nearby pad. 'I think we are ready to draw the pattern on paper. Do you want to help?'

'Yes, please!'

For the next hour they worked happily together. Libby helped Holly draw the pattern onto the paper and then Holly watched Libby's every move, which gave her a warm glow inside. They were having fun making the dress together and Libby was enjoying spending time with the little girl. After they had pinned the fabric pieces together, Libby carefully took each section over to the sewing machine and began to sew the dress. Holly was at her side the whole time and Libby taught her how to hold the material steady as it went through the machine.

'It's like magic,' exclaimed Holly, watching the material feed through the machine. 'And now it's sewn together.'

'It is, and that's why making your own clothes is so exciting. You can create your own designs and wear whatever you want.'

In what felt like no time at all, the dress was finished and hanging on the mannequin. 'What do you think?' Libby asked.

'It's so pretty!'

'Isn't it just,' Libby replied. The beam on Holly's face made her heart swell. 'I'm just going to steam it to get rid of the creases, then do you want to try it on?'

'Yes, please! I can't wait to wear it for the wedding ... but I wish Daddy was going to see me in my dress,' Holly said, suddenly looking sad.

Libby took the iron from the cupboard and began to steam the creases out of the dress.

'I'm sure your dad will see you in your dress,' Libby said supportively, trying to smooth away Holly's worry but aware that if Guy's split with his ex wasn't amicable, it would be difficult for him to go to the wedding, even for Holly's sake.

Holly shook her head. 'Daddy can't come and he's fallen out with Auntie Lydia too. I'm going with Granny and Grandad. Daddy's arguing a lot with Granny.'

There were certainly no secrets when kids were around. Libby was unsure what to say. 'You can try it on for him later. I'm sure when he sees you in your dress, he'll love it.'

'It might make him change his mind,' Holly said hopefully, her eyes wide.

Libby stood back and looked over the dress, grateful that she didn't need to answer. 'There you go, it's all finished.' She turned off the iron and stood it on the table to cool. 'Time for you to try it on!'

Holly gave a little squeal as Libby carefully lifted the dress off the mannequin. 'Come on, this way, there's a changing area though here.'

Libby led Holly through a double wooden door, up three carpeted steps and into a magnificent cream room. In each corner were giant palm plants and there was a plush cream sofa and armchairs. Across the back of the room were a number of large changing cubicles with thick ivory curtains. Libby pulled back the curtain on one. 'Do you need any help?' she asked.

Holly shook her head and disappeared behind the curtain. While she was getting changed, Libby retrieved the tiara that Holly had admired from the cabinet.

'I'm ready!' Holly shouted a moment later.

As Libby pulled back the curtain she was met by Holly, holding the dress by the hem and dropping into a curtsy.

'Look at you!' Libby turned Holly around and zipped up the back of the dress then stepped back to take a better look. 'Come and have a look at yourself in the big mirrors.'

Holly ran towards the mirrors that lined the wall. She spun round and round. 'I love it. Thank you!'

'You're very welcome. And now for the finishing touch.' Libby placed the tiara on the top of the little girl's head. 'What do you think?'

Holly brought her hands up to her mouth in delighted surprise. 'I'm a proper princess.'

'You are.'

Holly stepped straight up to the mirror and stared at her reflection. 'You need to dress up too. We can both be princesses.' She pointed to the row of wedding dresses along the opposite wall.

'Come and help me choose. Which one do you like?'

Holly walked along the line of dresses, looking carefully at each one before glancing towards Libby. 'I think this one would look pretty on you.'

Libby looked at the dress that Holly had chosen. It oozed romance. 'I'll try it on,' she said, kicking off her boots and taking it from the rail before disappearing into the changing room. Closing the curtain behind her, Libby slipped out of her clothes.

Hearing one of her favourite songs on the radio, she danced her way into the dress. 'I love this song,' she shouted to Holly. 'But you'll have to excuse my singing, I'm not very good at it.'

She was still singing her heart out as she posed in the mirror. She could hear Holly giggling. Pulling the curtain back, Libby spun round, waving her arms in the air like she just didn't care and wiggling her backside.

Holly was now laughing uncontrollably.

'Kiss me, you sexy thing!' Libby sang at the top of her lungs. Her eyes were closed as she spun round towards Holly, and she was still busting her moves when she opened her eyes to see a very amused-looking Guy. She blew out a breath, then grinned. He'd changed from his earlier attire and was now wearing a navy blue jumper with a designer logo. It clung to his torso, which she admired for a second before averting her eyes. And there it was again, that tingle when she was in Guy's presence—the goosebumps and flutters in her stomach. He even made her a little nervous, but in a good way. There was just something about him.

'Is that an invitation?' asked Guy, with a glint in his eye.

'Huh?'

'"Kiss me, you sexy thing!"' Guy repeated, maintaining eye contact.

'You can't beat a little bit of lip syncing to Hot Chocolate. It's always my go-to fun song,' she said with a shrug, trying to ignore the burning desire that had just ignited within her to know what it would be like to kiss Guy Hart.

Guy grinned, holding Holly's hand. 'Wow!' He was unashamedly staring. 'You're absolutely breathtaking.'

Libby was wearing a simple but stunning wedding dress of sparkly dotted tulle, gathered at the waist and with a plunging V-neck line. The dress floated elegantly to the floor.

'Why thank you,' she replied with a smile on her face she couldn't control.

Taking her by surprise, he stepped forward and lightly kissed her on the cheek. She inhaled his woody aftershave and lowered her voice to say, 'You smell divine.'

'Any man would be lucky to have you on their arm.'

Libby gave him a beatific smile that lit up her whole face. 'We were just trying on dresses.'

'I can see that. You both look as gorgeous as each other.' Guy gave Libby one last, lingering look before turning towards Holly. 'This dress is amazing and you too look beautiful.'

Holly grabbed the bottom of her dress and looked down at herself. 'We made the dress together,' she said proudly. 'I can't wait to wear it for the wedding.'

'We did make the dress together and it was so much fun,' confirmed Libby, giving Holly a warm smile. 'And your sewing skills were amazing.'

'Take our photo, Daddy,' Holly insisted.

'I've left my camera and bag by the door.'

'I'll get it but I need the bathroom first.'

After watching Holly run to the bathroom Guy locked eyes

with Libby. 'You wouldn't look out of place on the front of a wedding magazine.'

'Strike a pose,' joked Libby.

'I mean it. Just look at you.'

'We could both be on the front cover of a magazine if Flynn gets his way. Look. We would make the perfect couple.' She nudged his elbow to turn him towards the mirror then stood next to him facing their reflections.

'Surely it wouldn't be that bad, spending some more time with me to help Flynn out?' She took the chance of risking a sideward glance.

Guy smiled at her.

'But while you're thinking about that ... there's just one more thing...'

'You can be so demanding. Do you know that?' he said with amusement, still watching her reflection in the mirror.

'I try my best.' She smiled. 'Could you fasten the buttons at my neck before I lose the dress?'

'I think that's a little too much to ask,' he replied, embracing the playful banter. His dark eyes were glistening at her and she was feeling nervous again, but in a good way.

Libby turned around and moved her hair to one side, leaving her neck exposed. Briefly she closed her eyes as Guy moved closer to her, which made her heart beat a little faster. There was an undeniable spark of attraction between them. Feeling his hand brush against the nape of her neck, she bit her lip. He fastened the buttons and Libby dared to glance over her shoulder, staring straight into his eyes before her gaze fell to his lips then locked with his again. The way he was looking at her as he slowly moved her hair from the side of her neck made a burst of adrenalin electrify her heart. She hadn't experienced anything like this in a long while.

'Daddy! Here's the camera.' Holly ran towards him, thrusting the camera into his hand. 'Let's dance,' she said, taking Libby's hand.

They began to dance around the room, and Guy perched on the edge of a coffee table, the lens of the camera fixed on them both. After snapping a few photos, he reached into his pocket and took out his phone. He began to video as Libby took Holly's hand and they spun round and round, holding each other tightly as they leaned backwards, their hair trailing. They squealed and laughed and, as the song came to an end, they fell to the floor to catch their breath. Libby opened her arms wide and Holly hugged her. The feeling of the little girl's arms wrapped around her neck made Libby come over all emotional. She liked it. A lone tear escaped and she quickly brushed it away with the back of her hand.

She caught Guy's eye as Holly pulled away slowly. He narrowed his eyes and mouthed, 'Are you okay?'

She nodded and took Holly's hand in hers. 'I've had just the best time. Thank you, Holly, for a wonderful afternoon. I've enjoyed every second of it.'

'Me too and thank you for my dress. I love it.'

'You're very welcome, and don't forget that if you ever need help making any of your clothes, you can just give me a shout.'

'I will. I promise.'

'Now let's get you changed.'

A few minutes later Holly handed the dress to Libby, who wrapped it up in blush-coloured tissue paper and placed it inside a fancy cardboard bag with rope handles. 'And for being my favourite helper...' Libby held up the tiara. 'A present from me to you.'

Holly gasped. 'You're the best.' She flung her arms again around Libby, who squeezed her tight.

'And so are you.'

'Daddy! Look what Libby has given me.'

'Yes, I can see, but please let me pay for that. You've already given up your time to make the dress. It's too much. Let me pay for both.'

'Absolutely not. This afternoon has been my pleasure.'

'That is very kind,' replied Guy, touching her arm. 'Thank you.'

Libby placed the tiara in its own special box, gave it to Holly then they headed into the main studio. Libby pointed outside. She'd spotted Cynthia through the window pulling Pickle on the sledge.

'Why don't you go back with Granny and I'll see you in a bit,' said Guy.

Rushing out of the door, Holly called, 'Granny! Pickle! Wait! I have a dress and a tiara.'

'Be careful of the ice,' Guy bellowed after her.

'I think she's excited,' said Libby, standing next to him. They watched Holly hand over the bag to Cynthia and budge Pickle out of the way as she climbed onto the sledge. Immediately, Pickle jumped back on and settled on Holly's lap, then Cynthia began to pull them both back towards the lodges.

'You're extremely talented,' Guy said as he turned towards Libby.

'Are we talking about my singing or my dancing?'

Guy laughed. 'I'm not quite sure about your singing.'

'Me neither,' she replied, smiling up at him.

'But I have to say I was impressed with your bum-waggling.' There was a sparkle in his eyes as he flashed Libby a gorgeous smile. He was definitely flirting a little and it made her heart skip a beat. He reached out and took her hand. 'Dance with me.'

'What, here? Don't be daft.'

'Yes, here. Why not?' he said softly. With both hands in his, Guy led Libby into the middle of the studio. 'I used to love to dance, but it's a long time since I've danced with anyone.'

Sheer pleasure mixed with apprehension ran through Libby's body. It had been a very long time since she'd danced with someone too. Her heart rate quickened instantly and she thought she was going to either melt or combust. There was something about his gentlemanly confidence that made her go weak at the knees. They moved together slowly, every inch of her tingling with desire as they floated weightlessly around the room. The intensity between them was like nothing she'd ever felt. He drew her in closer and Libby felt breathless. Snuggling into his chest, she buried her face in the soft wool of his jumper. She immediately felt safe with his arms wrapped around her—a feeling she realised she'd missed and could get used to again. As the song came to an end, she had to remind herself to breathe. For a moment, they stayed locked in each other's arms, then gazed at each other in a contemplative silence. Then—she couldn't help it—her eyes filled with tears.

'Hey, are you okay? My dancing wasn't that bad, was it?'

'Of course not, it was beautiful. It's just been a long time since anyone has held me like that.' Her voice wavered. The electricity between them was exhilarating but unsettling. He held her head gently in his hands, his thumb caressing her cheek.

'I can't quite believe that,' he replied tenderly.

Libby hadn't felt desire like this in such a long time. She was willing him to kiss her but knew how much that would complicate things between them.

'I suppose I better lose this dress,' she said softly, not taking her eyes from his.

'Those are words I wasn't expecting to hear today,' he said, giving her the most kissable smile she'd ever seen.

'You know what I mean,' she replied, rolling her eyes. 'But if you would be kind enough to undo my buttons…?' She turned slowly but kept her eyes on him. He stepped closer to her, making every nerve in her body tingle. Guy unhurriedly released the buttons.

'Thank you,' she said, and returned to the changing area, where she stepped into a cubicle and pulled the curtain across. Taking a moment, she stared at her reflection in the mirror. Her skin was glowing, she had a smile on her face that she'd not seen for a long time, and she felt happy—another feeling that had been buried deep inside.

When she pulled back the curtain, Guy was sitting on the edge of the table, looking at his phone. He turned it towards her. 'Take a look.'

'You've filmed us dancing!'

'I'd left it running, and just look at you. You dance so effortlessly and with such beauty.'

'This is exactly what Flynn is looking for in his promotional video. This is the image he's trying to create. And I bet you'd look good in a kilt.'

Guy switched off the video and looked at her. 'I didn't mean to walk out of Flynn's office. I just have a lot going on in my life at the moment and having to discuss weddings is a bitter pill to swallow.'

Libby perched on the table next to him. 'I'm a good listener,' she offered. 'A problem shared and all that.'

Guy looked like he was going to say something and changed his mind. 'It's just something I have to deal with myself.'

'I'm guessing it might have something to do with your ex-partner getting married? Have you been separated long?' Libby's tone was soft but she knew she'd hit on something because Guy suddenly looked uncomfortable.

'Four years.' Guy didn't elaborate but Libby could see his whole demeanour had changed. She knew immediately that this wasn't a conversation Guy wanted to have.

'It doesn't matter how amicable a break-up is, it still must be hard to see her marry someone else. Holly mentioned that she would love you to see her in her dress on the day. She was so excited when she tried it on and the first thing she thought of was you. Maybe it's worth reconsidering to make Holly's day?'

Libby hoped that Guy would soften his stance but from the look on his face she knew she'd said the wrong thing. He stood up and put his phone in his pocket.

'You have no clue what is going on in my life, but to add emotional blackmail… Don't even go there. Holly can go to the wedding with my parents. It's her mother's wedding and she should be there but there are other reasons I can't go with her … and I don't want to talk about them.'

'And your unnamed reasons matter more than a little girl's happiness? *Your* little girl's happiness?'

'It's me that's the decent man here and once again I'm

being judged by somebody who knows nothing about the situation.'

'I'm not judging you. I just know from experience that sometimes family is all you have to get you through the hardest times.' Libby was remembering the most difficult time of her life. 'Believe me, I know.'

'Once upon a time I'd have agreed with you. My family was my world and I lived and breathed them. Parents are meant to be your protectors, to support you no matter what. It's a joke. If a friend had done what they've done to me, you would be encouraging me to leave that toxic relationship well and truly in the past. Just because they are blood doesn't make them decent people. My mother is only here for Holly because she isn't enrolled in school and someone needs to look after her while I work.'

'Whatever it is, surely it can't be that bad? Weddings are joyous occasions. A time for celebrating, bringing family together.'

'Not this one.'

Libby took a deep breath. There was something very serious going on here but she couldn't figure out what it might be.

She kept her voice calm; she didn't like to see anyone hurting. 'I'm sorry, I didn't mean to upset you.' She reached out to touch his arm, but Guy moved away and began walking towards the door. Just before he reached it he turned around. 'You can't have an opinion on something you know nothing about. We can talk about careers, aspirations, books, movies and even politics, but not family.' His voice was flat. A tone that said he was not to be messed with.

They exchanged glances before the door shut behind him.

What the hell had just happened here? One minute they were dancing together like a couple that couldn't get enough of each other, the attraction between them fizzing away, ready to explode, and the next they'd butted heads and Guy had stormed off.

Standing there, Libby felt numb. It hadn't been her intention to upset him in any way. She knew he was hurting about something and she was simply curious to know what was really going on here. All she wanted to do was help.

Chapter Nine

Libby had tossed and turned all night, though whether it was due to high winds rattling around the lodge or the fact that Guy was constantly on her mind, she wasn't sure. Either way, the result was the same: she'd barely slept a wink.

She was unsure how today was going to pan out after yesterday's conversation with Guy, but there was only one way to find out and that was to get up and start her day.

Pulling on her dressing gown, Libby padded into the living room and sighed. It looked like a bomb had hit it. She'd worked past midnight on Julia's outfit and all the 3D flowers were scattered over the table along with leftover material and threads of cotton. In need of a strong coffee, she switched on the kettle and glanced over the day's schedule.

Later that morning there was a meeting with Miranda to discuss invitations. They were a priority as they needed to be posted in the next forty-eight hours. Family and friends usually had lots of commitments over the festive period and with the wedding taking place on Christmas Eve people would need as much notice as possible.

Early evening the happy couple were set to be filmed ice skating, though Libby had no idea whether either of them could ice skate; she assumed all that information was in the missing application form. Surely they both must be of an adequate standard if they'd agreed to it.

Thinking about ice skating, Libby's mind flicked back to her childhood. She had spent a lot of time at her grandparents' house, which had its own lake in the grounds. Every winter it was frozen solid and that was where her father Wilbur had taught her to ice skate. As soon as she knew the basics, she'd spent hours on the lake twirling in the figure eight. Even though it had been a long time since she'd had a pair of ice skates on her feet, it was like riding a bike, something she would never forget how to do. Despite her mother passing away when she was young, her father, along with her grandparents, had done an amazing job of creating warm memories like that for her to look back on. Yet another reason to be grateful for her wonderful family.

Just after 10.30am Libby grabbed her coat and headed to the studio. She'd been working on Julia's dress by the living-room window, making use of the natural light and hoping to get a glimpse of Guy taking Pickle for a sledge ride, but they were nowhere to be seen and she felt a little disappointed. When she got to the studio, she found Julia waiting near the door.

'Good morning!' Julia chirped, checking her watch. 'I was just checking in with you to see how it was going and whether everything was okay after Guy—'

'Yes, he's all good,' interrupted Libby, not wanting to share anything about their latest disagreement. 'I can't stop wondering how Miranda and David were chosen out of everyone,' she said, trying to change the subject.

'I know what you mean. Flynn wishes he'd kept a closer eye on the competition but he can't oversee everything that goes on at the hotel. He searched high and low for their application form, even pulling out the filing cabinet to check behind it, which was a mammoth task in itself.'

'Did he find anything?'

'Half a Kit-Kat, a dead spider and lots of fluff.'

'Eww. But it would certainly be interesting to see that form. Miranda is due in half an hour and then later on Guy is filming them ice skating.'

'Hopefully Guy will be able to get some footage from this evening that can be used in the promotional material.'

Libby nodded. 'I'm sure he will. This morning Miranda will be choosing the invitations, which shouldn't take long if it's plain black card. It just seems all very doom and gloom to me.'

'Flynn wanted me to tell you that he's emailed you a link to the main stationery supplier in Glensheil. All you need to do when Miranda has chosen her invites is to input the details of the wedding, day, time, when and where, et cetera into the form on their site. Have you got a list of names and addresses for the guests?'

'Yes, Miranda has written all those down.'

'That makes it a little easier. If you scan her notes and email them over to the printers, they've got an assistant who will input all the addresses on their system and get the invites sent out by tonight or tomorrow at the latest.'

'That's just made my day; it would have taken me hours otherwise.'

'I thought that might put a smile on your face. Oh, and before I forget, I've just bumped into Florrie. She'd made up numerous bouquet samples that she thought you could show to the bride. They were absolutely gorgeous and would you believe she'd made up the very bouquet that I've got in my scrapbook? It was *stunning*. I'll have my dream wedding. One day...'

'That you will,' said Libby, smiling secretly at the thought of her little project. She couldn't wait to see Julia's face when she surprised her with the outfit just before she left for New York. 'And did you share with Florrie the colour scheme for Miranda and David's wedding?'

'I did, but at first she didn't believe me.'

'I'm not surprised. I'm guessing the bouquets Florrie made up won't be suitable?'

'No, and the colourless bouquet that Miranda wants may present a bit of a challenge but let's hope Florrie can pull it off.'

'Fingers crossed.'

'Going back to Guy.' Apparently Julia wasn't letting her off the hook that easily. 'Did you happen to persuade him to do some wedding modelling and be a pretend groom? You do know how good you pair look together, right?'

Libby did know exactly how good they looked together. She'd caught sight of them both in the mirrors while they danced together. Remembering exactly how it felt when he held her so close, all she could think about was what it would be like to be on Guy's arm for real. 'I'm working on it,' she replied, still not ready to share any more information from yesterday.

As soon as she saw him today she was going to apologise and put things right between them. Even though her intentions had been good, Guy was right, she knew nothing about the situation. Libby didn't like any sort of confrontation and it didn't sit right with her that she'd upset him. Hopefully he would accept her apology and they could put it behind them.

'Here's Guy now,' Julia said as she looked through the window. 'I need to make a move.'

'I'll catch up with you later.'

Julia and Guy passed each other on the doorstep and greeted one another before Julia took off down the path.

'Morning!' Libby chirped, determined to get things back on track between them. 'Did you sleep okay?' she asked, suspecting he'd also had trouble sleeping, since he looked as tired as she did.

'The wind kept me up. You?'

'Same,' she replied, watching him walk over to the corner of the room. Guy wasn't his friendly self and all Libby wanted to do was to rewind time to before she'd ever said a word. But on the other hand, knowing something was eating him up inside, she still wanted to help. In her experience, talking to someone always helped.

'Guy…'

He'd already started setting up the video equipment and glanced back over his shoulder towards her.

'I'm really sorry I upset you yesterday. I didn't mean to. You're right, I don't know anything about the situation and it is none of my business.' She took a breath. 'I just got carried away with the afternoon but it still wasn't right or fair for me to impose my opinions on the situation.'

Guy's face softened. 'Thanks for that. Apology accepted.'

'I'd had such a wonderful afternoon with Holly, she's the

best. It was just that she looked sad when she said...' Libby raised her hands. 'Sorry, it's nothing to do with me.'

'I do agree with you. Holly is the best but I am a little biased.'

'Can we just get back to yesterday before all that happened?' asked Libby with a hopeful smile.

'Of course,' he replied. 'And thank you. The apology means a lot.' He placed the camera on top of the tripod. 'If we're going back to yesterday does that mean you're going to slip back into that dress and look absolutely stunning again?' he teased.

As he took off his coat and hung it on the stand in the corner of the room Libby's eyes quickly ran over his body. He'd definitely got that handsome, sultry, brooding look going on. He was the kind of guy that would turn heads wherever he went. With a good eye for fashion too, he was the whole package. Libby knew she was staring but she couldn't help it. His tight white shirt fitted him perfectly and showed off his abs.

'If it puts that gorgeous smile of yours back on your face, I'm willing to do anything.'

'Anything?' Guy asked, giving her a lopsided grin.

'Within reason,' she teased, thankful that the tension between them had been removed. 'Shall we hug it out?'

'That might make everything better.' He opened his arms wide.

As she stepped into his embrace, there it was again, that overwhelming feeling of closeness. Libby briefly closed her eyes. 'I'm glad we're friends again.'

'Me too. I have to tell you the truth about something: it wasn't the wind that kept me up all night—'

'I know,' Libby interrupted. 'I couldn't sleep either. All I kept thinking about was us and the argument. It was the only thing on my mind.'

'I was going to say it was Pickle! She snores!' A smile tweaked his lips and Libby playfully swiped his arm.

'Honestly, not only does she snore, but she also wants to sleep stretched out, right in the middle of the bed. There was no room for me.' Guy rolled his eyes. 'And "us", you say?'

She gave him one last squeeze before changing the subject. 'You fit perfectly into that shirt,' she whispered in his ear as she slowly pulled away.

'Are you flirting with me?'

She pinched her forefinger and thumb together. 'Maybe just a little.'

Feeling a blast of cold air, they both spun round. The door to the studio opened and in breezed Miranda, dressed from head to toe in her favourite colour: black. Knowing that she was standing extremely close to Guy, Libby quicky took a couple of steps backwards, but Miranda didn't miss it. She waggled her finger at them.

'I was saying to David only last night that you would make a lovely couple if you aren't one already.'

Even though Libby was secretly chuffed at the compliment she was quick to put Miranda straight. 'We're not together. We're just work colleagues, friends. Let me take your coat and then we can start looking at the invitations. If we choose today, we can get the invitations posted hopefully as quickly as tomorrow,' she added, steering the conversation in another—safer—direction. She heard the beep from the corner of the room and knew Guy had started recording.

A moment later, Libby and Miranda were sitting in front of

the computer. The link that Flynn had set up for the invitation was easy to access and soon different designs were loaded on the screen. Libby typed 'black invitations' into the search bar and immediately a number of options appeared, all with embellishments around the edging.

'Just plain black with no fancy borders,' stated Miranda. 'That's the one. Plain and simple.' She tapped the screen.

It was exactly that. Just a plain black card with no frills or borders. With just a few clicks, Libby was able to begin typing all the wedding details onto the invitation, to be displayed on the screen. She pressed the font button and the wording was transformed into posh-looking handwriting in white.

'That was easy enough.'

It wasn't something that Libby would have ever chosen, but Miranda seemed genuinely happy with her choice and that was all that mattered. In fact, Libby was beginning to warm to her. Miranda's choices might not match her own but Libby admired her for knowing her own mind. She was pulling together the wedding she'd always dreamed of, regardless of what anyone else might think or say.

'Why don't you double-check the details while I nip to the bathroom and then we can get it sent off,' Libby suggested as she stood. Looking towards the camera she saw Guy had slipped out of the back of the studio and was talking animatedly on the phone outside.

After returning from the bathroom she found Guy sitting back behind the camera, but noticed he was preoccupied and looking at his phone.

'All the details are just fine,' confirmed Miranda.

'Excellent. Let's get those sent.' Libby pressed the button

and with a whoosh the email was off to the printers. 'The invitations will be sent out within the next forty-eight hours.'

'I can't wait for them to land.'

'I'll co-ordinate the RSVPs as they come in and we can look at table plans closer to the day when we have a firm idea of numbers. And next we have the most exciting part: your dress! We've got a rail of beautiful dresses for you to choose from, come and take a look.'

Libby led Miranda towards the dresses. 'Now, I know the colours will not be right for you but I can recreate any of these in black. Are you thinking something slinky or a full Cinderella dress? This one is a replica of a Vera Wang gown from the her autumn collection a couple of years back, complete with a fitted bodice, plunging neckline and layered tulle skirt.' Libby pulled out the dress for Miranda to take a look at it. 'But personally, this one is my favourite. This, to me, oozes classy, not trashy. This dress screams, "Marry me and love me for ever."' Libby took from the rail the dress that she'd worn yesterday and held it up against her body. 'Wearing this will make you feel like you're the most beautiful woman in the world.' Suddenly feeling the same flush of warmth run through her veins that she'd felt yesterday wrapped up in Guy's arms, she bashfully looked up through her fringe in his direction. His mood had evidently lifted as his eyes were shining, which gave her a glowing feeling inside.

'I'm thinking slimmer and slinkier. No embroidery or lace. Plain as can be with a black veil and a long black train,' Miranda said decisively.

What she'd described wasn't a fashion designer's dream by any stretch of the imagination and a plain black dress with no added frills would have not been Libby's choice, but it didn't have to be her choice.

'It won't take me long to make a dress like that. I'll just source a few different samples of material first and then we can see which one you prefer.'

'You're a woman of many talents. Planning weddings, designing and making dresses... Where did the management of Starcross Manor find you? They have fallen on their feet.'

'My brother Flynn is the owner,' Libby shared.

Miranda paused. 'Flynn Carter is your brother?'

'Yes.'

Miranda appeared momentarily thrown by this snippet of information. Finally she offered, 'I'd never have guessed. Two talented individuals from the same family. I am impressed.'

'Thank you,' Libby replied. 'Now, I think that's all we need to do today. As soon as the material is delivered, I'll give you a call. In the meantime, I'm looking forward to an evening of ice skating.'

'It should be fun,' Miranda agreed.

Libby held out Miranda's coat and she slipped her arms into it. 'We'll see you later. Make sure you wrap up warm.'

As soon as the door closed behind Miranda, Libby sighed. 'A plain black dress with no shimmer, no sparkles...' She looked towards Guy, who'd stopped filming and was staring at his phone once more.

'Are you okay?' she asked.

'Yes, it's just my mum. I can't seem to get a minute of peace, and it's frustrating as she knows I'm working.'

'As long as everything is all right?' she replied, noticing movement through the window just before Flynn walked through the door.

'Good morning! What brings you here?' Libby asked.

Flynn kissed his sister on her cheek before acknowledging Guy. 'I knew you had an appointment with Miranda this morning and I wanted to come and say hello. No, that's a lie. If I'm being entirely honest I wanted to discreetly try and discover what set them apart from the rest of the couples. I'm not sure why but there's something not sitting right with me. Jenny knew the brief. This wedding was meant to be all about winter elegance, the winter wedding of the century, a wedding fit for the royals … and a colourless wedding certainly doesn't fit the bill. If only I could confirm whether they lied on the application form. I've searched high and low and not only can I not find it, I also can't find any of the other forms.'

'That's strange,' said Libby.

'Are you thinking there's some sort of foul play?' asked Guy.

'I'm not sure, but like Libby just said, it's very strange, especially when there were clear instructions about how romantic I wanted this wedding to be.'

'I do get where you're coming from,' agreed Libby. 'This wedding is just not fitting the vibe you wanted. The theme Miranda and David have chosen isn't going to be marketable at all. We've just talked dresses and she wants it to be plain black and no frills. Plus, the invitations are just plain black. On your part, it's a lot of expense for almost no gain.'

'Exactly, and because of the competition I've already had some national magazines and the local press wanting to feature the wedding. It's exactly what I wanted to happen as the publicity would be brilliant for us … or at least it would have been.'

'Unfortunately, there isn't much you can do about it now,'

Guy said, 'except work with what we have. I'll do my best to get some special footage while I'm here that hopefully you can use across your own social media channels.'

'Thanks, mate.' Flynn nodded his appreciation. 'I need to get back to work.'

As Flynn stood up Libby gave him a hug. 'Honestly, we will try and get some usable moments. We know you've gone to a lot of expense for this.'

As soon as Flynn left, Libby turned towards Guy. 'What do you make of all that?'

'I agree with Flynn, something doesn't seem quite right, but Jenny's idea of an extraordinary wedding could have been totally different from Flynn's vision and it just got lost in communication,' replied Guy.

Their phones pinged at the same time.

'It's Florrie, she wants to talk flowers,' Libby reported, looking down at her phone.

'And I've got to go,' said Guy, looking at his. 'But I'll see you later at the rink.' He gave her a heart-melting smile as he looked up from under his fringe and headed towards the door.

Libby watched him through the window until he was out of sight. She was already counting the hours until she saw him next.

'Florrie!' Libby gasped. 'Look at all these wonderful bouquets.' She was standing in the doorway of Buttercup Barn and could barely see Florrie behind the counter, hidden as she was by a wonderful array of blooms.

'Aren't they just!' Florrie smiled warmly.

As usual she was wrapped up in many layers and standing next to a small heater behind the counter that was blasting out warm air. She handed a huge bouquet to Libby, who immediately closed her eyes and inhaled the scent. 'These are gorgeous.'

'They are, and that one you're holding is full of Julia's favourites.'

'These were the samples for the competition winners, weren't they?'

Florrie nodded. 'I took a punt on different colour themes and thought if I put the bouquets together it would help the bride to decide what she might like. But it seems as though I was getting ahead of myself, especially now I know the colour scheme … or should I say *lack* of colour scheme.'

'Dare I ask, have we got any flowers that might work for that colourless scheme?' Libby began picking up each bouquet and taking in their aroma.

'If we're looking for a dark, moody, romantic feel, I think we are best with…' Florrie leaned under the counter and pulled out an oversized book. 'This is my flower bible, it illustrates every flower one could possibly want.' She began to turn the pages then turned the book around towards Libby. 'We could have a black artificial rose, which would look great. What do you think?'

Even though the colour scheme wasn't very exciting, the roses staring back at Libby looked beautiful and very realistic. 'This could definitely work.'

'I was thinking I could entwine those with inky-centre anemones and fill the rest of the bouquet with moody dahlias, dark chocolate cosmos and dark foliage.' Florrie continued to turn the pages and pointed out each flower. 'We can even put in some artificial black berries and pine cones to create an enhancing effect rich in texture. What do you think?'

'You're a gem, Florrie! This all sounds so perfect.' Given Florrie's expertise, Libby was certain that Miranda was going to be pleased with her suggestions. 'But I have to say this oversize bouquet of white spray roses, lisianthuses and waxflowers is more up my street,' she admitted, picking up the last of the bouquets that Florrie had made up.

'And mine,' replied Florrie. 'Earthy greenery is winter-ready with the addition of pretty pine cones, roses and winter berries.'

'A gorgeous winter creation,' Libby agreed.

'I'll contact the suppliers this afternoon regarding the flowers for Miranda's bouquet, then drop you a text with an approximate delivery time, and we can take it from there.'

'That's a perfect plan. And I have to say, Julia has good taste. I can see her walking down the aisle holding this beautiful arrangement.' Libby picked up the flowers and held them with both hands as she took small steps and began singing, 'Here comes the bride.'

Florrie laughed. 'It's my favourite arrangement too. Maybe you'll find a perfect man in New York and I can make you one in the near future. I've never been and I do envy you. It's going to be such a lifestyle change and an adventure.'

'It is,' Libby replied, handing the bouquet back to Florrie.

When Libby was offered the job, it was all she could think about, but in the last couple of days New York had barely crossed her mind … and she knew exactly why.

'Julia was saying only yesterday that you're the only person she knows who has escaped the Heartcross curse. It got me good and proper. I've not been here that long but I can't imagine ever living anywhere else now. The community has become my extended family.'

'Are you living in the village?' asked Libby.

'I'm renting one of the whitewashed terraces on Love Heart Lane, just opposite Bonnie's Teashop, but I have to say it's not good for my waistline because I find myself always nipping in for breakfast or on my way home. The best part is waking up and opening my curtains and the first thing I see is Heartcross Mountain. It puts a smile on my face every morning. And with all that fresh air, I'd never slept so well as I have since moving in.'

'It sounds like bliss,' replied Libby, suddenly thinking of the hustle and bustle of New York City.

'I couldn't imagine leaving my family behind, I'd miss them too much. You're very brave.'

'I'll definitely miss them,' Libby agreed, suddenly thinking about the reality of leaving them behind.

Just at that moment, the bell above the door tinkled and a couple of customers walked into the shop. 'I'll catch you later; speak soon,' said Libby.

After leaving Buttercup Barn Libby walked down the long drive of Foxglove Farm. Despite the plummeting temperatures, everywhere she looked was beautifully picturesque. She stopped walking and took a moment to gaze at the mountain. With the peak covered in snow it was picture-postcard perfect. Standing there looking at the scenery Libby turned Florrie's words over in her mind. She'd been swept away in the excitement of the new job but hadn't thought about the reality of moving halfway across the world. This is where her family was and if she needed them, they weren't just going to be a train journey away anymore. Her dad wasn't getting any younger, either … and suddenly she couldn't wait for him to get back from his cruise so they could all spend Christmas together as a family. She missed him desperately.

Giving herself a little shake, she reminded herself she'd been recognised for her individuality in a very competitive industry and landed her dream job, something she should be thrilled about. But there it was again … a tiny hint of doubt creeping in. And it wasn't just her family that was playing on her mind; there was Guy as well. She hadn't known him long but now she couldn't stop thinking about him … and what it might be like not to see him every day.

Chapter Ten

Libby couldn't believe how fast her day had gone. Her afternoon had been as busy as the morning and she'd enjoyed every second of it. She'd spent time in the studio working on the next stage of Julia's surprise wedding outfit. The material she'd chosen was elegant and easy to work with, which was always a bonus. After tracing the pattern and cutting the material, Libby had pinned it loosely to the mannequin. Taking a step back and admiring her work. she thought this might end up being one of the most beautiful garments she'd ever made, and was already feeling proud. Gathering all the delicate 3D flowers, Libby switched on the radio and poured herself a glass of fizz then sat in the window seat and began to sew the flowers by hand. Time flew by and before she knew it there was only an hour before she was due to meet Miranda and David at the ice rink. Just as she was about to leave the studio an email pinged. It was from the printers to confirm that all the invitations for the wedding had been sent out.

'That was easy enough,' Libby murmured, grateful that one of the most important and time-sensitive jobs had been ticked off the list. As soon as the RSVPs began to land, she could start co-ordinating the seating plans, and once Miranda had chosen her material for her dress, that was next on the list to sew.

By early evening the temperature had dropped to minus one so Libby put on an extra layer of thermals to keep warm under her coat and grabbed her gloves. As she opened the front door she found Guy standing there, holding hands with Holly.

'I hope you don't mind but we have a little helper for filming tonight.' Guy smiled as he jokingly pulled off Holly's bobble hat.

'Dad!' Holly exclaimed, grabbing the hat back from him and pulling it down past her ears.

'I don't mind at all,' Libby replied, smiling.

'Mum has a phone call to make and Pickle is fast asleep.'

'He's worn out with all the sledging,' Holly said sagely.

Libby laughed. 'I bet he is. Miranda and David are meeting us at the rink,' she continued to Guy, checking her watch to ensure they weren't running late. 'It doesn't officially open to the public until tomorrow but Flynn texted me to say it's all been set up and tonight will be the perfect opportunity to check everything is up and running properly. He's also roped in some extras from a local agency to create a buzz around the ice rink and make it look busy.'

'Good plan bringing in some extras. I was going to say it would look very empty with just the wedding couple on the ice.'

'Would I be able to have a go, Daddy?' asked Holly, looking up at him with those adorable eyes.

'We'll see.'

Holly sighed and glanced at Libby. '"We'll see" always means no.'

'No, it doesn't, you cheeky monkey!' cut in Guy. 'It means, we'll see! There needs to be ice skates that fit, and it depends how cold you get standing around during the filming. If not tonight we'll be able to go another time. Not that I'm looking forward to it,' he said as an aside to Libby. 'I've only been ice skating once in my life and that didn't go well.' He rolled his eyes.

'Tell me more,' she encouraged him, wanting to hear all about it.

'I was seventeen and thought I was cool and that skating would be easy. I mean, how hard can it be to walk on blades and balance?'

Libby knew exactly how hard it was, given that she'd spent many a winter on the frozen lake behind her grandparents' place perfecting her technique. It wasn't something that happened overnight; it had taken her years.

'Very hard, let me tell you,' Guy continued. 'I thought I could do anything and after asking the head girl out on a date, I took her to the local ice rink. Big mistake! Everyone made it look so easy. The other skaters were whizzing around, hand in hand, and she stepped onto the ice first and skated right into the middle with ease. And what did I do?'

Libby knew what was coming next; she could already imagine him with his arms flailing then his legs shooting off in different directions before he landed on his backside.

'I put on the skates, wobbled up to the rink and launched

myself. Immediately my legs went from underneath me, and I fell backwards and saw stars. I woke up in an ambulance. I'd cut my head open as I'd cracked it on the edge of the rink.'

Libby threw back her head and laughed. 'Oh you poor thing! And what about the girl?'

'Never saw her again. She was dating the captain of the rugby team before I'd even got out of hospital. I guess it just wasn't meant to be.' He laughed.

'I think you'll probably do best to keep your feet on the snowy ground this evening, never mind the ice,' Libby teased.

'All I can say is thank God it was during the time before social media, because if that had been captured on video, it would have gone viral.'

As they turned the corner and the rink came into view, the magic of the space took Libby's breath away. Flynn had pulled out all the stops and it had paid off.

'It's Christmas!' Holly squealed.

'Just look at this,' Libby said admiringly.

The rink was lit by a soft glow, the trees surrounding it decked out in twinkly fairy lights, and Christmas music filtered out from the wooden hut next to the skate shack. The extras were scattered all around, some huddled in groups at the side of the rink cradling hot chocolate and mulled wine while others bustled on and off the ice, some in groups and in couples holding hands. Even though this was a staged event and the rink didn't open until tomorrow there was tangible excitement.

Libby shivered as the cold tickled her cheeks, and stuffed her hands firmly inside her pockets as they made their way to the hot chocolate shack. 'Can you see Miranda and David anywhere?' she asked, scanning the area.

'Not yet,' replied Guy. 'Hot chocolate with marshmallows all round?'

Holly squealed and ran ahead towards the counter. 'I think that was a yes.' Guy laughed.

Standing behind Holly, Libby burrowed her chin in the collar of her coat and shuffled from side to side to keep warm. 'The temperature is dropping fast.'

'Here, take this,' said Guy, unwinding his scarf from his neck and slowly wrapping it around Libby's.

She smiled. 'Thank you.'

He caught her eye and for a moment they stared at each other.

'Dad, are you having one?' asked Holly, interrupting the moment.

'Two more please,' confirmed Guy, his gaze still on Libby for a second longer. As he turned to pay he noticed a bunch of mistletoe dangling just above their heads. It had been tied to the top of the hatch of the drinks hut. He smiled as Libby spotted it at almost exactly the same time and they exchanged a playful glance.

'Shall we take a seat on the bench over there?' Libby pointed. 'While we drink these and wait for Miranda and David.'

'Great plan, that will be a perfect spot to set up the camera too.'

With their hands wrapped tightly around their cups Holly sat down next to Libby on the bench and shuffled in close. Libby wrapped her arm around Holly's shoulders and pulled her in to keep her warm.

'Here they are.' Libby nodded towards Miranda and David

who were making their way around the rink, walking hand in hand.

'And dressed for the part,' added Guy.

Miranda was sporting a huge black Shapka on her head with a matching black coat and gloves. She looked elegant and turned heads as she made her way through the extras. David, on the other hand, was turning heads for a different reason. With his bright neon green bomber jacket and matching hat and gloves, David was not going to be lost in a crowd any time soon.

'Now that's a jacket and a half. As a fashion designer, would you say that jacket is on trend?' Guy asked merrily.

'Keep your voice down or they'll hear you,' Libby whispered, smiling and passing her hot chocolate to him for a second while she stood up and greeted the couple.

'Look at this place, how romantic,' Miranda trilled. 'This must have taken some organising to have an ice rink with all these gorgeous huts and Christmas lights.' Miranda spotted the next hut along. 'David, a mulled wine is a must.' She pointed and without a pause or question David was on his way to the hut.

It was then that Miranda noticed all the huts had hanging mistletoe.

'Oh David,' she called, quickly at his heels. He turned round and Miranda planted her bright blood-red lips on his then pointed to the mistletoe above. 'Never miss an opportunity for a kiss.'

'Eww,' said Holly out loud, making Libby bite her lip to suppress a smile.

'Holly.' Guy gave her a warning glance.

'And who is this?' Miranda had spun around and was looking at Holly.

'Holly,' replied Holly.

'This must be your daughter,' Miranda said as she looked between Holly and Libby. 'Such a resemblance.'

'I'm not Holly's mum, just a good friend,' Libby quickly corrected her, gesturing towards Guy. 'Guy is Holly's father.'

'So sorry, my mistake.' Miranda held her hand out. 'Pleased to meet you.'

Holly stared up at Miranda's hat. 'That's a very big hat.'

'It is and it keeps me very warm.'

'Kids, they always say what they think. Please accept my apologies,' Guy jumped in quickly.

'There's no need to apologise, it *is* a big hat,' Miranda replied with a warm smile, taking the mulled wine from David and glancing across the ice rink. 'And where have all these people come from? We thought the rink didn't open until tomorrow.'

'Flynn organised it with the agency in town. They're extras —actors. You can hire them to make an event look professional for shooting videos, et cetera,' Libby explained.

'Isn't that a good idea?' she replied, still looking out over the rink.

'I'm all set here,' Guy confirmed. 'I can film you walking towards the skate hut and lacing up your skates. Dare I ask, can you both ice skate?'

'It's been a while,' admitted David. 'But I'm sure we will be able to lap the rink a few times.'

'And how long have we got the extras for?' asked Guy, looking towards Libby, who was checking her watch.

'Flynn booked everyone for an hour. All the huts and lights will close and turn off just after they leave.'

Guy nodded. 'Plenty of time to get a few laps of you both skating. Make sure you keep interacting with each other, talking and laughing. Are we ready?' he asked.

'Yes,' chorused Miranda and David, both swigging back their mulled wine before heading to the skate shack hand in hand.

'You stay there with Libby for a moment,' said Guy to Holly.

'Daddy, I'm getting cold.'

'I'm not surprised. It does feel a lot colder than when we first came out. Keep shuffling your feet from side to side. I'm just going to follow Miranda and David to the skate shack and then I'll be back.' With the camera on his shoulder he called, 'Let's roll!'

Right on cue, Miranda and David walked hand in hand, in joyous conversation, to collect their ice skates.

Libby and Holly sat back down on the bench, both swinging their legs to keep warm.

'Are you Daddy's girlfriend?' asked Holly, looking up at Libby.

'No, we're just friends,' Libby reassured her, smiling.

'You make him smile. I know he likes you.'

'He makes me smile too and is good fun to work with.'

'I like it when he smiles.'

Libby studied the little girl closely. Her face had saddened.

'It seems hard being a grown-up.'

'It is sometimes,' replied Libby.

'I wish I had friends of my own.'

'You must have some friends?'

Holly shook her head. 'I want to go to school but no one listens to me.' Holly shrugged. 'Everyone is always arguing, but Daddy has been smiling since we've been here. I like it here.'

'Heartcross is a lovely place,' agreed Libby. 'It makes everyone smile.'

'I think that's because you're here.'

Libby looked at the little girl. 'You think your dad is smiling because I'm here?'

Holly nodded. 'He talks about you a lot. My dad is very nice, you know.'

Libby laughed. 'I know and you know what else I know?'

Holly shrugged.

'That he has a beautiful little girl.'

Holly's smile grew wider as Libby put her hand on Holly's knee and gave it a little squeeze.

'You're very pretty. I love your curly hair,' said Holly with admiration.

'Thank you, but it's hard to tame, especially when I have a bobble hat on. Watch this!' Libby pulled her bobble hat clean off her head and all the curls sprang up on end, catapulting in different directions, causing Holly to laugh hysterically.

'They have a mind of their own,' Libby confirmed, pulling her hat back on quickly and digging her chin further into Guy's scarf. She inhaled his scent, the same aftershave he'd worn every day since she'd met him.

Guy reappeared and placed the video camera on the tripod. 'What are you two chatting about?'

'Nothing,' Libby and Holly replied at the same time. They gave each other a knowing look before their faces broke into huge smiles.

'Mmm, why do I think there is something going on here?'

'We were just saying how good it is to smile,' Libby offered, watching Guy fix the camera on its stand at the side of the rink.

'Come on, Holly, you can operate the camera. If you stand on this crate you'll be able to see.'

Holly jumped down from the bench and stood on a crate that Guy had just retrieved from beside one of the huts. Guy was extremely warm, kind and patient as he explained, 'If you move the camera slowly like this you can follow Miranda and David around the ice. Have a go.'

Listening to every word and with a little help from her dad, Holly followed his instructions. Watching them interact, Libby felt that tiny pang in her heart again. Even though that was something she would never have, such a closeness with her own flesh and blood, she focused on the positives. When the time was right there would be other options for her. She knew she had so much love to give.

Miranda and David took to the ice. Libby could follow them quite easily with Guy's neon green coat as they whirl laps of the rink. After only a few stumbles they began to skate with ease. Hand in hand they picked up the pace, weaving in and out of the other skaters.

'Look at them go!' exclaimed Guy, looking back over his shoulder. 'Who'd have thought they could skate better than me?'

'It's not that difficult when you make more than just the one attempt at skating,' Libby teased. 'I'm actually quite impressed,' she admitted. 'They're pretty good.'

'And it looks like they're having fun,' said Guy, helping Holly to slowly move the video camera. 'I think we've already got plenty of footage for their wedding video.'

'Here's Granny,' exclaimed Holly, looking through the lens. Cynthia was walking around the edge of the rink and waved in their direction. Holly jumped down from the crate and ran towards her grandmother, throwing her arms around her.

'You're freezing,' she exclaimed, kissing the tip of Holly's nose before saying hello to Libby and Guy. 'I finished my phone call so I thought I'd come and grab Holly to get her back in the warmth.'

Libby noticed the puffiness of Cynthia's eyes and wondered if she'd been crying.

Guy didn't seem to notice anything as he looked towards Holly. 'Are you ready to go back or would you like a go at skating?' he asked.

'Maybe tomorrow,' she replied, holding Cynthia's hand. 'It's a bit cold.'

'Okay, I'll be back soon,' he said.

While Cynthia headed off with Holly, there seemed to be some sort of commotion on the ice. Turning back to the rink, Libby and Guy could see a crowd of skaters huddled in the centre.

'What's going on?' Libby asked, concerned.

'It looks like someone is down,' replied Guy, straining to see over the crowd of people.

'It's David!' Libby exclaimed, noticing the neon green coat lying on the ice. 'What's happened? We only took our eyes off them for a second.'

Within moments David was being helped up off the ice by his fellow skaters. His face had paled, matching the colour of the ice as they carefully manoeuvred him to a nearby bench.

'He went down with a thud, could possibly be a dislocated shoulder,' relayed one of the extras. 'Nasty bang.'

'Libby! We need a first-aider and fast,' Miranda ordered as Libby rushed to the couple's side.

'I'm so sorry but there are no first-aiders to hand as the rink isn't officially meant to open until tomorrow.'

Miranda looked at Libby in outrage. 'What do you mean, there are no first-aiders? David is hurt and needs his shoulder looked at. Are you really telling me there's no one at all to take a look at him?' Miranda's face had reddened and she looked angry. 'You've put us in unnecessary danger with no medics to hand.'

Libby was a little taken aback by her tone of voice but avoided confrontation. She could see Miranda was angry, and she wanted to keep the situation as calm as possible. 'I'll call an ambulance right now,' she said, soothingly. She pulled off a glove and reached inside her pocket for her mobile phone.

'We haven't got time to wait to wait for an ambulance. Can't you see how much pain he's in? It'll be quicker if I take him to the hospital.'

'Let us help.' Libby looked towards Guy. 'Can you go and fetch their shoes from the hut?'

David was crying out in pain, gripping his shoulder with his other hand. 'I actually feel sick.'

Libby started to unlace his ice skates while Guy headed towards the skate hut.

As soon as they had their shoes back on Libby asked, 'Where's your car?'

'Over there.' Miranda pointed to the vehicle parked near the trees on the other side of the rink. 'I'll get him to the car myself.' Her tone was curt.

'Let me know what happens at the hospital,' Libby urged, watching as Miranda linked her arm through David's good one and they began to walk slowly towards the car. Libby turned towards Guy. 'I feel dreadful. It never even crossed my mind that we would need a first-aider on hand. Miranda was so angry.'

They could still hear unhappy mumblings from Miranda until they reached the car. As soon as David was sitting in the passenger seat and his seatbelt was fastened, Miranda slammed the door shut and within seconds the car sped away.

'Don't worry,' said Guy, touching her arm. 'I'm sure he'll be okay.'

'It's not the point though, is it?' Libby felt awful.

'Let's get rid of all these extras. It's a wrap,' he shouted, bringing back some order after the commotion. His words led to instant movement as all the extras began swapping their skates for their own footwear and the staff behind the huts began closing up. Within fifteen minutes everyone had headed home, leaving Libby and Guy at the side of the rink.

'Well, that wasn't the ending I was expecting to the evening,' Guy remarked, looking through the lens of the video camera. He wound back the footage. 'Let's have a look at what happened.'

They both stood and watched as David raced in front of Miranda on the ice.

'My gosh. He's picking up speed,' Libby murmured.

In a pirouette-like manoeuvre, David lifted his arms above his head and, taking one foot off the ice, he attempted to spin. He didn't even make a full turn, but fell straight to the ice with a thud.

Guy grimaced. 'Ouch! It even sounds painful. But who attempts to pirouette on ice if they don't know what they're doing? All we wanted them to do was a few laps of the rink, not to pretend they're Torvill and Dean.'

'Let's hope it's not a serious injury,' she replied, tossing her empty hot chocolate cup into the recycling bin.

'Do the fairy lights stay on or do we need to switch them off?' Guy asked, looking all around.

'I think they're on a timer,' she replied, subdued.

'Hey, come on, cheer up, it's not your fault. It was just one of those things.'

'I know, but everyone was in such good spirits and then it all went downhill.'

Guy held out his arms and Libby stepped into them. She hugged him tight.

'How about I attempt to put a smile back on your face?'

She glanced up at him. 'And how are you going to do that?'

He nodded towards the rink. 'I could attempt skating for the second time in my life.'

'You'd do that for me?'

'I'll give it a go for you, but I don't want to be joining David in A&E,' he joked.

'I promise I won't let anything happen to you!' Feeling her mood lift, Libby pointed to his feet. 'Size nine or ten?'

'Nine,' Guy confirmed, watching Libby walk over to the skate hut. Soon she was heading back towards him holding up two pairs of skates.

Leaning against the wooden bench Libby slipped her feet into the white, bladed boots, pulled the laces tight and tied them in a double knot. 'Make sure they're tight around your ankles; they need support. Trust me.'

'You sound like you know what you're talking about.'

Even though skating had been Guy's suggestion, Libby could see sheer panic written all over his face.

'I'll warm up while you lace up your boots.' She pretended to wobble as she walked towards the ice, and Guy lunged forward to try and steady her, but his mouth fell open as Libby launched herself onto the ice, powering one skate in front of the other.

'Woah!' Guy was mesmerised. 'How did you learn to skate like that?' he shouted after her but Libby was already on the other side of the rink.

He watched in awe as she moved; he couldn't take his eyes off her. She was the most beautiful girl he had ever seen.

Libby skated gracefully to the middle of the rink and began to spin on one foot with her other leg extended behind her. Her flexibility was extraordinary. When the spinning slowed Libby took off again around the ice. This time she skated forward slowly, extending her arms to either side. She then bent her left knee, followed by her right.

With the camera still set up Guy began to film, watching as Libby crossed the outer blade with her inside skate, moving effortlessly around the ice. She then began to skate on one leg, swinging the free leg through while jumping in the air, making him gasp. Landing on the toe pick of the opposite leg she stepped back onto the flat blade of the take-off foot, executing the move to perfection. She lapped the ring one last time—this time skating backwards—then stopped in front of Guy at the barrier.

'I loved every second of that,' she gushed.

'You were magnificent. You looked amazing, beautiful, everything was so effortless. Are you sure you aren't a secret Olympic ice skater posing as a wedding planner?'

Libby laughed as she caught her breath.

'And where did you learn to skate like that?' he asked. 'Professional training, surely? You're a woman of many talents.'

'My grandparents used to have the most magnificent house up in the mountains with its own lake that used to freeze solid in the winter. There wasn't much else to do there during the cold bleak winter days so my dad taught me how to skate.'

'Time well spent,' Guy said, approvingly. 'It's not very often I'm lost for words but I couldn't take my eyes off of you. You were breathtaking.'

'Why thank you,' she replied, feeling warm jitters as the compliments kept coming. 'And now it's my turn not to take my eyes off of you because you were right, we don't want to spend the rest of the night in A&E. Are you ready? I promise I won't let anything happen to you.'

The skates felt heavy on his feet and Guy wobbled as he attempted to stand. 'You made it look so easy.'

'You can do it! Now, let's get you on the ice.' Libby held out her hand and Guy reluctantly placed his in hers. She guided him along the barrier towards her.

'Are you ready?' she asked.

'As ready as I'll ever be,' he replied, still looking hesitant.

'Come on then, let's see your best Bambi impression.'

'Libby!'

'I'm only joking!' she teased, holding her hands up and making Guy wobble.

'Do not let go of my hand,' he said in panic, reaching out to grab her.

'Sorry! It won't happen again. Come on. You've got this.

And remember to just relax … because more bones can be broken if you're tense.'

'You're not funny.'

'Maybe just a little?' She grinned. 'And despite your nerves you're still standing upright, that's a great start.'

'Time will tell how long I'll be standing.'

'You've got to have faith.'

Libby stood in front of him and took both his hands in hers. 'Don't worry about moving your feet on the ice just yet. I'm going to pull you slowly along until you have your balance.'

Guy smiled nervously, and stared down at his feet.

'It's easier if you look where you're going, or just face forward and look into my eyes.'

With his eyes firmly gazing into hers she immediately felt her pulse begin to race. Feeling the crunch of the metal blade against the ice beneath him, Guy tensed again.

'I've got you.' Her voice was barely a whisper. Libby skated slowly in front of Guy and began to pull him along. 'Try standing up a little straighter and don't arch your back. Like this.' She demonstrated and Guy mirrored her posture.

With his eyes still firmly fixed on her, Libby finally felt him relax and the panicked look on his face slowly faded away as he began to grin.

'It actually feels magical,' he admitted, still concentrating but smiling.

'You're doing fantastically and Bambi hasn't even made an appearance.'

'Don't speak too soon.'

After Libby had pulled him one whole lap of the rink, she encouraged him to lift one foot off the ice and push. Guy bit his lip, hesitating, then, finally biting the bullet, he lifted his foot and placed it on the ice in front of him. Then he did the same with the other foot.

'Fantastic,' encouraged Libby. 'That's it, you've got it.'

As Guy smiled back at her, his eyes sparkled. He actually looked like he was enjoying himself.

'I can't believe it. I've not ended up on my backside just yet.'

'You're doing great! Now, I'm going to move to the side of you but I won't let go.'

Libby was true to her word. She grasped his hand tightly and slowly moved beside him. They carried on skating. 'It's a great feeling, isn't it?'

The next twenty minutes flew by as hand in hand they lapped the rink together. 'Are you having fun?' Libby knew that she was. It was a wonderful feeling teaching Guy to skate. Still holding one hand, Libby moved slowly in front of him again and began to skate backwards. After another lap they began to float towards the barrier.

'Now don't be scared, I'm going to let go slowly and I want you to just head straight in front of you.'

Placing one foot in front of the other Guy slowly loosened his grip on her hand.

'I'm skating!' he exclaimed, heading straight towards the barrier and grabbing hold of it before spinning round towards Libby.

'I can't believe I actually enjoyed it and I've not broken any limbs.'

'I'm glad to hear it.'

'In fact, this is probably the most fun I've had in a long time.'

'Want to take it a step further?' she asked, with a glint in her eye.

'And that means…'

'Setting off on your own and skating a short distance by yourself to…' Libby looked around the rink consideringly, then pointed. 'To that red button over on that barrier.'

Guy looked over.

'You can do this.'

'Can I?'

'Of course you can, and I'll be right behind you.'

'Okay,' he replied. He counted to three out loud before setting off and Libby smiled to herself. That's exactly what she always did as child when she was learning to skate. She had to psych herself up first.

Guy pushed off slowly.

'Don't overthink it and keep moving,' she said encouragingly. It wasn't long before Guy was picking up speed and Libby was impressed. 'You've got this.'

She watched as Guy pushed his skates harder and harder. He was skating faster and faster. Then, when he was just a few feet from the barrier, he wobbled and, reaching out, hit the round red button on the side of the barrier.

'Woah! What's that for?' he asked, alarmed. 'Is it some sort of emergency button?'

Libby shrugged. 'I'm not sure,' she replied.

All of a sudden there was a whirling sound followed by a clanking noise. They looked at each other before turning their gazes to a large aluminium contraption at the back of one of the huts.

'Is it some sort of generator to keep the electricity going?'

Libby queried, watching and waiting to see if anything would happen.

With a huge blast, artificial snow suddenly shot from the top of a funnel into the air and began to slowly float all around.

Libby threw her head back and laughed. 'Just look at that. It's like the real stuff. How romantic.'

She met Guy's gaze.

He smiled at her.

'Come here,' he said softly, taking off his glove and leaning tentatively towards her. 'You've got snow in your hair.' He gently brushed the snowflakes from her hair then from the tip of her nose. His eyes never left hers and he watched as she dropped her gaze towards his lips. Her heart was hammering against her chest and her whole body tingled as she took his hand and lapped the rink one last time while the snow was falling all around them. Skating towards the middle of the rink, they both slowed. Reaching into the pocket of his coat Guy revealed a hidden sprig of mistletoe and held it above their heads. Libby closed her eyes briefly and tilted her face towards his. Feeling all warm and fuzzy inside, Guy lowered his lips to hers. Every inch of her body tingled as he kissed her softly on the lips.

Suddenly, there was the sound of rapturous applause coming from the side of the rink. Immediately their lips parted and their heads turned towards the source of the noise.

'It's a wrap,' Flynn shouted from where he was standing next to the camera. He was staring right through the lens. 'This is amazing footage. You two are superstars!'

Hand in hand they silently skated towards Flynn.

'How long have you been standing there?' she asked, knowing full well that he must have seen everything.

'Since just before the snow machine erupted,' he replied. 'And I didn't know you could skate,' he said, looking at Guy.

'Neither did I until your sister talked me into it.'

Flynn touched both their arms. 'I really can't thank you both enough.'

Guy and Libby looked at each other, puzzled. 'What for?' asked Libby.

'All this. You know how much it meant to me to get a decent promotional video out of this whole competition disaster … and the footage of you two is just magical. I know this is going above and beyond the call of duty but this is exactly the image I'm trying to create for Starcross Manor. This footage could go viral!'

For a second Libby was speechless. She hadn't realised the camera was still rolling but as Flynn rewound the footage, there she was with Guy, lighting up the screen.

'And the way you look into each other's eyes. Wait for it… Right about now…' Flynn said pointing at the screen. There it was, the moment Guy had gently brushed away the snowflakes from Libby's hair, then her nose, before they skated to the centre and he slowly lifted the mistletoe above their heads. Just watching the kiss made Libby want to kiss him again. He had the softest lips she'd ever felt.

'Thank you again,' continued Flynn, 'for agreeing to be the pretend bride and groom.'

Libby was lost for words, not sure what to say, and was pleasantly surprised when Guy came to her rescue.

'We couldn't let you down. Starcross Manor deserves to be the number one wedding venue in this part of the world and if we can help you achieve that dream then it's our pleasure. Isn't that right, Libby?'

'Of course,' she immediately replied. 'We couldn't let you down.' Libby looked up at Guy, who simply smiled serenely back at her. She wondered why the sudden turnaround but then the penny dropped. He'd wanted to kiss her as much as she'd wanted to kiss him but he didn't want to explain that to Flynn.

Making the most of the situation that they had landed themselves in, Libby playfully smacked Guy's backside. 'Tomorrow, this one gets to try on the wedding attire. Kilts…' she said with a mischievous look on her face. 'And I'm curious to discover whether or not he's a true Scotsman.' She gave him a cheeky wink.

Guy shook his head good-humouredly, both of them relieved that Flynn seemed to be unaware that he'd caught then sharing a real moment on the ice. He thought it had all been for him.

'I'll turn off the lights and everything while you two take your skates off. Then let's get a drink at the hotel bar.'

Even though Libby didn't want the night to be over, going home now would be the perfect end to her evening.

'I'm going to pass but you boys have a good time.'

'Are you sure?' Flynn and Guy asked in unison.

'Yes,' she replied, knowing there was a hot bubble bath with her name on it, and then she could continue sewing a few more flowers for Julia's wedding outfit.

'Well, I'll see you tomorrow for my kilt fitting,' Guy said with a playful look in his eyes.

'I can't wait.'

After the lights were switched off and Flynn had made sure all the huts were locked, they headed towards the manor.

'Are you sure we can't twist your arm and convince you to join us?' Flynn asked, touching Libby's arm.

She shook her head. 'I've got a secret mission I want to be getting on with.' Giving away nothing else, Libby left them on the steps of the entrance to Starcross Manor.

In the short time since meeting Guy, she'd begun to feel different. She was strangely at ease in his presence and, holding his hand and skating around the rink, she'd felt an overwhelming sense of happiness and belonging.

And that's when it hit her: she missed being part of a couple. Knowing by the way he'd kissed her that he must be feeling the same gave Libby an all-over warm glow. It was a feeling she barely recognised—the first flush of love. This was going to complicate things immensely.

Chapter Eleven

The snow was coming down with bold grace when Libby drew back the curtains. The fast-falling snowflakes instantly transported her back to last night and the moment when Guy had accidently started the snow machine. She smiled to herself, thinking of the time they'd spent together, skating hand in hand around the rink, and the intense look in his eyes when he stared into hers.

After she'd left Flynn and Guy last night her thoughts were chaotic, darting all over the place. All she could think about was what could have happened if Flynn hadn't turned up. What would she and Guy have said to each other after the kiss? Would they have kissed again? Libby knew she'd wanted to ... but as soon she arrived back at the lodge she checked her emails and was brought back to reality. Two videos had been sent to her from her new boss at the fashion house in New York, and after curling up on the settee she opened the first one.

Her boss spoke directly into the camera, saying she was

standing on the third floor of the fashion house and was going to give Libby a virtual tour. 'Come and see your office. We can't wait for you to arrive!' The view changed as Francesca turned the camera to face forward and walked through the busy office towards a door. When the door opened the camera panned across a number of people standing behind the work table, one with his arm wrapped around the mannequin's neck, making Libby laugh. 'Let me introduce you to your staff.' Libby gave a little gasp. She had her very own team working with her? She had thought she'd be on her own in the beginning and a team would come later. But no, she had a runner, who literally ran about after anything she needed, a marketing assistant who was a social media expert and would help sell her designs online, and what they called an intern who was going to be Libby's shadow and learn everything that Libby could share with her.

After each staff member introduced themselves, Francesca came back on screen and said, 'Get ready for part two.' Everyone waved goodbye and the video clicked off.

Opening the second video she saw Francesca was standing in a new room. She panned the camera to show the floor-to-ceiling windows then focused on the view outside. Libby sat up and stared at the screen. Before her was the Hudson River and the heart of Manhattan. She could make out many iconic sites, including the Empire State Building and sprawling Central Park. 'Libby Carter, welcome to your brand-new New York apartment! It's ready and waiting for you!'

Libby's jaw dropped as Francesca gave her a tour. 'Your lease is for one year to start and then you can renew or move elsewhere; the choice is entirely yours. It's a five-minute walk to work and has a view to die for. We all can't wait for you to arrive and see it for yourself!'

For the rest of the evening, Libby had tried to concentrate on Julia's outfit but the thought of the new job and the kiss with Guy were both very much on her mind. She kept trying to remind herself – with not much luck – that whatever was going on here between her and Guy was short-term, and New York was waiting for her to arrive and start the rest of her life. After successfully sewing all the flowers onto Julia's outfit she finally climbed into bed just before midnight. She knew she was in for a restless night.

Her new job was one hell of an opportunity. It would catapult her name and designs into a global arena. She would be featured in magazines around the world and her name would stand alongside some of the greats in the industry. But mixed with this acknowledgement was a feeling of trepidation. Taking the job meant leaving her family behind, a disconcerting thought she couldn't shake off.

Now, in need of coffee, Libby headed to the kitchen. Guy's scarf was draped over the back of the settee and she picked it up, briefly closing her eyes and inhaling his scent. 'What are you doing, you absolute weirdo?' she said out loud, putting the scarf back before catching sight of her reflection in the mirror on the wall. Her bed hair would need a lot of taming today. Her curls were springing in every direction.

As she waited for the kettle to boil, she leaned on the worktop with folded arms and looked out across the stunning scenery. Only a few weeks ago the trees had been heaven-blended browns and caramels but now they were frosted with a lacy brilliant white.

She had a list of jobs that needed to be done this morning

for Miranda and David's wedding but as she started mentally running through it she felt a twinge of panic followed by guilt. Libby hadn't given David a second thought since Miranda had carted him off to the hospital yesterday. She'd been so wrapped up in thinking about the kiss with Guy that she'd forgotten to check on her clients! Just as she was about to text Miranda for an update there was a continuous and somewhat frantic knock on the front door.

Taking a quick peep out of the window, she saw Flynn pacing up and down the porch. Libby took a quick glance around the room, glad she'd moved Julia's wedding outfit into the bedroom last night. The last thing she wanted was for Flynn to stumble on his future bride's outfit when it was meant to be a surprise for both of them.

'Where's the fire?' Libby asked, opening the door wide.

'Everyone is talking about it.'

Libby had no clue what Flynn meant. 'Talking about what? What's going on?' she asked, confused.

'I've just been for my early morning walk to the village shop where I overheard a bunch of tourists talking about Starcross Manor and some sort of accident on the ice last night. Then I bumped into Meredith and she told me that last night there were rumours circulating in the pub that there had been a freak accident at the ice rink and because there was no first-aider or any health and safety measures in place, a man had to go to hospital.'

'I'm so sorry, Flynn, it totally slipped my mind to tell you. We did have a minor mishap last night.'

'My phone hasn't stopped ringing. Even Drew was on to me first thing asking what happened. What *did* happen?'

Libby took a breath. 'I promise it was nothing too major but

David slipped on the ice during filming. Miranda wasn't happy because of the lack of first-aiders on hand and she drove him to hospital to get checked out, in case it was something more serious than what it initially appeared to be.'

'And you didn't tell me this because...?'

'Because I wanted a chance to try and make things right with Miranda and David before telling you. But it wasn't a freak accident as such. David attempted a pirouette and he fell over, landing on his shoulder.'

'Are you sure there's nothing more to it? Because the rumours are making it sound worse than that and the suggestion is that the staff at Starcross Manor are incompetent at best and negligent at worst.'

'I give you my word. It was a minor accident and I'm sure he's going to be fine.'

'If these rumours get out of hand it can have an effect on business. I'm thinking of nipping it in the bud and putting a statement out.'

'I'd suggest you don't fuel the fire. Let's see how David is first. If you put a statement out now it could possibly spark more interest and it'll keep people talking about something that really isn't anything to worry about. It's just a misunderstanding that's been exaggerated.'

Flynn thought for a second. 'Yes, you're probably right.'

'You have nothing to worry about. Like I said, you can see the footage for yourself.'

'I just don't want these rumours to spread on social media as then they can circulate like wildfire.'

'I'll give Miranda a ring and get an update.'

'Thank you. I'm still getting an uneasy feeling about this competition. It seems like it's been doomed from the start.'

'And you still haven't been able to locate the application forms?'

Flynn shook his head. 'There's something that just doesn't feel right to me.'

'I'm sure there's nothing to worry about and everything will be plain sailing from now on.'

Flynn didn't look convinced.

Libby's phone pinged and Miranda's name flashed up on the screen. 'It's a text from Miranda.'

Flynn stared at the phone. 'What does it say?'

The hospital confirmed that David's shoulder was bruised. He will be resting for the next couple of days.

Libby read out the text then looked at Flynn. 'At least it's not broken. No one will think a bruised shoulder is anything to worry or get up in arms about. And let's not forget it was his choice to attempt a pirouette. We can't be held responsible for that.'

'Yes, you're right,' Flynn said, looking relieved. 'Let's hope that's the end of it … but if you hear anything else, you'll let me know, right?'

'Of course, but I think it's gossip that will die down very quickly.'

'The main thing is that David is okay. For a second I thought there had been a horrific accident and I was going to be sued.'

'It's all good. I'll send some flowers with our best wishes for a speedy recovery. Now put it to the back of your mind and rest assured that when that ice rink opens tonight it will be a success.'

'Thanks, Lib, and thank you again—both you and Guy—for agreeing to do the video.'

'You're welcome,' she replied, answering for both of them even though she hadn't had a conversation with Guy since Flynn saw them skating together and got the wrong end of the stick. 'Now don't worry about a thing.'

As soon as Flynn left, Libby's thoughts turned to Guy and that kiss. She was nervous about seeing him this morning but also couldn't wait to be close to him again. She looked over Miranda and David's wedding planning schedule one more time before getting ready to head to the wedding studio. Hopefully the RSVPs would start rolling in soon so she could start working on the seating plan.

As she locked up the lodge an hour later, she noticed the curtains of Guy's were still drawn.

Libby decided to take a walk before work, as a jaunt around the grounds of Starcross Manor then through the woods leading to Primrose Park might help her get her thoughts straight. But no matter how hard she tried, there was only one thing on her mind: that kiss. She'd willed it to happen but now she didn't know what, if anything, would happen next. Was it just an in-the-moment kiss or was it one that would lead to another? Still thinking about how close she'd felt to Guy in that moment, Libby headed towards the frozen lake, which sparked memories of her grandparents' house. It held a special place in her heart and she was glad the house was still in the family, now owned by her father, somewhere she was able to visit often. In the past, she and Flynn had often talked about one day taking their own children there for holidays. Libby couldn't wait for Flynn and Julia to have children; they would make the best parents and she was going to be the best auntie.

Then another thought suddenly consumed her. How was she going to feel being on the other side of the world when they did have children? She wanted to share every moment with them. She wanted to be waiting at the hospital when Julia was in labour. She wanted to be one of the first to smother the baby in kisses and cuddles. Libby didn't want to be one of those aunties that sent a Christmas and birthday card every year and didn't really know the child; she wanted to be present in the baby's life.

Trying to shake the spiralling panic, Libby was pleased to see Cynthia up ahead, sitting on a bench. Huddled inside her coat and with her chin buried under her scarf, she was staring out towards the mountains.

'Hi, Cynthia, how are you?' Libby asked as she approached Guy's mum.

Startled, Cynthia jumped. Libby noticed a puffiness around her eyes and couldn't help thinking she looked like she had the weight of the world on her shoulders. 'Sorry, I didn't mean to surprise you.' Libby pointed to the bench. 'May I sit?' She didn't want to pry but Cynthia looked like she could probably use a friend right about now.

'Yes, of course, it's a bit nippy out here this morning. Here…' she said, standing up and spreading out the blanket she was sitting on, 'you don't want a cold bum.'

'You've come prepared,' Libby observed. 'Thank you,' she said, sitting down. 'What are you doing out here?'

'I just needed some time to myself,' Cynthia confessed.

'Of course. I can go, if you'd like? Honestly, I don't want to intrude.'

'It's okay, it's nice to see a different—happier—face first thing in the morning, if I'm honest.'

Libby assumed she was referring to Guy but didn't think it appropriate to ask any personal questions. So she stared straight ahead, just as Cynthia was doing.

'I'm out here to think too,' Libby finally ventured.

They sat just taking in the view for a while before Cynthia broke the silence. 'I always thought being a parent was going to be the most wonderful job in the world,' she said, taking Libby by surprise.

'I've always thought it would be too. Are you saying it's not?' Libby asked tentatively, noticing the tears welling up in Cynthia's eyes. Libby reached inside her pocket and offered her a tissue.

Dabbing her eyes, Cynthia said, 'I thought at this stage of my life I'd be sitting back enjoying retirement and making memories with my family, but instead I've been in the middle of World War Three for a few years and there's no sign of any side surrendering soon.'

'Are things that bad?'

Cynthia nodded. 'I'm in the middle of it all, just trying to get through the situation as best I can. There's nothing worse than seeing your own children feuding, tearing each other apart when you can't seem to do anything to put it right. I don't know *how* to put it right.'

For a moment, Libby placed a supportive hand on Cynthia's knee. 'Is there any chance that Guy and his sister could put whatever it is behind them and agree to leave it in the past?' she asked softly.

'I wish they could, but I really don't think so. I'm not sure how I would have coped if my own sister had done to me what Guy's has done to him … and I'm not saying that lightly.'

Libby didn't have a clue what his sister had done to him but it must have been bad if even Cynthia couldn't see a way forward.

'He expected me to cut her off, but she's my daughter and I still love them both as much as I did before. Your child is your child and the whole thing is breaking my heart. I don't know what to do.' Cynthia dabbed her eyes with the tissue. 'It really is a mess. Lydia has health problems at the moment and I'm overloaded with worry. I'd just like some sort of reconciliation between them.'

Whatever was going on in the family feud, anyone could see that Cynthia couldn't take much more.

'I know you don't know me very well, but I'm happy to lend a shoulder for you to lean on while you're here.'

'Thank you, that is very kind of you. For now, I'd best be off.'

Cynthia stood up and Libby shifted off the blanket. Watching Cynthia walk away Libby couldn't imagine being in her position, stuck between two children who were fighting over goodness knows what. Even after spending such a short time with Guy, Libby knew that he was a reasonable person. She'd seen the love he had for his daughter and his kind and caring nature. But he must be swamped in hurt and pain because of whatever was going on if he saw no chance to end the feud. As she carried on walking through Primrose Park, she noticed the signposted path towards The Little Blue Boathouse. She followed the trail down to the river, where she hopped onto the water taxi into town with a plan to grab a coffee and a pastry from one of the cafés as soon as she reached the other side of the river.

The boat docked and Libby headed towards a side street off the main road. The last time she was here she'd stumbled across a tiny coffee house that sold cinnamon rolls to die for. Despite the weather the street was busy and there was a small queue outside the coffee house, which she joined. Soon after, she spotted Florrie standing on the street corner a little further up. She was in conversation with a woman and Libby immediately recognised the long, flame-red hair of the woman from the car park outside Buttercup Barn. It was Jenny. She watched as Jenny touched Florrie's arm before disappearing into the building behind them. If Libby remembered rightly, it was a care home for the elderly. Florrie was now heading her way and Libby called out to her.

'Florrie!' She waved.

Florrie looked up and immediately smiled. 'You've got the right idea,' she said, joining Libby in the queue. 'I think I'll grab a coffee before I head back. I was actually going to text you. The flowers have arrived. I have to say it was a bit of a task but I got there in the end. I'll have a couple of bouquets made up for Friday.'

'Miranda will be pleased. This wedding is coming together effortlessly after the initial shock of the colour scheme.'

'And how is everything? I believe things got a little scary last night?'

Libby looked puzzled. 'Scary? What am I missing?'

'The ice-skating accident. Jenny was just telling me all about it. It doesn't sound good.'

'Jenny was telling you all about it?'

'Yes, the whole town is talking about it. I heard David

nearly lost his fingers on the ice and there's possibly going to be an investigation into health and safety measures up at Starcross Manor.'

Libby immediately came to Flynn's defence.

'None of that is true.' Annoyed, she didn't hesitate to put the record straight. 'I was there. David didn't nearly lose a finger. He fell over on the ice when he was skating and jarred his shoulder and Miranda drove him to the hospital to get it checked out as a precaution. There was nothing more to it. Where have these rumours come from?'

'I'm not sure, but everyone was talking about it up at The Heart of the Village when I went to put the heaters on in the shop early this morning, and it was the first thing Jenny said to me just now.'

'Rumours like this can escalate and cause damage to businesses.'

'The gossip mill has a lot to answer for,' replied Florrie.

'It certainly does,' Libby said as they reached the front of the queue. After they bought their coffees and pastries they wandered back out onto the street. 'Do you want a lift back?' asked Florrie. 'I'm heading that way.'

'Thank you but I feel like a walk. Let's catch up as soon as the samples are made up?'

'Perfect.'

With their conversation playing very much on her mind, Libby headed in the direction of the care home. There was a low stone wall opposite, on which she perched to drink her coffee. Libby didn't like the fact that wrong information about last night seemed to be circulating fast; gossip was lethal. Thinking back to her earlier conversation with Flynn, she remembered how he'd said something wasn't sitting quite right with him about this wedding. It made her wonder: were the untrue rumours circulating *not* coincidental or was Libby beginning to overthink things too?

Tucking into the cinnamon roll, she looked over at the care home as her thoughts turned to Jenny. Had she resigned from her job because she'd been successful in gaining another position? But given what Florrie had previously said about the Starcross Manor job being Jenny's dream, it didn't make sense that she would have been job-hunting elsewhere. Still glancing in the direction of the care home, she saw the door open and Jenny walk out.

She felt compelled to introduce herself and ask Jenny how she had heard about the skating incident—but would that be adding fuel to the fire, which was exactly what she'd advised Flynn against? Maybe she could have a general chat about the wedding and during the conversation mention the missing entry form. Before she could make up her mind a car pulled up beside Jenny and, though Libby couldn't see who the driver was, she recognised the car as the same one she'd spotted with Jenny in The Heart of the Village.

Jenny climbed into the passenger seat and the car sped off down the street, leaving Libby with no option but to head back without answers.

As Libby walked briskly back towards Starcross Manor, the breeze was bitter but the view was stunning. Heartcross Castle with snow on its turrets and gardens looked peaceful and picturesque. It didn't take long to walk across the bridge and reach the track on the other side, and soon she was walking through the gates of the manor. The first thing on today's agenda was checking her emails and logging any RSVPs, followed by planning the layout of the tables in The Grand

Hall for the wedding so she could run them past Miranda and David. The third thing on her list was researching wedding cocktails that could be served at the wedding in the secret garden.

With the lodges in sight, she noticed that Guy's curtains were now open. Of course she wanted to see him again after last night but she felt sick with nervousness about how to handle the situation. She had no reason to be knocking on his door but a couple of seconds later that was exactly what she did. She heard the click of the lock and then the door opened and Guy was beaming back at her, immediately putting her at ease.

'Hello! I was just thinking about you! Come on in, come and take a look at this.'

Guy led Libby through the lodge to an area that had been set up as a mini office. 'No Pickle?' asked Libby, waiting to be jumped on then licked to death.

'He's out with Mum and Holly; they've gone to explore the town.'

'That's exactly where I've just been but I didn't see them. I did bump into your mum earlier on though.'

'She never said. She's always been one for an early-morning walk. It's her favourite time of the day and she says it's good for the soul, especially when you a have a little human tied to you for most of the day. I really do think Holly would enjoy hanging around people of her own age and she would enjoy school. Anyway...' he said, steering the conversation in a different direction. 'What do you think of this so far? Take a seat.'

The corner of the room reminded Libby of a recording studio. Guy sat down next to her. 'This looks all very technical,' she remarked, taking in the cameras and a control panel with rows of small black knobs, which lay before a TV screen.

'It's all my video and editing equipment,' he replied, pressing some buttons on the remote control. 'This is what I've put together so far for Flynn's promotional video. See what you think.'

Libby sat back, crossed her legs and waited for the video to start. As soon as the vision of Starcross Manor flashed on the screen she gave a tiny gasp. The entrance to the manor house looked enchanting as the camera moved along the snowy driveway capturing the magical festive feel. Next came the footage of the baby deer following the herd as they lolloped majestically across the untouched snowy ground. There was a glimpse of the look-out tower and a small clip of the two of them sharing the moment they'd spotted the herd. The camera then moved to the woods, the path leading to the studio, then the lodges with their twinkly fairy lights and finally the ice-skating rink. There were people bustling on and off the ice, the beautiful huts with the hanging mistletoe … and then there she was, gliding across the ice looking almost like a professional skater. It felt surreal watching herself. Taking a sideward glance at Guy, she noticed he hadn't taken his eyes off the screen.

Up next was Guy and they started skating together, laughing and joking, looking like a happy couple and very much in love. The film oozed romance and chemistry and Libby knew exactly what was coming next.

Goosebumps erupted all over her skin as their skating slowed towards the middle of the ice rink. Libby could see the look in his eyes as he held up the mistletoe and his lips dropped softly onto hers. They were lost in that moment and it was clear they'd both wanted it to happen. She knew she wanted him to do it again and she tried to banish the thought that she would soon be leaving for New York. The editing of the footage was outstanding, and the scenes had been set perfectly to music. Libby knew this was exactly what Flynn had been looking for to market Starcross Manor's wedding services.

'And that's as far as I've got. What do you think?' asked Guy, pressing a button on the remote control before looking in her direction. 'Oh my God, I didn't mean to make you cry!' He frantically grabbed a tissue from the box on the window sill.

Dabbing her cheeks with the tissue, she said, 'I'm so sorry. Ignore me, I'm just being silly.'

He reached over and placed his hand on top of hers. 'You're not being silly.'

'It's just that that was so beautiful, I've come over all emotional.' She fanned her hand in front of her face. 'It felt like I was watching a romantic movie about a couple falling in love. You captured everything so perfectly, I got lost in the moment there for a second. I can categorically say that Flynn will be bowled over. This is exactly the type of thing he was looking for. There is just one thing though…'

'And what's that?' asked Guy, his eyes not leaving hers.

'That's the beginning of the love story but how does it end?' The words had left Libby's mouth before she could stop them.

'With a winter wedding at Starcross Manor,' replied Guy, making Libby laugh. 'Come here, you daft bugger.' He opened his arms wide and as she leaned in to him, he hugged her tight.

'I really enjoyed myself last night,' he said, pulling away from her slowly.

'Me too, but I have to say my heart was racing when I saw Flynn standing there and he assumed we were filming for his promotional video. After putting this together for him you must be okay with that now?'

'You captivated me by your skating. I think you could talk me into anything. I'm now putty in your hands,' he declared. 'There's something about you—'

'Likewise,' she interrupted.

He paused. 'I'm not having an easy time of it at the minute but you have made my days a lot brighter.'

Libby wanted to ask him to explain what he meant, but she also didn't want to press him to talk if he wasn't up for it. The last time she'd given her opinion without knowing all the facts, it had led to a heated argument. She was going to let Guy open up in his own time and if and when he did she would be ready to listen.

'You have surprised me,' he said softly, taking hold of her hand.

'In what way?' she asked.

'In the past few years, I've found it difficult to open up or get on with anyone new. But I find it easy to be around you.'

Libby knew exactly what he was saying because she felt the same. Since Daniel, she'd found it difficult to let anyone completely in. She'd built her walls high, not letting anyone get close to her after what she'd been through. Guy was the first man she'd felt comfortable around in a long, long time.

'I think we may be a bit similar in that respect. Can I ask how you're feeling after last night?' Libby had been wanting to ask the question since she'd arrived.

'It just felt the most natural thing in the world to do. I hope that was okay by you.'

'Perfectly okay,' she replied.

'And would you mind if I did it again?'

With a racing heart Libby leaned forward and pressed her lips to his in response. It was exactly how she remembered it and the same feeling immediately exploded inside her. She didn't pull away, but in the back of her mind there was a small feeling of guilt that she hadn't told Guy she was leaving soon. It was only fair that he knew all the facts before things went any further, so he could decide if he still wanted to kiss her again. She needed to be honest with him, because despite all the self-preservation she'd practised over the years, she was falling for him fast.

Building up the courage, Libby pulled away slowly and took a deep breath. 'Guy…' But she didn't get a chance to finish her sentence as just then the front door flew open. Pickle barked the second he noticed Libby and ran towards her, launching straight onto her lap while frantically trying to lick her face.

Holly was in fits of giggles. 'Pickle loves you!' she exclaimed, shaking off her coat and handing it to Cynthia who hung it up.

'And who couldn't love Pickle back,' replied Libby, placing her down on the floor.

'Has Daddy shown you the video?' asked Holly, looking at the paused screen on the monitor. 'You look like a ballerina on skates.'

'But without the tutu,' added Guy with a grin, then mouthed to Libby, 'Don't worry, she hasn't seen it all.'

Holly began to gracefully dance around the room with her

arms open wide. 'I want to learn to skate. Will you teach me?' she asked as she stopped in front of Libby.

'I'm sure Libby is busy with all the wedding preparations,' Guy said, giving Holly a look to make it clear she wasn't to push the issue.

Libby noticed the smile slide off Holly's face and decided to put it right back on. 'I'm sure we can find time for a couple of lessons.'

Instantly, Holly threw her arms around Libby's neck and hugged her tight. 'Thank you!'

The look on Guy's face was heart-warming as Libby glanced at him over Holly's shoulder.

'Now let me get you a snack and a drink,' he said. 'You must be freezing. Go sit by the fire and get warm.'

'Daddy, can we pick a Christmas tree this afternoon?' Holly's eyes were wide and hopeful.

'How can you resist such an adorable face?' Libby whispered.

'Pleeeease. Libby could come too.'

'They've got freshly cut Christmas trees up at Foxglove Farm,' added Cynthia, switching on the kettle. 'Or Drew is offering tractor trailer rides to the forest where you can pick your own tree and he'll transport it back for you.'

'Can we do that, Daddy?'

'We'll see,' he answered with a big smile on his face.

Libby gave Holly a wink and leaned in towards Guy. 'Go on, you know you want to.'

'You're all ganging up on me!' he objected. 'Next Saturday. I promise we can go and get the tree then.'

'We called in at Bonnie's Teashop on the way back,' said Cynthia. 'Starcross Manor is the talk of the village.'

Libby knew what she was going to say next and realised she hadn't had a chance to tell Guy about her conversations with Flynn or Florrie this morning.

'Everyone was talking about the skating incident last night.'

'There was no incident,' Libby was quick to point out. 'Just after you left, David fell over on the ice, which happens all the time in skating.'

'There were a bunch of reporters hanging around the teashop. Apparently something has been posted about it online. They were asking questions.'

'What sort of questions?' Libby probed.

'Just whether anyone was present last night and what they had witnessed.'

'Unbelievable! Nothing happened that was newsworthy.'

'These vultures like to make up stories from the slightest of mishaps,' Cynthia said sympathetically.

'It really has been blown out of all proportion.' Libby shook her head in disbelief. 'I best leave you all to it.' She suddenly wanted to get back to the lodge and see if she could find any comments online. Standing up she noticed Holly tugging on Guy's sleeve and whispering something in his ear.

'She may be busy,' replied Guy.

Whatever it was, Holly wasn't giving up. Her eyes were wide and she was tilting her head between her dad and Libby.

'Go on, ask her,' Holly urged.

'Libby, if you have nowhere you need to be next Saturday, would you like to join us to go and pick a Christmas tree?'

Holly looked towards Libby with her fingers crossed.

'I'd love to!' replied Libby, noticing the smile hitch on Guy's face as well as Holly's.

'Perfect,' he replied. 'Are you happy now?' he said, smiling warmly at Holly. 'I'll walk you to the door,' he added, looking back at Libby who then said goodbye to Holly and Cynthia.

'Sorry, I didn't mean to put you on the spot then. I know Holly can be a little enthusiastic. You can change your mind about the Christmas tree…'

'Do you want me to change my mind?' she asked quietly.

'Absolutely not. Holly really likes you. She never stops talking about you.'

'I really like her too.'

Guy took her hand, his fingers entwining around hers for a moment. 'I'm looking forward to it.'

'It's a date,' she whispered. Taking a quick glance over her shoulder to make sure no one was looking, she pressed a swift kiss to his cheek before leaving him standing in the doorway. Once inside her lodge, she caught sight of her reflection in the hallway mirror. The smile on her face said it all. She couldn't wait to spend more time with Guy and Holly.

Chapter Twelve

Three weeks until Christmas

The following week was a busy one. The material had been chosen for Miranda's wedding dress; David—now recovered from his bruised shoulder—had picked out his attire for the wedding and Miranda had chosen her bouquet from Florrie's suggestions.

Thankfully, the press had decided there wasn't a story to report, after Flynn invited them in and showed them Guy's footage. There was no freak accident, just a falling over, which happens all the time on the ice.

This morning, Libby was working from the lodge but soon she would be meeting Guy and Holly to go and pick their Christmas tree. She hummed as she checked her emails, pleased to note that the RSVPs for Miranda and David's big day were rolling in. She had begun to co-ordinate the list of confirmed guests and as soon as the majority of replies were back, she would send the bulk over to the printers for their names to be printed on place cards. Everything was on track and the arrangements for the wedding were coming along nicely.

Hearing her phone ping, she looked at the screen to see her father's name. He'd sent her more photographs from his cruise and she was pleased to see he looked relaxed, his smile wide and his face tanned. Libby couldn't wait for him to arrive home in time for Christmas. She thought back to the moment she'd told him she was moving to New York. He hadn't flinched. Instead, he'd thrown his arms around her and squeezed her tight, telling her how proud he was that she was chasing her dreams and following her heart. She stared closely at one of the photos he had sent. Wilbur's face was a map of wrinkles, each line telling a story or representing an adventure he'd been on. He'd lived a colourful life, enjoying every second of it, and that's what he'd always encouraged her and Flynn to do. But he wasn't getting any younger, and the thought that maybe she would only see him a couple of times a year was beginning to weigh on Libby's mind.

At two o'clock, Guy and Holly were ready and waiting outside the lodge. As soon as Holly saw Libby open her door, she began to pull on Guy's arm. 'Come on, you two!'

'I think someone is very excited,' Guy mused.

'We'll be late! Granny said the trailer leaves in fifteen minutes.'

'We have plenty of time,' Guy reassured her.

Together, they took the short walk to Love Heart Lane where Drew's tractor was waiting in the lay-by just outside the entrance to Foxglove Farm. As soon as he spotted Libby and Guy, Drew jumped down from the cab.

'Good afternoon, what are you doing here?' asked Drew. 'Are you coming to choose a Christmas tree?'

'We are. I'm staying in one of the lodges at Starcross Manor until Christmas Eve and as this one thinks it should have a tree, who am I to argue?'

'Everyone has to have a tree, Dad, you're so bah humbug.'

'This is Holly,' introduced Guy. 'My bossy little human.'

'Pleased to meet you,' said Drew with a warm smile. 'Let me help you up on the trailer. The first stop is the other side of the bridge where a few more from the town usually jump on board.'

There were numerous hay bales grouped in a horseshoe shape and a pile of tartan rugs scattered on them.

'Wrap yourself in a blanket, it's about a ten-minute ride to the Christmas tree fields,' Drew said cheerily. 'And be warned: it may be a little bumpy as we go over the track towards the bridge so hold on tight.'

Drew had been right. Holly sat in between Guy and Libby and as the trailer bounced over the uneven track she started giggling uncontrollably. Guy had slid his arm around her shoulders and exchanged a look with Libby that melted her heart. Just as Drew had anticipated, more people clambered on board on the other side of the bridge, but in no time at all he'd pulled the tractor into a designated parking spot, switched off the engine then jumped onto the trailer.

'Welcome to the Christmas tree plantation. A place where there is a magical Christmas tree for everyone who loves Christmas.' Drew smiled in Holly's direction before he continued. 'Put your hand up if you love Christmas,' he insisted.

Libby and Holly's hands immediately shot up in the air,

making them both laugh. They looked at Guy and together they each firmly grabbed one of his arms and thrust it up into the air.

Guy grinned. 'Look at you two ganging up on me!'

'Now, the trees have been planted in sections according to their different varieties.'

'There are different varieties?' Guy questioned. 'I thought a Christmas tree was a just that: a Christmas tree.'

'Dad! You know nothing,' piped up Holly. The whole trailer of people was now looking in her direction. 'There are three main types of Christmas trees.' Holly looked towards Drew who nodded in encouragement. 'There's fir trees, spruce trees and pine trees. Their needles grow in clusters.'

Guy looked impressed. 'How do you know that?' He noticed Holly give Drew a look, and Drew wink back. 'Mmm, I'm beginning to think you've actually met before.'

Holly giggled. 'Last week with Granny. We were talking with Drew and learning all about the trees and Granny said we should go for a pine tree, as their needles grow in clusters and look prettier.'

'Did she now?' replied Guy, pulling Holly in for a hug.

Drew smiled as he continued issuing instructions. 'Once you've picked your tree, all you need to do is write your name and address on a star.' Drew was holding a up a pile of stars and pens. He began to hand them out. 'Then hang the star on your tree. The guys over there…' Drew pointed to a number of forest workers wearing hi-vis vests and hard hats standing in a group by a wooden hut. They were fully kitted out in sturdy boots and gloves and each standing by a chainsaw. 'They will cut down your tree, wrap it up and attach the star to the front. And then, just like your presents on Christmas Eve, the tree will miraculously appear at your home address by this evening. It's as simple as that. And for all of you that especially love Christmas, Santa has left a few of his reindeer to the side of the hot chocolate hut for you to meet. If anyone would like to feed them, you will find reindeer food in buckets just by the fence.'

'Reindeer, Dad! Please can we feed them first?' asked Holly, springing to her feet.

Holly's excitement was infectious as she tugged at Guy and Libby to stand up.

'We sure can!' he replied, grasping the star and pen Drew had handed to him.

Everyone scattered off the trailer in different directions, and in a matter of seconds Holly was haring off towards the small paddock at the side of the hut, leaving Guy and Libby following behind. A dozen or so reindeer were standing munching hay. The woman looking after them was dressed up in a Mrs Santa Claus outfit, her red hat clashing with her bright red candy-cane-coloured hair. She beckoned to Holly to come and feed the reindeer.

'Dad, can you see Rudolf?'

'How cute,' Libby whispered to Guy.

'Rudolf isn't here,' replied Mrs Claus. 'He's with Santa in the North Pole.'

Watching Holly take a couple of carrots from a sack leaning against the fence, Libby linked her arm through Guy's and leaned her head on his shoulder. 'Aww, just look at her.'

Holly held the woman's hand and stepped into the paddock. She held out a carrot to the nearest reindeer, who immediately began chomping on it.

'Very cute,' admitted Guy, glancing between Libby and

Holly. 'Given that life has been very difficult of late, these family moments melt my heart.'

Libby had a burning question on the tip of her tongue and even though she thought she already knew the answer, she asked it before she could stop herself. 'Do you want more children one day?' she asked, still staring in Holly's direction.

Without hesitation, Guy said, 'Of course. If I had my way, I'd have a whole football team—but this time I'd hope it would be with the person I'm going to spend the rest of my life with.'

It had been the same answer that Daniel had given her. Part of her instantly felt inadequate, her emotional insecurities creeping into her thoughts again.

Knowing she should practise her coping mechanisms when these feelings surfaced, she tried her best to keep them under control. She knew this was partly why she shied away from getting close to anyone: because the face-to-face conversation explaining that she couldn't have children had led to her being abandoned once, and she feared that it would happen again. 'Us men also want our happily ever after, you know.' His eyes twinkled.

There was so many questions that Libby wanted to ask, the main one being: what had caused the break-up of his relationship with Holly's mum?

'And how about you?' he asked.

'That's the dream,' she answered, avoiding giving a direct answer. It was clear now that whatever this was between them, she needed to try and curb her feelings for him, because his dream of more children wasn't something she could give him.

'I think you'd make an excellent mother. I've seen how you are with Holly and I have to say, when she came back from the studio, she wouldn't shut up, talking about how wonderful you are and how she wants to make dresses like you one day.'

'That's lovely. I think she's an adorable little girl,' said Libby, trying to resist the depression that had suddenly engulfed her. She didn't want to feel glum and ruin the next few hours they all had together just because Guy had expressed his desire to have more children. Why wouldn't he? He was a fantastic dad and the relationship he had with Holly was heart-warming to watch. Libby knew she had no right to feel sad about that, and that it was time to put some distance between them, if she was to avoid ending up with a broken heart.

She unhooked her arm from his. He looked at her. 'You okay? You suddenly look—'

There was no time for Guy to finish his sentence because Mrs Santa Claus interrupted. 'You have a very delightful little girl,' she said to Guy and Libby, opening the gate to the paddock and delivering Holly back to them.

'Thank you,' replied Guy, not putting her right. 'But believe me, she has her moments.'

'Don't they all,' she replied, smiling before turning back towards Holly. 'And don't you worry, I'll make sure Santa knows exactly which house to deliver your presents to.' She gave Guy a wink. 'Santa always gets it right.'

They walked away towards the trees, Holly in the middle, holding hands with both Guy and Libby. 'What did Mrs Claus mean by "She'll make sure Santa delivers your presents to the right house"?' Guy asked.

Holly looked down at the ground and attempted to ignore the question. Guy gave Libby a puzzled look and she shrugged.

'Holly?' Guy stopped and bent down next to his daughter. 'Come on, tell me what's on your mind.'

'Santa might miss out my presents because I don't know where I'll be on Christmas Eve. I might be at Granny's house, or with Mummy, or with you.'

'You will see us all at some point on Christmas Day,' Guy said reassuringly.

Holly nodded. She clearly already knew that, but Libby could see she wanted a plan, so she didn't have to worry about her presents not being there when she woke up in the morning.

Libby also crouched down. 'I think what Holly wants to know is where she will be sleeping on Christmas Eve, so she isn't worrying whether she will be missed by Santa Claus.'

Holly nodded and Libby gave her hand a little squeeze.

Guy took both of her hands. 'You can wake up wherever you want to on Christmas morning and I'll personally make sure that wherever you are, Santa knows where to deliver your presents.'

'Promise?' asked Holly.

'I promise,' replied Guy, giving his little girl a hug. 'Let's talk about it tonight and make some proper plans. Is that okay?'

Holly smiled.

'Good. Now let's go and pick a tree. I need to show you all that I'm not bah humbug.'

As they walked on, Holly ran in front and began weaving herself in and out of the trees. 'What about this one?' she shouted.

'Too big! We'll never get it through the door,' Guy bellowed back. 'Go to the smaller section over there, and stay in sight.'

'Just smell that,' said Libby, inhaling the rich, sweet scent.

'And look at those pine cones on those branches.' She noticed that Guy was lost in thought. 'How are you feeling about Christmas?' she asked tentatively, knowing that the holiday season was meant to be a joyous time for families, but for many was a time of pain and stress. She was sure it was something that was preying on Cynthia's mind, too.

'I'm actually not sure,' he admitted. 'It's just not easy trying to please everyone. My ideal would be to spend it with Holly by myself, but that's just me being selfish. I do know she needs to see her mum and my parents, and I know there's going to be a part of the day when I'll be sitting on my own.' Guy looked into the distance. 'Sometimes I wish I had a magic wand… But no matter what, I'll make sure Holly does what she wants to do and wakes up where she wants to wake up.'

'That's all you can do,' Libby replied. She noticed that Guy looked pensive.

'And you're still here Christmas Eve?'

'I am. I'm spending Christmas at Starcross Manor so please don't think you're on your own; there's always room for extras at our table.' She bumped her shoulder against his.

'I might take you up on that, thank you.'

'You're very welcome.'

'Dad, come on. I've found one! This one is perfect.'

The tree Holly had chosen was near the edge of the field and as Guy and Libby caught up with her, they heard her give a tiny squeal and jump forward. She clutched Guy's hand as a squirrel popped its head out of the branches then scampered down the trunk and across the ground. It stopped in a pool of sunlight in front of them and none of them moved, standing like statues and watching as the squirrel found a nut and popped it into its mouth. With its fluffy tail quivering behind it, it raced off and was soon out of sight.

'We nearly got a free squirrel with that tree,' Guy joked.

'It frightened me at first but it's so cute,' Holly said, finally letting go of Guy's hand.

'I'm not sure Pickle would be impressed if we took a tree with its own resident back to the lodge so it's probably best he's headed back to his own home. Now, this tree is beautiful. It's the right size and the right shape.' Guy walked around it. 'This is the one,' he declared, handing the pen and star to Holly. 'Why don't you write our name on there and I'll write the address. We need to hang it on the tree before anyone else chooses it.'

Holly ran to a nearby bench, rested the star on her knee and began to write. She was soon back by Guy's side and handed him the star. His face lit up. 'You cutie,' he said, pulling the bobble on the top her hat. He showed the star to Libby, who didn't have the heart to tell Holly that she had spelled the words incorrectly.

Me, Daddy and Libby for a majical crismas.

Guy added the address then gave the star back to Holly, who hung it proudly on the tree.

'We will see you soon,' she whispered to it. 'And I can't wait to decorate you.'

Libby's heart swelled with happiness as she stared at the star on the tree swinging lightly in the chilly breeze. This was exactly what Libby had always hoped her life would be like: spending quality time on family outings, sharing fun and laughter with a man she loved and a child of her own. Then that sudden sadness crept up on her again, and she tried to thrust it out of her mind so it wouldn't spoil the moment.

'I've had a thought,' declared Holly. 'Would it be possible to have Christmas at the lodge and everyone can come to visit us? That means we can see Libby.' Holly cupped her hands around her mouth. 'You need to get her a present too.'

Guy didn't have time to answer as a forest worker appeared beside the tree and asked them to stand back before he started up the chainsaw. Holly put her hands over her ears in anticipation of the loud noise and took off towards the trailer, leaving Guy and Libby following behind.

'What are your thoughts about having Christmas at the lodge?' she prompted. 'Might be an idea, so you don't have to travel back home.' Libby would also selfishly love to see them both on Christmas Day, even if it was only for a while. 'And where is home, by the way?'

'At the minute I'm in the worst possible situation ever. I'm staying with my parents as Holly's mum is still currently living in our family home. It's one of the reasons why I took this job, to get some breathing space. But now because my father is ill and my ex-partner has decided to take off doing whatever she's doing, my mother has ended up here.' He rolled his eyes. 'Between you and me, I've been looking at buying Weathervane Cottage, at the foot of Heartcross Mountain, but with the situation I'm in at the minute and with Holly, everything is up in the air.'

Libby wasn't sure what he meant by that and didn't want to pry. 'Heartcross is a beautiful place to live. I'm quite envious.'

'It is,' he agreed. 'And maybe it is worth thinking about

staying here for Christmas.' He caught her eye and gave her a warm smile.

Libby's heart began to race. 'I'd love that,' she admitted. 'And I don't want to speak out of turn here but maybe you could offer an olive branch? With your dad not being well, it might be nice to invite them so your mum doesn't have to worry about any of the Christmas preparations. She has a lot on her mind, especially with your sister's health problems too.'

Guy stopped dead in his tracks, his smile gone in an instant. He checked to see that Holly was on the back of the trailer before he returned Libby's gaze. 'How do you know about that?'

By the look on Guy's face, she'd put her foot right in it. Again. She hesitated. 'Oh God, I've said something I shouldn't have, haven't I?'

'I don't know, have you?'

'When I met Cynthia, she was upset and she mentioned—'

'You met my mum? Was this a planned meeting to talk about me?' Guy's tone was defensive and he looked visibly upset. 'Why is it everyone always goes behind my back?'

'Honestly, that's not what happened. I was just out for a walk and we bumped into each other.'

'But she managed to confide in you about my sister's health.'

Libby swallowed. Whatever she said she knew that it was most likely going to be misinterpreted. 'Speak to your mum. All I know is that she's upset about the situation too and wishes things were different but she's stuck in the middle between her children.' She kept her voice calm and warm yet her heart was beating nineteen to the dozen, and not at all like the racing heart she'd felt only moments earlier.

'We need to go,' he said.

Guy's good mood had completely evaporated, and all she could do was paint a smile on her face for Holly's sake. Climbing onto the back of the trailer she sat down next to the little girl, who was thankfully oblivious to the sudden change in atmosphere.

Just at that moment Libby's phone pinged and she rummaged in her pocket to find it. There were two messages on her screen, one from Flynn and one from Florrie. She read Flynn's first.

Meetings are all done for the day. There are more RSVPs flooding in so we need to confirm menu options and I'm hoping it's not going to be just black food. Otherwise Andrew will have to burn everything!

Libby smiled. *At least he hasn't lost his sense his humour*, she thought as she flicked onto Florrie's message.

Sample table decorations have been made up to match the bouquet.

Deciding to respond later, she slipped her phone back into her pocket and took a sideward glance at Guy. She realised she'd put her foot in it and she could kick herself knowing that Cynthia was going to take the brunt of Guy's sudden change in mood when he arrived back at the lodge.

'I can't wait to tell Granny all about the reindeer and that Rudolf is resting with Santa.'

'And I bet she can't wait to hear all about it,' replied Libby.

'Are you going to help us decorate the tree when it arrives?' asked Holly.

'Thank you for the very kind thought, but I think your dad and granny are looking forward to doing that with you. This evening I have some work I need to be getting on with.'

'But we'll see you tomorrow, so I can show you the tree?'

'Of course. I can't wait to see it.'

Holly slipped her hand into Libby's and soon afterwards Drew started the engine. By the look of happiness on Holly's face Libby knew the little girl had enjoyed every second of the afternoon, unlike Guy, who was now preoccupied with his own thoughts. She wished she could turn back time. All she could do was hope that she hadn't made the situation worse between him and Cynthia.

Chapter Thirteen

F eeling down in the dumps, Libby spent the rest of the evening working on Julia's surprise wedding outfit and surfing the Internet. She noticed Drew had delivered the Christmas tree to Guy's lodge and hoped they were spending some quality time together decorating it.

Checking her emails she saw that there were no outstanding RSVPs, which was a miracle as she had thought that part of the wedding was going to be the most challenging. Now she could report back the confirmed numbers to Flynn and organise the menus with the chef and Miranda and David by the end of the week.

Thinking of food made Libby feel a little peckish. Opening the fridge she found leftover chicken, and she cut up a few potatoes to make chips. After a drizzle of vegetable oil and a sprinkle of salt and pepper she placed them on a baking tray and turned the oven up to its highest setting. While waiting for the chips to cook, she looked out of the back window. It was already dark but the security lights had been activated.

Everywhere was calm and looked icy cold. She was about to turn away when she thought she saw a movement on the other side of the fence at the bottom of the decking. She narrowed her eyes and focused. Yes, there it was again. Grabbing her coat and slipping on her shoes, Libby opened the back door. It was freezing, and she shivered. Hearing a whimpering sound, she hurried towards the fence.

'Holly, what are you doing out here?' Libby was astonished to see the little girl huddled up on a bench looking upset. 'You're going to catch your death. Let me get you back inside. Your dad will be worried about you.'

She shook her head. 'They've haven't even noticed I've gone.'

'How long have you been out here?' asked Libby, touching Holly's hand with the back of hers. 'You're freezing.' She dropped her gaze and noticed the little girl was wearing slippers.

'I don't want to go back inside.' Holly pulled her knees up to her chest, and rested her chin on top of them.

Libby looked towards Guy's lodge. There was no sign of him through the window. 'How about you come inside with me and I'll make us a hot chocolate and you can get warm by the fire.'

Holly nodded.

'And if you're hungry I've got some chips cooking in the oven. But you can't walk through the snow in your slippers.' Libby turned around and bent down. 'Stand on the bench and climb on. I'll give you a piggyback.' She smiled at Holly over her shoulder.

The little girl wrapped her arms around Libby's neck, and Libby pushed her up on her back and headed into the warmth.

She lowered Holly onto the chair next to the fire. 'You get warm and I'll get you a drink.'

After she'd checked on the chips and seen that they weren't quite ready, Libby made two calorific hot chocolates topped with marshmallows and cream before making herself comfy on the rug next to the fire. 'You do know I need to tell your dad where you are, right? He'll be worried when he finds you missing.'

Holly nodded and Libby quickly punched out a text to Guy. As soon as Holly had finished her hot chocolate, she would take her home. Hopefully Guy wouldn't be too mad and they could talk things through calmly and put right whatever was going on.

'Did you decorate your tree? I can't wait to come and see it,' said Libby.

'We were about to but Granny and Daddy started arguing about Auntie Lydia again and Christmas.'

Libby could see how sad Holly looked.

'Remember when I hung the star on your Christmas tree?'

'I do,' replied Libby.

'I wished for my family to be happy at Christmas.'

Libby didn't know what to say. She'd never been in this situation before and hearing those words coming from Holly was heartbreaking.

'You're the only person who hasn't shouted since I met you. I like you.'

'I like you too,' replied Libby, watching Holly scoop up a spoonful of cream packed with tiny marshmallows and plunge it into her mouth.

As soon as Holly had demolished the cream and marshmallows, she took a sip of the hot chocolate and placed it on the table. 'What's that?' she asked, pointing. Libby glanced towards the table at the post she'd received today, including a brochure about her new apartment along with the lease agreement.

'It's an apartment in New York City,' said Libby, deciding not to share that it was *her* apartment.

'Is that in America? It's a long, long way away.'

'It is, isn't it?' replied Libby, having realised over the past couple of weeks exactly how far away it was.

'Daddy wants to live in Heartcross. There's a cottage by the mountain. He said if we do, I can have a goat, to help keep the grass down.'

'And do you think Pickle will like that?'

Holly thought for a moment. 'They'd become best friends. I wish I had a best friend. Do you have a best friend?'

Libby thought for a moment. 'I have my brother, Flynn,' she replied, thinking how sad it was that Holly felt she didn't have a best friend. It broke Libby's heart.

'Maybe we could be best friends?' Holly said with hope.

'I'd like that,' replied Libby, feeling guilty because she knew that very soon she would be leaving. But there was no reason why she couldn't write old-fashioned letters to Holly and send her photos and presents from the Big Apple. But the now familiar niggle was troubling her and she found herself wondering if she was doing the right thing.

'Let me check on those chips.'

As Libby stood up there was a loud knock on the door. 'I think that's going to be your dad.' She gave Holly an encouraging smile. 'It will be okay. Just tell him what you've told me and explain how you feel. He's your dad. He'll understand. I promise.'

Opening the door, she found Guy looking worried. 'I've just received your text. Is Holly here? I thought she was in her bedroom.'

'You thought wrong,' Libby said in a hushed whisper. 'I found her outside, sitting on the bench in the freezing cold with only her slippers on her feet, and all because you're arguing again with your mother. She had a wonderful afternoon and it would have been lovely for her to end the day decorating your tree as a family. This isn't fair on Holly and it needs to be put right. Not only is she sad about the arguing, but she's also sad because she has no friends. All she has is her family and with you guys continuously at each other's throats, what effect do you think it's having on her? I know I haven't got kids but—'

'That's right, you haven't,' Guy cut in. 'So you'd best leave the parenting to me.' His tone was curt.

Libby exhaled and held her hands up in a gesture of surrender. 'I'm just saying that I promised you'd listen to her,' she said placatingly as Guy walked into the living room.

'Hey,' he said.

Holly was still sitting on the chair, cuddling a cushion.

'I'm sorry, Granny and I didn't mean to argue.' Guy knelt at the side of the chair. 'I was really worried when I'd realised you had gone. You have to promise not to do that again.'

Holly nodded.

'I know you've had a good chat to Libby and I've promised I'll listen to what you have to say.' He stood up and stretched out his hand. Holly reached out and slipped her hand into his. 'Please thank Libby for having you.'

'Thank you, Libby, and thank you for being my new best friend.'

It was the most adorable thing anyone had ever said to her. 'I'll see you tomorrow.'

'You will,' replied Holly, looking over her shoulder and giving her a gorgeous smile as they headed towards the door.

Guy picked her up. 'You can't walk out in your slippers,' he said. Just as they reached the door, he turned back to Libby. 'Can I smell something burning?'

'Blooming heck! I've left the chips in the oven,' she said, hurrying into the kitchen and grabbing the oven gloves. 'It's okay, you two get yourselves home,' she shouted after them. As she pulled the oven door down she was hit with a smoky blast of hot air. Turning the oven off she pulled out a tray of chips that wouldn't look out of place at Miranda and David's wedding. Black as coal. Just her luck.

'Hotel restaurant it is,' she murmured, tipping the burnt potatoes straight into the bin before grabbing her coat and keys. As she walked out of her front door she glanced through the front window of Guy's lodge. The curtains were wide open and she could see the Christmas tree standing in the middle of the room. Guy was holding fairy lights and Cynthia a large glass of wine. Holly was standing on a chair, ready to start hanging the baubles. Libby smiled. She hoped they could all get past whatever was going on and have a good family night together.

Heading towards the hotel restaurant, Libby knew things were starting to get on top of her and promptly texted Isla.

Are you free tomorrow morning for breakfast? I need a friend.

Immediately Isla replied.

I am. Are you okay?

I am but I'm not. Can you meet me in the bar at Starcross Manor around 9.30?

See you there.

Libby felt relieved. Maybe after a good night's sleep and a chat with Isla, everything would become a lot clearer.

Chapter Fourteen

L ibby had been curled up in bed for half an hour. Granted, it was only just after 9pm, but she still couldn't gather her thoughts. She'd lived on her own since Daniel had walked out all those years ago and she quite liked her own company but the reality of moving to the other side of the world was getting closer and the thought was beginning to scare her a little.

Taking a notepad from her bedside cabinet, Libby picked up a pen and drew a line down the middle of the page, then wrote 'pros' and 'cons' at the top of each column. She began to make a list.

Pros:

> *Fantastic career opportunity.*
> *Living in New York City.*
> *Working alongside the best in the industry.*
> *Financial stability.*

Cons:

> *Will miss my home and family.*
> *Will miss Guy.*
> *Social stability.*

She stared at the page. Both sections were short and sweet and the words 'family' and 'career' were turning over in her mind. Why couldn't she have it all? But how would that even be possible? Placing the notepad back on the bedside cabinet she thought of Guy and his family. She knew how lucky she was to have grown up with Flynn and her father. The death of her mother could have had a profound effect on her wellbeing, but her father and Flynn had been strong in their support and Libby loved them unconditionally for shaping her into the person she was today.

Switching off the light and pulling the duvet up around her chin, Libby closed her eyes. Minutes later, she was woken by a tapping sound. She opened her eyes and listened. There it was again. Sitting bolt upright in bed, she switched on the light. There was someone at the door. Quickly grabbing her dressing gown she pulled the belt around her body and hurried into the living room. Taking a peep through the curtain, she saw Guy standing outside with Pickle under his arm.

Opening the door, her first thought was that he looked dreadful: exhausted and visibly upset. 'Come in,' she said. 'Are you okay?'

'I'm so sorry, you're dressed for bed.'

'I was in bed,' she confessed. 'And woke up when you knocked.'

'I can go.' Guy gestured back towards his own lodge.

'Don't be daft, you're here now and I'm awake. Let me make a cuppa.'

'Thank you,' he replied, taking off his boots and hanging up his coat. 'Sorry, I had to bring Pickle because otherwise she would have just been barking at the front door and Holly is in bed.'

'You and Pickle are most welcome anytime. You get the fire going and I'll switch the kettle on.'

After greeting Libby, Pickle jumped up on a chair and immediately settled down. Ten minutes later she was asleep and Guy and Libby were sitting on the sofa in front of a roaring fire, their hands cupped around mugs of hot, milky tea.

'I'm sorry about earlier. I didn't mean...' said Guy, genuinely upset. 'I feel like I'm losing myself and I just have no one to turn to.'

'You do,' Libby replied tentatively. 'I'm always here for you, And you don't need to apologise.'

'Thank you, but I do. I didn't mean to speak to you the way I did before. It was out of line and undeserved.'

'Apology accepted,' she said warmly. 'Now, do you want to tell me what's really going on here?'

'I think I do,' he said, taking a sip of tea. 'I'm going to be truly honest with you, although it hasn't seemed to get me anywhere in the past.'

'Let's hope that changes then,' said Libby, tucking her leg underneath her and resting her elbow on the back of the settee. 'It's good to talk.'

'And it's so easy with you, which I wasn't expecting. You've taken me completely by surprise.'

'In a good way or a bad way?'

'Obviously a good way. The first time we met—'

'Don't remind me. I was standing in the snow in a bikini and bobble hat. How embarrassing!'

'You were a sight for sore eyes. I couldn't quite believe my luck that you were going to be my neighbour for the next few weeks, especially when I didn't even want to take this job in the first place. After I took Pickle back inside the lodge, I gave her a kiss and screamed, "There is a God!"'

The mood was lightened and they both laughed and glanced towards Pickle, whose eyes were firmly shut, her front paws twitching as she dreamed.

'Did you really?' questioned Libby, not sure if Guy was exaggerating.

'Absolutely I did. Pickle's timing was perfect for me, though maybe not for you. And by the way, those springy curls trying to escape from underneath your hat were just as sexy as that bikini.'

Libby rolled her eyes in jest and Guy took hold of her hand.

'Was the reason you didn't want this job because your ex has moved on and is getting married?' Libby was trying to gauge if Guy was unable to move on because he still felt some romantic attachment to his former partner.

'Believe me, I'm sick to my back teeth of hearing about weddings, but not for the reasons you're thinking. I've had a lot on my plate recently, and when Flynn needed someone, I thought that even though the job wasn't to my taste it would give me my own space for a few weeks and a break from the situation.'

Pickle suddenly emitted a loud snore, and they both laughed.

'I've been living with my parents since I left the family home. Sophie, Holly's mum, and I met just after I left university. I'd landed a job with a film company and we were put on the same project, a safari documentary for a TV channel, which we filmed in Africa. After that we worked on a couple more jobs together and eventually decided to go freelance together. Everything was going so well, and soon afterwards we bought a flat. At the time I couldn't have been happier. I was living the dream with a job I loved ... and then my girlfriend announced she was pregnant. At first, I was shocked and couldn't quite believe it, but of course I embraced it. We upgraded our flat to a beautiful country cottage, the perfect place and village to raise our child, and I had visions of pigs, chickens and Shetland ponies accompanying us in our life's journey. The only thing was, at that point Sophie still hadn't met my family.' Guy paused, rubbed his hand over his face and then took a breath.

Libby could see that whatever he was about to share had hurt him deeply.

'My family loved her. She fitted in so well it was unbelievable. She didn't have a family of her own and so she quickly became close to my parents. We all took good care of her during the pregnancy and things were going so well that I wanted to make us a proper family. I proposed and she said yes. My family and I were over the moon. Then, all of a sudden, our life became about one thing: organising the wedding. My sister became the wedding planner and Sophie spent more and more time with Lydia. But after twelve months of supposedly planning the wedding, there was still no venue booked. I thought it was odd but Sophie assured me it was just a matter of finding the perfect place, and besides, she wanted time to lose her baby fat and look her best for the big day.

'I asked to be involved in the planning but Sophie and my sister wouldn't hear of it, even though it was meant to be my wedding too. Time ticked on and Sophie and Holly were practically living at my parents. Every time I arrived home late from work I'd find our house empty as they'd had dinner with my family and then stayed over because Holly had fallen asleep and Sophie didn't want to disturb her. My family was becoming more involved in my daughter's life than I was. It became a little soul-destroying.'

Guy's voice cracked, and Libby knew he was building up to something.

'I spoke to my mum about the way I was feeling, which was mainly left-out and a little jealous. I know it sounds daft— these people are my family and it was good for Holly to be surrounded by her auntie and grandparents. My mum explained that becoming a new mum was difficult and that Sophie was lucky to have the support while I was out at work. But by this point Holly was two, and the family home had been standing empty for most of those two years. Holly had her own bedroom at my parents' and Sophie was sleeping in the other spare room. My sister took me out for lunch and convinced me I was over-reacting and putting too much pressure on the situation. Honestly, Libby, I thought I was going mad. I'm not normally a selfish or jealous person and yet my whole life was becoming affected. Then my dream of the perfect family life—the house, the child and the marriage— turned into my worst nightmare.'

Guy placed his empty mug on the table. 'Have you got anything stronger?'

'Wine or whisky?' asked Libby, standing up.

'A drop of whisky would be perfect.'

Libby walked over to the fridge, dropped a couple of ice-cubes in a glass then poured in some whisky from a decanter on the sideboard. She watched as Guy swirled the amber liquid around in the glass then took a huge swig.

'I was filming down in Kent. I finished the job early and instead of spending the evening sitting on my own in the hotel I headed home … well, to my parents' house, as I knew that's where Sophie and Holly would be. It was just past 11pm and my parents go to bed early so the house was in darkness. But I knew Sophie was there as her car was on the drive. I let myself in with my key, thinking I'd surprise her. I'd made a plan. I'd take on less work and not travel long distance. Family was more important than my career and money.'

'That's exactly right,' Libby said, watching Guy drain his glass. His words resonated; it was exactly what she'd been thinking about earlier.

'I checked in on Holly first and she was fast asleep in her bed in the tiny boxroom. She looked perfect lying there and I pressed a kiss to her forehead.' His voice faltered. 'She was beautiful and I knew I'd made the right decision to limit my jobs. After watching Holly sleep for a moment, I headed to the spare room. The door was ajar and the bed was empty. My initial thought was that maybe Sophie couldn't sleep and was in the snug downstairs or the bathroom, but I checked both and there was no sign of her. I texted her, asking her where she was, and I heard her phone beep. Then I heard hushed whispers from my sister's room. After knocking on the door and being met with complete silence I opened it slowly … and discovered that the reason my wife-to-be was always at my parents' house was not because she needed help with Holly, but because she was in a relationship with my sister.'

Libby's eyes widened and she stared at Guy open-mouthed. She had not been expecting that revelation! No wonder he was struggling with his family. It was bad enough coming to terms with the betrayal of a fiancée but when that betrayal was with your own sister? It was the worst situation imaginable.

Libby's hand moved to her heart. 'I'm so sorry, Guy. I don't know what to say.' She was still trying to digest it all. The situation was a complete mess and she wouldn't wish on anyone the hurt and anger that Guy must have experienced. Then the penny dropped. 'Oh, Guy, Sophie's wedding... She's marrying your sister, isn't she?'

All Guy could manage was a nod as he stood up and walked over to the decanter. After refilling his glass, he sat back down next to Libby.

'Yes, and my daughter is a bridesmaid, and my father is walking both Lydia and Sophie down the aisle. I feel like I'm in the middle of a weird reality TV show.'

Libby could understand why.

'And it gets better. My ex-fiancée and sister are now living together in the house Sophie and I bought, and I'm back with my parents. My daughter's auntie will soon become her step-mum and my parents haven't taken any stance on the situation.'

Libby could see how difficult this was from both sides. Cynthia and her husband were caught in the middle: their daughter had found happiness but at the expense of their son's, and they were trying to deal with everyone's emotions, including their own.

'I know it's daft but I feel abandoned by everyone: my sister, my parents and of course Sophie. I can live with her betrayal, but my own sister?

'I haven't spoken to anyone about the situation. I hoped it would all go away, but now that they've announced their wedding and the save-the-date cards have gone out, I feel ten times as humiliated.'

'You really do need some breathing space. This must consume your thoughts every day.'

'Exactly that. But my parents think I should put it all behind me and move on. They think I should go to the wedding. It's not that I'm still harbouring any love for Sophie —believe me, that died on the spot—and I know she has to be in my life because of Holly, but Lydia... I can't get over her betrayal. She should have put me and Holly first; we're her blood. I've tried to move on but every day the deceit of those two is rubbed in my face. I don't need or want the constant reminder.'

'And you've had no support, or anyone to talk to?' At least when she was going through her break-up and the devastation of an early menopause Libby had had her family. She couldn't have got through it without them.

'No one. I've never spoken about it before.'

Guy's eyes filled with tears. Libby opened her arms wide and he immediately fell into them.

'I've got you,' she whispered.

'Thank you,' he murmured.

It was definitely all a mess.

According to the clock above the fire it was two in the morning. It took Libby a second to realise she'd fallen asleep on the couch with two strapping arms wrapped around her, and Pickle fast asleep at their feet. Cuddling into the warmth of Guy's jumper, Libby inhaled his aftershave. It felt good being in his arms. She felt safe. She was happy that Guy trusted her enough to open up his heart. What must it have been like for him during the last few years? Devastating. And it still was. She believed him when he said that he no longer had any romantic feelings about his ex, but she understood that he didn't want the new relationship rubbed in his face either.

Libby wanted to help, to make everything okay for him, but she had no clue how to do so. Guy had two options: either he could try and forgive his sister for the sake of Holly and his parents, or he didn't, and things would carry on much as they were. But she didn't know how—or if—he could live his life like that.

She felt Guy's arms squeeze her lightly as he kissed the top of her head.

'Hey,' she said softly. 'We fell asleep on the couch.'

'Mmm, I have to say it feels good,' he murmured.

'I was just thinking the same thing.' Libby held on to him, not wanting him to move. 'Everything is going to be okay; I've just got that feeling.'

'I've got that feeling too.'

'Don't shoot me when I say this…'

He pulled away a little to look at her.

'How about I come with you to the wedding, so you would at least have some support?' As soon as the words left her mouth Libby began to worry. She might have just offered to do something she couldn't go through with. She'd not asked when the wedding was. Maybe she wasn't even going to be in the country.

Guy was silent for a moment. 'You'd do that for me?'

'Yes, of course. I'll help out in any way I can. Sometimes things can be less difficult with someone else by your side. I can scrub up pretty well when I need to. But don't make a decision now, have a think about it.'

'Thank you, Libby. That has given me a little bit of faith.'

'I'm glad.'

'I vowed never to let anyone in again after this happened, but talking with you is so easy and it's helped me getting a lot of it off my chest.'

'I'm glad.' Libby tilted her face up to his and kissed him softly on the lips. She could already see she was breaking down his barriers and she hoped his opening up about his situation would help him work through his feelings. 'Apparently Heartcross is well known for mending broken hearts and getting lives back on track.'

'And once you arrive, you never want to leave, I heard.'

For a moment, they lay in silence, lost in their own thoughts, Libby feeling guilty that she still hadn't shared any details of her past life or any future plans with him. She wasn't sure why.

'I don't want to go, but I think I need to. If I wake up after Holly and she wanders into my room, she'll see my bed hasn't been slept in.'

Libby kissed him softly again. 'It's okay, I understand,' she whispered, pulling away slowly. But before she could swing her legs to the floor and sit up, Guy pulled her back into him. Even in the darkness Libby could feel his face close to hers.

She'd never felt attraction like this to anyone before. The electricity was sparking between them as Guy kissed her, stealing every breath from her body. Embracing the tingling pleasure that flooded her, she kissed him back. Fifteen more minutes wouldn't hurt.

Chapter Fifteen

Libby was already sitting in the restaurant waiting when Isla breezed in with a big smile on her face and headed towards the table. Taking off her coat she handed it to a nearby waiter and sat down.

'Good morning!' trilled Libby.

'How are you?' asked Isla. 'I was worried about you all last night.'

'Honestly, I'm okay. I was just having a wobble.'

Attempting to be upbeat and pretending that life was hunky-dory clearly wasn't fooling Isla, who gave her a sceptical look.

'I suspect you're still having that wobble. Let's order some food and you can tell me all about it.'

The waiter arrived and took their order of two full Scottish breakfasts with a pot of tea each. Then Isla folded her arms and leaned on the table. 'What's going on?'

Libby trusted Isla. She knew whatever she confided in her friend would be in the strictest confidence, but she needed to be careful not to break Guy's trust. It wasn't her place to tell anyone his story.

'I don't know what I'm doing,' she admitted. 'I thought I did and now I don't.' She didn't say any more while the waiter placed two pots of tea and cups on the table. As soon as he was gone she continued, 'For the past ten years, I've looked after myself and my mental health after...' Every time she began to mention the early menopause, she found herself close to tears.

Isla reached across the table and placed her hand on top of Libby's. Isla knew about everything that Libby had gone through. She'd confided in her a few years ago when they'd gone back to Isla's after a night out and the conversation had turned towards Libby's love life. Isla couldn't believe she was single and after Libby revealed that was her choice, the conversation had moved on to the reasons why.

'I vowed not to let anyone hurt me again. My relationship ended because I wasn't a full woman.'

'Stop right there. Your relationship ended because your ex was an asshole. End of. And I don't ever want to hear you blame yourself.' Isla was firm. 'Do you hear me?'

Libby nodded. She knew that Isla was right but every time she thought about the past, she wondered, would they still be together if she could have children? What if?

'I can say this until I'm blue in the face but you *have* to know your own self-worth. He was not good enough for you.'

'I love you,' said Libby, laughing. 'You put everything into perspective.'

'That's what good friends do.' Isla grinned. 'So, after you vowed never to entertain a man again...'

'I threw myself into work.'

'And became a blooming talented fashion designer, with a

brand-new job in New York City. A place I've never been!' Isla poured them both a cup of tea. 'But why are you suddenly looking glum about that? This is everything you've worked for. Or am I wrong?' Isla was watching her closely.

'There's no other way to say it. I'm in a mess, a big fat mess, and I can't believe I'm going to share this with you now…' Libby stopped in her tracks as the waiter put their breakfasts down in front of them and brought further condiments to the table. Then he walked away and they were free to continue the conversation, knowing they wouldn't be overheard.

'And this big fat mess?' prompted Isla.

'I don't know if I can go to New York,' Libby admitted.

'But this is everything you've worked for and the job of your dreams. What's changed?'

'Being here. Spending time with my family. Flynn and Julia are about to start their life together and have a family, and my dad isn't getting any younger. If something happens, I'll be miles away.'

'I do understand what you're saying but you knew all this when you applied and accepted the job.'

Libby nodded. 'I know. It's what I thought I wanted but as the time to leave gets closer I'm not sure how I feel about it anymore.' She looked around the room. 'There's something about this place. The people, the community…'

'It's the Heartcross curse taking hold of you. I knew you wouldn't get away from it,' said Isla cheerfully. 'But what's the worst that can happen? You go for six months and if it's not for you, you come home. At least then you've given it a go.'

'I know what you're saying, and I've had that scenario in my head many times. The people in New York have already made me feel so welcome…'

'But…?' said Isla. 'What's the part you aren't telling me?'

'But I've got feelings I've not experienced in a very long time and I don't know what to do because it's complicated.'

'How complicated?'

'I can't hinder what someone else wants in life, and I know it's too soon to be even thinking we might have a future, but if we can't, he deserves to know.'

'You're talking about Guy?' Isla guessed.

'I am. I didn't come here thinking I was going to meet someone or start developing feelings towards them … but I have.'

'It always happens when you least expect it,' confirmed Isla. 'Does he feel the same?'

'I'm getting the same vibe back.'

'So apart from the fact that it's still early days, why do you think there's no future to it? There's always a possibility.'

'Because it came up in conversation that he wants more kids. In fact, a football team. I can't give him that. The closer we get, the more likely it is that both of us are going to get hurt.'

'He'll understand when you explain everything to him. If your feelings are this strong you need to talk to him about it. It's like the job in New York; what's the worst that can happen?'

'I've been in this position before and look how that ended.' Libby's voice cracked. 'Maybe it's just better if I go.'

'How does he feel about your job in New York?'

Libby was silent.

'You haven't mentioned it, have you?'

'Not yet. And I'm struggling with that fact. Why wouldn't I share this information if it's what I wanted most in the world?'

'Because you're keeping your options open,' said Isla firmly. 'These things have a way of working themselves out, but if you aren't open and honest and then he discovers you've kept this from him, he could walk away anyway.'

Libby knew Isla was right and she needed to be honest with Guy the way he had been with her. Last night, he'd opened up to her about his life. He'd made himself vulnerable, and Libby knew she needed to do the same, but fear of rejection held her back. She couldn't alter the fact that she was unable to have children, and she couldn't expect Guy to change what he wanted in life.

'I know I have to tell him, and I will. Today.'

'Things will become a lot clearer when you do.'

'Thanks, Isla.'

'You're very welcome. I have to say this breakfast was a very good choice. These sausages are just the best!' Isla stabbed one and held it up on her fork.

'Because they're from your farm!' Libby laughed.

As they finished their breakfasts and drank their tea Libby felt a lot better for having shared her thoughts with Isla and for deciding to speak to Guy tonight. Isla was right: she needed to put herself in that vulnerable position and be open and honest with him.

Isla took out her purse to pay the bill but Libby raised a hand. 'This one is on me ... well, actually Flynn. I don't have to pay for meals. One of the perks of the job.'

'Only if you're sure?'

'I am, put your purse away.'

'Thank you. I've got to get back to the farm but if you need anything or want to talk again, just text me.'

'I will.' Libby got up and hugged Isla. This was what she

was missing in life: a genuine friend who was there for her no matter what. After the waiter brought Isla's coat, she headed towards the foyer and Libby watched her make her way down the steps of Starcross Manor. She was amazed to see a long line of expensive cars pulling up in front of the entrance. There must be a function about to start at the hotel as there were hordes of people walking in. Everyone was dressed to impress, their suits smart, their party dresses stunning. It was all glitz and glamour.

Libby wandered into the snug off The Grand Hall. The open fire was roaring and she seated herself in the wingback chair in front of it after ordering another pot of tea. She was thinking about Guy, the way he'd confided with her about the last few years, the way they'd snuggled together on the settee, their bodies fitting perfectly together like jigsaw pieces ... and the kisses. Her feelings were genuine but she was conflicted. Was New York really meant for her? How would she feel, leaving Heartcross, her family and Guy? There were so many questions whirling around in her mind and the answers were unclear, but Isla was right, things had a way of working themselves out.

Her thoughts were interrupted by a commotion at reception. All the guests who had just arrived seemed to be huddled together, talking in loud voices. The receptionist looked frazzled, her head turning from guest to guest as if she was watching a frantic tennis match. Libby wondered what was going on. The general manager appeared at the side of the reception, followed by Flynn, who was looking over a card that a guest had just handed him. Libby watched as Flynn punched in something on his mobile phone and was surprised when her own phone rang.

'I can see you,' she answered.

'Where are you?' he asked, glancing around the reception.

'I'm in the snug.'

Flynn's gaze swung towards her and Libby waved at him as he hung up the call. She watched as he addressed the guests. 'Please follow the general manager into the bar area, where complimentary tea and coffee will be served while I look into this.'

There were a lot of disgruntled noises from the guests as they shuffled into the bar area on the other side of the lobby. Flynn strode towards Libby and thrust an invitation into her hand.

'What's going on?' she asked. 'Why have you given me one of Miranda and David's wedding invitations?' Confused, she glanced at the invitation then back at Flynn.

'I was going to ask you the same thing. There's approximately one hundred and twenty guests in the foyer that have turned up for a wedding that's meant to be happening at eleven this morning.'

'You've lost me. Who's getting married?'

'Miranda and David!' Flynn looked at his wits' end.

Libby took a closer look at the invitation. 'Oh no. There's been some sort of printing mistake.'

'How has this happened? I've got the majority of the wedding guests dressed up to the nines sipping tea and coffee in the function bar expecting a wedding to take place.'

Libby was still looking at the invitation. 'I don't understand. I input all the correct information onto the invitations and Miranda double-checked it before we hit send. It has to be a mistake at the printer's end. No wonder all the RSVPs came back so soon; I did think that was strange.'

'It doesn't matter how it happened. It's carnage out there and I've got to explain to all those guests that there is to be no wedding—well, not until Christmas Eve. Can you get on to the printers and check what the hell has gone on? Because unless a new batch of invites is posted with the correct details, our winning competition winners may not have any guests at their real wedding.' Flynn blew out a breath.

Libby watched him walk towards the lion's den, raking his hands through his hair, something he only did when he was nervous. How had the mix-up happened? She knew she'd double-checked everything so it had to be a mistake at the printers.

Scrolling through the list of numbers in her phone, she rang them and was relieved when the call was picked up within three rings.

'Hi, it's Libby from Starcross Manor. I'm not quite sure how to say this but there's been an issue with those invitations I ordered that were sent out for the wedding on Christmas Eve. Everyone has turned up today instead. There's nothing that can be done about the mix-up now, but would it be possible to check the original email I pinged across with the order, please?'

At the end of the phone the assistant went quiet for a moment and Libby could hear the tapping of the keys on a computer. 'I'm sorry to tell you, there's no mistake at our end. The details in the email clearly state today's date. I can send the original email back to you so you can see?'

Libby thanked the assistant and waited for the email to land. After ordering another batch to go out for the correct day and time she hung up the phone, utterly perplexed. The email landed and there it was, in black and white, today's date and time. She watched the hordes of unhappy guests trailing back through the reception, their loud, disgruntled mutterings making it clear that this was unacceptable and they wanted compensation for the time they'd had to take off work. Libby knew that Flynn wasn't going to be happy when she confessed that it must have somehow been her mistake, though she didn't have any idea how.

'What's going on? Flynn has a riot on his hands out there.' Guy was suddenly standing at the side of her chair.

'You aren't going to believe this. All these people have turned up for Miranda and David's wedding.'

'They're a bit early,' said Guy. 'How has that happened?'

'It seems it's somehow my mistake. I input the wrong date on the invitations and, hey presto, here they are.'

'Surely not?'

'I don't know how it happened, because I definitely double-checked the details.'

'Flynn doesn't look happy,' observed Guy.

'Who can blame him?'

'Hopefully this will help a little … maybe.' Guy held up a pink frosted cupcake with the initial L on the top. 'From Holly and she—well, we—would like to know if you would like to come for tea?'

'I'd love to,' she answered before she could stop herself.

'Holly is making a very special tea, she said, for her new friend.'

Now Libby felt guilty; it wasn't just Guy's feelings she could be hurting, it was Holly's too. 'Guy, we need to talk.'

'Of course. Are you okay?' he replied just as a harassed Flynn headed towards them.

'Unbelievable, half the guests want some sort of compensation! As soon as one piped up, then the next and the next joined in. I can't believe the printers got this so wrong.'

Libby scrunched up her face. 'I don't know how—and that's not an excuse—but it appears it was my mistake. I sent the wrong date when we ordered the invites. I'm sorry, Flynn.' Yet even as the words left her mouth, she didn't believe it *was* her mistake.

Flynn exhaled. 'There's nothing we can do about it now. It was just a genuine mistake.'

'I've asked the printers to send out the invitations for the correct day and time. I hope that's okay.'

'It'll have to be. This wedding is becoming a headache and very costly.'

Libby apologised again. It was all she could do.

'Don't worry. Just put it down to experience and move on. Oh and before I forget, your house is well and truly packed up and emptied. I've put the stuff into storage except some of your personal stuff, which is ready for the move to New York.'

Libby's heart began to race. She immediately felt Guy's eyes fixed on her.

'What's this about New York? Holiday?' he asked.

'Libby's landed a great job and a fantastic apartment. We'll miss her when she leaves after Christmas, but what an adventure!' chipped in Flynn. 'I need to get back to my office. I've still got my morning calls to make.'

Libby's heart raced and she briefly closed her eyes. Damn. Why had Flynn dropped that into the conversation *now*? This was not how she wanted Guy to find out.

'Were you even going to tell me you're leaving for New York?'

'I was going to tell you.'

'What, after you'd left?'

'No, honestly, I was. Only this morning I had breakfast with Isla and we had a good chat about everything. I was going to tell you today.'

'You've been discussing me with Isla?' Guy looked betrayed. 'I told you everything in confidence. I don't believe this.'

'Guy, no. You've got this wrong. I'd never discuss your personal life, please don't think that.' Libby felt her pulse racing for all the wrong reasons. 'It was just that I was going away and confused…'

But Guy didn't hear. He was too busy shaking his head in disbelief and walking away.

Tears of frustration brimmed her eyes as the door swung shut behind him. All she wanted to do was put it right. Holding the pink frosted cupcake, Libby followed him.

Chapter Sixteen

S potting Guy walking down the driveway of Starcross Manor, Libby shouted after him, 'Guy, please wait.'

He was heading out of the main gates and Libby did her best to catch him up but as she'd thought she was only going to the hotel for breakfast, she was wearing entirely the wrong footwear. Her feet slid from underneath her on the icy path, and with a squeal she landed on her backside, the cupcake flying into the air.

'Damn,' she muttered, feeling a throbbing pain as she held her wrist.

'Are you okay?' Guy was soon at her side. 'Two-second rule,' he said, rescuing the cupcake. 'You can still eat it.'

'Do I look okay?' replied Libby, ignoring the remark about the cupcake. 'I would be if you weren't tearing off like a ridiculous toddler having a tantrum. My wrist hurts.'

'These icy paths can be lethal.' Linking his arm through hers, he pulled Libby to her feet. 'You've not got the right shoes on for this weather.' He pointed to her footwear.

'You don't say,' she replied sarcastically, slipping on the ice again.

Guy steadied her. 'Let's get you back to your lodge and you can see how your wrist feels. Maybe get some ice on it. There's enough of it around.' Guy did his very best to lighten the mood.

'You're not funny and I don't feel like laughing. You walked off without letting me explain.'

'I know. I'm sorry. But in my defence, hearing those words came as a shock and I didn't like it.' With his arm still linked through hers, they began to navigate the icy path back to the lodge.

'For what it's worth, I didn't like you hearing it either.'

It wasn't long before they were standing at the door of Libby's lodge. 'Do you want to come in?' she asked.

'If it's okay with you.'

Unlocking the door and opening it wide, Guy stepped inside. 'How's the wrist feeling?'

'Just a little sore but I'm sure it's nothing worse than a bruise.' She gestured to Guy to sit down. The atmosphere felt very different from when she'd woken up in the early hours of the morning wrapped in his arms. 'I'll put the kettle on.'

Soon they were sitting next to each on the settee.

'I honestly don't know what to say because I really don't know where to start.' She paused. 'Last night you opened up to me and I didn't mean to keep my stuff from you.'

'And your stuff is?' he prompted.

'As Flynn mentioned, I've been offered my dream job in New York with the chance for my designs to be walking down the Fashion Week catwalk. It's what I've worked towards for the past ten years and now … the thing is … I'm confused.'

'About?'

'Going,' she replied. She paused, finding this difficult to talk about but knowing she owed Guy the truth. 'It's my turn to be honest with you.' She looked Guy straight in the eyes. 'Many years ago I was engaged and planning my dream wedding. I thought my life was mapped out, just like you did, and then also like you, things changed for me. The wedding was off and the man who I thought was my soulmate left me and made me feel I was worthless as a woman.' Libby heard her voice crack. 'I threw myself into my business as I picked up the pieces and I vowed never to let anyone else hurt me like that ever again. My business went from strength to strength; my designs were being worn by celebrities and new commissions were coming in thick and fast. I applied for the job in New York knowing there would be a mass of applicants and I can't describe the feeling when I was first invited for an interview and then, a couple of weeks later, received the job offer. It was one of the best moments in my life. It came with an apartment for a year. And finally I was going to see humans every day rather than be locked up in my spare room alone. Don't get me wrong, the safety of my home has helped me heal, helped me to build up the strength to believe in myself and know my own worth as a woman, but it came at a cost and I was thrilled to think I'd soon be surrounded by people once again.'

Guy reached across and took her hand. 'You're a beautiful woman and a gorgeous human being and don't ever let anyone tell you different.' He hesitated. 'Was it infidelity?'

Libby shook her head. 'Not to my knowledge. Anyway, Flynn's wedding planner let him down, and I agreed to come to Heartcross, plan the wedding for him and spend Christmas with my family before I jetted off to my brand-new life. I was looking forward to it all but something has changed. That's the reason I had breakfast with Isla: I wanted to talk over how I was feeling.'

'And how are you feeling?' Guy asked tentatively.

'Confused, scared, unsure if I'm doing the right thing. I'm going to be miles from my family. My dad is back from his cruise on Christmas Eve and, like I said to Isla, he's not getting any younger. Do I really want to be that far from everyone I love so much? I don't know.'

'But you said it was your dream job?'

'I know but since arriving here I've felt so settled, in a way I never expected. I have my family close by and I've stumbled across you.' There, she'd said it now. 'I know this is early days but it's been a long time since I've felt these kinds of feelings. I like spending time with you and Holly. When she said I could be her best friend, all I kept thinking about was the fact that I'd be leaving soon and I might let her down. I wouldn't want to upset anyone.'

'Holly would understand. And just because you move to the other side of the world it doesn't mean she can't speak to you.' Guy sipped his tea. 'I admit I was shocked when Flynn said the words "New York", and rather annoyed, if I'm honest with you. I admitted to you that it feels like people leave me— and here we are about to go again. I didn't think I'd have these feelings again either, but it's just so easy and enjoyable being around you. Your offer to come to the wedding with me was the nicest thing anyone has offered to do for me in a long time. I know I need to put Holly first...'

'But you have to look after you, too. Your mental health is important as you have to be able to function to be the best version of yourself and get through this difficult time. If attending the wedding is going to set you back then don't do it. You know what you can deal with and what you can't.'

'You're the first person who has understood this. Thank you.'

Guy opened his arms and Libby hugged him tight. 'I didn't mean to keep anything from you,' she murmured. 'I just don't know what to do.'

'You have to follow your heart. I know I'm feeling what I'm feeling, but I'd never stop you going after your dream. You've worked so hard for your career. There will be a way for everything to work out.'

'Your kindness is overwhelming.' Libby swallowed. It was time. She needed to share the reason why her last relationship had ended. 'And I could never stop you going for your dream too and that's why—even though I think you've got the same feelings as me, that this could be the start of something new— it just can't be. You will always need more than I can give you.'

Guy pulled away slowly. 'What do you mean? I don't understand.'

Libby swallowed a lump. She knew her emotions would wash over her any second, even as she tried her best to keep her composure. 'Your situation is tough and you're always going to be reminded of it because there's never going to be any getting away from it, but I think once you meet someone and you have them by your side, championing you, it will get easier.'

'But you don't think you're that person?'

'You made it clear that in the future you wanted as many children as possible, a football team, in fact—'

'I may have run away with myself a little bit there,' he interrupted.

'But if that's what you want then you should have the chance to meet someone that can give you that. I can't. Guy, the reason I have chosen to be on my own since my fiancé left me was because of the reason he left me. It has taken a long time to come to terms with the fact...' She hesitated and Guy placed a supportive hand on her knee.

'He left because I went through early menopause. Guy, I can't have children,' she said, laying all of her cards on the table.

It was out in the open now and Libby couldn't hold on to her emotions anymore. A tsunami of tears began to roll down her cheeks. Guy had made such an impact on her life in such a short time and she'd just risked it all by being honest, but there was no other way.

'Oh Lib,' Guy said, holding her tight as she sobbed.

Chapter Seventeen

Libby had a very full day ahead. She was meeting with Miranda to fit her dress and finalise the cake design; David and his best man had their final suit fitting at the tailors in Glensheil and Libby had spent the last hour sourcing black chair covers and tablecloths for the wedding day.

Overnight there had been fresh snowfall and thankfully Drew had delivered a pile of logs to the lodges to keep the fires burning. Now sitting in front of the roaring log burner with a tray balanced on her knees, she tucked into her breakfast of scrambled eggs on buttery granary toast.

The past few days had been extremely busy and Libby had spent most of her free time with Guy. They were getting closer by the second. He'd been everything that she'd imagined he would be and his warm heart had blown her away. Libby felt that sharing her past had lifted a huge weight from her shoulders. There were no secrets between them now.

Placing the tray on the table, she finished her morning coffee. She had a couple of hours before she needed to be in the studio to meet Miranda, which would give her plenty of time to finish Julia's wedding outfit. Hearing the crunch of snow on the path outside, she swung her gaze towards the window and saw Guy walking to her front door. She jumped up to answer his knock.

'You're early. We have another two hours before we meet the bride.' Libby leaned forward and kissed him on his lips but then noticed the serious look on Guy's face. 'What's up? What's happened?' She opened the door wide and Guy stepped inside. He handed her the newspaper.

'I think you should see this. Have a look at page four and be warned, you might not like it.'

Walking into the living room, Libby took the newspaper from him and sat down on the settee. She read the headline.

Starcross Manor's Wedding Planner makes a huge blunder.

'Blooming heck. Flynn is going to lose his mind,' Libby exclaimed.

'The first line is brutal.'

Libby read out loud, 'After staff walked out of Starcross Manor leaving Flynn Carter floundering to organise the wedding of competition winners Miranda Jones and David Mellor, he roped in his sister whose blunder has cost Starcross Manor a small fortune after wedding guests were issued invitations with the wrong day listed.' Her jaw seemed to have fallen past her knees. 'Oh my God. This is terrible.'

'Isn't it just. I take it Flynn hasn't seen it yet?'

Libby picked up her phone. 'It appears not. I have no messages or missed calls.'

They both stared at the newspaper article, which was now

lying on the table. 'I suppose with over a hundred guests turning up, one of them has thought it was newsworthy,' added Guy.

'It certainly looks that way but...' Libby tapped the article. 'It says here that ex-wedding planner Jenny Hughes has commented: "This is a huge blunder for Starcross Manor and future brides and grooms will question whether they have full trust in the wedding service they offer." Why would Jenny say something like that? All Flynn has ever done is sing her praises. This feels like a right stab in the back.'

'I agree with you.'

Libby checked her watch. 'What are you doing now?'

'Nothing, I'm just hanging around until we have to film the fitting of Miranda's wedding dress.'

'Do you fancy a walk into town? We could grab a coffee and catch the boat back.'

'Sounds like the perfect plan.'

Libby closed down her laptop and zipped up her coat. 'A brisk walk will do us good. I'll ring Flynn on the way out to warn him about the article.'

Walking down the path, Libby tried Flynn three times but there was no answer. She left him a voicemail and hoped he'd pick it up before he heard about the article from anyone else.

'He really isn't going to be happy,' she said, sliding her phone back in her bag.

'There's nothing you can do about it now,' Guy reassured her.

'It just seems so unfair. Yes, a mistake was made, but we're all human. I just feel like I've let Flynn down. He asked me to help and now look.' Guy slipped his hand into hers and gave it a squeeze. 'Something isn't sitting right with me. I'd still swear the information on the invites was correct.'

As they walked over Heartcross Bridge into the town, Guy slowed down and looked out across the water. 'Look at that view. I can already picture Holly enjoying the summer, learning how to kayak, taking picnics by the river and hikes up the mountain. This is going to be a good place to live.'

'It is a beautiful place.'

'Holly and I had a good talk. She loves it here and I think it's the perfect place to bring her up. She wants to go to school and it's a chat I'm going to have to have with her mum.'

'How do you think that will go down?' Libby asked tentatively.

'Sophie and Lydia tend to do what they want, when they want, without any regard for Holly, and she needs stability. If she agrees, I want Holly to live with me, here. They want to go travelling and I think it'll do me the world of good if they do. Everyone needs a breather. I'm prepared to take projects that I can work on from home, so that I can pick Holly up from school.'

'It sounds like you have it all worked out.'

'I have, if everyone agrees.'

'I've got everything crossed for you,' said Libby, feeling a tiny bit envious.

They carried on walking. 'I'll miss you when you leave, you know.'

'Me too,' replied Libby, knowing that every day her move to New York was getting closer.

'Timing is not in our favour, is it?'

'I don't even want to think about it. I just want to spend as much time with you as possible. However difficult it is, we can work it out as we go along.' He bowed his head and pressed a soft kiss to her lips.

Libby wanted the dream job, but her feelings for Guy were growing stronger by the second. She didn't want to give him up.

Hearing his phone ring, Guy looked at the screen and promptly answered the call. By the look on his face and the way he was intently listening and nodding his head, Libby knew it was something important. Then he beamed widely. 'That's brilliant, thanks so much!' He hung up the call. 'I can't quite believe it.'

'Good news?' probed Libby.

'The best news!' He picked Libby up off the ground and spun her round.

She laughed. 'Come on, tell me. Don't leave me in suspense.'

'I put in an offer on Weathervane Cottage and it's been accepted. I'm getting my fresh start!'

'Guy! That is brilliant news! Your luck is changing. I can feel it. I'm so happy for you. Living in Heartcross is living the dream.'

She knew as soon as the words left her mouth that she meant every single one. Being in Heartcross *was* living the dream. It was the perfect place to live: the community and the village had everything anyone needed and the views were to die for.

'Wait until I tell Holly; she'll be so excited.'

'A new home to decorate how you please,' she added.

'I know and we'll be able to send you updates as we go along. The whole cottage needs a little tender loving care and I can't wait to see it become a happy home.'

'That would be lovely. I can't wait to see the transformation.' Libby was genuinely pleased. This was just the fresh start he needed and it would give him something to focus on.

The traffic through the town was quieter than usual, probably due to the weather, but Libby noticed a bus on the high street slowing down at the traffic lights. They stopped to cross the road and Libby glanced up to the top deck. Jenny looked out of the window.

'There's Jenny,' Libby exclaimed. 'She's on the bus.' She took hold of Guy's hand and dragged him after the bus.

'What are you doing?'

'The next stop is the care home.'

'And?'

'I don't know. I'm going to see if there's an opportunity to have a chat. Introduce myself. Maybe ask her why she said those things about Starcross Manor.'

'Are you sure that's the right thing to do?' Guy asked.

'No, but I'm going to do it anyway.'

'What do you want me do?'

Libby thought about it for a second. 'It might be better if I'm on my own. There's a coffee shop down that side street. I'll meet you in there.'

'Okay,' he agreed, kissing her on the cheek as the bus pulled up at the stop outside the care home.

Libby wasn't sure what she was going to do or say. She watched Jenny step off the bus and begin to walk towards the entrance of the care home.

Deciding what to do next was taken out of Libby's hands. Just as she was about to call out, Jenny's phone rang and she answered the call. Libby perched on the same stone wall as last time and watched.

Jenny was upbeat as she answered the call but her mood deteriorated fast. She stood on the edge of the pavement and looked up the road. Libby followed her gaze. The same car she'd seen Jenny with a couple of times before pulled up at Jenny's side—and David stepped out. Libby couldn't believe her eyes. Jenny looked alarmed and there was a heated exchange before David grabbed hold of her wrist, which she promptly shook free. Her voice was raised as she said, 'You promised me the money. My mum's fees need paying. You promised.'

David shushed her and leaned in. Libby couldn't hear what he was saying but Jenny was visibly upset. A moment later David got back in the car and sped off, leaving Jenny evidently changing her mind about heading into the care home. She was now briskly walking down the street in the opposite direction. What the hell had just happened here? How did David know Jenny? Whatever was going on between them didn't look pleasant. Libby took her chance and rang Flynn.

'I think there's something suspicious going on,' she said as soon as Flynn picked up his mobile.

'I know! I've just seen the newspaper. I'm fuming.'

'Never mind that for now. Flynn, I've just seen something that may be of interest.'

'Go on.'

'David Mellor and Jenny. Together. Having some sort of argument in the street and it was possibly about money.'

There was a short silence on the other end of the phone.

'I don't think it's a coincidence,' added Libby. 'There's something not quite right here.'

'I agree. The application forms are missing; the rumours regarding the skating were exaggerated and now there's this article in the newspaper.'

'I heard Jenny say that David promised her money and that her mum's fees need paying. Why would David be paying the fees? What's the connection between them? Are they related, do you think?'

'I don't know but I think I'm going to pay her a visit. Do you fancy coming with me?'

'Can do, but…' A thought suddenly struck Libby. 'I need to check something out first before Miranda turns up for her dress fitting. Let's go this afternoon.'

Libby hung up and hurried towards the coffee shop, where she found Guy had ordered a couple of pastries and coffees. 'We need to get these for takeaway.' Libby waved towards the assistant.

Guy glanced up. 'Where's the fire?'

'I've just had a thought and we've not got long to check it out.'

Thanking the assistant, who passed Libby a coffee and a cinnamon swirl inside a white paper bag, Guy followed Libby out of the coffee shop.

'What's going on?' he asked, trying to keep up.

'I've just witnessed David and Jenny arguing in the street over money and I'm now convinced those invitations were tampered with. Those guests were invited on the wrong day to put Starcross Manor in a bad light, for some reason.'

'But for what reason?' quizzed Guy.

'That I'm not sure of yet.'

'And how are we going to know whether the invitations were or weren't tampered with?'

'Because you were filming in the studio when I sent the email to the printers. You may have captured something on the video that can help us check!'

Fifteen minutes later, they arrived back at Guy's lodge and he pulled up two chairs in front of the monitor. He selected the right video footage and hooked it up to the TV.

'Here we go, the moment of truth,' said Guy, pressing play on the remote control and sitting back with his arms folded.

They watched as Libby selected the invitations on the screen, which Miranda approved, and then Libby typed in the details. 'Is it possible to zoom in to see the information I'm typing on the invitation?'

Guy pressed a couple of buttons and the image on the screen enlarged. Libby gave a tiny gasp. 'See, it's there in black and white. I've entered the correct details.'

'You have indeed,' confirmed Guy, sitting up straighter, still watching the video closely as he zoomed back out. 'So how did it get changed?'

With their eyes fixed firmly at the screen, they watched Libby stand up and excuse herself before she headed to the bathroom. 'But you're still there,' murmured Libby.

'No, I was outside for this. I got a phone call and headed out just before you did,' Guy said, taking a sideward glance towards Libby. 'This could be interesting.'

'Oh my God. Look!' Libby grabbed on to Guy's arm as they watched Miranda take a quick look towards the doors before typing on the keyboard. 'She's actually changing the date and the time. We have got to show this to Flynn. He isn't going to like it but I'm still confused about why she would do that.'

'Flynn can show Miranda the video while he's asking her that very question. I'd think that this violates the competition agreement as it's clear evidence that the bride was attempting to sabotage things. He would be able to cancel the wedding. Look, there's more. Miranda is making a call.'

Guy turned the volume up.

'David, it's me, I've managed to change the date and time. It's done.' Miranda gave a cackle like a pantomime villain then hung up the phone. She then sat back in her chair with a look on her face like butter wouldn't melt. She never even flinched when Libby walked back into the room and asked if it all looked okay. 'I can't believe I didn't check it over once more before pressing send.'

'Flynn's gut feeling was right, but why would they want to sabotage their own wedding and/or attempt to ruin Starcross Manor's reputation?' Guy asked. 'What are they gaining from it?'

'That's what we need to find out.' Libby was thinking fast. 'We know that David knows Jenny, so what's the connection between them and does it have something to do with why Jenny resigned?'

'And we still need to find out what happened with the application form.'

'I'm going to ask Miranda to bring in identification and a copy of their application form when she comes for her dress fitting appointment today.'

'And if she asks why?' probed Guy.

'Because they've won a major competition worth thousands

of pounds and we need to verify they are who they say they are.'

'Good thinking, then we can do a little snooping.'

'We?' Libby questioned.

'Oh, I'm completely invested in uncovering what these two are up to,' Guy confirmed.

'I'm going with Flynn to see Jenny this afternoon after Miranda has been for her dress fitting.'

'Looks like we may both have an afternoon of it after the fitting...' Guy rolled his eyes and exhaled. 'Sophie rang while I was in the coffee shop. We've arranged to meet this afternoon to discuss Holly's future living arrangements and schooling. I have to say I'm not looking forward to it.'

Libby could see that Guy was worried. 'I've got a good feeling about it,' she said encouragingly. 'Just stay positive.'

'I'm glad I have you on my side.'

'You better believe it,' she replied, leaning in for a kiss like it was the most natural thing in the world.

Chapter Eighteen

S itting waiting for Miranda to arrive, Libby knew she needed to keep what they had discovered under wraps. As discussed with Guy, Libby had rung ahead of today's appointment and asked her to bring in identification and a copy of the application form. Miranda was on time and breezed in through the door.

'Good morning,' chirped Libby, making sure she sounded as bright as possible to avoid arousing any suspicion. 'How are you? I'm looking forward to the fitting. We just need to confirm the measurements before I sew it all together.' Libby gestured towards the dress that was pinned together on the mannequin.

Miranda gasped. 'It's beautiful and the quality of the material... It hangs so elegantly.'

'Doesn't it?' replied Libby. 'Before we get started, have you got your identification with you and a copy of the application form?'

Miranda reached in her bag. 'Passports and driver's

licence.' She handed them over. 'But I'm sorry we don't have a copy of the form.'

'Oh, that's okay then. I'll just get a quick photocopy of each of these and then we can make a start. Help yourself to tea and coffee.'

Five minutes later, with the photocopies stored safely in a drawer, Libby carefully took Miranda's final measurements, knowing full well that as soon as Flynn set eyes on the video of Miranda tampering with the invitations, he would put a stop to this wedding. But in the meantime, Libby had to continue being as professional as possible.

After adjusting the dress on the mannequin Libby turned towards Miranda. 'Now, if you could carefully try it on so I can confirm a few final touches, then I can begin sewing it all together.'

As soon as the curtain was shut behind her, Libby took the photocopies out of the drawer, quickly snapped a photo of each and pinged them over to Flynn along with a text.

There is some interesting footage you need to see.

Once the door was firmly closed behind Miranda, Libby looked over at Guy.

'What do you make of that? I really wanted to say something.'

'It was bizarre. I keep wondering if we imagined that footage of her changing the date. And the weirdest thing is that she's never referred to the mix-up with the date. If hundreds of your friends turned up for a wedding on the wrong day, surely you would be questioning what the hell had happened?'

'Yeah, you're absolutely right.'

'Here's Flynn now,' he said, looking out the window from where he stood wrapping up the camera equipment.

The door opened, and Flynn waved his phone in the air. 'Two upcoming weddings booked for the end of spring have cancelled their bookings.'

'Why?' asked Libby.

'I'm assuming because they have got wind of the article and social media posts. But it gets a lot worse—'

'It does,' cut in Libby.

Flynn raised his eyebrows. 'What do you know?'

'We have video evidence that Miranda tampered with the invites before they were sent to the printers. She was the reason her own guests turned up on the wrong day.'

Flynn's eyes widened. 'This is starting to make sense now. Look at this.' He walked over to the computer and began typing in the search engine. Libby and Guy stood behind him, waiting for the page to load. 'Aidy Redfern, the local reporter, contacted me as he thought I should take a look at something. He got wind of an old renovated barn in the area that is being converted into a wedding venue. Apparently, it's due to open next spring and he sent me a link to the website. See?'

'The Glensheil Wedding Barn. The number one wedding venue in the Scottish Highlands…' Libby read out. 'Where is this place? I've never heard of it.'

'It's on the other side of the river, at the edge of town. It backs onto the rural lane with the mountainous terrain behind. It's a stunning area and the land was bought around a year ago. I was under the impression that it had possibly been purchased to develop a couple of houses but no, they've turned it to an olde worlde wedding venue.'

'I know you don't want to hear this but it looks beautiful,' remarked Libby.

'I agree the photos are stunning, but look at these, showing the sunny, mountainous terrain and the lush green grass.'

'Gorgeous,' replied Libby.

'Take a closer look.' Flynn tapped the screen. 'That isn't a view from the Glensheil Wedding Barn. For one thing, when these photographs were taken it would have still been a building site.'

'I recognise that view,' Guy suddenly exclaimed. 'It's from the back of Starcross Manor! It's the view over the deer park and the walled flower garden.'

'Exactly,' Flynn confirmed.

'Bloody hell, isn't that what you call false advertising?' Libby asked.

'It gets better.' He clicked on the menu at the top of the web page. 'Wait until you see this.' Flynn clicked again on the 'About Us' tab. 'Meet the team.'

Libby gave a tiny gasp. Staring back at them were the faces of two very familiar people: Miranda and David.

'No way!' Libby exclaimed.

'Yes way. They are not only the management team, but also the owners.'

'I don't get it. Why are they getting married at Starcross Manor when they've got their own venue?' asked Libby.

'I'm assuming because they want to discover how it works here and sabotage my business at the same time, or perhaps they're hoping to steal my contacts and undercut my contracts with suppliers, so that they have exclusivity and become the number one venue in the area.'

Guy raised an eyebrow. 'The sly dogs. That would explain changing the invites and feeding the story to the newspaper.'

'Exactly. And I suspect it's no coincidence that their application form went missing because I don't think they ever even entered the competition. Based on what you've seen, Lib, I think they got to Jenny. There's only one way to find out. We're going to pay her a visit.'

'I'll get my coat,' Libby replied, grabbing it from the coat stand.

Flynn looked over at the black wedding dress on the mannequin. 'Is this Miranda's dress?'

Libby nodded.

'You can stop working on it. Their contract is void and there will be no wedding. Starcross Manor and its team had nothing to do with anything that went wrong. We have the evidence that Miranda and David are competitors and that Miranda tampered with invites. My guess is they started the rumours about the skating incident. In fact, I'm going to call a meeting with Aidy. He can write an article exposing their scheme using the video evidence. They aren't getting away with this.'

Libby agreed. 'Good idea. Give them a taste of their own medicine.'

'In the meantime, let's go and pay Jenny a visit and see what she has to say.' Flynn was clearly rattled by the discovery of the new wedding barn and Miranda and David's deception.

'I'm ready. Looks like we're going to be in for an interesting afternoon,' Libby said before turning towards Guy and taking his hands in hers. 'And I hope all goes well with you this afternoon. I'll be thinking of you. Let's catch up later?'

'Sounds good to me,' Guy answered, leaning in and kissing her on the lips.

Taken by surprise, Flynn cocked an eyebrow and pointed at the pair. 'What am I missing here? Is something going on between you?' His face broke into a smile. 'There is, isn't there?'

'Never mind us, I'll fill you in later,' Libby replied, gently shoving Flynn towards the door.

'Just when I think nothing else can surprise me,' Flynn marvelled, still with an astonished look on his face as he stepped outside.

Libby gave Guy a warm smile over her shoulder. 'See you later,' she mouthed.

Chapter Nineteen

Climbing into Flynn's car, which was parked outside the main entrance of Starcross Manor, they set off towards the High Street, Flynn repeatedly taking sideward glances at Libby and smiling.

'Do you know how you can sense that someone wants to say something? Come on, out with it!' Libby playfully rolled her eyes.

'Damn right I want to say something! You've kept that quiet.' Flynn indicated left and the car bounced across the track before reaching the bridge that led them into the town. 'What's going on?'

'We just kind of fell into each other… I don't know what it means or even what is happening between us. It's a tricky one. I'm meant to be leaving soon…'

'Meant?' questioned Flynn straightaway.

'Figure of speech. My plan is still to go. It's been something I've been working towards for a long time.'

'It is and it's something you truly deserve after everything you've been through and all your hard work.'

'But I was never meant to start falling for someone; that wasn't part of the plan. It's still early days but it's just so easy. It feels so right when I'm in his company.'

'That's how it should be. What does he think about you going away?'

'That I have to do what I want to do, chase my dreams, live my best life…'

'There will be a way to make it work if it's meant to be.'

'I'm having a chat about it with Dad tonight when the cruise ship docks. I'm hoping with all his wisdom he has a suggestion for how I could make this work. I just keep hoping there's a way to have both the job and the … Guy.' They both laughed. 'But Guy has Holly. It's not as though he can just take a few months off work and come and stay with me in New York. He's also got a number of things going on in his life at the moment. At least one of them is good though: he's made an offer on Weathervane Cottage and it's been accepted.'

'No way, that's a fantastic cottage! Needs a bit of work but it's in a great location and that view of the mountain is superb. He never mentioned he was thinking of staying here permanently. That is brilliant.'

'It is…' Libby paused. 'Do you know when you get a good feeling about someone but the timing isn't quite right?'

'I do. I really feel for you as it's not an easy situation you're in. Julia is my life and if she were to move to the other side of the world then I'd follow her. But then, I don't have a daughter with someone else and all the responsibilities that come with that.'

'You can't even coordinate your diaries to get married,' Libby said with a laugh.

'I can and I will. I'm making it my priority. Having you here has given me food for thought. Work and making money used to be the most important things in the world to me, but when you find your special person, that all changes. We've not been able to coordinate our diaries because of workloads but we should have been putting us first. So that's what I'm going to be doing.'

'You two are just adorable together. Do you think you'll wait long to start a family after marriage?' asked Libby. Knowing her brother would be conscious of not wanting to hurt her feelings, she added, 'I hope not. I can't wait to be an auntie.'

'You'll make the best auntie. How do you feel about Guy having a child?'

Libby had already thought about this and didn't hesitate. 'I think they come as a beautiful package, but he's mentioned he wants more children and that's not something I can give him. Is it a non-starter before it's even got going?'

Flynn instantly began to shake his head. 'I think you have to take every step as it comes. I love Julia and it would be wonderful if we had children but if it doesn't happen or can't happen, Julia will always be enough for me. You get through it. Together. Don't put too much pressure on yourself. It's still early days for you and Guy. Enjoy the moments as they happen and let it develop naturally.'

Libby knew that Flynn was right … but every day that passed was a day closer to getting on that plane and potentially leaving Guy and Holly behind.

'I'll do my best,' she replied.

'Good,' he said, navigating into a side road and pulling the car to a stop. 'We're here.'

He looked at the row of terraced houses before them. The pavement was littered with bin bags and beer cans. 'Are you sure Jenny lives here?' Libby asked, looking up and down the street.

Flynn nodded and pointed. 'It's that red door there. I think this house has been turned into flats.' There was an intercom at the side of the door with the flat numbers.

'If we press that she'll know it's us and may not let us in to talk.'

'What do you suggest then?' Flynn asked. 'How are we going to get in?'

'I think we just got lucky.' Libby gave Flynn an encouraging look and nodded towards a young woman pushing a pram, battling to open the door from the inside. Libby was quick on her feet. 'Let me help you,' she said, holding the door open for the woman, who thanked her before carrying on up the pavement.

Flynn and Libby sneaked inside and the door shut behind them. There were two flats on the ground floor and more upstairs. The entryway was dark with no natural light flooding into the tiny space. They could hear a TV blaring from somewhere and heavy metal thumping from the flat to their left.

'Did you know she lived in a place like this?' asked Libby, thankful that Flynn was with her.

He shook his head as they turned to the door on the right. 'It's this one.'

Libby put her ear to the door and narrowed her eyes. She

concentrated for a moment and whispered. 'I'm sure I can hear someone in there.'

Flynn knocked but there was only deadly silence.

'What do we do now?' Libby mouthed.

Flynn shrugged then gestured for Libby to stay where she was. He opened the front door and immediately shut it again with a bang. A couple of seconds later they heard the slide of a chain and a key turning slowly in a lock. A frightened-looking Jenny peeped around the edge of the door.

'It's okay. It's me, Flynn, your old boss, and this is my sister, Libby. We've just come to come to check if you're okay.' Flynn's voice was warm.

'I don't want to speak to anyone,' she said, about to close the door.

'No, please wait,' said Libby. 'We just want to make sure everything is okay because we know how much you loved your job and yet you suddenly resigned.'

Jenny gaze strayed to the ground. She was tearful and her hand trembled a little as she held on to the chain.

'Can we help in any way?' Libby kept her voice soft.

'I can't talk to you.' She looked towards the main entrance.

'I'm not quite sure what is going on here, but please let us help.'

Jenny met Libby's gaze. She looked exhausted.

'Let me be honest with you. We want to talk about the selection of the competition winners. We can't find any of the application forms.' Libby wanted to add that they knew Miranda and David were business rivals but she wanted Jenny to come forward on her own with any information she had.

'Do you know where they are and would you be able to tell us how you selected the winners for the competition? You aren't in trouble; we just want to understand what's going on. Please,' Flynn beseeched.

'I can't.'

'Come on, this is me you're talking to. You've worked for me for many years and I've always looked after my staff. I gave you time off to look after your mum when she fell ill and didn't have anyone else to look after her. All your line managers have said how loyal and hardworking you are and that they wouldn't hesitate to promote you and have you in their team. You were successful in landing the job as the wedding planner and you were so happy. What's changed?' asked Flynn.

'If there's any sort of problem, let us help to put it right.' Libby could see that Jenny looked like she wanted to talk but there was something holding her back.

Jenny closed the door and a second later they heard the chain sliding across and a click. The door opened wider and Jenny looked at them both. 'I've let you down, Flynn, and I'm sorry. I can't put it right.'

With the door open wide, Jenny stood to one side and gestured for them to come in. Flynn and Libby looked at each other before stepping inside. The room was small and open plan, with a small kitchen, tiny living room and bedroom merged into one. The decor, if it could be called that, was minimalist, but it was clean and tidy and the first thing Flynn noticed was Jenny's Starcross Manor uniform hanging on the side of the wardrobe.

Flynn and Libby sat down on the settee and Jenny perched on the edge of the chair. 'I'm sorry I can't offer you tea or coffee; I've run out of milk.'

'That's okay, don't worry about that,' replied Flynn. 'We're here because we're worried about you. Why do you think you've let me down?'

'Because I have and I've lost everything. The job I loved...'

'But you resigned. We just thought you'd been successful in another position, because your career was flying.'

Jenny looked hesitant.

'I'm going to be truthful with you, Jenny. We've discovered that the competition winners are business rivals. Did they ask you to rig the competition?'

The look of guilt was written all over Jenny's face but she remained silent.

Flynn continued. 'There are no application forms for any entries and we have evidence that they've been trying to sabotage my business. This is something I can't overlook.' His voice was now firm. 'I'm a fair man, but I need some answers and I've got no alternative but to go to the police and ask them to investigate what I already know.'

'Miranda and David approached me directly,' Jenny finally began. 'They offered me a lump sum to sway the competition in their favour.'

'Why would you do that?'

'I needed the money.'

Libby and Flynn looked at each other then back towards Jenny.

'I loved my job and working at Starcross Manor. I took pride in my work and in pushing myself to be the best I possibly could. But my personal life has been difficult. My mum's health had been deteriorating and I was struggling to look after her by myself. I was thrilled to have landed the promotion to become the new wedding planner at the manor and hoped the bump in salary would make things easier. The day after that, Miranda bumped into me on the water taxi on the way to work. She sat in the seat next to me and we got talking. She asked me what I did for a living, but looking back now, she already knew. It was all a set-up.'

Libby dared to take a sideward glance at Flynn, who was listening intently.

'For the next few weeks she was always on the boat. I even looked forward to seeing her. I liked her company, especially given the difficult time I was having with Mum, whose behaviour was becoming increasingly erratic. I'd enquired about putting her into a care home but I had no savings and the weekly cost was way out of my league.' She exhaled. 'Miranda told me she'd bought some land with her partner, David. They were in the events business, mainly horseracing and motor days. I didn't pay too much attention until she told me that the next business venture was a wedding venue on the other side of town. Then she dropped into the conversation that they wanted to talk to me about a job at the new wedding barn they were opening. I told her I was very happy where I was. Then, on the closing day of the competition, Miranda was yet again on my journey to work. I'd had a dreadful night with my mother and felt I really couldn't take much more, and when I confessed this to Miranda she came up with a plan. She said that if I swung the competition in her and David's favour, in return they would give me six months' worth of fees for the care home up front, and a job working at the new wedding barn when it opened. They said if I resigned as soon as the winners were announced then that would leave you in the lurch and give them a greater shot at making a success of their business. I'm so sorry.' Jenny wiped away her tears with the back of her hand. 'They wanted to sabotage their own wedding so they could spread rumours that would potentially ruin future business for Starcross Manor. I was blinded by greed and I feel so stupid. You and Julia have always looked out for me and I've done nothing but stab you in the back.'

Thinking of the conversation she'd overheard outside the care home, Libby asked, 'Did they pay you the money?'

Jenny shook her head. 'As soon as they were announced as the winners, the goal posts started changing. First, they said they would pay me after I helped to spread rumours of the skating incident. Then they said they would pay me after I planted the story of the invitation blunder in the paper.'

'Unbelievable,' replied Flynn. 'These two need the book thrown at them.'

'I telephoned David on a couple of occasions asking where my money was and when it didn't turn up, I threatened to expose them to you. That's when he began following me in his car and telling me I was up to my neck in it. I had to sell my car to pay the initial deposit to the care home as Mum had already moved in and it needed to be paid. I know now that there was never going to be a job at the new wedding barn. It had all been lies.'

'Did you sign any sort of contract with them?' Flynn asked. 'Something that specifies that they would pay you money and give you a job in exchange for them winning the competition?'

Jenny shook her head. 'We only had a verbal contract, but when the money still hadn't arrived I recorded a phone conversation with David and he laughed, telling me there was no money or job.'

Flynn's eyes widened. 'Would it be possible to listen to that conversation?'

Jenny reached on to the sideboard behind her and grabbed

her phone. 'Of course,' she said, pressing play on the recording.

What followed was a calm start to a conversation followed by an explosive argument, in which David degraded Jenny in every way possible: telling her she was stupid, there was no job or money, they had used her so they could sabotage the good reputation of Starcross Manor and become the number one wedding venue in the Scottish Highlands. She'd thrown the competition and that was her choice.

Libby was flabbergasted. 'I can't believe such awful people exist in this world.'

'I'm deeply sorry, Flynn. I really am.' Jenny was remorseful and tearful.

'Oh Jenny, you should have gone to Flynn and told him what was going on.'

'How could I? I made a bad choice and now I have to pay the consequences. I'm really sorry for letting you down.' Jenny looked towards Flynn.

'Can you send me that recording?' Flynn asked.

Jenny immediately handed over her phone and Flynn sent the recording to his phone before handing hers back.

'Can I just confirm that they didn't fill in any sort of application form for the competition?'

Jenny shook her head. 'No, they didn't.'

'Okay, this is what we are going to do,' Flynn stated. 'Firstly, you're going to come back to work at Starcross Manor and we are going to sort out the payment for your mum's care home.'

The look on Jenny's face made it clear she couldn't believe what she was hearing. 'Why would you do that for me? After everything I've done to you?' she stuttered.

'Because I don't like to see anyone being taken advantage of and you have been a member of my staff for a long time. I know how hard you work. You made a bad call, but it's obvious to me they targeted you and used you as part of their plan.'

Jenny became tearful. 'I don't know what to say, except that I don't deserve this.' Her voice quivered and her hands were shaking.

'The only thing I ask in return is loyalty and honesty. I appreciate things have got on top of you with a sick parent and then you trusted someone you shouldn't have, but everyone deserves a second chance.'

'And what are we going to do about Miranda and David?' asked Libby.

'Hang them out to dry and expose them for what they are.'

'Good,' replied Libby. 'That's exactly what they deserve.'

'Do you think they would have actually gone through with the wedding?' Flynn pondered.

'No,' confirmed Jenny. 'They were going to carry on and sabotage everything—the flowers, the cake, the dress—and then sell the story that due to the incompetence of the wedding venue they cancelled the wedding and decided to open their own wedding venue to give future brides and grooms the wedding they deserve.'

'The cheek of them both. I'll be pursuing legal action against them for slander and money lost,' Flynn said. 'We'll need your help with that, Jenny, if you're up for it?'

Jenny nodded. 'It's the least I can do.'

'Good. Now, try not to worry about anything.'

'I worry they'll come looking for me.' Jenny looked around the small open-plan flat. 'It's a little scary on my own.'

'Let's get you out of here then. Pack a bag; you're coming back to Starcross Manor with us. There will be a spare room in the staff quarters. You can settle back in and start work on Monday.'

'Are you serious?' Jenny questioned.

'Absolutely.'

'I can't thank you enough.' Jenny smiled through her tears. Without hesitation she took down a suitcase from the top of the wardrobe.

'We'll wait for you outside,' said Flynn, standing up.

Standing next to her brother on the pavement Libby gave him a look of admiration. He hadn't gone in with all guns blazing; he'd assessed the situation and tempered his response accordingly, acknowledging that even though Jenny had made a poor decision, he could see the reason why.

'Do you know how much I love you?' She bumped her shoulder against his. 'Everyone needs a Flynn in in their life. You're so kind and considerate, giving her a place to stay and her job back.'

'Anyone would have done the same thing.'

'They really wouldn't have. I have the best family.'

Thirty minutes later Jenny was unpacking her belongings in her room at Starcross Manor while Flynn and Libby headed to the bar to sit in front of the roaring fire sharing a bottle of wine, after Flynn had made a phone call to the police.

'That was a hell of an afternoon,' said Libby, taking a sip of her drink.

'And it looks like you and Guy are out of a job. At least you can relax a bit now before jet-setting to the other side of the world.'

Libby had had the same thought. She couldn't wait to spend more time with Guy and was determined to enjoy every moment of the run-up to Christmas. Her mind had also been ticking over as she thought about her own future. She'd had an idea that she wanted to run past her father before speaking to anyone else about it.

'It's a shame to let The Grand Hall go to waste. Maybe we could advertise for a Christmas Eve gala and put on a three-course meal with music? The hotel will be full of guests and we could invite all our friends. It would be the perfect get-together and a chance for you to see everyone before you leave,' suggested Flynn.

Suddenly, Libby stared at Flynn, the cogs turning in her mind.

'Are you okay? You look kind of weird.'

'Flynn!' Libby couldn't hide her enthusiasm. 'I've got the *best* suggestion.' She flung her arms towards The Grand Hall. 'We are not letting the date go to waste and I can still do my job.'

'What are you talking about?' He sat forward in his chair.

'You and Julia!' Libby couldn't get her words out fast enough. 'You can get married on Christmas Eve, a surprise winter wedding for Julia! I can coordinate everything because I know exactly the wedding she wants. I have her scrapbook of her dream wedding and if everything she's outlined is okay with you, I can make it all happen. You and Julia can get married on Christmas Eve with all your friends and family!' she said excitedly. 'What do you think? Please say yes?' Libby's heart had begun to race with anticipation.

'But what about Julia's dress? How would we organise that?'

'Believe me, Julia's outfit will not be a problem. All you have to do is organise your own kilt and turn up. I'll sort the rest. A winter wedding at Starcross Manor is Julia's dream. Please say yes!'

'Of course! Yes!' he exclaimed without hesitation, throwing his arms wide open for a hug.

'Yay!' Leaning over she hugged Flynn with all her might. 'This is going to be brilliant. And top secret. I'll organise a pamper morning for us with hair and make-up so we can keep her out of the way of preparations here. She's going to look stunning!'

Flynn was beaming. 'This is a brilliant idea.'

'I'll get Isla and Guy roped in and then we can get the villagers organised. Honestly, what better way to promote Starcross Manor as a top wedding venue than with its very own hotel mogul getting married here. The pictures and videos will be *amazing*!'

'Are you sure we're going to be able to pull this off?' Flynn queried. 'It's only a little over two weeks until Christmas.'

'You better believe it!' Libby chinked her glass against Flynn's.

'You better believe what?'

They both spun round to see Julia standing behind them.

'You better believe that this is going to be the best Christmas ever!' stated Flynn, standing up and lifting Julia off the ground before spinning her around.

Laughing, she asked, 'How much have you two had to drink? Put me down.'

With their secret still very much a secret, Flynn winked at

Libby as he placed Julia firmly back on the ground. 'Grab yourself a glass. Wait until we tell you about our afternoon. You aren't going to believe it.'

'I'm intrigued,' replied Julia, narrowing her eyes. 'I can't leave the pair of you alone for a minute, can I?'

As Julia grabbed a glass from behind the bar, Flynn whispered to Libby, 'She doesn't know the half of it. I can't believe I'm getting married in just a matter of weeks.'

'Me neither!' Libby whispered. 'This is going to be the best Christmas ever!'

Chapter Twenty

Walking back through the snow to the lodge, Libby wondered how Guy's afternoon had gone. She'd checked her phone several times throughout the day but there had been no word from him. If he didn't get in touch within the next hour, she was going to drop him a text. Arriving at her front door she found an envelope addressed to her. She tore it open to discover a note from Guy.

Meet me at the deer observation tower 7pm.

Allowing herself a discreet smile in case she was being watched, Libby let herself into her lodge. She glimpsed herself in the mirror. The crisp air had reddened her nose and enhanced the pink glow of her cheeks. She didn't know what Guy had planned but it wouldn't be long until she found out.

After a lovely soak in the bath, she frantically rummaged through her clothes, trying to find something to wear for the evening. She wasn't sure what to expect when she arrived at the deer observatory but knew that the dress code would be warm.

So, wearing her thermals and with an hour to go until she met Guy, she settled down on the settee with a cup of tea and willed her phone to ring. Right on cue, she saw her dad was FaceTiming her. Quickly picking up the phone she was greeted by his familiar cheery smile.

'Dad! It's great to see you!'

Wilbur was wearing his favourite straw hat and held up a cocktail. 'Cheers!'

'You're having the time of your life, aren't you?'

'Absolutely I am. You have to do what makes you happy and a cruise on the ocean waves with a cocktail in my hand is right where I want to be. Now, how are you? What is it you want to talk to me about?'

'Dad, I don't know where I want to be. I'm in a mess. I need your advice.'

Wilbur put up his hand out to flag down a passing waiter. 'Something tells me I might need another.' He smiled warmly at his daughter. 'Tell me all about it.'

An hour later, with a fizz of excitement, she grabbed a torch, locked the door and followed the snowy path towards the observation tower. Wilbur had given Libby the lift she'd needed and a scenario for her future, which she was keeping close to her chest for the time being. She couldn't wait to hear everything about Guy's afternoon. She was hoping his day hadn't been too traumatic and that they could relax together this evening.

Walking fast she discovered lanterns lighting the way through the woods. With a huge smile on her face, she approached the observation tower. She couldn't wait to see what Guy had planned. Fairy lights were wrapped around the wooden rail leading her up the gritted steps to the door. Opening it, she discovered two chairs either side of a table in the middle of the room, the red linen tablecloth topped with two wine glasses. Dozens of tealights were dotted over the floor. Guy was sitting on a chair in the corner. Her heart was beating nineteen to the dozen. He looked drop-dead gorgeous.

'Hello,' she said. 'What's all this?'

'Dinner,' he replied, standing up and kissing her on her cheek. 'Well, more of a picnic and a glass of wine.'

The air was charged between them.

'It looks lovely. Are we celebrating?' she asked, noticing a bottle of champagne.

'Maybe,' he said. 'It's been a very eventful day.'

'I'm not sure who is going to win in the most eventful day stakes.'

'I can't wait to hear all about it, but come and look at this first.' Guy took her hand and led her to the window. Feeling his presence so close, and the way he looked at her, gave Libby a jittery feeling in the pit of her stomach, and goosebumps all over.

'It's a very different view from daytime.'

Libby gave a tiny gasp as she looked out. The observation

tower delivered a spectacular unobstructed view of the village of Heartcross with the castle standing tall above it.

'It's the best night-time view of the town from up here.'

Houses in the distance had lights shining from their windows, cars snaked along the roads, and the lights of Starcross Manor twinkled brightly.

'Drink?' he asked, draping a warm blanket around her shoulders.

'Yes please, that would be lovely.'

With a gorgeous smile he popped the cork of the champagne bottle, poured and handed her a glass. 'Here's to new beginnings and a wonderful evening,' he said, clinking his glass against hers.

'New beginnings? Was today a successful day then? And look at all this.' Libby was impressed. On a nearby side table were salad, crusty bread and a variety of meats, cheeses and pickles.

'Tuck in,' said Guy.

'This looks amazing.'

'It's mainly from the farm shop up at Foxglove Farm. And you can't beat the bread from The Old Bakehouse.' They both began to load their plates. Guy pulled out a chair for Libby, and they both sat down, their legs touching under the table

Libby gave Guy an encouraging smile. 'So how was today?'

'Today it felt … different. I approached the situation with a new strength.'

'That sounds promising.'

'It was hard being in the same room as Sophie and Lydia. I can't believe I'm saying this but I could see they were happy together and the situation isn't going to change. I've got to focus on what's next for me and what's good for me.'

'Who is this Guy I see before me?' she gently teased.

'A new, improved version of myself,' he replied, the eye contact strong between them. 'The past is something we can't change but we can learn from it. Since meeting you I seem to be letting go a little more,' he admitted. 'It doesn't seem as raw, if that makes sense.'

'It does. Once you let yourself start living again and there's hope for the future, everything seems calmer.'

'You're right. I wasn't happy with life but this place makes me feel settled, like I'm meant to be here. Having had my offer accepted on the cottage, I finally feel I'm going to have a base, a place that is mine and a home for Holly.'

'Did you tell Sophie and Lydia about the cottage?'

Guy nodded. 'It all started off a little tense with small talk but as I was about to go in with my suggestion about Holly's future, they beat me to it.'

Libby wasn't sure from the look on Guy's face what was coming next.

'Lydia has had some health problems caused by the whole situation. I hadn't realised she'd been off work for six months because of the stress. She didn't even tell Mum and Dad until recently. The guilt of the situation has consumed her and she broke down.'

'How did you feel hearing that?'

Guy swallowed. 'It's hard to see anyone in that state, especially when it's your sister. It was heart-wrenching.' He paused. 'I've been hurting because of her actions and so has she. She looked tormented; she's lost lots of weight and she said she knew it would take a long time for us to get back to anything like normal, but she asked for forgiveness.'

'And can you forgive her?'

Guy remained silent.

'I know it's not easy but forgiveness can lead to healthier relationships, less anxiety for all of you, less stress and hostility … for Holly's sake,' Libby said tenderly. 'Even though I know it's extremely hard after all the betrayal.'

Guy smiled at her. 'It's a little easier when I have someone to talk to about it. That's what I like about you, you always have the right answers. I know it would make Mum and Dad's life easier if I at least try. I was so frustrated that they didn't wholly support me but I suppose they've seen Lydia struggle because of her own actions.'

'It's not been easy for any of you. It won't be fixed overnight but hopefully with time everything will get easier.'

He nodded. 'Which leads to the next part of the conversation. Sophie has got the opportunity of a six-month posting in London.'

'Gosh, I wasn't expecting that. What does that mean for Holly?'

'We've had a long talk and Sophie has agreed that if Holly wants to go to mainstream school, then that's what she should do. Lydia is going to go with Sophie. I really think it will do everyone the world of good to break their normal routine, reset and start again when they don't feel so hurt.'

'Does this mean that Holly can stay with you at Weathervane Cottage?'

Guy broke into a broad smile. 'It does. We're going to make our home there. Then, after the six months is up, Sophie and Lydia want a fresh start somewhere new. They will be looking for a place—maybe on the other side of town—so we can sort out proper custody on their return. While they're in London, Holly is going to see them every other weekend and we will organise school holidays as and when. I'm going to take jobs that fit in with Holly.'

'It's all coming together!' exclaimed Libby.

'It is and I feel relieved. After I met with them, I had a meeting with the headmaster at the local school about a place for Holly. I've not told her yet but she will be able to start after Christmas. It will be good for her to make new friends and have a proper routine.'

'It will be good for you both. I'm genuinely happy for you.'

'Heartcross is a lovely village with a brilliant community and it will be good for me to have some stability and a supportive network. I've been feeling as if my whole world has collapsed but now...' He reached across the table and took hold of her hand. 'And then there's you.'

Suddenly emotional, Libby gulped. This was the first man in a very long time that she'd had genuine feelings for.

'I think about us ... a lot,' he admitted. 'And the circumstances we're in.' He paused. 'After I'd discovered the betrayal of Sophie and Lydia, not only did I think I'd never bounce back but I also made a promise never to get entangled with another woman again. But then, who could resist a gorgeous woman standing in the snow, wearing a bikini and a red bobble hat? It's every man's dream.'

Libby laughed. 'I couldn't believe my luck either. Standing there, semi-naked. It was embarrassing.'

'There's something about you, Libby Carter. I just can't get you off my mind. You're like no one I've met before. You're fun, vibrant, drop-dead gorgeous... I wasn't interested in finding anyone, but you're...'

She whirled a finger around, urging him to continue. 'Keep those compliments coming.'

He smiled. 'And I knew the kindest thing would be not to get involved in your life but in just this short time my feelings have grown hugely. I find myself thinking about you more and more ... but in the situation we are in, it's damn near impossible to date or have a relationship.'

'Damn near impossible but not impossible...' Libby was harbouring an idea, thanks to her dad, but before she talked about it with Guy there was an important phone call she needed to make. 'We have to keep the faith.' Even though a few weeks ago she could never have imagined being in this situation, she might now have come up with the perfect solution, one that she hoped would protect her heart from shattering into hundreds of pieces.

'We have to find a way, though I've no clue how to make that happen. I don't want you to give up on your dream but I don't want you to walk out of my life either. If I didn't have Holly, I'd be jumping on that plane with you and spending time with you in New York.'

'You would have done that for me?' Libby's smile grew. He'd actually thought about it.

'Of course I would. Maybe once Sophie and Lydia are settled, I can come out and spend time with you. There are ways to keep in touch—FaceTime and WhatsApp... I really want to see where this goes.'

Libby's heart was melting. Guy was wearing his heart on his sleeve, being open and honest with his feelings, and she was feeling the same. She didn't want to let him go but she also knew that while this was lovely to hear, there were bigger factors they would need to address.

'New York isn't that far.' He was trying to make a joke of it but his voice cracked.

Libby reached across the table and took his hand. 'I know it's very early days but, distance aside, there's a difficult conversation we need to have.'

Guy nodded. 'I know.'

Libby's voice was soft. 'You know I can't have children. It's heart-breaking for me but I've had a long time to come to terms with it. You really need to think what is best for you and your future. I don't want to be the one who takes your dreams away from you.'

Guy was quiet for a moment. 'There are options.'

'There are but you need to be sure you're okay with them. I can't go through the pain of getting close to someone again, only to have them leave me later when the going gets tough.' Libby's voice wavered.

'I'm not the type of person who would leave when the going gets tough.'

'I know, but it's a huge decision to make and not one I want you to make now. You need time to digest this and decide what you truly want...' She swallowed. It was difficult to give him an out like this but she knew it had to be said.

Guy nodded. He understood.

For the past ten years Libby had found it difficult to move on, memories from the dark times in her life often resurfacing, but since she'd met Guy all that had begun changing. She too had hope for the future, but they needed to figure out how to make it work.

'I appreciate that,' said Guy, 'and I promise I'll give it serious thought. For now, let's lift this mood and enjoy our time together. Do you need to get back tonight?' He raised his eyes playfully. 'Holly is staying at her mum's with Pickle so I have the night to myself.'

'You don't have to be by yourself.'

Standing up, he reached out and took Libby's hand. They stood close together and he rested his head against hers. 'There is something telling me we have to give this a go.'

'I feel the same way.'

With his arms wrapped around her, they stared out across the clear night sky. They stayed silent as they watched the lights of houses in the far distance. 'Quick, look.' Guy's voice rose and he pointed directly in front of them.

Libby swung her gaze upwards, to see the most wonderful sight. 'Oh my... It's amazing!' In the darkness, the white light shone all the brighter.

'A shooting star. Make a wish,' whispered Guy.

Libby squeezed her eyes shut and made a wish.

'And what did you wish for?' asked Guy, hugging her tight.

She looked up and kissed him on his lips. 'I can't tell you that, otherwise it won't come true.' And this was one wish that Libby desperately hoped would come true.

'I think we're going to be okay,' he whispered.

Enfolded in Guy's arms, she stared at the night sky for a moment longer. Even with the uncertainty hanging over them, this was the happiest she had been for a long time. She knew difficult roads led to beautiful destinations, and after everything the pair of them had gone through, she hoped they could overcome any obstacles and make it work between them. Tilting her gaze towards his, their eyes locked, and the flickering glow and shadows of the candlelight passed across the contours of their faces. Guy smiled at her. One thing she knew for sure: being wrapped up in Guy's arms tonight couldn't come soon enough.

Waking up snuggled into Guy's chest, she glanced at the clock. It was 6am. Guy was fast asleep and Libby watched him for a few seconds before she closed her eyes. Lying next to him she felt content, safe and the happiest girl on the planet. She had wanted last night as much as he had. She knew there were still talks they needed to have, but at least they'd made a start on the difficult conversations. Now all she could do was take one day at a time.

Wide awake now, she gently removed Guy's arm from around her body, silently slipped out of bed and padded into the kitchen. After making a cup of tea and lighting the fire, she pulled a blanket across her legs and picked up Julia's wedding scrapbook.

As soon as Flynn had agreed to the surprise wedding, Libby had scheduled a top secret meeting in the wedding studio with their closest friends in the village. She knew the whole community would get on board to make this the wedding of the year. Guy would capture every moment on video. The outfit was made and Flynn was going to sneak a few items of clothing from Julia's wardrobe so that Libby could get the measurements spot-on. She was leaving nothing to chance.

Taking her phone, she began to snap photos of the relevant pages, which she was going to distribute at the meeting. The main challenge would be to get the whole community to Starcross Manor on Christmas Eve without Julia discovering that they were all there for her and Flynn.

'Hey, what are you doing? I woke up and you were gone.' Guy was standing in the doorway.

'I just woke up.'

'That's good. You haven't run out on me.'

'Don't be daft! Where would I run to? This is my lodge.' She smiled.

'Oh yeah, I forgot that bit. What are you doing?'

'Looking at Julia's wedding scrapbook.' Libby lifted the edge of the blanket and Guy slipped onto the couch next to her.

'Girls actually have scrapbooks about their ideal wedding?'

'Some,' replied Libby. 'But this is going to make my life a hell of a lot easier. I still can't believe that Flynn is going to re-propose on the morning of Christmas Eve. Julia has no clue that by midday she will be married!'

'Has anyone considered she might say no?'

'Don't be ridiculous!' Libby swiped his arm playfully. 'It's going to be magical watching her walk down the aisle.' She fanned her face. 'I'm getting emotional just thinking about it.'

'You daft sod,' said Guy, pulling her in for a hug. 'You do have a lovely family. Don't worry, when you're not here, I'll look after them all.'

'That makes me even more emotional but…'—Libby smiled —'if things are meant to be, things are meant to be.'

He gave her a puzzled look. 'What is that meant to mean?'

'I can't tell you just yet.'

Guy tilted his head, then began to tickle her. In a fit of giggles, she moved the scrapbook to one side and kicked her legs in the air. 'Get off me! I'm ticklish.'

'I can see.'

'Now, can we get back to bed?'

He stopped tickling her and gave her a cheeky wink. Standing up, he dropped his boxer shorts to the floor, then ran naked across the room, treating her to a sexy rear view. She laughed as she admired his broad shoulders and toned thighs. He stopped in the doorway and held out his hand to her. 'I want to ravish you every moment I get.'

Libby had no objections whatsoever. She was up on her feet at once, and followed him into the bedroom.

Chapter Twenty-One

Two weeks until Christmas

L ibby and Guy had spent the last hour getting the studio ready for the secret meeting. Jenny had organised a buffet from the kitchens at Starcross Manor and brought over cups and saucers from the bar as well as a number of chairs, which were now set out in a couple of rows. Earlier that morning Libby had sent out a cryptic text to Flynn and to Julia's closest friends …

You're invited to a top secret meeting at 2pm at the wedding studio at Starcross Manor. Do not breathe a word to anyone. I mean it!

She was bursting with excitement and couldn't wait to share the reason why she was bringing them all together.

Jenny was the first to arrive. As she slipped off her coat,

Libby noticed she was wearing her Starcross Manor uniform and a smile. 'It's good to be back.'

'How's your mum?' asked Libby.

'Settled, thankfully. Flynn has helped me so much in the last forty-eight hours. I just can't believe how this time last week I was at rock bottom and now...'

'All of us are always here to help. Remember that.'

'Thank you. I suppose you've already seen the news?'

'I haven't.'

'Miranda and David have made the front page. "Scandal! Bogus competition winners attempt sabotage on Starcross Manor's wedding plans,"' she read from the paper she'd brought with her. 'Aidy Redfern wrote the article and it certainly makes for an interesting read.'

'Miranda and David have been arrested for fraud and are being sued by Flynn,' Libby said after scanning the article, which was accompanied by a photo of David being escorted towards a police car.

'And cancelled bookings and stranded local suppliers have left the new wedding barn potentially out of business before it's even begun,' Guy said, looking it over.

'Let's hope they just disappear and we never have to see those people around town ever again,' Libby added as the church clock chimed two. She clapped her hands together in excitement as she noticed everyone walking down the path towards the studio.

Opening the door wide, Libby welcomed everyone as they stepped inside.

'This is all very cloak and dagger,' remarked Rona, the owner of Bonnie's Teashop, narrowing her eyes at Libby. 'What's going on?'

'You look like the cat that's got the cream,' observed Florrie.

'If you all want to grab yourselves a drink then I can share the biggest secret ever to hit Heartcross!'

There was excited chatter all around. As soon as everyone was sitting down, Libby instructed Guy to keep a look-out at the window just in case Julia decided to come and visit. Jenny slipped into a chair next to Eleni, Julia's right-hand woman at the B&B.

Libby looked over the sea of faces as everyone fell silent. All eyes were on her.

'Thank you all for coming. I know you must be wondering why I've invited you here. Eleni! Please tell me you haven't told a soul you're here, not even Julia?'

Eleni looked puzzled. 'Scout's honour, I've not told Julia or anyone else that I'm here. Why?'

'Because…' Libby took a deep breath, letting the tension in the room build. 'I am about to take on the biggest secret challenge of my life and I need your help!'

'This is intriguing,' said Isla, looking towards Rona, who shrugged.

Picking up the newspaper that Jenny had brought with her, Libby held up the front page. 'This couple were the couple who were meant to be getting married here on Christmas Eve. However, they were trying to sabotage Flynn's business and ruin his reputation because they planned to open their own wedding business in the area.'

'What a cheek they both had,' commented Isla.

'Unbelievable! Thankfully, I had already given Flynn exclusivity for wedding flowers at Starcross Manor,' chipped in Florrie.

'And I won't be baking any wedding cakes for them. They won't get any help from this community,' confirmed Rona.

'Here, here,' everyone chorused.

'And that's what I love about this community, we all look after each other,' Libby continued. 'Which is the reason I've invited you today... You're all invited to a wedding!' she announced, a wide smile on her face.

There was excited chatter.

'I love a good wedding, but whose?' asked Isla.

'This is the good part and it's top secret and I can't stress this enough...' Libby took another deep breath. 'It's Flynn and Julia's wedding and it's going to take place on Christmas Eve!'

There was a ripple of excitement around the room.

'How marvellous! This is exciting news! But why is it secret?' asked Rona, not fully understanding.

'My guess is because Julia doesn't know,' chipped in Eleni. 'She has always wanted a winter wedding. How exactly are we going to pull this off? She might want her wedding to be a certain theme, or colour. We don't want her to be disappointed.'

'Agreed,' reassured Libby. 'And I'm about to share how we are going to pull this off. But for this to happen, I really do need your help. Firstly, can I have a show of hands? Who can help?'

Everyone in the room raised an arm. Eleni raised two. 'This is going to be the best Christmas and wedding ever!' Libby clapped her hands together excitedly before holding up Julia's scrapbook. 'The answer to Eleni's question is right here. Julia has made a scrapbook with everything in it and with this we can make every wish come true.' She turned towards Guy, who stood up and picked up a remote control. He'd erected a screen at the front of the studio and pressed play on the remote.

'Let's take a look at what Julia would like.'

On the screen were scans of the diagrams and pictures in Julia's scrapbook. 'Here we have the flowers.' Libby looked towards Florrie. 'Is this doable for Christmas Eve along with all the Christmas cranberry garlands, buttonholes and mistletoe? Oh and white blossom trees. That's a firm must.'

'It will be my pleasure,' answered Florrie.

'Thank you,' Libby said happily.

'Then we have the cake, and I'm hoping you can help us out with this, Rona.'

'Of course, without a doubt.'

As soon as the drawing of the cake flashed up everyone gave a murmur of appreciation. Julia had designed the cake herself and every detail was written on the drawing projected on to the screen.

'The cake has elegantly designed festive details. With the sugar-coated cranberries, winter florals and frosting it will be a stunning work of art. I can't wait to get started,' Rona enthused.

'Thank you, Rona. You're a marvel.'

'Jenny and Isla, would it be possible to work together on the stationery? Flynn will have a guest list that mainly consists of the wonderful community in Heartcross.'

Guy pressed the remote again and Libby pointed to the screen. 'According to this the theme is cranberry, mulberry and winter white. Think handwritten calligraphy, silver envelopes, winter berries and parcel string. The RSVPs need to come back to my email at Starcross Manor within ten days at the max so I can co-ordinate table plans, which leads me on to table decorations and candles. Julia loves candles and crystal baubles.' Libby looked towards Grace, who had lived at Heartcross Castle for the last few years.

'Grace, I believe that you have decorated a room at the castle with something similar. Is that right?'

'I have indeed. Those crystal bauble centrepieces reflect candlelight so beautifully and make the atmosphere magical. I'll take a look at how many we will need and get everything ordered.'

'You're a superstar. And now over to your other half.' Libby smiled at Andrew Glossop. He was a good friend of Flynn's and a world-famous chef with his own cooking show on TV. 'There's only one person we could possibly ask to cook the menu but I do appreciate this is Christmas Eve...'

'As if I'm going to let you down. It will be my pleasure to take care of all the food and winter cocktails.'

'We need Christmas trees for The Grand Hall...'

'Drew will take care of that,' volunteered Isla.

'The secret garden will also need to be decorated. And, according to this scrapbook, which is the most romantic thing I have ever seen, Julia wants to walk up the aisle under an archway of sparklers.'

Everyone oohed in unison.

'We need bagpipers, which I believe you could source from Heartcross Castle?'

'We can indeed,' confirmed Grace.

'And reindeer?'

'We can organise those, too.'

'Flynn's best man is Drew, so he is going to organise the

suits for them, my dad and the ushers. I'm already working on Julia's wedding outfit, which then leaves the bridesmaids: Eleni, Isla and myself.'

'This is going to be so magical,' enthused Isla. 'Do we know what we're wearing?'

'Oh I do, and you are both going to look gorgeous. Think winter cosy. Beautiful shrugs will complement our dresses in neutral tones of cream, mink and beige, perfect for a winter's day. I'll need you in for a fitting sometime by Wednesday, and Eleni, I need you to be extra careful not to let anything slip at work. I've already co-ordinated with Julia's hairdresser to come over to the lodge the morning of the wedding. We'll all have our hair and make-up done and leave together in the reindeer-pulled carriage. My dad, Wilbur, will be giving Julia away and he arrives back first thing that day. Oh and before I forget, I've set up a private WhatsApp group, which you should all now be a part of. Also, thank you all. This couldn't happen without you. I love it when a plan comes together. This Christmas is going to be so magical.'

A couple of hours later Guy and Libby were tucking into sandwiches. It was going to be a busy time pulling the wedding together but they couldn't wait for the moment when Julia walked down the aisle with Flynn waiting at the altar for her.

There was a knock on the door and Libby waved through the window. Holly was standing on the doorstep. 'It's a little girl about this high, with beautiful hair, and it looks like she's holding some post.'

Guy was up on his feet and as soon as the door was open, he picked up Holly and spun her round. 'Here she is! I've missed you!' he said, blowing a raspberry on her cheek.

'Dad, get off me,' she squealed, pretending to wipe it away. 'You always do this.'

'Where has my little girl gone? You've been away for one night and come back all grown up.'

'I'm still here; I just don't want sloppy kisses.'

Libby smiled, watching the father and daughter bond. 'How was your night?' she asked. 'Did you have a good time?'

Holly nodded. 'Pickle has been naughty though. She chewed up the post. Granny said this is for you.'

'Why thank you. Would you like a drink? There's a jug of juice over there.'

'Yes, please.'

Guy poured Holly a drink while Libby looked at the envelope in her hand. Tearing it open she discovered a letter from her new boss, Francesca, and there, staring back at her, was her one-way plane ticket to John F Kennedy International Airport. She glanced towards Holly and Guy, who were chatting away, then checked her phone. She'd left a voicemail for Francesca just before midday and was hoping that her new boss would return her call very soon. Libby had put forward a proposition for what her new job might look like and it was one she hoped would be agreed to.

'Please ask her, Dad, I want her to be our first visitor.'

Libby suspected she knew exactly what Holly wanted Guy to ask her.

Holly continued. 'I'll help to make dinner and we can buy a cake as you're rubbish at making cakes.'

'Hey, I'll have you know I'm not that bad,' he objected.

'And I know you're excited about your new home but it needs a lot of work done on it before we can make those plans. Thankfully, I do have some other news that I know you're going to love. You will be starting school very soon.'

Holly's smile widened and she began jumping up and down. 'Will you and Libby pick me up on my first day? Please, Dad.'

Guy looked across at Libby and took in her expression. 'Everything okay?'

'What have you got there?' asked Holly before Libby had a chance to answer. 'Mummy has a ticket like that. She's going away with Auntie Lydia and I get to live with Daddy in Heartcross, which means we can see you all the time.'

Libby looked towards Guy for guidance and she noticed him briefly close his eyes before he bent down next to Holly.

'Holly, we can't wait for you to start school as I know it's something you've wanted for a while, and I promise I'll be there to pick you up on your first day, but Libby has some very good news that might make it hard for her to join me. You know how fantastic Libby is at making clothes? Well, she has a new job. A job that she has worked hard for. Libby is going to get to do what she loves the most, designing dresses and making clothes for a lot of famous people … in New York City.'

'But New York is far away. I know that because you read me a bedtime story where a monkey flies to New York City by mistake, and it's thousands of miles away. When will we see you?' Holly's eyes were wide and the smile had fallen from her face. She looked at Libby then back at Guy.

'We have lots of technology so we can see Libby all the time and catch up over FaceTime or on phone calls.'

'But it's not the same.' Holly's lip began to quiver and she ran out of the front door.

'I have to go.' Guy touched Libby's arm before he went after Holly, leaving Libby clutching her one-way ticket to New York. Picking up her phone, she willed Francesca to return her call.

Chapter Twenty-Two

L ibby had been feeling dispirited for the past couple of days. She hadn't seen Guy, as he was under the weather, and even though she had no reason to doubt him, it crossed her mind that he might be creating some distance between them for Holly's sake. Trying to rally herself, she focused on what still needed to be done. Isla was due for a bridesmaid's fitting and the next few days were going to be full on with Libby's sewing machine working flat out.

'I'm here!' Isla jigged through the door of the wedding studio. There was a blast of cold air as she stepped inside and kicked off her boots. 'Thank God it's toasty in here. It's freezing out there.'

'That's Scotland for you,' remarked Libby, thrusting a mug of coffee into Isla's hand.

'This is just what I needed,' Isla said, wrapping her cold hands around the mug. 'I've already stocked the farm shop with fresh produce this morning and didn't have time to even make a cuppa, so this is very welcome. But I've just had a close call. Julia popped into the shop. She said she had an afternoon to herself and wanted to do lunch as Flynn had a prior engagement.'

'Suit fittings! He, Drew and the rest of the ushers are off to the tailors in town then Flynn is off to the jewellers to pick out the rings,' confirmed Libby.

'It's just so exciting! I admit I became a little flustered when I saw her walking into the shop, as I'd only just been chatting about the wedding with Florrie, but thankfully she didn't hear a thing. Fair warning though, she did say she was going to call in on you.'

Libby looked towards the window. 'Julia can't catch us both here because she'll wonder what we're up to. Let's work in the back part of the studio.' She hurried to the window and pulled down the blinds before locking the door. 'No one's getting in here,' she declared. 'Now come and have a look at the design and tell me what you think.'

They walked through to the wedding dress area and in the middle of the room was a mannequin clothed in a dress straight out of a wonderful dream. With a beautiful halter neckline, a tightly gathered mink tulle bodice and matching flowy tulle skirt, the dress was accompanied by a cream shrug for warmth.

'I've been working on this for the last couple of days. It's just pinned together but won't take any time to sew.'

'It's utterly gorgeous. I'm going to feel like a Hollywood superstar wearing this. It's just perfect.' Isla walked around the mannequin. 'You're extremely clever. You must be looking forward to the wedding so much, especially after you've pulled it all together.'

Libby knew it was going to the best day of Flynn and Julia's life and she couldn't wait to see them married. Working together with all their friends, she was going to make sure that everything was magical, but there was a tiny anxious feeling swirling around in the pit of her stomach: Francesca had not phoned her back.

'And how is everything with you?' asked Isla.

Libby perched on the carpeted step next to the mannequin and Isla sat beside her. 'I have something I need to tell someone, and I thought I'd have some news by now but I haven't.'

'News? What sort of news?'

Libby took a breath. 'Since arriving I've been battling with my head, my heart and my career. My feelings for Guy have grown fast.'

'You two are made for each other,' Isla confirmed. 'I love a good love story.'

'Let's not get ahead of ourselves too much…'

'Who are you trying to kid? The chemistry between the two of you could light up the whole of Scotland.'

Libby laughed. 'When I came to Heartcross, I wasn't expecting to meet anyone, never mind have these kinds of feelings. I've waited nearly ten years for someone to cross my path—and of course it happens the moment I'm meant to be leaving the country. Talking it all over with my dad, I've realised that my main concern about factoring Guy and Holly into my plans is: what if I don't go to New York and then Guy and I aren't compatible?'

'And what if you are?'

'This is exactly what's been going around in my head. I've also worked so damn hard for this job.'

'It is a huge decision. I wouldn't want to be in your shoes. What does Guy say?'

'He said he feels the same. He wasn't expecting anyone to cross his path and it's come as a shock. He's moving into Weathervane Cottage with Holly and she's going to be starting school in the village.'

'Oh, wonderful, that's great news.'

'And there are Holly's feelings to consider. She got upset when she knew I was leaving for New York and I haven't seen them since I told them, as Guy is unwell.'

'There's got to be some sort of compromise.'

'That's what Dad said and advised. That's the phone call I'm waiting for.'

'What do you mean?' Isla asked. 'Come on, tell me.'

'I rang my boss and left her a voicemail. I explained the situation, how I was feeling, leaving my family behind. It's a big move but I still want the job and so I asked whether there was any possibility of working out in New York for a few months and then here for a few months. I could flit between the two, having the best of both worlds. But as yet my boss hasn't phoned me back, and I don't want to say anything to Guy until I've had the conversation with her and know what my options are.'

'You definitely did the right thing. After all, if you don't ask, you don't get. This would be the perfect solution.'

'Every time my phone rings, I'm a nervous wreck in case it's her.'

'But it might be the news you want. Come here, I think you need a hug.'

As they pulled away from the hug they heard a rap on the door and nearly jumped out of their skins.

'Who's that?' mouthed Isla.

Libby shrugged. 'It's a good job we closed the curtains,' she whispered.

They watched as the door handle twisted. Thank God they'd locked the door.

'Libby, are you in there?' shouted Julia.

Libby flapped her hand frantically in front of her face and pointed to her phone on the desk. Quickly hot-footing it over to the phone she managed to switch it on to silent just before Julia's name flashed across the screen. Libby pressed a hand over her swiftly beating heart. 'That was close,' she mouthed. Julia would definitely have heard the phone ring if Libby hadn't managed to silence it.

As soon as the phone stopped ringing, Libby received a text message.

Where is everyone? Have all the villagers been captured by aliens?

Libby bit her lip, stifling her laughter. 'Aww bless her,' she said, showing Isla the text. 'Do you think she's gone?'

Tiptoeing to the window, Libby carefully peeped out of the side of the blind. Julia was at the top of the path then disappeared around the corner. They both breathed a sigh of relief.

'She's gone! That was a close call!'

'My heart is racing,' Isla agreed. 'Could you imagine if we blew the surprise?'

'We didn't, thankfully! But we are keeping that door locked. Now, let's get you measured properly and I can start sewing this beautiful dress. You're going to look stunning!'

A few hours later, armed with homemade chicken soup from the manor's kitchen, Libby knocked on the door of Guy's lodge. She heard the rustle of keys and finally the door opened to reveal Guy standing there wearing a tired smile and a pair of lounge pants, his hair wild and sticking up in every direction.

'How's the patient? I brought soup!' She held up the container.

'You're a sight for sore eyes.' He grinned, opening the door wide. 'Enter at your own risk.'

'I think I'll take the chance,' she said, walking past him and pressing a swift kiss to his cheek. 'Where is everyone?' she asked, looking around the room.

'Mum and Holly didn't want to catch the dreaded bug and now my father is feeling better they've gone back there for a few days. And Pickle...' He pointed to the log fire and Libby looked over to find that Pickle had bagged herself the best place in the lodge: stretched out on the faux fur rug in front of the fire toasting her little body.

'That's what you call a hot dog.'

After handing the soup over, she asked, 'How is Holly? I've ... I've missed seeing you both.'

'I'm sorry. My intention was to come and see you the day after we talked but then this bug came from nowhere. My head hurt; I was dizzy and sick, and I've only just been feeling human again this morning. I've even had a shower. Promise!'

Libby laughed. 'That's good to hear,' she said, sitting down on the sofa.

'Holly was upset. I think she thought she would see you

every day. She also thought the lodge was your home. I explained that you came here, like I did, to work for Flynn for a short time and just like us you'll be going home when it's done—only home now happens to be New York. She had a little cry but I promised her that you wouldn't get rid of us that easily and that I liked you and we would be doing everything possible to keep in touch. I did mention a couple of things'—he screwed up his face—'and I know I should have checked it with you first…'

'Go on…'

'That, if it was possible, we could come and visit when you've settled in.'

'It would be my pleasure and I insist you stay with me.'

'I was hoping you would say that.' He slipped his arm around her shoulder and pulled her towards him.

'And the second thing I've told Holly is that I'll go to Lydia and Sophie's wedding because I wouldn't miss seeing her in her dress.'

'I'm happy you've come to that decision.' Libby knew it must have taken a lot of courage to begin making his peace with Sophie and Lydia. It would be worth it for everyone's sake, especially Holly's.

'Me too. And if your offer of coming to the wedding with me still stands, I'd very much appreciate it.'

'Of course it does. I wouldn't miss seeing Holly in her dress either.'

Smiling, they stared into each other's eyes. 'I've missed you these last two days,' admitted Guy. 'And this is only going to be as hard as we make it so let's make it as easy as possible.'

'I agree,' she said, leaning forward and kissing him on his

lips. 'Are your mum and Holly arriving back today?' she murmured.

'Sometime after tea,' he responded, in between kisses.

'What are we waiting for then?' she whispered.

Standing up, he lifted Libby, who began giggling. 'Don't drop me!'

'The only place I'm going to drop you is on my bed,' he replied with a wicked glint in his eye.

Pickle looked up then, wondering what all the commotion was about. 'You stay there,' Guy ordered before closing the bedroom door behind them.

Chapter Twenty-Three

With only twenty-four hours to go before Flynn and Julia's wedding, Libby and Guy had spent the entire day overseeing the final details, double- and triple-checking all the suppliers to ensure that there would be no last-minute hiccups. Tomorrow morning, Florrie would deliver the flowers to Starcross Manor along with the buttonholes and sprigs of mistletoe. Rona had baked the cake, which was already hiding in the kitchen of Starcross Manor, ready for final touch-ups just before the ceremony; Andrew had prepared a feast, the secret garden had been dressed with hundreds of fairy lights, and warm blankets and winter cocktails were ready to be served.

'The tables are dressed to perfection.'

Libby and Guy spun around to see Flynn standing behind them. His smile was broad.

'I have to say all this looks amazing. We've pulled this together, haven't we? I'm really getting married tomorrow.'

'You are!' replied Libby, kissing her brother's cheek. 'And Jenny has worked wonders in helping to get everything organised. Honestly, she's been my right-hand woman and is worth her weight in gold.'

'I knew all she needed was another chance,' replied Flynn, looking around the room.

'And Guy has every secret mission recorded on video so Julia can see how we've all sneaked behind her back to bring this together.'

'Perfect. She won't believe it when she sees everything is exactly how she planned it.' He held out his hand. 'And look at me, I'm shaking with excitement. I've got to try and keep all this under wraps until tomorrow morning. It's been difficult because I keep disappearing and she's getting suspicious. I'm picking Dad up from the airport later tonight and I keep panicking I've lost the rings, but thankfully these have come through in time.'

'What have you there?' Libby asked.

'Honeymoon tickets. Not the proper honeymoon but something to be going on with. It's a short break in a couple of weeks' time.'

'Are we allowed to know where you're going?' asked Libby, intrigued, looking at the envelope.

'New York!' Flynn grinned. 'I thought we'd fly over and see how my favourite sister is settling in. Then you have Dad coming out a couple of weeks after. You will be sick of the sight of us.'

Libby threw her arms around her brother. 'You're the best, do you know that?'

'You're not too bad yourself. Thank you, Libby, for all this. Julia is going to be blown away. It's just oozes winter wedding Christmas magic.'

'And thankfully there's not a hint of black in sight,' put

in Guy.

'Did you see that Miranda and David have now made the national papers? The story is spreading like wildfire and it's gone viral on social media,' Flynn said.

'It couldn't have happened to nicer people. Got to love karma.' Libby smiled.

'There is just one thing that might put a spanner in the works tomorrow…' Flynn said, suddenly looking worried.

'What's that?' asked Libby, wondering what she'd missed.

'What happens if Julia says she doesn't want to get married?'

Libby and Guy laughed.

'I don't think there's much chance of that, you daft bugger. Is the plan still the same for the morning?' asked Libby.

'Yes. You need to get Julia to the lodge by 9am.'

'Understood.'

'I'll see you both then, then.' Flynn turned and began to walk away. 'I'm getting married in the morning,' he sang loudly as he disappeared out of the door.

Chapter Twenty-Four

Christmas Eve

As the early alarm sounded, Guy and Libby sat bolt upright in bed. 'It's today! It's finally here!'

Guy attempted to pull Libby back under the duvet. 'It's way too early to be getting up. Surely we can have another couple of hours in bed,' he said, with a suggestive look on his face.

'No! There's no time,' she replied, swiping him playfully and wriggling free. 'You know what day it is!'

'Spoilsport,' he said with a grin, watching her draw back the curtain. Pickle was sprawled out at the bottom of the bed and made her disgust at the abrupt wake-up call very clear.

'What time are Holly and Cynthia arriving?' Libby asked.

'Literally an hour before Julia walks down the aisle. Which gives me plenty of time to help you with any last-minute jobs that might need doing.'

'Aww, thank you,' she said, placing a kiss on his lips.

'Are you sure there aren't any I could help you with right now?'

'Ha, ha. No! But if I tell you I have a special present later for you this evening, would you be happy with that?' She lightly caressed his face and gave him a passionate kiss. 'Just be patient,' she added, pointing to the window. 'See how beautiful it looks out there.' A fresh layer of snow had fallen over night, sprinkling Starcross Manor with a fine layer of white powder. 'Julia had always dreamed of a winter wedding in a beautiful manor house. Look at this perfect backdrop for their special day.'

Libby couldn't wait for Julia to arrive at the lodge just after 8.30am. She thought she'd been invited for a Christmas Eve breakfast; little did she know that she was about to find out this was her wedding day. Libby had spent the last ten days planning every detail of the winter wonderland wedding, from the elegant bouquet to delicate snowflake decorations to the candles, cocktails and wedding outfits. Everything had been replicated from the ideas and plans outlined in Julia's scrapbook to create the perfect winter wedding ambiance, and now the day had arrived Libby was filled with excitement and anticipation. She was about to watch her brother get married, and with Guy by her side she couldn't wait for the day to begin. Julia's wedding outfit was hanging in the next room, all ready to go. Libby knew that she was going look stunning with her hair styled in loose waves and a delicate, sparkly tiara that would glimmer in the soft winter light. This was going to be a day to remember.

'I'm going to jump in the shower and you're going to get Pickle out on the sledge,' ordered Libby.

'I'd rather be joining you in the shower.' He grinned as Libby gently pushed him out of bed before hot-footing it into the bathroom and locking the door behind her.

'*Such* a spoilsport.'

'I can't hear you,' she shouted, laughing and turning the water on in the shower to drown Guy's protests.

Two hours later, Libby's phoned pinged. 'It's Flynn! Julia is on her way. She left five minutes ago. Quick, everyone, behind the counter, and move the glasses,' Libby ordered.

Isla, Eleni, Drew and Guy were hiding behind the counter in the kitchen. They couldn't wait to see Julia's face the second she realised today was going to be her wedding day.

'Do not breathe,' Libby ordered. 'Flynn is following her, so he'll arrive soon after and I'll keep Julia in the living room in the meantime.' She looked out of the window. 'She's here!'

Her heart was racing as she opened the door to Julia. 'Merry Christmas Eve!' she trilled. 'What a beautiful morning.' She kissed Julia on both cheeks.

'And Merry Christmas Eve to you to too! Thanks for the invite to this Christmas Eve breakfast; I can't wait for a glass of fizz,' said Julia, heading straight towards the kitchen.

'No! You sit down,' ordered Libby.

Julia raised an eyebrow. 'Are you okay? You seem very on edge.'

'Of course I'm okay! It's Christmas! And I get to spend it with my family. You sit there, next to the fire, and I'll get us a drink.'

Walking into the kitchen, Libby did her best to ignore the

four people crouched behind the counter pulling faces at her to try and make her laugh. 'Behave!' she mouthed, before grabbing two glasses and a bottle of fizz.

'I'll let you warm up before I serve breakfast,' she said to Julia. 'I hope Flynn didn't mind you coming across this morning?'

'I have to say he's been in a weird mood recently. He's been disappearing left, right and centre. I keep catching him whispering on his phone. Something isn't right, I can feel it. Honestly, the last two weeks I feel like I've had the plague. Everywhere I go people are acting strange. Eleni keeps disappearing from work and her excuses are lame, and I feel like Isla is avoiding me. Every time I suggest lunch, she makes an excuse, but when has Isla ever turned down a lunch date?'

'I'm sure it's all in your imagination,' Libby said, humouring her.

There was a knock at the door.

'Are we expecting company?' asked Julia.

Libby shrugged nonchalantly. 'Not to my knowledge.'

Opening the door Libby gave her brother a quick hug and pushed him ahead of her into the living room. 'Look who it is.'

Julia looked up, puzzled. 'I just left you. Why didn't you say you were coming here?'

Flynn smiled. 'Because I didn't want you to know.'

'You've lost me now. Your weirdness is getting weirder.'

'I have to agree with you,' replied Flynn, taking hold of Julia's hand as she stood up. 'You know, over a year ago I proposed to you and you said yes.'

'Yes,' she replied slowly, taking a sideward glance towards Libby, who had moved out of the way and was now leaning against the worktop in the kitchen.

'You know how you've always wanted a winter wedding?'

'Yes.'

'Would you do me the honour of marrying me today?' Flynn asked, his face beaming with hope.

Julia stood open-mouthed. 'I don't understand. We can't get married today. What about the venue, the food, my outfit, the guests...'

'What if I tell you everything is taken care of and all you have to do is say yes?'

Julia looked towards Libby once again. 'Say yes!' Libby urged. 'Please say yes.'

'Okay!' she said, looking back at Flynn. 'Yes!'

Flynn took her in his arms and kissed her on the lips. 'I'm getting married! Today!'

Just at that moment the gang behind the worktop stood up and cheered, making Julia scream and put her hands on her heart. 'I'm not sure I can take much more. What are you all doing here?'

'Waiting for you to say yes!' exclaimed Isla, rushing across to give Julia and Flynn a kiss and a hug. 'There's going to be a wedding! Three cheers for Flynn and Julia. Hip, hip, hooray!'

Everyone was hugging the happy couple. 'Is this the reason everyone has been acting weird? Eleni, how did you keep this from me?'

'With great difficulty!' replied Eleni, pouring a glass of fizz. 'And I didn't think my excuses were lame.' She grinned.

'Am I actually getting married today?'

'YES!' everyone chorused.

'You certainly are! Boys, you need to be leaving. We have the hairdresser and beautician arriving any second.' Libby began to shoo them towards the door. 'We'll see you at the altar at midday!'

Julia was still in a state of shock as Flynn kissed her one last time. 'See you in a bit, Mrs Carter-to-be!'

Libby saw Guy to the door. 'Be outside to film us leaving around eleven-thirty.'

'In the words of the Jackson Five, "I'll be there". See you later!' He kissed her then followed the other men while Libby returned to the living room.

As the door shut behind them Julia held out her hand; it was shaking. 'I never expected this at all.'

'How are you feeling?' asked Libby.

'Shocked, happy, I don't really know... Libby, I didn't want to say anything in front of Flynn but I had my heart set on my own wedding outfit design.'

'You didn't think I'd let you down, did you? Of course you're going to get married in your dream outfit. Wait there!'

Libby wheeled the first mannequin from the bedroom into the living room. Julia gasped and happy tears began rolling down her cheeks. 'I'm lost for words. I don't believe it. You made this?' Julia walked over to the mannequin, which presented the exact design from her scrapbook. 'Have you sewn all of these on?' she asked, running her hand gently over the 3D florals.

'I have and it was worth all the blood, sweat and tears to see that look on your face.'

'It's absolutely... I can't speak. I'm lost for words.'

'We have the long lace bubble sleeves and the high boat neckline and it's finished perfectly with the pearl clasps down the back. The wide trousers are so elegant ... and what do you think of the plume feather jacket?'

'I think I have the best sister-in-law-to-be in the whole wide world. You must have been working non-stop since you arrived. This is exactly my design. Thank you.' She hugged Libby.

'And next up we have the bridesmaids' dresses! Just in case you didn't realise, you have three bridesmaids.'

Libby, Isla and Eleni curtsied at the same time. Then Eleni wheeled out the bridesmaids' dresses.

Once again Julia gasped. 'They're exactly like my designs. When I woke up this morning, I never imagined—' She was interrupted by a knock on the door.

'Come in!' shouted Libby.

They watched as Florrie brought the most beautiful blooms into the room. 'I believe someone is getting married today!' she said.

'Oh my gosh, I can't take any more. My heart is beating so fast. Florrie! These are exactly what I wanted.'

'I know, it's a good job you made that scrapbook.' She kissed Julia on both cheeks. 'Congratulations! I'll just bring in the bridesmaids' posies and then I'm off to finish dressing The Grand Hall. Oh, and before I forget, a little sprig of mistletoe for you each, just in case any of you fancy stealing a kiss today!'

'And here's the hairdresser arriving,' exclaimed Libby. 'Drink your fizz and let the celebration begin.'

A couple of hours later there were collective gasps from the bridesmaids as Julia walked into the room wearing her wedding outfit.

'You look absolutely gorgeous. Dare I say it, my brother is punching way above his weight,' Libby teased. 'He's going to be blown away.'

She looked at her phone to check the time. Guy had texted that he was ready when they were, and she could see him standing outside with a camera, waiting to film Julia as she left for her wedding. 'I'm just going to check on your carriage.'

'My carriage? I thought I was getting married at Starcross Manor.'

'You are, but you still need a carriage!'

Libby opened the door and her heart missed several beats when she saw Guy standing there dressed in a kilt, dirk and sporran. His three-button waistcoat, white shirt and cranberry-coloured tartan bow tie pulled the whole outfit together and left Libby's heart a-flutter. 'How blooming handsome are you?' she gushed, immediately holding the mistletoe over his head and giving him a huge kiss. 'Phwoar!' she added, pulling away.

'And you, Libby Carter, have literally taken my breath away. You're stunning.' Guy held her hands and kissed her cheek before glancing back over her dress. 'Beautiful,' he said, kissing her once more.

'What I want to know is whether you're a true Scotsman,' she said, moving to pull up his kilt.

Guy laughed and quickly pushed her hand down. 'You can find that out later.' He winked. 'Now is the bride ready? Her carriage awaits.'

Julia stepped out of the lodge into a winter wonderland, every inch of Starcross Manor covered in snow, wispy flakes swirling like feathers to the ground. Guy pointed through the trees to the clearing where six reindeer were ready to pull the sledge-like wooden carriage towards the red-carpeted stone steps of Starcross Manor.

'Can this day get any better? I'm so emotional,' Julia admitted.

'Hold on to those tears, we don't want your make-up ruined!' added Eleni.

Guy filmed the bride and her bridesmaids making their way towards the sleigh, where they sat on heated throws while the footman made sure they were ready before pulling on the reins. Bells wrapped around the reindeers' antlers jingled as they stepped in time and began to pull the sleigh towards the Manor. As soon as they were out of sight. Guy quickly made his way through the back of the hotel and headed towards reception. He spotted Flynn and Drew in the doorway of The Grand Hall. 'Go inside! Julia is on her way!'

Guy positioned himself alongside one of the Christmas trees at the top of the stone steps. He could hear the jingle of the bells and as soon the sleigh was in sight he began to film again. The footman slowed the sleigh and the reindeer halted at the foot of the steps. With perfect timing, a peal of bells rang out from the stone spire of the church in the distance.

'Are you ready?' Libby asked, touching Julia's arm as they stepped out of the sleigh.

'I think so.'

Libby nodded towards Guy, who knocked on the oak door, which immediately opened. Through the doors came five pipers and a drummer, all dressed in traditional costume. They stood next to the Christmas tree along with a Highland choir. The conductor painted a picture as elegantly as an artist as he swirled his baton gracefully and instantly the sound of Julia's favourite Christmas carol rang out, 'God Rest Ye Merry Gentlemen'. Everything was pitch- and picture-perfect, like a scene from a Christmas card, and as Julia began to walk up the steps there was another surprise waiting at the top for her: Wilbur.

'Wilbur! You're home.' Tears sprang to her eyes as she threw her arms around him. 'I mustn't cry.' She hugged him tight.

'Would it be possible to have the honour of walking you down the aisle?' he asked.

'Yes! It would be my honour too,' Julia replied with a hand on her heart as Libby hugged her dad.

'Welcome home,' she said.

'I can't leave you kids alone for a minute, can I?' he said with a smile. 'Are we ready? Everyone is waiting for you.'

Julia and Wilbur led the way towards The Grand Hall, the bridesmaids walking behind. Libby gave Guy a quick kiss as she passed him. 'See you on the other side.'

As they approached the room, they could hear laughter and chatter echoing all around. Libby glowed with pleasure as the doors opened and she spotted Flynn at the altar with Drew standing by his side. The room looked spectacular: dressed chairs set in rows, with an aisle in the middle leading to the altar, which was flanked by two giant Christmas trees decorated in cranberries and gold, and with a roaring log fire just behind the officiant. The room was filled with Flynn and Julia's family and friends and everyone had dressed for the occasion, in kilts, tuxedos and glamorous winter dresses and gowns.

Suddenly the room was filled with the sound of soft

classical music, creating a romantic atmosphere that made everyone feel as though they were in a fairytale. Flynn beamed as he clapped eyes on his bride for the first time in her finery.

All eyes turned towards the back of the room as Guy slipped down the aisle to catch every magical moment on video. As soon as he was in position under an archway of sparklers, Wilbur walked Julia down the aisle. There wasn't a dry eye in the place.

Christmas Day

It was just past midnight and Holly's arms were slumped around Guy's neck as he did his best to give her a piggyback without waking her. It had been a wonderful day. After an emotional, beautiful wedding, everyone had danced their hearts out, drunk winter cocktails and devoured a magnificent feast. It had been one of the best days of Libby's life.

With the lodges in sight, Guy whispered, 'I'm just going to slip Holly into bed and make sure Mum doesn't have another sherry.'

'Hey, cheeky,' objected Cynthia, with a smile. She looked at Libby. 'You have a wonderful family. Merry Christmas and thank you for inviting us today. Everyone was just so lovely.'

'They are, aren't they?' replied Libby.

'You're good for this one,' she observed, nodding towards her son.

'Merry Christmas to you, Cynthia. Sleep well.'

Guy winked at Libby. 'I'll see you in a minute.'

Fifteen minutes later, Guy sank on the settee next to Libby, who hadn't even removed her shrug or shoes.

'I'm feeling a little tipsy,' she said. 'Wasn't that just the best day?'

'All I kept thinking was that your dad can't half move on that dancefloor. Even at my age I haven't got that much energy!' Guy laughed.

'I think I did Flynn and Julia proud.'

'Everything was exactly like in Julia's scrapbook, down to the archway of sparklers and the secret garden. And the winter cocktails went down a treat. You should be proud of yourself.'

'I am. Never did I think when I started to organise Miranda and David's wedding that it would end up being Flynn and Julia's. I'm so pleased it all came together and everyone seemed to have a great time. I know I had far too much to eat and drink. I don't think I can face more turkey in a few hours' time.'

Guy laughed. 'You'll be fine after a sleep.'

'Dare I say it ... everything seems to be okay with your mum now. Is that the case?'

'I think tonight was just what we needed: a fun time, with no reminders of the past, just the future. She really likes you.'

'And I really like her,' Libby replied, standing up.

'Where are you going?'

'It's gone midnight.' She reached under the tree and pulled out an envelope wrapped with a red ribbon. 'Your Christmas present. Merry Christmas!' She kissed him on the cheek and sat down next to him. 'Here.'

'Oh my, I didn't think about it being Christmas... I've not got—'

'You don't need to get me a present,' Libby interrupted.

'Of course I did. As if I'd forget.' He reached inside his pocket and pulled out a small oblong box. 'You first,' he said.

Libby bit her lip as she pulled on the ribbon. Once it was undone, she looked at the box.

'Go on, open it,' he encouraged.

With slightly shaky fingers Libby opened the box. Resting on the silver paper was a key. Libby picked it up and turned it over in her hand before looking at Guy.

'This is a key to Pickle's kennel, so whenever you're back from New York, you can feel free to take her for a walk.'

She swiped him playfully. 'You idiot!'

Guy laughed. 'Only joking. This key is actually the key to my heart.'

Libby pulled a face. 'You should do stand-up.'

'No, honestly, it is...' He took the key and placed it on the table. 'I might be a little drunk but ... Libby Carter, you have turned me around. You have given me hope. You have made me laugh again. You have made me want to get up in the morning and hold my head high. You've helped me to realise that I am worthy, I deserve love and I have so much to share with someone. And just in case you're in any doubt, I hope that someone is you.'

'That's good to know.'

'The chances of you walking into my life when I was in such a bad place were definitely slim, but thank God I decided to help Flynn out and thank God Pickle escaped into your hot tub that day. No one can wear a bikini and bobble hat like you. Joking aside, I know you're going to be on the other side of the world, but you deserve every bit of success that's coming your way, and Holly and I will be championing you every step of the way.' He paused. 'You pulled off the best wedding today. Everything ran like clockwork. You're a very special person.'

Hearing all those heartfelt words, Libby's heart melted with happiness. 'You'll be making me cry in a minute.'

'Now, in all seriousness, it's actually a copy of the key to next door's lodge because I've arranged with Flynn to stay there until the cottage is ready. So whenever you're back, you're more than welcome to use it.'

Libby leaned in and gave him a long, lingering kiss. 'I can't tell you how much this means to me.' She held the key tightly in her hand. 'Now open your present.'

Guy looked down at the envelope and carefully opened it. 'Tickets?'

'Plane tickets,' Libby confirmed. 'One for you and one for Holly. I've already checked with Cynthia that the dates work. It's for Holly's half-term in February. If it's okay with you, I'd like you both to fly out.'

'No way! This is the best present. This is brilliant. Holly will love this.'

'I thought I'd show her the magic of the fashion house where the designs are created. During that time my designs will actually be featured on the catwalk at a local fashion show and I'd love you to come with me.'

'Of course! We'd love that!'

'And we can do the sights.'

'But wait … there's three tickets here,' Guy noticed.

'There are. Look at the last one.'

Guy stared at a return ticket with Libby's name printed on it.

'I know I may have had a little too much to drink but I don't understand.'

Libby smiled. 'It's mine. I'm flying back with you at the end of your trip. Dad planted a seed and it grew into a clear vision of what I want my future to be. I'm already successful in my field and attracting celebrities to my brand, which is why I was successful in the job interview. But I can do the job anywhere. I spoke to my boss about how I was feeling—my worries about being so far away from friends and family—and she was brilliant and understood this is a major move. She agreed that if I go for an initial two months to meet the team, build a rapport and gain the experience of working alongside everyone, after that I can be flexible about where I'm located. Flynn has agreed to set me up a studio here so I can split my time between New York and Heartcross.'

'I can't believe what I'm hearing. Are you sure this is what you want?'

'Yes. Today was the best day. I love my family and I want to be near my dad, Flynn and Julia. My friends are here, and you and Holly are going to be here, and as far as the apartment in New York goes … it's mine for a year whatever I decide.'

Guy raked his hand through his hair. 'I'm lost for words. This is just amazing. I knew we could work this out. I wanted to work it out. You, Libby Carter, are my enough.'

'Enough?'

'Yes, my enough,' he confirmed. 'I know we are going to have a lot of things to work through but what I'm trying to say is that I've got everything I need and want: you and Holly.'

This was the reassurance Libby hadn't realised she needed, and she knew she'd made the right choice. She threw her arms around him and whispered, 'And you and Holly are my enough.'

They locked eyes and Libby leaned in to kiss him. 'Oh my gosh, you have to go,' she said, springing up from the settee. 'Go! You have to go!'

'What do you mean? Why? What's going on? I thought we could find out whether I'm a true Scotsman,' Guy said, looking a little hurt.

Still pushing him towards the door, Libby thrust a Santa's hat into his hand. 'It's Christmas Eve … correction, Christmas Day. You need to make sure all of Holly's presents are waiting for her in the morning.'

'Oh my God! It slipped my mind.' Guy pulled on the Santa hat.

'Good job it didn't slip mine. We can't have a broken-hearted little girl in the morning.'

Guy pointed at Libby. 'Did you just say "we"?'

'I did. Guy Hart, we are a team.'

'I like the sound of that.' He kissed her quickly. 'I'll be back!'

'That's good because I still need to find out if you're a true Scotsman!'

As Guy hurried out the door, Libby cheekily attempted to lift his kilt but failed. 'You make sure you hurry back!'

It wasn't long before Guy slipped into bed next to her. With his arms wrapped around her body he kissed her. 'This is the best Christmas I've ever had.'

'Me, too,' she replied, her lips finding his. Running her hands up his thighs she dared to venture higher. 'I'm glad to discover you're a true Scotsman. Merry Christmas!'

As their hands started exploring each other's bodies, Libby

reached over and switched off the bedside lamp. Flynn and Julia's winter wedding was a memory that would stay with her and Guy for ever, a day filled with magic, romance and the promise of a bright future together. After their conversation, she knew she was going to be enough for Guy, and as she contemplated spending the rest of her life by his side, she felt as if her heart would burst with happiness.

Acknowledgements

I can't quite believe my nineteenth book is published. As ever this book is a team effort and the hugest of thanks to editor extraordinaire Laura McCallen who works her magic and makes my books the best they can be. Laura is an absolute pleasure to work with and long may this fabulous partnership continue. This extends to the brilliant team at One More Chapter especially Charlotte Ledger who is the captain of this fabulous ship. Charlotte's love of romantic novels shines through and it's wonderful to see this genre championed within the industry. She is without a doubt, one of the loveliest people in this industry.

A massive thank you to my children, Emily, Jack, Ruby, and Tilly who of course are my greatest achievements in life. I'm proud of you all.

Big love to Woody (my mad Cocker Spaniel) who has been my writing partner in crime from my very first book and Nellie (my loony Labradoodle) who is extremely hairy but lovable.

Thank you Anita Redfern. Everyone has a friend during each stage of life. But only lucky ones have the same friend in all stages of life – I'm the lucky one.

A good friend is like a four-leaf clover. Hard to find and lucky to have. Julie Wetherill is my four-leaf clover and usually turns up with gin in her hand. Squad goals!

This book was inspired by a week away in Devon with the

truly inspirational Estelle Maher. Thank you for putting up with me and my dislocated knee!

Deep gratitude to all my readers, reviewers, retailers, librarians, and fellow authors who have supported me throughout my career. Authors would be lost without you and I am truly grateful for your continuous support.

I have without a doubt enjoyed writing this latest instalment in the Love Heart Lane Series and I really hope you enjoy *A Winter Wedding at Starcross Manor*.

Warm wishes,

Christie x

PS. I think this is my favourite book cover so far!

ONE MORE CHAPTER

The author and One More Chapter would like to thank everyone who contributed to the publication of this story...

Analytics
James Brackin
Abigail Fryer
Maria Osa

Audio
Fionnuala Barrett
Ciara Briggs

Contracts
Sasha Duszynska
Lewis

Design
Lucy Bennett
Fiona Greenway
Liane Payne
Dean Russell

Digital Sales
Lydia Grainge
Hannah Lismore
Emily Scorer

Editorial
Arsalan Isa
Charlotte Ledger
Laura McCallen
Jennie Rothwell
Tony Russell
Caroline Scott-
Bowden

Harper360
Emily Gerbner
Jean Marie Kelly
emma sullivan
Sophia Wilhelm

International Sales
Peter Borcsok
Bethan Moore

Marketing & Publicity
Chloe Cummings
Emma Petfield

Operations
Melissa Okusanya
Hannah Stamp

Production
Denis Manson
Simon Moore
Francesca Tuzzeo

Rights
Vasiliki Machaira
Rachel McCarron
Hany Sheikh
Mohamed
Zoe Shine

**The HarperCollins
Distribution Team**

**The HarperCollins
Finance & Royalties
Team**

**The HarperCollins
Legal Team**

**The HarperCollins
Technology Team**

Trade Marketing
Ben Hurd

UK Sales
Laura Carpenter
Isabel Coburn
Jay Cochrane
Sabina Lewis
Holly Martin
Erin White
Harriet Williams
Leah Woods

**And every other
essential link in the
chain from delivery
drivers to booksellers
to librarians and
beyond!**

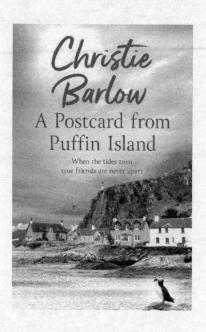

Verity Callaway is running away.
From her job.
From her quiet life in the Midlands.
And most of all from her ex-fiancée… who has just become her
newest neighbour.

The plan is simple: hop in her reliable camper van and cross the Channel, headed for a rendezvous with her best friend in Amsterdam to kick off six months of travel. But when Verity stumbles across a decades-old postcard while preparing her cottage for its temporary tenants, her life takes an unexpected turn, and she finds herself on a ferry to Puffin Island instead.

Available to order now!

Love Heart Lane Series

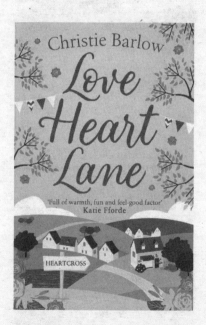

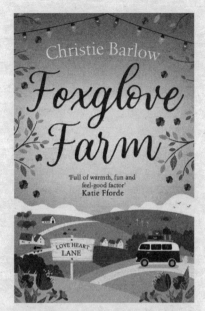

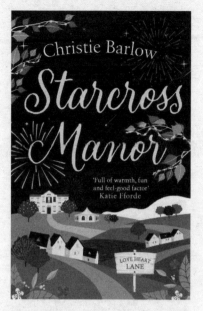

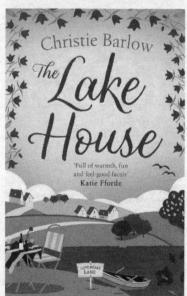

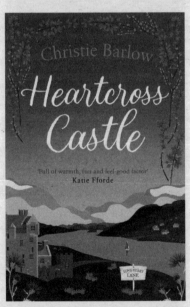

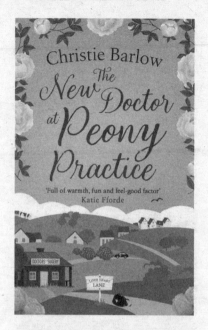

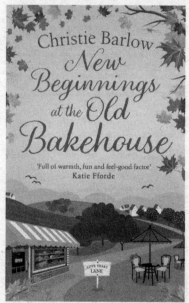

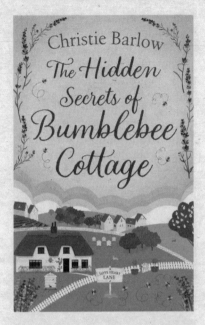

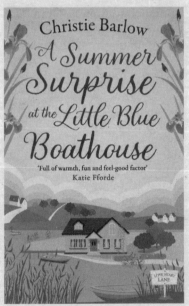

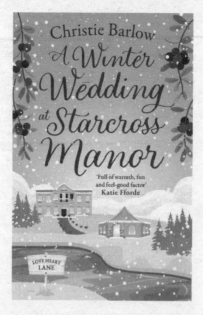

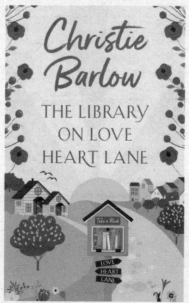

YOUR NUMBER ONE STOP

ONE MORE CHAPTER

FOR PAGETURNING BOOKS

One More Chapter is an
award-winning global
division of HarperCollins.

Sign up to our newsletter to get our
latest eBook deals and stay up to date
with our weekly Book Club!
<u>Subscribe here.</u>

Meet the team at
<u>www.onemorechapter.com</u>

Follow us!
 <u>@OneMoreChapter_</u>
 <u>@OneMoreChapter</u>
@onemorechapterhc

Do you write unputdownable fiction?
We love to hear from new voices.
Find out how to submit your novel at
<u>www.onemorechapter.com/submissions</u>